CASTER

CAS

TER

ELSIE CHAPMAN

Scholastic Press New York

Library of Congress Cataloging-in-Publication Data

Names: Chapman, Elsie, author.
Title: Caster / Elsie Chapman.
Description: First edition. | New York: Scholastic Press, 2019. | Summary: Aza Wu knows that casting magic can kill—it killed her sister—but she needs money desperately to pay off Saint Willow, who controls her sector of Lotusland, and save the family teahouse, so she secretly enters an underground casting tournament—and finds herself competing against other castors with "full magic," and where even victory could cause her to lose her freedom, her magic, and her life.
Identifiers: LCCN 2018060381 (print) | LCCN 2019000903 (ebook) | ISBN 9781338332636 (Ebook) | ISBN 9781338332629 (hardcover)
Subjects: LCSH: Magic—Juvenile fiction. | Sisters—Juvenile fiction. | Contests—Juvenile fiction. | Competition (Psychology)—Juvenile fiction. | Young adult fiction. | CYAC: Magic—Fiction. | Sisters—Fiction. | Contests—Fiction. | Competition (Psychology)—Fiction.
Classification: LCC PZ7.C36665 (ebook) | LCC PZ7.C36665 Cas 2019 (print) | DDC [Fic]—dc23
LC record available at https://lccn.loc.gov/2018060381

10 9 8 7 6 5 4 3 2 1   19 20 21 22 23

Printed in the U.S.A.   23
First edition, September 2019

Book design by Maeve Norton

FOR MY FOLKS. MOM,
HERE'S THE NEXT, LIKE YOU'RE
ALWAYS ASKING. AND DAD,
YOU WOULD HAVE ESPECIALLY
LIKED THIS ONE.

ONE

I take the coins and am compelled to remind my buyer how things can still go wrong. I thought I was over botching my last mind wipe, but apparently not.

"Like I said before, there are no guarantees," I say. The corners of the square coins dig into my hand as I riffle through them, counting the number of marks. Removing time from someone's memory is burning down a single tree in a thick forest—sometimes there's smoke damage to other trees nearby. "Mind wipes are tricky."

The last time, I didn't just wipe out a weekend as requested, but the whole week. Rudy pointed out it had more to do with the nature of the spell than my control. Mostly I believe him, if only because Rudy's not one for trying to make me feel better.

Coral nods. Her name's not really Coral—I never want to know their actual names—but it's what I call her on account of the lipstick she wore on our first meeting, the same shade she's wearing now. "Still, I'm just asking for one specific day to be gone," she says, nervously twirling the ends of her brown hair. "But if you can't do it . . ."

Annoyance flickers across her face even as her eyes stay hopeful.

The conflict comes as no surprise. It's how most of those with leftover magic feel about casters of full magic, unable to decide if they loathe us or envy us. If they need us or hate us. We're dangerous, forever having to hide who we are. Only one thing is certain—they can't do what we can. Full magic.

"Any other caster of full magic will tell you the same," I say. "No guarantees. And if they say otherwise, they're lying." I slide her a cool look, hoping nothing on my face gives away that another caster might be more confident with their magic. How they might've done more than the few mind wipes I have. How I'm actually doing this because I still need to be better.

I hold out my hand, offering back the marks. "But be my guest, if you'd like to spend the time searching for someone else."

She flushes. The network of rumored full magic casters in Lotusland is thin—holes and dead ends—and it took her months to find me, a caster willing to cast for marks. And needing marks the way I do, I let myself be found.

Still uncertain, Coral picks at her nail. She's careful to work around the material painted onto the tip. It's a trend, embedding bits of spell starters right onto your nails so you only have to curl your fingers into your palm to cast magic. The downside is that a lot of starters need to be replenished, so you're always repainting. Like most casters of any magic, I just use a basic starter bag. Blending in is good.

I do my best to hide how nervous I am as doubt continues to cloud her expression. She takes in my age—I'm sixteen, not exactly a responsible adult—my worn clothing that says I might just be trying to hustle her, and then my casting arm. Like there are signs in the limb and its palm that would give away my true control over magic.

I hope she can't tell I'm still working on perfecting that control, the consequences of which could mean disaster for me or the fragile ecosystem around us.

Finally Coral waves her hand, exasperated. "I've paid, so whatever—let's just get on with it. I have a meeting in a few minutes and need to get back to my office." She touches one of her starter-embedded nails to her palm and her hair smooths itself back, though we are indoors and there is no wind. It's leftover magic, weak enough to exact no cost on its caster.

I shove the marks into the pocket of my jeans and glance around the washroom.

We agreed to meet here secretly, this room of silver-papered walls and warm mahogany doors and ceramic-framed mirrors. We're in one of the dozens of high-rise office buildings that make up the Tower Sector of the city, and for a second my skin goes clammy.

It was not even a year ago that Shire fell from one of these buildings—maybe it was even *this* building, I don't know. It was a job gone beyond wrong—her casting full magic.

The memory of our last time speaking, the raised voices. The disagreement. I would mind wipe myself of that argument, if I wasn't too scared of losing more of Shire. She died too young, and I don't have memories to spare.

Coral clears her throat. "What's the worst that can happen again?"

I check the washroom stalls once more, though they're just as empty as they've been since I got here. "We've already covered that."

"Humor me. This isn't an easy decision."

"Fine," I say.

"I lose a lot more time than a day, right?"

"Possibly."

"It doesn't work at all?"

"Maybe."

She swallows, curls in her pinky, and hastily casts another leftover spell. The shoulders of her suit jacket neaten themselves. "I forget everything."

"Highly unlikely." Even I couldn't do that, especially not by accident. A caster would have to have zero control over their full magic for that to happen. Brand-new to their power, caught completely unaware. I think back to the day I found out I wasn't a typical caster of leftover magic, and repress a shudder.

I step into one of the stalls and she follows me. I lock the door and then lean back against it, hoping it all goes well. I'm not worried about someone interfering. Casting full magic hurts. There's always a price to pay, sometimes forever, so I'd prefer to be out of sight for this.

Leftover magic requires a starter, just like the ones embedded in Coral's nails. And it's cast by placing the starter in the palm of the casting arm.

But for *full* magic, we cast with a spell star, tracing the shape in the palm. The rule is that the more points to a star, the more magic is pulled from the earth. It's why casting real magic is illegal now. The pain that follows is a limitation, too—draw a star with too many points and you could be dead before the spell's even run out.

A mind wipe the way Coral wants it is a seven-pointed star. That's the amount of magic I'm going to need.

I *could* chance six points—I'm only wiping one day. But six usually means a nosebleed for me, and it'd be awkward to move across a crowded lunchtime lobby while bleeding from my face. Seven will give me a bad headache that I usually like to sleep off when I can. Except it's the middle of the day and my parents already think I'll be out until late, working at a job that has nothing to do with casting full magic. A job I don't actually have.

Which is why I keep a jar of healing meds in my starter bag. They're not a surefire fix, and they won't work on a bloody nose, but they should help with a casting migraine. I mean to head to Rudy's from here anyway—if I'm really still hurting, there's no better place to be than his apothecary.

If he were here, he'd remind me to be careful. To not draw any extra attention to myself. To never forget that secrecy is imperative when casting is illegal.

Shire would tell me the same. She'd remind me of Scouts and their department within the police dedicated to hunting us down. Some of those Scouts are casters just like me. But full magic never guarantees loyalty, and they've turned because of pay, or because they worry about the earth caving in while they still stand on it, or simply because they believe it's the right thing to do.

But Shire is dead. She faced the pain of casting too much magic and died.

I push back harder against the stall door, needing it to keep feeling steady. I pull out a green leaf from the starter bag I wear slung over my shoulder.

"Last chance," I say to Coral.

She's sitting on the closed lid of the toilet. Her eyes are huge. There's fear in them now, crowding out need and envy and hate. The look in them says despite her being here, it's right that my kind of magic is now banished, that casters like me no longer have a place in this world.

She exhales. "I'm in."

"Then play out the day in your head for me to find." I draw a seven-pointed star on my palm with my finger, lay down the leaf in the center, and cast.

TWO

The floor beneath me rumbles just the slightest. My feet grow hot. The heat climbs up my legs and torso until it's pooling in my hands, making them feel heavy and languid. I'd almost expect to go up in flames if I were new to how full magic works. The sensation's still odd, though, so much heat without pain.

I've learned that the pain comes later.

It's said that earth's magic doesn't have a physical form, but even so it fills my veins. Full magic glows inside, a red that's brighter and hotter than any blood, desperate for escape. A thin buzz fills my ears. My heartbeat collects in my throat, thick and pounding.

It's like stoking a fire, Shire once said to me, a conversation I go back to again and again. *The magic you draw is its fuel, but you control how high you want its flames, Aza. What you want the fire to burn. Where you want it to go.*

I paint a picture of my power—this strange red amorphous *thing*, real and not real, wonderful yet terrible—in my mind. At the same time, I make sure to meet Coral's eyes, the connection necessary for me to work a spell on her mind.

I drive—*stoke*—my magic forward. It enters her head as fire, red and pointed. There's a wind behind it, pushing the flames of that magic straight along its intended path. The fire seeps through the bone of her skull and then deep into her brain, where it's soft and vulnerable. Malleable. It curls into the recesses of her living mind, into its tiny hills and valleys that are full of memories and stories and *time*, all of them shaped like trees. One tree sticks out above the rest. It's *that* day, the reason why I'm casting banned magic in a bathroom stall. I will the red fire that is my power toward the tree and set it alight. A final black swirl of smoke and my job is done.

The skin of my hand burns. Full magic might have no real form, but it sits in my palm anyway, alive as a flame.

Pain shoots through my head. If not for the door I'm still leaning against, I'd be stumbling back with the intensity of it. Waves of nausea come, and I barely keep from retching. The fire that lit up my skin cools and disappears.

I drop the leaf. Used up now, it's gone all autumn on me, brown and crisp. It shatters into dust as it hits the bathroom floor.

"Did it work?" Coral licks her lips. "How do I know if it worked?"

"It worked," I whisper. Hammers are alive in my brain, and they're all going at once. I drag a shaking hand across my face. Cold sweat, nerves, deep relief, and sickness—they all wash over me.

"You can't know that for sure."

"I know because you're asking."

"How do I know if you accidentally wiped out too much?"

"It went as well as it could, trust me." I think of the last job and how it *didn't* go so well and shiver. "Anyway, does it matter? It's too late now."

I unlock the door of the stall and stagger out, not wanting any more questions, not caring if anyone else has come into the washroom. I pull out the tiny jar of healing meds and frown when I see that there's only one left.

I found it in Shire's room, a jar clearly from Rudy's apothecary, and kept it for myself. I knew I was going to take over for Shire, and that casting magic would hurt—being able to recharge faster just meant I could fit in more jobs. I also figured out pretty quickly that Rudy must have used full magic to make the pills. Even the times they only half work, it's still better than what nonmagic medication can do.

I'll have to get more from Rudy today. I wash down the pill with water from the tap and drop the empty jar back into my bag.

"I can cast you better," Coral says. Her voice comes way too close to my ear, and I wince. "A simple skin spell for pain. I can cast those, too, just like you."

I nearly laugh, but I'm still afraid of throwing up. Her weak magic *can* cast skin spells. She can also cast bone spells, and blood, and breath ones. Just like me, but so much *less*, only able to ease a sore muscle instead of erasing someone's mind. To get rid of an ache in a bone, not clear it of disease; to form a tiny scab, not knit skin back together; to help fill a lung, not crush it.

"Won't work," I whisper. "Leftover magic isn't strong enough."

I don't tell her that pain from casting is just one way we're affected. How for some full magic casters, all their damage *comes back*. And it comes back all at once, like being stampeded over. Becoming an Ivor—the condition goes by the name of the first caster in history known for it—can happen anytime after casting full magic. Maybe weeks later, or months, or years. And for Ivors, the change is forever, their magic as good as gone, their bodies no longer able to handle even one more casting. If they're lucky, it's only on the inside that they're broken. If not, it's never too long before Scouts find them and take away their magic. Before they lock them up and display them as warnings to other full magic casters.

I used to worry about ending up an Ivor. But I don't worry about it as much anymore. I actually think most full magic casters don't. I think we worry way more about accidentally destroying a part of the world. I think we worry about the smog we're breathing in all the time, about earth being too weak to sustain the magic that we hold.

"Well, then why can't you just cast yourself better?" Coral sounds nearly as put out as she does concerned—*I have a meeting, and it's very important that I be on time.* "Wouldn't that be faster than any medication?"

I shut my eyes against the bright lighting of the room. Already the hammers are quieting down a bit. But it can't hurt to keep Coral away from wondering about such effective pills, away from wondering about who might make them and how.

"Casting another spell at this point would only mean more pain." I have to recover enough first, or the effect compounds. And then I'd be in serious trouble.

"Right. That makes sense." Then I hear her breath catch.

I open my eyes, already knowing what I'll see. The shock in that single caught breath gives it away.

A long crack splits across the tiled washroom floor, as thin as string but impossible to ignore. It's as though the opposite sides of the room are tectonic plates and there's been a shift from a quake.

This quake is because I pulled full magic from the ground.

The earth isn't too happy about it.

"So it's all true." There's disgust in Coral's voice. "It's *not* just enough that *you* hurt while casting. You have to hurt *us*, too."

"Oh, please." I manage a sneer even as the crack slowly begins to widen. "*You* came to *me*, asking for full magic. You knew the cost. You know how magic and this world work."

"But I've never seen it for myself before. It's always just been the Scouts warning us about full magic." She gazes down at the crack, then back at me, her eyes full of disdain. "How we're never going to be really safe until all casters like you are locked up or your magic is taken away. Books and the news, reminding us how it's full magic that ruined the air and oceans, so that the earth had to turn it against you."

I clench my hands over my starter bag. It was once Shire's. I struggle to think of what she might say to this weakling of magic. Shire, who was always nicer and better than me, with her discipline, her views, her ideas—even our parents think so.

But my mind stays blank even while it continues to pound. Because nothing Coral's said is untrue. I can blame her for hiring me and giving me a reason to cast—but it doesn't change that *I'm still casting*. I'm still slowly breaking apart small bits of the world, spell by spell. Shire did the same, and I guess that's why her words don't come to me, either.

I move toward the washroom door, staring at Coral as I go. "Don't forget, one word of this and Scouts will be on you just as fast as they will be on me. They might not do to you what they'll do to me, but they'll definitely haul you in anyway." It's not just the casters of full magic that are banned but full magic itself. Whether it's cast or bought is beside the point. Our power can be the end of everything.

Coral's gone pale. "I promise."

"Also, you might want to get out of here before the fire department comes to inspect. The crack's only getting wider and once Scouts get word, they'll have questions for anyone caught in the area."

I pull my smog mask from my back pocket and tug it on over my nose and mouth. With my stomach still rolling and my tongue as bitter as ash, I push the door open and step out of the washroom. I cross the lobby, and just before I step outside, I yank the lever for the fire alarm.

I hit the street running, ignoring how my head still hurts. The distant ringing of the office building's fire alarm fades behind me, and I think about what I need to do next.

Namely, bug Rudy for more about magic.

I want to be as good as Shire was. No, better, because I don't want to die casting magic for marks. And he was her instructor, teaching her to be good enough with her magic that she made the marks to keep our family's business going. Now that's on me.

Never mind that Rudy would rather be left alone, saying that he wants to focus on running his apothecary. Or that he says my personality is the very opposite of Shire's, that he actually liked having her around. Or that when I beg him to show me new magic,

I always somehow just end up helping out around the shop instead. I've stocked shelves, pestle and mortared, filled jars, plus other way more mundane chores I don't even have to do at the teahouse anymore—and I still can't figure out how Rudy gets me to work for him when it's supposed to be the other way around.

He owes *me*.

I also still haven't decided if I even like him, considering the circumstances.

He was there when Shire died. He was the one unable to save her. He was the one to make her think she could use the amount of power that killed her.

Also, I know of no other caster of full magic. There's no one else but Rudy Shen.

His apothecary is in the Tobacco Sector, which lies west of Tower, two sectors over. It's summer, but Lotusland summers are still cold and full of rain, seeing that we hug the Pacifik on the whole west side. Breezes that blow off its surface hit you in the face with damp and salt, and you remember all over again how it's the coldest ocean in the world.

Normally I walk everywhere because I like being able to choose where I go as much as I can. I like imagining I can disappear if I feel like it, for my face to blend into the myriads of shades of skin—gold like mine, but also white, black, brown—that are the people of Lotusland.

But I'm not in the mood for crowds today, or for the rain that's starting to fall. Not for the gray air that never fully leaves, either, so that half the city wears smog masks that cover their noses and mouths while outside. And my head still hurts a bit. My rider's pass still has enough marks on it for a final trip, so I decide to chance the train and hop on a westbound one.

The city can never keep up with system repairs, meaning there are usually lots of detours and stoppages around broken-up asphalt and parts of the track undergoing construction. Or the passenger cars just die on you because the city hasn't upgraded them for years, and you end up somewhere you don't want to be. Or someone has cast real magic nearby, and the earth deflates a bit more.

I only have to glance out the windows to hear Coral's words all over again.

The air and oceans and forests, ruined because of casters like me. No more blues and greens but smog and rust and dull gray concrete. All true. Lakes and rivers carry mutant fish that ate up all the normal fish, and wildfires keep burning up forests all over the world because of freak weather. Every time a caster uses full magic, we are cracking open the earth that much more.

We're considered earth's biggest threat.

Still, real magic has been dying out more and more with each generation. Five hundred years ago, every person alive could heal or mind wipe. Now we're just a fraction.

The train motors along, and we're still in the Government Sector when the engine gives out and an announcement comes on, telling us to get off and catch a different westbound train. But the rain's stopped now, as well as my headache, so I decide to walk the rest of the way over. I know this part of the city well, since it borders the Tea Sector, which is home. And the Tobacco Sector is no more than ten blocks away, then Rudy's shop another five more heading south.

I've just reached the outer edge of Tea when I spot him. Half a block away, standing on the corner. He's wearing one of his perpetual black suits and bright white sneakers, a combination I see now in my nightmares.

Jihen.

THREE

I can tell by the way he's waiting that he spotted me first.

I freeze, my heartbeat a dull thud in my ears, debating for a handful of wild, desperate seconds if I can run fast enough to escape for another day. Or if I've recovered enough yet from the effects of casting the mind wipe to safely cast more magic to escape that way.

It'd be a temporary reprieve, though—anyone who lives in the Tea Sector is never entirely free of Jihen and the rest of his gang. Jihen works for Saint Willow, and it's Saint Willow who runs the area. It's been like this since the sectors were first formed.

The only person who really owns property in Tea is Saint Willow—the rest of us just pay to stay here. The world might call it "rent," but people in the sectors know it as paying *honor* marks. If not for his protection, other gangs would move in, and then where would it all be? Saint Willow promises we don't want to know. The gangs have always had their own say about how the sectors are run, and cops who sometimes forget this end up disappearing as a reminder.

As though Jihen can read my frozen mind about trying to slip away, he moves first, closing the gap between us as quick as the oiled snake I know him to be.

"Hello, Aza," he says, smiling greasily. More than half of Tea's population is Chinese, and this includes Jihen, and so his skin is as gold as mine. He's also nearly as short as I am, but thick as a barrel through the middle.

Not that his heft matters either way. His being a distant cousin of Saint Willow's is all that's needed to give him power. It's why he got assigned the job of watching the lagging Wu family. Of dogging me to make sure we pay up as everyone else in Tea has to.

Without the marks Shire was bringing in, our honor debt is only growing, day by day.

"Jihen," I say.

"You have our marks?" He pats at his waxed black hair. The movement lifts his jacket. I can't miss his knife, tucked into his side. It's mostly for show—Saint Willow usually deals with problems more creatively—but the threat remains.

"I just paid you a bunch of marks two days ago." Jihen's what we call a squeezer, the person Saint Willow employs to chase down debts still owed to him.

"Two days ago was two days ago. Your family's debt continues to grow. Must we go through this each time we meet?"

"We wouldn't meet so much if you gave me room to work."

Jihen smiles. "Just as you must work, so must I."

"Running a teahouse is work—stealing from its profits is just robbery."

"Yet both are enterprises, and enterprises have deadlines. Your family's year is nearly up, Aza."

Stories in the sector are that Saint Willow has a principle about money owed—that a year is all he chooses to tolerate. He even has a calendar to mark down the day. One year. That's when he gets creative about getting him what is owed, if creativity means choosing between methods of torture.

"I have one more week," I say defiantly.

We managed eight months of stalling after Shire died. She was steady in paying Wu Teas's honor marks through her casting secretly for years before her death. Then it was two months of Jihen being assigned to come around the tea shop, "observing" the business until we couldn't put off paying any longer. Finally, I lied. To keep him away from my parents and the teahouse, I told him he was wasting his time because *I* was the one in charge of my family's finances.

He's been shadowing me ever since. Two months now.

"It's been awhile since I've said hello to your fou-mou." His voice goes silky over the Chinese word for parents. "Perhaps I need to pay a visit to your mama and baba at the teahouse, to stay and nem cha."

The marks I made from the mind wipe are still in my pocket. I'll have to give them over because the mention of Jihen dropping by for tea makes any other choice futile. But anger flows anyway, hot and thick in my chest. I spin on my heel, just needing a second to reclaim my own space.

His hand whips out and grasps my arm, stopping me. "Aza, *beauty*"—Jihen's still smiling and it makes my skin prickle with cold—"let's not do anything drastic. Saint Willow won't be pleased."

His calling me *beauty* is a joke. Shire was the pretty one. She and I had the same bones beneath because we're sisters, but it's like a great sculptor spent extra time polishing her face while I never got fully finished. She dressed in colorful and showy things, but it wouldn't have mattered if they'd been as drab as the sky—if they'd all been as pink as the scar on her cheek—because she looked the way she did.

I try to turn again, but Jihen's grip is still firm on my arm. "I'll pay you, all right?" I say to him. "Just . . . not right here."

"Where are we going?"

I start walking as an answer, heading deeper into Tea while still keeping away from the teahouse. I *want* to head toward the Tobacco Sector, but I don't want him to start thinking too hard about where else in the city I go. Tea is safe because it's what he expects. He already knows to look for me around home, always somewhere nearby, waiting and following and making sure I pay whatever I have on me.

This can't go on much longer.

I have to think of something to save us.

Because the truth looms, and it comes at me in stabs:

The growing shadow of Saint Willow. The jobs where my magic felt like a stranger's. Advice Rudy doles out like it hurts him to talk. The faces of my parents, miserable because our family legacy now rests entirely on me.

Jihen sighs deeply. His fingers squeeze my arm as we walk. We're still blocks from the teahouse, but the whole area smells deeply of tea anyway. Wu Teas is just one of dozens of teahouses in the sector, hence the sector's name. Housing and supply businesses and restaurants fill the spaces in between, but one sniff and there's no doubt which part of Lotusland you're in.

"This whole sector has sure gone downhill, that's for sure," Jihen says conversationally. Like we're close to friends. "This economy has gone to si, been that way for decades now. It's too bad Wu Teas has gone down right along with it."

"No other teahouse is any different. Demand's down, while supply remains."

"Good thing you are able to find work. Tea might never be needed the way you Wus would like it to be, but there's always going to be a need for teachers. Leftover magic can only do so much."

"Tutor, not teacher," I mutter, fighting a grim temptation to cast full magic on Jihen as I yank a leaf from a boxwood hedge along the sidewalk. Starters work on the things they create, so a leaf works on paper, fabric, *skin*—because just as trees are of the earth, casters are of the earth, too. And I want him to stop talking, even if it would only last for a moment, and even if most skin spells could never pass for leftover magic.

Being a tutor is the lie I had to tell Jihen to cover for my not being at the teahouse all day long and somehow still making marks. Shire was able to hide the marks she made from magic by claiming they were a part of the shop's profits. And Jihen hadn't been watching her. Saint Willow hadn't needed to send anyone then. Honor marks from Wu Teas were still coming in as scheduled.

"Tutor, not teacher, my mistake," he says. "Math?"

I drop the leaf. "A bit of everything," I lie again.

"See, I watch you, Aza. I stay in Tea because I know you'll always have to come back. But I see you come and go at all times, all over the city, in all the sectors. I know you're getting jobs. I know you're making marks. My job, on behalf of Saint Willow, is to get those marks into our hands more regularly, and in larger amounts."

"I can't control who decides to hire me."

He plucks a plum from a tree as we pass. It's unripe, as green as a lime. He casts leftover magic, huffing a warm breath into his palm.

The plum turns a deep purple.

There's another story that goes around the sector having to do with Saint Willow, and it's one about magic. How the gang leader might have marks and power and everyone's fear, but he'll never have what he wants most, which is full magic.

The whispers say that over the years he's tried to keep full magic casters under his employ, but is so overly demanding with their casting that they never last. Some have died, some quit, and some have even wiped themselves from Saint Willow's mind, if you believe the rumors.

If Saint Willow had any clue he had a caster of full magic already squirming right beneath his thumb, I bet I'd be even more chained to him than I already am.

Jihen bites into the ripened plum. "I still remember the stories our grandparents would tell us about Wu Teas. Stories their grandparents told *them*. How emperors and empresses from overseas served your ancestors' teas to their royal guests. How they would pay with bars of gold and nuggets of silver—all for your family's *tea*."

"Don't forget about castles and temples," I add, my voice stiff as I keep walking. "They stocked our blends, too."

"Now look at you Wus, with your emperors and empresses and fancy gilded palaces, castles, and temples all long gone. Swallowed up by quakes, drowned out by floods. Then other teahouses moving in, so you have to lower your prices more and more. Your family, begging for diners and shops to carry a blend or two, for handfuls of marks instead of armfuls of riches." He sighs again, a parody of sympathy for my family's troubles. "Ah, business is so mah-fung, no?"

I run my finger along a shop windowsill and sweep the small shard of broken ceramic into my palm before Jihen notices. Ceramic starter. Good for a bone spell. Rage is a hot fist in my chest as I imagine all the horrific full magic spells I could cast on him, ones I could never do without giving my secret away.

Each of his limbs twisted into the shape of a pretzel.

Bones turned to putty inside his body.

His skull turned inside out.

"The marks, Aza," Jihen says now, tucking the plum pit into his chest pocket. I've seen him keep other starters there, ones like rocks and leaves, dirt pellets and water capsules. My guess is that carrying a weapon on his side leaves little room for a starter bag. His fingers squeeze my arm until it hurts. "Hand them over."

I tell myself I'm not scared.

The truth is, Saint Willow and I have actually entered into a strange kind of partnership. Deep down, he doesn't *really* want to see Wu Teas gone—our teas might not be served to royalty anymore, but visitors to Tea still make a point of coming to his sector just for our teahouse.

Another family could take us over, but then it would not be Wu Teas.

And as for me, Saint Willow knows I would do almost anything to save my family's legacy, business, and home, and milking desperation is always more profitable than a family that has given up.

"Your boss still requiring everyone in the sector to pay honor marks isn't helping anyone's business," I say to Jihen, slowing down. We're less than three blocks from the teahouse now, from our apartment that makes up its rear, and I don't want to bring Jihen any closer to my parents.

"Saint Willow is running a business, too," he says. "A business that has even deeper roots here in Lotusland than Wu Teas. Our family's marks are why your family—why *all* the families running businesses here—got the chance to make marks of their own. Aza, beauty—"

"Don't call me that."

"—*you owe us.*"

His words are an echo of my own, the way I think about Rudy, and I tug at my arm to get away, sickened that I could have anything in common with a man like Saint Willow.

I dig out coins from my pocket and thrust out my hand. "This is all that I have."

Finally my arm is free as he lets go to take the marks. He counts, once, twice. "You really want me to go back to Saint Willow with this?" Fury turns him red. "Have you forgotten I can walk into your family's teahouse anytime I want? I don't need to ask."

I look away. "Please don't. I'll have more tomorrow."

"Any family would be happy to live in your apartment. To be given a teahouse with a nice legacy to run. It doesn't have to be yours, Aza. Not at all."

Dread's a lump in my throat as I try to stay convinced it's nothing but talk. I push the faces of my parents out of my head. "I *said* I'll pay you tomorrow."

Now he leans close, his smile overly kind, and whiffs of tea and hair wax and aftershave cloud my nose.

"You Wus were so much better at paying when your sister was alive," Jihen says softly. "On time, in full amounts. It was all so pleasant. Your sister, so much better than *you* at keeping the teahouse going. If only she were still alive, then maybe your family wouldn't be in such trouble."

I shove my hands into my pockets to find some kind of warmth, suddenly cold all over despite the midday sun. Inside the pocket where I kept the marks, my fingers hit something sharp. The corner of a mark I missed.

"Such a sad accident, falling from a balcony the way she did," Jihen says. "Twenty stories, wasn't it?"

I yank out the mark and cast. Copper coin for a copper starter. Good for a bone spell, even if it has to be a minor one. Good for painless leftover magic, because no one's supposed to know what kind of caster I really am.

I toss the mark at Jihen—I almost want to keep it; rigid starters can be used again, and it's a *mark*; but there's something about hurling it at his head that just feels so good—and run.

"Aza, I'm not done yet! Get over—!"

A yell as my magic makes his knee give out and he topples to the pavement.

FOUR

I get within sight of Shen Apothecary, keeping up running at first before letting myself slow to a half-rushed walk. My hair and clothes and even my skin smell like smoke by the time I hit the corner of his block. The Tobacco Sector is really a mix of scents—from ash to tobacco to moss—but put together the overwhelming one is simply smoke. Only having the breezy Pacifik as its west side border does anything to make a difference. And each time I leave here for home in Tea, I take the roundabout way. I head west until I hit the shore, hoping the spray from the salty ocean will wash away the smoke scent. My parents haven't forgotten where Rudy works.

I'm nearing the entrance to the apothecary when I notice the guy in a baseball cap across the street. I notice him because of two reasons.

One is, he's trying so hard to not be obvious how he's scoping out a place that he's nothing *but* obvious. He's standing near the curb, skin white beneath the cap, checking his phone every fifteen seconds or so, like he's expecting someone and they're late. But in between checking his phone, he lifts his head and stares into the front window of Rudy's shop.

This makes something in my stomach flutter, and I slow down, unsure of what to think.

The second reason I notice Baseball Cap is because he's a cop.

He thinks the silver armband is hidden beneath his sleeve, but he's oblivious about the breeze.

This makes my mouth go dry.

Why would a cop be watching Rudy's place? Sure, businesses in the Tobacco Sector have been known to be fronts, putting up a facade to sell all kinds of illegal items out their back doors.

But Rudy's legit, always sure to renew his licenses on time. And his formulas—his nonmagic ones, that is, the ones that stand in for the full magic formulas he actually sells—all meet grade. He's careful mostly because he's a full magic caster and he knows how to avoid getting noticed by suits of any kind. He knows how to get around the law.

Like with Shire—Rudy was the one who called in her death. He knew a sleazy medical examiner willing to be bribed to falsify a medical report that made sure not to include anything about her casting magic—only reporting her death as due to an accidental high fall.

Rudy still hasn't told me which spell—or spells—she'd been attempting to cast from up there. I still don't know the actual physical reason why she died. I don't know how much pain she must have been in, or if she died before it could even fully hit her.

Why were you even there, Rudy? She always sold magic alone. It was the middle of the night! Who would buy magic in the middle of the night? On top of a building?

Fresh anger builds in my throat, while a huge wave of missing my sister brings tears to the backs of my eyes. Rudy has no right to keep any of this from me. And Shire—she should have known better.

Shire, why would you try casting more magic than you could control? Why would you chance something like that when I was always right there, wanting to help?

Something else hits me then, and it twists my stomach into a huge knot.

The year anniversary of Shire's death is nearly here. If that guy is a cop and he's here to ask Rudy about Shire, how long before that cop's coming to my parents to talk to *them*? Cops hate having a case on their books for more than a year, and the pressure goes up to solve them. Many innocents have gone down just so some Scout can clear an unsolved case.

How much would my parents be forced to bend before they'd break and give away the truth about what Shire was doing? How long before they give away *me* and my full magic?

My heart's thudding hard as I force myself to walk past Baseball Cap's line of vision and into the shop.

Inside, I lean back against a wall, taking off my smog mask and folding it back into my pocket. I breathe deep to calm down so I can tell Rudy about the cop without freaking out. I glance around, searching for him.

It's the middle of the afternoon on a weekday, and the apothecary has just a few customers. Here the smoke scent of the sector lifts completely and another deep breath brings ginseng and eucalyptus to my nose, cinnamon and mint and honey. Shining amber bottles line floor-to-ceiling shelves. The air is tinged with a haze, the perpetual vapors and mists from Rudy's mixing and concocting that never seem to dissipate entirely. The place reminds of another time, an easier and mellower era in the past—maybe it's a time when full magic and casters like Rudy and me weren't quite so feared.

As a person who likes helping to heal people, he's not the greatest at separating his full magic from his store stock. Even hurting from making the good stuff doesn't stop him. His effective medications are definitely why his shop isn't wanting for customers. They're why his customers are so loyal to a lot of his remedies.

I'd tell him he should be more careful, but Rudy wouldn't listen to me. Only Shire being gone keeps him from barring me from his apothecary altogether. I've made a point to come in at random times so he can never figure out how to avoid me.

But I'll tell him about the cop outside. Because now that I'm here seeing his customers, maybe it's *not* that surprising that the cop is watching Rudy. All these years he's run this apothecary, doctoring up some of his medications with full magic and selling them as typical ones—maybe he's finally caught.

I wait for him to finish serving the last customer at the counter and then walk up.

"Rudy, there's something I have to—"

He cuts me off with a tired, heavy sigh, not looking up from a pad of paper he's scribbling on. He's older, in his forties, maybe even in his fifties. His black hair is going gray, and all his clothing always seems a size too big. His starter bag is slung around his waist, and the words START ME UP! are printed across it.

"Aza, I'm busy. Can we do this another time?"

I fight back a spurt of irritation. "No, because there's a cop outside and he's watching the shop."

Rudy stops scribbling and looks up sharply at me. "What did you say?"

He shoves his white-framed glasses higher on his nose. He's nearsighted but has never used his magic to fix the condition. Instead he likes to collect different-style frames, the way some people collect purses or shoes. From behind the glasses his gaze is startled, shaken.

I only really know Rudy as brusque, and reluctant, and border-line rude. Except for that one terrible night when he was in tears.

Closer up gives away how his eyes are bloodshot, how the bags directly underneath them are purple. His skin is more sallow than gold, and his cheeks seem more gaunt than normal. Even his hair seems grayer than the last time I saw him. I glance again at his baggy clothing—maybe I'm misremembering about it always being too big. Maybe he's been losing weight or something.

I wonder if he's having problems eating, or sleeping. I wonder if guilt can pervade even dreams so that you can be *afraid* to sleep. I wonder why I feel bad about it instead of satisfied.

I lean in. "I said, there's a cop outside and he's—"

He moves out from behind the counter and goes to peer out the window. I follow and look over his shoulder. The cop's still out there, his face turned right in our direction.

Rudy steps back, deeper into the shadows of the apothecary. "No, you're wrong. It's a cop, but he's watching the place next door."

My thoughts scramble to recall what shop is next door, but nothing comes.

I squint out the window again. "What do you mean? He's staring right over here."

"It might be hard to tell, but it's definitely next door." Rudy's voice sounds wrong—too stiff. Careful.

"What's next door?"

"It's a snuff place, but they've already been caught selling opium and pipes and stuff. The cops are probably just waiting for one more incident in order to close them down for good."

Before I can say anything to that, Rudy heads off toward one of the shop shelves and begins to rearrange tins and bottles.

I can't deny I now doubt what I saw out there, but I'm still annoyed as I follow him over. Because I'm a bit embarrassed about jumping to conclusions so fast. Because it's always so easy for him to dismiss me over nearly everything, exactly the way he just did. Because I hate how I always have to *follow* him. How even if he's using me as much as I'm using him—I'm picking his brain and he's assuaging his guilt—he never forgets to remind me just how much I still have to learn.

Sometimes I think it's worth trying to break down his defenses. How if I could make him like me the way he liked Shire, I'd learn to trust him the way she did, too.

But I never think it for long. I see him and I think of Shire dying and all the questions he hasn't actually answered. I see him and I think of my parents and how their deep grief keeps them from even really wanting to know. All that matters to them is that the daughter who's left is the one who's barely been any help at all.

"Okay, so you know why I'm here," I say to Rudy when I walk up to him.

Like before, he's too busy to look away from his work. "Thanks for telling me about the cop. I'm glad you were wrong, but it was still good to know."

I glare at him hard enough that the side of his face must be burning. "You know that's not the only reason why."

He moves glass amber bottles around on the shelf, making them clink against one another. I have no clue how he's trying to organize them. It all seems very haphazard when normally he's practically berating me to be nothing but exact whenever I'm doing some kind of chore around here. *Powder up this package of roots, will you? But make sure you use the mortar and pestle just this way with your wrist, each and every time. Otherwise the grind will be too coarse and you'll only have to do it over again.*

"Well, I think I've pretty much helped you out as much as I can, Aza," he says now, still only looking at the bottles and sliding them around and not bothering to face me. "I don't know what else I can tell you."

"You were Shire's instructor for nearly eight years!"

I can't make myself stop. Jihen, Saint Willow, my parents' despair whenever they look at me, the once-majestic legacy of a family business now needing rescue—I feel them all, breathing down my neck. And here's Rudy, trying to run away from me when he's my last hope. "Eight years! But I come here for not even one and *it's supposed to be enough*? You're not going to get rid of me that easily, okay? I—"

Rudy clamps his hand over my mouth so I can't say anything else. *You owe me you owe me you should have died instead of Shire* plays out silently in my head as he drags me behind the counter and into the shop's supply room.

He slams the door shut behind us. I'm expecting him to be furious, but instead he just looks even more tired, and much older than I know he is. A flicker of worry comes, of shame that I'm here when he just wants to be left in peace. To maybe get over Shire his own way, on his own, without her sister reminding him every day how he messed up.

But I stamp out those feelings and keep glaring at him. I'm too desperate for sympathy. Sympathy doesn't pay.

"Aza, you need to be more careful. You can't just be out there saying stuff like—"

"I wouldn't, if you'd just help me."

"I *have* helped," he snaps. He shoves his glasses up. "What else do you want from me?"

"Answers." Medicinal smells waft out from the rows of bottles and stacks of tins that fill the shelves lining the room.

"I've answered all I can."

"So how have you helped me, exactly? You've had me be your shop helper is what you've been doing. Shelving ointments, bottling tonics—how does any of that help me learn how to control magic?"

"You can cast now, can't you?"

"That's not the same thing as learning control."

He throws up his arms. "Then don't cast at all, I don't know. Make marks some other way. Go get a job at a Guz-n-Go. I know the pay is crap, but you can't be charging that much for spells yet anyway, given how recently you started."

I laugh and it's shrill. "I can't believe she liked working with you."

"No one's making you stay."

Shire makes me stay. Saint Willow and *his* family legacy make me stay. *Magic* makes me stay.

Rudy rubs his face and swears. "Look, you come here unannounced whenever you feel like it and demand advice, answers. And I'm here working, Aza, at this shop that is supposed to be just any other shop in the city. I'm doing my best to pretend I'm leftover magic because that's what we have to do."

"Then pretend. Why does that mean you can't help me?"

"Because sometimes I get *tired* of full magic, all right? Sometimes I even hate it, the way it controls you if you don't control it. And maybe I want to quit while I'm ahead of the game and not end up an Ivor, waking up with my body completely twisted up inside my skin and maybe even getting caged and put up for display by a Scout because of it."

I shake my head, surprised. "Really? You're scared of going Ivor? You're probably more likely to get struck by light—"

"So you coming here, reminding me all the time how we have to live—you're not making it any easier, that's all."

"I guess Shire being gone doesn't make it easier, either. Since casting full magic is what killed her. Since *you're* the one who taught her." Then my voice hitches and I don't know who's more surprised, Rudy or me. My eyes get hot. The rows of glass and tins all shimmer and waver. "Once I know I can beat the spell that she couldn't, I promise I'll leave you alone, all right? And you—you should *want* to teach me that, don't you think?"

Rudy's gone still. Like my words have frozen him. Finally, he rubs his face again. He cleans his glasses using the front of his shirt. His eyes are more bloodshot than ever, and I can't tell if it's him just being exhausted for whatever reason or because his eyes sting like mine still do.

He puts his glasses back on and points to a row of boxes on a low shelf. "Those need to be unpacked and sorted and then repacked."

I stiffen as he heads toward the door that takes him back into the apothecary. "Are you kidding me?"

"Aza." Rudy stops at the door. "One more thing before you start yelling."

I'm almost numb. Everything I just said and it's like he didn't hear me at all. Panic wells while a crushing kind of defeat leaves me hollow. All I can do is look at him.

"Stop overthinking it. You complaining that I'm just having you help out around the shop instead of teaching you how to control your magic? Shire used to say the same thing—before she finally understood."

FIVE

I take down all the boxes and line them up on the floor. Inside each is a jumbled mix of supplies—more bottles and tins, droppers and vials. There are packages of dried flower buds and rhubarb roots and tiny glass jars full of clear syrups.

I sit down and stare at the mess in front of me, my thoughts racing. I'm still hollow inside from the idea of defeat...but not so much anymore.

So Shire trained just this way, too—organizing and sorting, measuring and pouring—and I never had a clue. I always just assumed she practiced by casting real magic. How she learned to deal with the pain and then recover before doing it again.

I can blame my parents for making it part of their deal, agreeing to let Shire cast magic for marks as long as she didn't tell me anything about training with Rudy. I know they did it to discourage me from thinking I could go along, too. How they did it out of worry for me as much as for practical reasons, since I really wasn't ready at all. They only had to look at Shire's scar to remind themselves of that, to look at the scant amount of marks in the till as the teahouse went through repairs.

And after a while, I got used to not asking questions anymore. I got used to Shire heading out and coming back and the shop's honor marks getting paid on time. Just like I got used to her staying in her room for hours, quietly suffering as she healed from her last casting.

But I'm no longer willing to look the other way.

I take a deep breath and begin to empty the boxes. Something steely fills my blood, settles my racing mind—hope, determination, maybe just delusion if that's what it takes.

Shire, I'm going to figure this out. I stand bottles on the floor, stack jars and tins. *You're dead, but I'm not, and I'm going to save us from Saint Willow.*

When I finally have Rudy's boxed apothecary supplies laid out in front of me on the floor, I sit back and stare at them again, frowning and wondering what it all means when it comes to magic. The answer feels slippery, just out of grasp.

I will the panic to stay away for a bit longer. Reach again for that steeliness I need so badly to stay with me.

"C'mon, you stupid hunk of glass . . ." I whisper, reaching for one of the bottles. The coolness of its neck is soothing in my fingers. "What are you supposed to help me understand?"

I decide to start sorting, as Rudy asked. I *could* think all of this is just another chore. That nothing has changed from when I was here last time or the time before. But he's asked me to do this for a reason. I know that now.

I set the bottle down behind me where there's room on the floor, and reach for another. I start a new pile for each different kind of item, and before long, I've settled into a groove and barely think as I work. It's mindless once you get the pattern down and just follow it.

Bottles here, jars here, *green* bottles here, vials here—

I stop moving and slowly set down the vial I was holding.

My thoughts start to race again.

All those times he made me organize shelves, taking every single item off and placing them all back down. My one shoulder—the shoulder of my casting arm—was sore the next day from repeating the same motion too many times.

The dozens of bottles he had me fill with one of his formulas for treating a bad cough. So that by the time I was done, I didn't even have to think about double-checking the amount I was using because I just knew it was fine.

The rows of ingredients he had me memorize, knowing exactly where each item was just by picturing the layout in my head. A clear vision in my mind. Everything I could need, right at my fingertips.

A laugh bursts free, flooding the last of the hollowness that'd still been nestled inside me even as its echo bounces across the room. I can't miss the relief in it, the note of startled amazement.

"Really, Rudy?" I start sorting again, rushing to finish now that I understand. "Couldn't you have just *told* me?"

But I know why he didn't. I would have listened and not really believed I needed to do any of it. I would have gone out to cast full magic without worry, sure I already knew everything.

I might not have even made it to this point.

The earth might be half gone.

I slow down the sorting on purpose now, taking more care with each item as I set it in its right place. The motions of my hands move like cogs turning in a wristwatch—the kind full magic casters don't really wear anymore because each casting burns up the mechanisms inside—smooth in their repetition, from here to here and then back again.

My heartbeat runs low and gentle, an idling motor. Even the flow of my blood seems to slow. A soft, steady hum fills my ears.

But don't just sit and watch the flames dance, Aza. You have to remember to stoke the fire, too. To keep it going for as long as you need it.

It's Shire's voice in my head. It's the memory I still go back to whenever I cast full magic, from that day years ago when we were both still kids. How she talked to me about controlling magic while we built a fire in the workroom of the teahouse, a room that's hidden from the eyes of customers out front. Not just a typical fire but a *red* fire, the gentlest fire that exists. It's one of our family secrets, passed down from the ancestors who first created Wu teas centuries ago—that only a red fire be allowed to dry the delicate buds used in a Wu blend.

My mind reels back in time.

The workroom still smelled of fresh wood and paint. The new countertop around the open fireplace gleamed. Repairs had just finished days ago and the repairmen were finally gone. My parents and Shire were already back to using the room as heavily as they had before—business went on and teas still had to be blended for sale—but things had changed just the slightest.

My parents looked at me with fear. I had to tell them whenever I used a fire.

And Shire had her scar.

It was still pink and healing as I followed her into the workroom, my arms full of fragrant flower branches—chrysanthemums, wisteria, rhododendrons, jasmine—all carefully preserved as they dried so that smoke from their fires would smell of their blooms. She said it didn't hurt anymore, but I wasn't sure I believed her.

"I'm supposed to tell Mom and Dad," I said to Shire, "whenever I come in here to—"

"No, it's okay," Shire said, opening up the vents along the wall. "I'm here with you. Want to start up the fire?"

I set my armful of branches down on the counter beside the fireplace. Some houses had material around to start fires without using magic. But most houses had nothing, because even leftover magic was enough to ignite tinder.

There was some on the grate already, tufts of shaved-up wood. There was also kindling on the side, ready to be added as soon as the fire began to take.

"No, you do it," I said. I hadn't lit a fire since the accident. Since the workroom had been fixed, I'd barely come in. But I still remembered how the magic had felt. Like I was sick with a bad fever.

"You're only lighting it. Use your leftover magic, like before."

I shook my head, still unsure. What if it had changed again and I didn't know it? "Will you do it? Please?"

Shire knew it wasn't leftover magic on my mind. "You can't be scared of your own magic," she said. "It's full magic. It's rare, just like mine."

"I can't control it."

"One day, you will. I just know it."

The memory of the heat I felt was so strong even then. "Not today, though."

Shire was twelve to my eight and still mostly patient with me.

She rolled her eyes and cast the fire alight with a breath on her palm.

We built up the fire slowly, keeping it gentle with the flower branches we chose as its fuel, by stoking it with the fire rod at exactly the right time, and only just so. The flames glowed a red as bright as poppies.

I asked the question I still hadn't learned not to ask. "So is Rudy a good magic teacher?"

Shire smiled. "Rudy doesn't teach 'magic'—he teaches *control*."

I picked bark free from a wisteria branch. "That's what I said."

She frowned and poked the fire with the rod. "I can't tell you anything. I promised Mom and Dad."

"A hint? I won't tell."

"Oh, Aza." I could sense her patience wavering with the flames. She huffed out a sigh and tucked her long black hair behind an ear. "How about I tell you something I got on my own? Something about controlling magic?"

I nodded, deciding it was a good swap.

"It's like stoking a fire. The magic you draw is its fuel, but you control how high you want the flames, Aza." She took the wisteria branch from my hands, dropped it in, and the fire grew. "What you want it to burn." Shire poked the bed of wood and it spilled over. The flames shot sideways. "Where you want it to go."

I backed up a step. The skin of my arms was hot, nearly as though I were casting magic again. The flames danced closer to yellow than red—too hot for drying stuff for tea now. "What do you mean?" My sister stepped back with me and grinned. The spread of the scar on her cheek went in and out of shadow. "Well, that's the part Rudy's going to teach me."

The memory ends and time is today again. The medicinal smells of Rudy's apothecary replace the floral ones—chrysanthemums, wisteria, rhododendrons, jasmine—of the teahouse's workroom of eight years ago.

Shire, now I know how, too. If only we could have talked about it together. Maybe we could have made each other stronger. Maybe you'd be alive still.

SIX

I start moving the supplies back into the boxes, careful to keep everything sorted. And just like before, soon enough the work becomes mindless, a pattern of motions I do while barely having to think about it. Green bottles in this box, amber ones here, rhubarb roots in this one . . .

When I'm done I return the now re-sorted boxes to the shelf and head out to the shop.

It's empty except for Rudy. He's doing inventory, checking his stock of medicated oils and soaps against information he's looking at in a binder. The light coming in through the main window is a gauzy dark gray, revealing it's nearly evening. Which means it's nearly dinner. I have to get home soon—as far as my parents know, I should have been done with work by now.

"Why are you still here?" I walk over and pick up a thick bar of black soap. I sniff but can't place the scent. "Doesn't the shop close around this time?"

"Pine tar," Rudy mutters as he writes something down in the binder. He sounds even more tired than he did earlier. "For rashes."

"What?"

"The soap."

I put the bar back, wondering how to say thank you. It should be easy, now that I finally have some answers. But I still have questions, ones about Shire that I'm beginning to doubt Rudy will ever tell me.

"So I figured out why you've been having me do chores around this place," I say.

No reaction. He just keeps writing, eyes planted firmly on his paper. It's like the Rudy from the supply room who gave me back a small piece of my sister never happened.

"You don't care that I know now?" My voice is stiff. The note of pleading in there surprises even me, and the skin of my neck burns.

"Only if it means you'll stop coming back." Still writing. "You can practice on your own now. There's really nothing else you need from me, Aza."

The heat around my neck climbs until my face is just as hot. I don't even mind that much—I'm used to being angry with Rudy instead of grateful. And maybe he's the same way, too. If my being here keeps being a bother, he won't have to feel bad about everything he hides from me.

"Practice on my own or not, I still need to know the spell that killed Shire. Which *you* know because you were actually there when she cast it."

Rudy shuts the binder and finally faces me. He looks like hell. Guilt slips in—I know a lot of that hell is because of me—and I drop my gaze. I can't let it matter, can't let it convince me to back off. Just a little more time is all I need, I almost want to beg him. One more week and it's over either way—Saint Willow pays the teahouse a personal visit or I'll have made enough marks from magic to clear our debt.

"I can't tell you anything else," he says quietly. He pushes up his glasses and begins to move away. "The shop's closed now, so good-bye, Aza."

He's already disappeared into the supply room before I can make myself leave. My face is still hot, and an ugly mix of fury and humiliation slicks the back of my mouth, turning it bitter.

I yank open the front door and rush outside. Smoke-scented air washes over me, immediately smothering the cleaner scents of rosemary, camphor, and ginger. It's drizzling and cold out because it's Lotusland, and I start walking as fast as I can down the sidewalk, like I'm trying to chase something down or maybe even escape from it—Rudy's secrets, Shire's, my own, I can't tell.

Baseball Cap hasn't left. At the last second, I remember to turn to check and there he is, still across the street. Except now he's inside the breakfast-all-day diner that's opposite Rudy's place. He's sitting at a window table, his head turned in the direction of the apothecary. Our eyes meet as I pass, and whatever it is I see in his, I'm suddenly sure that Rudy's wrong about the cop not keeping watch on him and his shop.

Sweat pops up on my brow as I swing my gaze forward and keep walking, pretending I haven't taken real notice of Baseball Cap in any way. And now my thoughts swivel, going from recalling all the reasons why I'm right for resenting Rudy, to breaking down why it makes sense a cop's on him and how he could be in very bad trouble.

I have to tell him.

Shire would want me to.

And the thing is, if this *is* about him lying on record about how Shire died, then I'm in trouble, too. And so are my parents.

I stop abruptly at the end of the block and make a show of searching for something in my pockets and coming up empty.

I turn right back around and keep going until I'm once again at the apothecary. I keep from looking at the cop across the street, hoping that Rudy hasn't already locked up and left. It feels too important to not tell him right away.

I pull the front door open and call out his name. "Rudy?"

At first glance, the shop seems empty. He's not even hunched over behind the counter, counting marks or gathering up the day's bills of sale.

But the door wasn't locked, so he must still be here.

The supply room.

I head over, calling out as I stuff my mask away—"It's me, Aza, where are you?"—so I don't accidentally startle him into a heart attack or something.

"Rudy, it's me," I say loudly. The echo of my voice rings off the walls, emphasizing how it's so quiet here otherwise. I go behind the counter and step into the supply room. "Hey, about that cop, I think—"

He's on the floor, lying on his back. His eyes are shut and he's as pale as porcelain. Supplies lie scattered all around him—whatever happened, it was sudden.

"Rudy!" My pulse is thudding in the back of my throat as I rush over and get down to my knees. "Are you okay? What happened?"

All I can think about is how I saw that he looked unwell, and still I pushed him. I bothered him and refused to leave him alone.

How much of this is my fault?

What if all of it is?

I'm considering patting parts of his body to see if he's injured, but I have no idea how to even tell. He's not awake to scream in pain or anything.

Panic turns my stomach icy, and I have to shake myself to focus. Where should I start? Torso? Okay, torso.

His eyes open, but just slightly. "Aza?" My name is a slow whisper.

"Rudy, what happened? Do you want me to call an ambulance? The shop must have a landline, right?" Full-time casters often have cells just because it draws attention if we don't, but most of the time, they're not working; we kill them each and every time. I've been carrying around a dead one for months. If anyone asks, I just say I'm on my way to get it repaired.

"No ambulance," Rudy says. His words are jagged, full of pain. "Knew . . . this was coming. Can't be helped."

"What are you talking about?"

"I'm sick. Been sick for years. My heart . . . is bad."

Rudy, dying? How can he—? He's always been—

"No." I clutch his shoulder with a cold hand. My blood runs colder. "No, you're going to be fine. Let me call—"

"Listen." A cough, and there's blood rushing out, and I realize that this is all real. "The cop outside, Aza. He's here for me, okay?"

"What? Why? What did you do?"

"Shire . . . the night she died . . ."

More blood, gushes of it. Panic hits me in waves. "Rudy, stop talking, I have to think. Let me try magic—"

He shakes his head. "*No.* It'll hurt you. And it's too late. I'm dying."

"*Rudy*—"

"Listen to me." He coughs again, and more blood comes. "Wanted to teach you more, but . . . scared to. Meant to enter . . . meant to finish what I started." His eyes drift shut. "Meant it as payback . . . for Shire."

Everything he's saying is a tangled mess in my brain. "Enter what? What do you mean, payback for Shire?"

"I'm sorry, Aza."

Then Rudy dies.

SEVEN

For a long time, I just sit there, unable to move because I've gone numb. From outside there's the sound of traffic, the occasional honk of a horn. One of the glass bottles on the supply room floor has shattered open and the entire room smells of rosemary, a scent I might never smell again without thinking of this moment.

Rudy's lying on his back, half-covered in blood. He's still very much dead.

I stare at him and wonder if I ever knew him at all.

Wanted to teach you more, but scared.

Meant to finish what I started.

Payback for Shire.

His words flash across my mind, leaving me more confused than ever. And then it comes: guilt, not just slipping in, but in huge washes and waves. Oceans of it, wishing it could revive a secret bad heart.

"Rudy," I whisper. "You should have told me. I would have—"

I would have done exactly the same. I would have kept coming still, choosing a ghost to avenge over the person I wanted to hold at fault for creating that ghost in the first place.

Shame makes me shiver. So how am I any better than Rudy? Who I resented so much—for all his cruel nonanswers, his cranky evasions to keep from helping me. I couldn't forgive him for letting Shire die. And now I'm the one here left with his body.

The answer is, I'm not any better. I'm worse.

I lay my hand over his heart, despite all the blood. "I'm sorry, too."

The cop outside, Aza. He's here for me, okay?

Shire, the night she died.

My stomach twists as I observe Rudy for another long, unmoving moment. I feel sick as the truth sinks in.

How this whole time, I've been right about him hiding something about Shire and the way she died.

"And so you got caught," I murmur as I stare down at his still face. "Which means it won't be long before some Scout comes around asking *me* about that night. Asking my parents."

Something contorts in my chest, making it hard to breathe. Guilt tangles with the same old anger. I might have killed Rudy, but it was from being kept in the dark—while his keeping secrets about my sister dying was absolutely on purpose.

I have to know what happened. The need for answers burns inside, just as hot as my banned magic does.

But where do I start?

"Getting away from here is one idea," I say out loud. Baseball Cap across the street saw me come in here but not leave. What if he decides to come check out the shop? And here I am with the dead body of the person he's been staking out.

I scramble to my feet, terror working like caffeine through my veins. Parts of me are shaking, turning my motions jagged and clumsy.

There's some blood on my pants, and it's not dark enough outside to hide the stains. I grab an acorn from my starter bag and cast the fabric clean. There's no pain, since leftover magic is enough for the spell.

How to leave the apothecary is another matter.

I *could* leave using the shop's back door—it's here in the supply room, between two of the shelves. Or cast myself invisible and then leave through the front.

But soon enough Rudy's body will be discovered, and Baseball Cap will know, and he'll wonder about the teenaged girl he saw go inside but not leave again.

Or I could use the front door and just let him watch me leave.

But that doesn't erase how I'd still be the girl he saw leave from a shop with a dead body inside.

So, the only option I have is to make the cop forget he ever saw me come here today, the day Rudy died. There's no escaping that I'm connected to the apothecary—my prints are all over it—but that's as a helper. I need to not be connected to his death.

My head buzzes.

To cast full magic on a cop is about the most reckless thing a caster could do. But I can't figure out another way to get out of here without ending up appearing suspicious over Rudy dying.

For a second I consider taking myself out of the cop's mind altogether. A total mind wipe, but of a person instead of a chunk of time.

But just as quickly, I drop the idea. It might save me from being questioned, but it wouldn't save my parents during his continued investigation of Shire's death. And to cast enough magic to wipe out all of us—

Cold sweat rises on my skin at the thought. That amount of magic is dangerous—to me, to the whole sector.

I leave the supply room and walk back into the shop, still unsure what spell to cast in order to escape. The light's changed again, and the inside of the apothecary is dim, nearly half-dark. I make my way over to the front window, making sure to stay off to the side to avoid being seen through the glass.

My heartbeat pounding high in my throat, I crane my head sideways and peek across the street so that the diner is in full view. A more experienced caster could do this while hidden away, but for me to do a mind wipe, I still need the person I'm casting magic on to be in clear sight.

Baseball Cap is still at the window table. I'd almost admire his doggedness if he weren't being so careless about showing it. What kind of cop is this, anyway? Maybe I'm worrying way too much about what he could possibly figure out . . .

I unzip my starter bag and dig out a small bit of bark. I draw a five-pointed star on my palm. It should be enough magic to wipe away the last few hours from the cop's memory. He'll be confused at first over the missing time. But he'll eventually forget that he can't remember how there's a small gap at all.

I place the bark in the middle of the star and envision parts of his memory being wiped clean. Like grit from a dirty windowpane, swept away with a rag.

The floor of the apothecary trembles. Heat collects in my sneakers and climbs up my legs and spreads into my hands. They grow heavy, as though I'm cradling invisible weights. My hand is on fire around the piece of bark, and the material begins to smoke just the slightest bit.

I glance up and over in the direction of the diner window to catch Baseball Cap's eye. Only once we see each other can I drive my magic into him.

But the cop's turned away now. There's a waitress at his table—he's ordering something from the menu.

Damn it.

A drawn-out casting doesn't add to the pain that comes afterward, but it *does* keep me burning up until I can finish the spell, and the building discomfort makes my head sway. Heat rolls off my skin and fills the room. Scents of apothecary supplies roll back at me, set off by the drastic temperature change—licorice, roses, beeswax, sandalwood. My vision wavers and the shop goes dreamlike, not quite real.

The waitress is laughing. Baseball Cap must have told a joke.

"C'mon," I mutter out loud. "Just finish the order and look over here."

My veins are flooded with full magic, this vast nebula of glowing red fire that only my mind's eye can see. It dances off my skin in swarms, circles me in a blood-tinged hug, looking for somewhere to land. The inside of my mouth is hot. My eyeballs feel singed, gone raw and red. My pulse is a thousand drums inside my ears, beating out a mad rhythm.

The waitress finally leaves and the cop turns and peers out the diner's window.

His eyes meet mine.

Magic surges.

EIGHT

I pull away, breathing raggedly. Out of Baseball Cap's head and back into mine. Immediately my skin grows cold, and where my veins were filled with magic, now they fill with pain.

Bruises bloom across my arms. They crawl out from beneath the sleeves of my shirt, patches of purple as dark as midnight, blotches of maroon as red as wine. I don't need to check beneath my jeans to know my legs are just as bad. There's a dull ache inside my limbs that feels close to a fever. I press my fingers all over my face. I'm lucky; only my left cheek and jaw hurt—my smog mask will cover most of that.

Five points—bruises until tomorrow, at the very earliest.

But it's done. I stagger back from the window, steadying my breath, and go back into the supply room.

The scent of blood wars with that of rosemary, and bile rises.

I go to check Rudy's body for signs that might give me away, grabbing a pair of safety gloves Rudy used when handling some of his more volatile ingredients. First, his wallet for any cards or whatever else might tie him to Wu Teas. But there's nothing. I'm about to put it back when I decide to take the marks that are inside. Rudy would want me to.

I check the rest of his pockets, and they're all empty except for his chest one.

A note. It's written in Rudy's handwriting, which I recognize from all over the apothecary.

Midnight
July 15th
987 Scalding Way
FC

That's it. Four lines. Midnight tonight. An address in the Meat Sector. Nothing more to explain what it means. The *FC* is even more mysterious. Someone's initials? A password of some kind?

I flip over the note and there's a small black coin taped to it. I take off the tape so the coin falls into my hand. Its shape and weight and thinness are about right for a mark, and it has the same center hole, but everything else is different. Black metal instead of copper or nickel, perfectly blank on both sides.

I have no clue what it is or what it could be for.

"You couldn't have elaborated on this a bit?" I gesture toward Rudy with the note and the coin. I tell myself he looks at peace. At least not sick anymore, anyway.

The note could mean something as simple as Rudy having plans tonight. Maybe it's the address of a friend? Maybe there's a party and Rudy had a date? Maybe it means nothing at all.

But his last words are again in my head.

Wanted to teach you more, but scared.

Meant to finish what I started.

Payback for Shire.

They're still cryptic. I can't tell what Rudy might have meant by them. The note doesn't help at all.

But to have an address, and a time, for something Rudy might have meant to be at. It eats at me—him dying with all his secrets about my sister, leaving new questions behind.

I fold up the note and tuck it and the strange black coin into my starter bag.

Tonight at midnight. Scalding Way. I'll figure out the FC part when I get there.

I touch Rudy's cold shoulder once more. *I wanted to trust you because Shire did, Rudy. But maybe she never really knew you, either.*

I get to my feet, tear off the gloves, make sure my sleeves are still hiding my arms, and pull on my smog mask to cover the bruises on my face. I slip out through the back door.

Outside, there are the sounds of an approaching fire truck, but I don't make the connection until I turn the corner.

It's an eruption of a stretch of asphalt. Cars are spiraled across the still-flat part of the road like toys, while pedestrians ogle from the sidewalks.

I walk along, trying to blend into the crowd, convinced at least some of them must realize they're seeing the result of full magic being cast somewhere. I'm careful to avoid meeting the eyes of any of them.

Of casters of leftover magic because they might detect my guilt.

Of casters of full because they might nod in understanding, giving us both away.

NINE

It hurts to walk—each step is like a slap on my bruises—so I take the short way home for once, cutting through the sector instead of going along the salty shore. I figure seeing the bruises will be enough to distract my parents from asking me why I smell like Tobacco instead of Tea.

My parents think I work for Saint Willow. On account of falling so behind on paying our honor marks, they think he hired me two months ago as a courier for his gang. That the marks I make doing this go toward paying our debt.

This is another lie I've told. And so while they think I'm going around to other businesses in the Tea Sector picking up and dropping off packages, I'm actually either at Rudy's apothecary or somewhere else, casting full magic for marks.

My parents believing I work for Saint Willow explains Jihen's sudden disappearance from their lives, his threatening presence no longer darkening the teahouse. That lie, in turn, rests on my lie to Jihen about being a tutor so he will stay away from my parents. Between my two fake jobs, nobody knows where I actually get my marks from—selling spells as a caster of banned full magic. Magic that if Saint Willow knew I could cast, he would make me cast for him, regardless of how I would suffer for it.

Sometimes I lie so much that I think I'll stop knowing what's real anymore. Or maybe it's just being surrounded by the lies of so many others that they change what truth even means.

Even my parents have lied to me. About what they let Shire do for them. For us. A lie by omission. *Don't tell Aza.* The thick scents of smoke and moss soon swirl away and the lighter ones of tea take over—images of green fields and orchards full of lushly leaved plants float across my mind. The sky's gone a clouded, deep charcoal by the time I reach the teahouse, and cold drizzle continues. The front window of the teahouse glows gold against the rain, so warm and cheery that it seems almost impossible people like Saint Willow and Jihen and a hungry cop looking for answers that will destroy us can also exist.

For a second, my throat goes tight at how everything's going wrong. Rudy's dead, his body probably still on the floor in his apothecary. I can't decide if I should warn my parents about Baseball Cap possibly showing up or just leave it in case I'm wrong and he was never on a trail leading right to our door. My desperation for marks is real, but no matter how many I might make, they won't bring Shire back. Nothing is the same.

One week.

A breeze comes right then, and I imagine it's Jihen, breathing close.

My mother pushes open the front door of the teahouse while I'm still climbing the steps. Her long black hair sweeps across her shoulders, and she places her hands at her hips. You have to really study her black silk trousers to notice how old the fabric's gotten. That same golden light from the now-closed-for-the-day teahouse flows out from behind her.

"You're very late, Aza."

As always, her tone is both soft and sharp, both concerned and irritated.

And your dead daughter's old instructor is dead, Mom. I'd tell you, but you'd ask how I know. I'd tell you, but you'd probably be glad, and I don't think I want to see you glad over something like that.

"Sorry," I say, taking off my smog mask and folding it back into my pocket.

"Dinner is . . ."

Her voice falls away as I reach the top step, and she glimpses the two bruises on my face. Her gaze immediately goes to my arms and she tugs up a sleeve, checking for more because she knows how pain from full magic works. Beneath the dimness of the sky, the blotches on my skin seem even darker. She blinks fast, as though she can't believe what she's seeing. Then she rushes me inside and slams the door shut.

"Casting full magic out in the open? *Why?* What were you thinking?"

I swipe rain off my forehead. I tug at the zipper of my starter bag, making sure it's still secure. Forcing my thoughts away from the mysterious note, I let go of the bag and take a deep breath. The inside of the teahouse always smells like a mix of tea and forests and dried flowers—it's the scent of legacy, of the ghosts of emperors and empresses and *security*. Sometimes it's comforting, and sometimes it's smothering.

"I'm okay, by the way," I say as I walk through the tidy retail area with its display cabinets and tall shelves. "They'll fade by tomorrow."

"I'm glad you're okay, of course," my mother insists as she walks alongside me. Her eyes flicker to my jaw and then flicker away. "It's just—"

"You worry."

"Every day."

On my other side is the teahouse's small dining area, with its main window that faces the sidewalk. During the day, customers sit here and order tea and pastries and buns.

Once it was a lot busier, not just with customers but also with family. We used to eat out here every night, after the teahouse closed and the space was ours again. But that was before Shire died, and now it's a rare thing for my parents and me to bother bringing dinner out here. Now we just sit around the beat-up wooden island in the cramped back kitchen and pretend we're really talking.

My father is already seated at the island in the kitchen, hunched over paperwork, a plate at one elbow and tea at his other. His face falls when he peers up at me. "Aza, what—?"

"Nothing happened," I lie. "I cast magic and the price is some bruises. A car was about to run a light and I had to help it slow down, so don't freak out." I pull out a stool, sit down, and start piling food on my plate. It's Thursday, so it's pork dumplings and broccoli salad and lemon rice. The stool beside me still feels huge in its emptiness.

He pours tea into a cup and pushes it toward me. "Is this why you're so late? Maybe we should finally get you a new cell so we can at least reach you while it's working."

I shake my head and take a sip of tea. It's our Conversation blend, which I think is ironic. "My last delivery was on the other side of the sector. It just took me a bit to walk back."

"You could have taken the train."

"Pass is used up, and I didn't want to spend any marks."

My mother sits down beside my father and picks up her chopsticks. But instead of eating, she just holds them over her plate. "That doesn't explain why you're casting. Why did they need your help so badly? That car would have likely stopped in time on its own."

I shrug. "Some people were slow to finish crossing."

My parents exchange a look.

"You're not ready," my mother says.

The food in my mouth turns dry, and I take a minute to wash it down with tea, wondering why I'm suddenly bothered. My mother *always* says I'm not ready. She says it as often as she says she just worries about me.

"I'm not eight anymore," I finally say. "I don't actually hurt someone each time I cast."

"And your surroundings? Did you check to see what you broke or just not bother?"

"Some asphalt fell apart. I might have done the city a favor—I'm pretty sure that road needed an upgrade anyway."

"No one was hurt?"

I shake my head again. There were no ambulances.

My mother slowly stirs her food, while my father just watches me. He's still holding the paperwork. I can see now it's the teahouse's files on our suppliers and distribution systems that we have in place in the city.

He points at my arms. "So maybe not hurt someone else, but what about *you* getting hurt?"

"This is—" I nearly laugh. "This is just part of it. You know there's a cost. It's nothing new."

"And your sister is dead from casting full magic. Have you thought about that?"

"It's pretty much all I think about, okay?" I stab apart a dumpling with my chopsticks. "Just like it's all you guys think about," I add under my breath.

"Aza," my mother starts, "we just—"

"Worry, I know. You worry because you don't want the same thing to happen to me, and that's why you won't let me cast to help out with all the bills." I break open another dumpling, hoping my face doesn't show how my stomach's gone tight.

"We *don't* want you getting hurt, and we're thankful you want to help. It just means we shouldn't ever forget how lucky we are that you get to work for Saint Willow."

"So you really sleep easier knowing I'm spending each day as a courier for the sector's gang leader instead of casting full magic?" The moment I say it, it hits me how furious I am with my parents for feeling this way. It's like they're okay if something bad happens to me, even if it's because of someone as evil as Saint Willow, as long as it's not because of full magic.

How much do they care about me staying safe, then?

My parents exchange another look.

"We know you're angry with us for not letting you go to Rudy," my father says, "but we just think you need a bit more time."

"Time for what? Saint Willow says we're nearly out of it."

"How can you learn how to control magic if you don't understand that magic in the first place? Can you ever be sure you're using magic and it's not using you?"

I eat salad to hide how my eyes are prickling. *I'm not eight anymore*, I want to scream again.

My mother clears her throat and casts to turn on the television we keep mounted to the front of the fridge. One of her favorite dramas starts playing. It's a Pearl of the Orient production, the kind she watches the most because she likes their tropes. *Liar's Lair* first came out when I was a kid, so I've seen it a bunch of times already. It's about two casters from rival gangs who each go undercover to infiltrate the other's in order to find secret intel.

It's always reminded me a bit of Lotusland just because of the gang thing, but my mother says Lotusland isn't nearly so brutal. We'd argue about it, about the rumors that spread throughout the city the way poisonous fungi pop up in the dark.

I heard that Earl Kingston demoted one of his own cousins the other day for trying to conspire against him. And you know what "demoted" means.

I've heard the stories, Aza. Just because a businessman operates with a firm hand doesn't mean he's a monster.

Well, the stories are true, Mom. A nice little drowning for poor Milo Kingston in the good ol' Sturgeon River.

That is not what "demoted" means. And Earl Kingston would never do that. He takes care of families in the Tobacco Sector as though they are his own. Just like Saint Willow takes care of all of us here in Tea.

It was only Earl Kingston's third cousin, twice removed, if that means anything.

Oh, Aza.

Paperwork rustles as my father looks away and starts once more to read the file, as my mother turns to watch her show.

So many ways they don't see me. How I'm not a kid who can't control her magic anymore. How, in the end, it still wasn't me who killed Shire.

I keep eating and drinking more tea, trying so hard not to think back to that day. But I fail, and soon my mind is no longer in the kitchen but instead in the workroom.

I'm eight again. And I remember it all.

TEN

I was holding fragrant branches in my arms—chrysanthemums, jasmine, rhododendrons, wisteria—each carefully dried under very specific conditions so their fires wouldn't smoke too much. Shire and I had been put in charge of drying the buds for our mother, who would be mixing up new teas that day.

It was also the first time my parents trusted us to build the red fire for the drying. To do it all on our own, without their supervision.

Watch for signs of yellow in the flames, girls. You must cool the fire a bit if it turns close to yellow. And if there is any blue at all, suppress the fire and start over again. Blue is too hot and will destroy anything.

Shire went around the workroom and opened the vents in the wall. Sunlight filtered in and danced off the smooth, unmarked skin of her face.

"Aza, want to check on the fireplace? Do we have enough of everything?"

I set the branches down on the counter and peered down. "Yes, there's lots of kindling *and* tinder."

My sister came over and moved some of the tufts of shaved-up wood around. "Okay, I'm going to start the fire now."

I nodded, stepping back to give her room to cast.

Shire cupped her hand and blew into it.

The kindling caught, and I reached for the fire rod to pass to Shire for her to poke in some of the tinder.

She shook her head and smiled. "Let's not use that today."

Full magic.

I grinned back, excited. I wanted to see Shire cast full magic more than anything. It wasn't often that our parents let her since the world said it wasn't allowed, and because it hurt her, too.

My excitement died down a bit. I didn't want her to hurt, either. And I didn't want her to get into trouble.

"Mom and Dad will get mad," I said. "Plus casting hurts you, remember?"

"Not very much. I'll use a spell that will just leave my bones sore for a bit. It's not permanent. And Mom and Dad won't even be able to tell."

I hesitated, torn. I trusted Shire because somehow she always knew how to keep our parents from getting mad, while I never did a very good job with that. And to feed a fire with full magic—it would be like making rain with a wish, like growing snow from your fingertips . . .

I tried once more to be obedient. "They don't like it when you use your magic for no good reason."

"There's never a good reason, then."

I grinned again and leaned the rod back against the wall. "Okay."

Shire picked up a stray shaving from the side of the fireplace. She drew a five-pointed star on her palm and placed the shaving in the middle of it. Then she stared hard at the pieces of tinder that lay on the hot grate. The tiny strands of red that were our fire had already raced themselves through the rest of the kindling.

The tinder slowly lifted up into the air. There, the thin pieces of wood hovered for a second before each slowly flipped once, twice. Then they flopped back down onto the strands of red. The edges of the tinder caught, began to glow.

"Shire," I whispered in awe—we wouldn't find out until later that day how earth had paid for our moment of fun, the wild blackberry bushes that lined the ditch behind the teahouse bent low to the ground as though a giant foot had come down from above and stomped on them. "All of that was you?"

My sister laughed, then winced. The pain had hit her bones. She slowly opened her hand, and the tiny bit of charred wood that was all that was left of her starter floated downward. "Of course it was me—who else?"

Sometimes my heart ached with how much I wanted full magic, too. I cast leftover magic all the time, but now it was no longer special. It felt dull, second best. I wanted to be like Shire, who was older, prettier, and better at so many things. It almost seemed unfair that she had full magic on top of all that, but I knew it wasn't up to her. She was just really lucky. I hoped I would be as lucky one day, too. And if I was, I would never become one of those casters who Scouts had to hunt down, the ones who destroyed bits of the earth at a time. I would never be terrible with my magic.

"That first time." I was staring at the fire, watching it grow. "Did you know the instant your leftover magic turned into full magic?"

I had no memory of Shire's discovery since I'd only been two when it happened. But I knew the story. How it'd been at breakfast, and how Shire had heated up a cup of water for tea—still a caster of leftover magic. But that's all such a caster can do with a breath spell—heating a single cup at most. So when she went on to heat a whole teapot, everyone knew.

"Well, you don't really lose your leftover magic," Shire said. She rubbed at her arms, checking the pain. "It's more like full magic comes and . . . swarms it up."

"That's what I meant."

"I told you how it gets hot while casting, right? Your whole body does. That's really the only difference, since you don't feel anything when you cast leftover magic."

"But that first time, could you tell *before* you cast that your magic had changed?"

She shook her head. "I can't really remember. I was only six. Mom and Dad would remember better if I told them anything then."

"There had to be something."

"I really can't remember, Aza. One day it was just there."

I frowned, wanting to believe her. But it seemed too simple. If it was so simple, why was full magic so powerful, then? I began to add some of the dried branches to the fire, wondering if I could help her remember, trying to come up with ideas. "Was it maybe like getting a burst of energy?"

"Sure, a burst of energy, just like that."

Shire didn't sound convinced. It sounded more like something she was saying because she knew I wanted to hear it.

"Maybe I should go look it up," I said. "Someone must have talked about it before, since every single caster on earth once used full magic. Right?"

"Really, Aza, it just happened all on its own." One day it was just there. And then as I got older, it grew stronger. Now she sounded nearly bored. It reminded me of how she was already twelve and I was only eight and how sometimes she seemed tired of me always being there. "You can't make it come or anything. It just means not everyone is meant to cast full magic—not anymore." She passed me another branch. "Here, one more. Last one, though—the fire's pretty much ready right now, and if it gets any hotter, we'll have to bank it back before we can dry anything. I'll be right back—we left the box of buds behind the front counter."

She left the workroom, and I stared at the red flames, feeling their gentle heat. Restlessness stirred.

I dropped the branch onto the flames and decided I had to at least *try* casting full magic. Shire hadn't had any warning before she found out, after all. What if I'd had full magic for *ages* and had just never known because I'd never tried it?

Then there was just *how much* magic I wanted to pull from the earth. Just how strong of a spell did I want to try casting? Shire's five-pointed star had pulled enough to make pieces of wood dance in the air.

Which meant ten might lift up the larger flower branches and make *them* dance.

Fifteen might make the *whole entire fire* dance.

My heart was beating fast, a pattern of notes of anticipation and hope, of dread and fear. I had to be fast. I knew if Shire got back and saw me trying that I would feel stupid. She wouldn't mean for me to, but I would anyway. Maybe if only I was better at *something* than Shire, or had something she didn't. But no.

I reached over and picked up a piece of fresh kindling that we'd missed.

I drew a star of fifteen points on my palm.

I laid the kindling in the middle of the star.

I looked up and stared at the red fire and imagined all those flames dancing in midair. I tried to imagine feeling suddenly energized. I told myself that I *was* energized. How I had all the energy of all the casters who ever existed, right there in my blood.

But nothing happened.

My palm stayed cool, the starter on it unburned. The red fire on the grate didn't dance.

I felt no differently than if I'd been trying to cast leftover magic.

Disappointment surged, surprising me with its force. I blinked back tears. So Shire wasn't lying. You really couldn't wish for it to happen. The earth was so different now, and not all casters were allowed to—

The red fire turned yellow.

My shoes, tingling with heat, the way kindling must as it ignites. My legs, crackling and snapping and smelling of char—they were tinder, feeding a fire. My hands were tangled bunches of fragrant branches that smelled of sweet blooms as they burned.

Aza!

Shire's voice came from somewhere far away, a wave of sound in my heated ears.

Aza!

My vision turned thick and blurry. I was jerked backward. It took forever for me to fall to the ground.

Shire's hazy outline as she faced the fireplace. The shimmer of her profile as she turned away.

I was eight, and on the grate in the workroom, blue fire exploded.

And then I am sixteen again, and on the television in the kitchen, rival gangs are hurling threats at one another.

I blink to shake myself out of the memory. The scent of fire is gone and smells of dinner come back. My plate still has food on it, and with numb hands, I begin to eat again. My parents are now looking at paperwork together, the teahouse's file opened up and some of its pages spread out on the wooden island.

"Maybe you can speak to them just once more?"

My mother, sounding worried again. But this time, it's not for me. Her expression is clouded as she reads something on one of the pages.

The tone in her voice forces the past from my mind.

"I've spoken to them over the phone a few times now," my father says. There are creases on the sides of his mouth I haven't noticed before. "I even offered to go over to the office so we could speak face-to-face. But Leafton said no, it wouldn't change anything."

Leafton is one of our longest-running suppliers. We've been getting a bunch of our tea ingredients from them for years. Without them, a handful of our most popular blends wouldn't be the same. Saint Willow owns them, too.

Back to reality, I ask, "What's going on?"

"Leafton is terminating its contract with us." My father's expression is as clouded as my mother's. "They're 'refocusing their customer base,' is the line we're being fed. Which doesn't say much, as it never does in business."

"We didn't get much warning," my mother says quietly. "Twenty-five years of working together, and they end it with a phone call. I'm actually a bit surprised with how they've handled this."

"Well, we'll just have to find a new supplier." My father shuffles papers together. "We need those ingredients."

A new suspicion comes, and suddenly I'm uneasy. The bruises on my arms and legs and face pound along with my pulse. "Doesn't Leafton have contracts with a few other teahouses here in the sector? Have you talked to them to see if they know what's going on?"

"We have." My mother pours more tea. "They're not affected. It's just us. You'd almost think it was intentional, but we've never had problems with Leafton before."

But we're having problems with Saint Willow now, aren't we?

My stomach churns, and I push my plate away. On the television screen, a gang member is screaming as he dies a painful death.

I wonder how much clout Jihen has with his boss. Did my casting him to trip hurt his ego so badly that he went to his cousin and told him to up the pressure?

Or maybe it's really all just Saint Willow. Maybe he got Leafton to cut ties with us so we wouldn't be able to pay. Maybe he likes to use his power in petty ways.

Maybe he's so angry with the pathetic amount of marks I paid him today that he's snapped.

"Let me guess," I say quietly. "Leafton is giving you one week before the process is finalized."

My father finishes shuffling papers and tucks them into the file. "How'd you know?"

"Like I said, just a guess." I start to get up to begin clearing dishes. Rudy's note and the strange black coin are still in my starter bag, their presence like live bugs contained in a jar, waiting to be released. I want to get to my room to look up directions for the address. Midnight can't come fast enough.

One week.

The ticking bomb grows louder each day.

"Aza, hold on a second." My father rips off a small piece of his napkin. He casts around it.

The pounding deep within my bruises recedes a tiny bit. I peek beneath one of my sleeves; blotches that were as dark as violets have gone a muted lavender.

"It might not be full magic," my father says, smiling, "but we still do what we can, don't we?"

ELEVEN

I leave the teahouse at eleven, sneaking out my window and trying not to wince as my bruises knock against the sill. My feet sink into the grass of our backyard, and I shut the window as quietly as I can. It can't be locked from the outside, and it's not worth the pain to cast it locked (and then unlocked when I get back), so I leave it as is.

Once, my mother locked it on me, exasperated to wake up in the middle of the night to find me gone and the apartment vulnerable. *You have a key to the door of the teahouse, Aza; simply leave that way instead of like a criminal.*

But I still sneak out, because of Jihen, who's been ordered to keep an eye on me, Jihen who my parents think is my coworker.

Slipping on my smog mask, I step over to the row of snowball bushes that grow so tightly together they act as our back fence, and peer through a tangle of branches.

No sign of Jihen.

I squeeze through the bushes and out into the alley, then turn and head toward the street.

The Tea Sector isn't really the section of the city most people aim to be late night—that's mostly Culture because of all its theaters and shows, and Electronics because of the arcades and opens-at-dusk shops—but pockets of it stay busy long after typical business hours. I take a more thorough look around, checking for the contrast of white sneakers against a dark suit on the sidewalk

patios of the late-night tea cafés and teatini bars that don't close until dawn. Jihen's like me, never sticking to a schedule or route to keep me guessing when I might run into him.

I also remember to check for signs of a cop wearing a baseball cap. Chances are that he's still in the Tobacco Sector and nowhere near here. If he's staking out the apothecary, it makes sense that he's checked into a motel near to it. Or if Rudy's body has been discovered, then he'd be there for that, too.

But still.

It's a waiting game now. If he's going to come looking for us, I just need him to find me before he finds my parents.

I walk, sweeping petals of snowball bush blooms from my hair and shoulders. I might be sneaking out now to hunt down this place on Rudy's note, but it used to be Rudy himself I'd sneak out for. I would leave home at dawn to make sure I got to the apothecary before it opened, cast full magic to let myself inside, and wait there for Rudy to arrive. So he could never forget I was always around with my questions. So one day he would have to give me the answers I needed. Because he failed in teaching Shire how to stay alive, so he owed it to both her and me to become *my* teacher.

I was Rudy's Jihen. His Saint Willow. His weak heart's worst enemy.

My own heart goes tight with this fact as I finish crossing the street. A chilly drizzle is coming down so finely that it hangs in the air like a mist, unsure of where to go. I turn the corner, that cold mist having nothing on the way I'm already like ice inside.

I know Rudy's dead because of me.

For all that I swore as a kid to never become terrible with my magic, here I am.

Rudy, whatever I'm going to find at this address—if it's anything to do with what you said about finishing something, I'll do it for you.

The Meat Sector makes up the northeast corner of the city, and is about as distant from Tea as you can get and still be within Lotusland limits. So I take the most direct route, cutting my way through the sectors that stand between us.

I leave behind Tea and I step into Government, where all the buildings look the same and the streets run neatly square to each other. I gradually angle my way north even as I keep east. Every few blocks or so I double-check for the dim glow of white sneakers, the curve of a baseball cap, wanting to see them before they see me.

The ring of aged marble statues in the middle of a courtyard lets me know I'm crossing the literal center of the sector. The statues are of the greats, the first seven casters the earth ever created. Together they once made up the Guild of Then. Each of them contributed something to the original magic system—skin spells, bone spells, blood spells, breath spells, the casting arm, the starter, the pointed star—and the statues were once considered the figurative center of the city. Casters came here to celebrate full magic and honor the Guild.

But then casters couldn't stop using all that magic. Over centuries they abused it, leaving the earth on the verge of collapse. So earth adapted to save itself before it fell apart by turning full magic back on its own casters. It made them bear the burden of their greedy powers. Over time, the number of casters of full magic dwindled, while that of leftover grew.

It's only half working.

Earth waited too long to get rid of full magic, so each time it's cast, more of the world still breaks. And its casters are still here, even if we're mostly pretending and hiding, and dying out.

I step around the garbage that's strewn across the ground and finish crossing the courtyard. It's all wrinkled flyers and torn posters—another protest must have just ended. The protests are always over the same issue—how the Guild of Then monument should be taken down. Or at the very least, amended. Why honor a magic system that's become a threat and is no longer the gift it once was?

I leave the Government Sector and walk along the street that divides Spice from Tower, keeping straight east for a bit. As with a lot of the city's sectors, Spice has its own distinctive scent, and the smells of bright peppers and tongue-stinging salts fill my nose. On my other side, lights from the high-rises that make up most of Tower's buildings wink against the dark. Then the road curves south, so I leave it and go north again, cutting into Spice proper and zigzagging my way through its streets. I'm twenty minutes away from 987 Scalding Way.

"Magic? Got magic for me? Who's got magic to spare?"

The faint call comes from the intersection just up ahead, through the thin sounds of late-night traffic.

It's a display caster. An Ivor. Road lights gleam off the steel bars of the human-sized cage that hangs from the tall lamppost on the corner.

"Magic, anyone? Cast me some magic to get me something to eat?"

It's a busy area, and gawkers loiter on the sidewalk nearby, standing outside twenty-four-hour pancake houses and all-night inhalant bars. One catcalls. Another asks if the display caster would take some marks instead. Someone else yells how all full magic casters should be locked away.

I look up as I near the cage to get a glimpse inside. The city keeps a display cage for every sector, and Scouts save them to display the worst of the Ivors they catch. Mostly repeat offenders, like casters who get recaptured after escaping lockup or those unlucky few who get on the bad side of a cop in a mood.

The Ivor leans toward the bars, pressing her forehead into them so she can peer down at me as I go by. She smiles, and there's too much fury in her expression for me to believe she's actually insane.

"Hello, little one," she croons. "I smell magic off you. Won't you share, since mine's all gone?"

I keep walking, stiff with discomfort at being noticed, at the risk I'm taking. I don't know if I could stay as furious and alive as that Ivor if I lost everything. What if I just faded away, nothing without full magic? What if all these risks I'm taking *is* magic using me instead of me using it, and there's no winning this game?

What if it's *right* that casters like me disappear?

I walk faster and push away the questions. More answers I might never find.

Smells of blood and grilling meat greet me as I enter the Meat Sector. I find a street that's more steakhouses, fish markets, and delis instead of processing plants and butchers, not wanting to see for myself if what they say about this part of the city is true—that from dusk until dawn, curbs from certain places turn red with runoff as they clean.

987 Scalding Way turns out to be an underground mall at the edge of a small retail area. Everything around it is closed except for a twenty-four-hour gas station a block down; the large clock on its display says it's five until midnight. I'm standing across the street, and the only parts of the mall that are visible from here are the length of its top floor and a cone of a roof that's like a small hat perched on an oversized head. The top floor is banded with wide windows that are covered up with paper from the inside.

After double-checking the address that's painted on the roof against the one that Rudy wrote down, I fold up the note, return it to my starter bag, and cross the street. I go down the mall's sunken front steps and walk up to the glass-fronted entrance. The glass is boarded up, covered over with plywood. The sign taped over it says the entire mall is set to be demolished in two weeks.

I'm not sure what's more surprising—that the address on Rudy's note is for a mall or that he might have actually meant to be here at midnight.

Midnight and malls don't mix.

I'm pretty sure *Rudy* and malls don't mix.

I tug at the handle of the door, feeling both ridiculous and annoyed. And of course the door's locked, so I let go of the handle and stand there for a moment, considering. Then I peer closer at the lock to see how much full magic it would take to open it.

Everything logical says I should turn around and just go home,

but there's no way I can leave this place without going inside. Rudy died while speaking of meaning to finish things, while having this note on his body—to leave this place now would be doing the very opposite of what I promised him while coming here tonight.

The lock is a typical one for an outer door. Meaning, as with all locks in public places, that leftover magic can't touch it. You either need its key or to cast full magic.

I take a small rock from my starter bag, draw a six-pointed star, and cast.

Nothing happens.

The ground stays asleep instead of sending the full magic I just called for. My feet aren't even remotely hot. The rock starter sitting in my palm is just as cold.

For a second, the world goes off-kilter: My full magic is gone. I'm transported back in time to a workroom and a red fire that wouldn't dance, to those few seconds when I was sure I would only ever cast leftover magic. Failure turns my mouth ashy.

My ears are roaring as I numbly open my starter bag and begin to riffle through it with unfeeling fingers: *Something else in here will work, something* must. As if ancient rules about how starters work have suddenly changed. Or a cure for lost magic can be found inside my *bag.*

The strange black coin clinks against my nails.

My heart pounds inside my chest as I pick up the coin. So much like a mark but not one at all—useless, then, unless you happen to know its real purpose. The world stays off-kilter as I hold the coin tightly enough for its edges to dig into my fingertips, a near kind of vertigo that still leaves me dizzy. Nothing seems real.

Oh, Rudy—what were you up to?

I draw a six-pointed star on my palm once more. I drop the coin into the middle of it.

There's a clicking sound as the lock of the door twists open.

I wait for the pain to come like it always does, a thrumming ache that starts behind the eyes and ends up a sting in my nose. Sometimes nosebleeds from casting gush and sometimes they don't—a six-pointed star for unlocking a door has a different effect than six points for a mind wipe—but their arrival is always the same.

The pain, when it comes, is a fraction of what I'm expecting. Here and then gone, a spark that doesn't catch fire.

I keep waiting for it, sure it's only delayed, not understanding. Full magic without pain is as disorienting as the sky without its robe of smog—it's impossible.

I look at the starter still in my palm. The black coin had been an oddity from the start, but only because I'd never seen anything like it before. Its strangeness feels different now. Like I'm about to encroach on something much bigger than I am. Something meant for someone stronger, more experienced.

What am I getting into here?

I drop the coin back into my bag with shaking fingers.

"Last chance," I mutter out loud. Just as I said to Coral this morning, which feels like an eternity ago. *So are you in or out?*

I release a shaky breath. "Guess I'm in."

I pull open the door and go inside.

The dark wavers but stays mostly solid—the paper covering the band of windows is thin, but so is the light from outside. It takes my eyes a minute to adjust to this part of the mall. The only sound in here is my breathing. I take off my mask and fold it away.

There's an elevator in the middle of the floor. A mall directory juts out from the floor beside it. A blur of deep shadow farther down is likely the escalator. That's all. There's nothing else.

I go to the directory, half-convinced someone's going to pop up from somewhere and know I'm not Rudy. Know I'm trespassing—a fake—and make me leave.

But no one does, and I squint in the half dark, reading for something to explain this weird night.

There are three more levels below this one—two of retail and a food court floor on the bottom. A typical setup.

Then my pulse speeds up.

Food court.

FC.

Everything I see says the power to the whole place has already been cut—the covered-up windows, boarded-up door, and a demolition date just two weeks away. The idea of walking down the escalator in the dark, step by step, feels like a terrible one. So I move over to the elevator to see if it's working.

I blow a breath into a cupped palm and cast leftover magic to call the elevator.

The motor stays silent.

Just as the lock outside did not twist open.

But now I know about the strange black coin.

The vertigo from earlier—that sense of things not being quite real—swims back. I fumble open my starter bag and fish out the coin. I cast.

The motor hums to life and the cab climbs. The elevator doors open with a ping.

I step inside before I can change my mind. I jab the button for the food court and cast around the coin again. The doors shut, the floor drops, and my stomach drops along with it.

Cold sweat films my skin. I shove the coin back into my bag and clutch it to me like it's some kind of lifeline.

"Yep," I mutter out loud. "I guess I'm definitely in."

TWELVE

I curse Rudy for dying with a cryptic note. Curse myself for finding it, for not being able to let things go.

Third floor.

Aza, what are you doing?

My own voice in my head, sounding panicked.

You're in a building you got into using magic that makes no sense. Go back.

The black coin's peculiarity, still on the skin of my palm like something alive. "I can't. I have to finish this."

Second floor.

Rudy didn't write that note for you.

"I know."

How is this going to help you with Saint Willow? Help you with the cop?

"I have no clue."

FC.

The ping sounds again, the elevator doors open, and I step into the food court.

Everything comes at me at once. I don't know where to look first as an already off-kilter world tilts even more.

You and parties at midnight, Rudy—I never would have guessed.

However this place appears during daylight hours, I'm willing to bet magic that it's far different.

People are everywhere—two hundred, maybe even three. Groups of them fill the middle of the floor, which has been cleared of the eating stations, having conversations and calling out names to those who pass by. Others are busy looking for empty spots at the tables and chairs pushed to the sides of the room.

There's a sense of anticipation here. The noise of a crowd that's waiting for something to happen. My own nerves buzz, wanting to understand what's going on. The room's setup reminds me of a show and its audience. Was Rudy coming to watch something?

I peer upward at the lights that float just beneath the ceiling, dozens of oversized bulbs, running on magic because the power to the mall has already been cut.

My mind struggles with the impossible, with the *possibility* of the impossible. What if there is a third kind of magic in this world? One that works when the others fail, and only with certain starters like the strange black coins? What if there's a kind of magic that's as powerful as full magic can be, but is kinder to its casters? Pain that is a brief eclipse instead of a long blackout?

Or maybe it's magic that works only at this address. Or only after midnight. Or according to rules I've yet to understand.

Rudy, did you know? Or would you have been here, just as stunned as I am? I think you'd agree with me that if either of us had to pull enough magic to keep all these light bulbs lit, we'd already be dead and the city burning.

". . . want to enter, make sure you're registered!"

I swivel at the raised voice, my pulse speeding up at the word *enter*. I hear Rudy again as he bled on the floor: *Meant to enter . . . meant to finish what I started . . .*

"Fighters, come get registered! You've got to register if you want to fight!"

Fighters? There's a *fight* tonight?

I *really* didn't know Rudy.

I follow the sound of the voice, weaving through the crowd, and soon I've crossed the floor and am at the restaurants lining the back of the food court.

The voice belongs to the guy who's standing behind the counter of a burger place. The word REGISTRATION is scrawled across the front menu in thick white chalk.

"Fighters," he calls out, "if you mean to enter, come get registered! As always, first fight opens as soon as we register fighter number fifty!"

I hesitate, unsure, wishing there were someone to ask. I'm only here because I'm supposed to know—will they kick me out if they realize it's Rudy's note, not mine? That would end my search for answers before it's begun.

A caster—a girl, White, younger than me—moves up to the counter.

"Fighter, here to enter," she calls out, her tone completely confident.

I move a step closer, listening as closely as I can without being obvious about it. Less obvious than Rudy's cop, anyway, I would hope.

"Ring name for the books?" The guy drags over a clipboard.

Ring name.

The name a boxer or wrestler uses for matches to keep their real name a secret.

Dread threatens. Boxing and wrestling—what do I know about either? And yet, Rudy was definitely neither, so why did he mean to come? And the girl doesn't seem to be any closer to being a boxer or wrestler than I do, but she's here entering without seeming scared at all.

What am I missing?

Maybe this isn't about boxing or wrestling at all. Maybe there's still magic somehow, if floating light bulbs and mysterious black coins mean anything . . .

"Kylin," the girl tells the guy behind the counter.

He nods and scrawls her name down on the clipboard. He uncaps a white pen and holds it out.

Kylin leans forward, her braid a stream of bright chestnut down her back, and the guy writes something on her face.

"Don't forget to get over to the starter counter as soon as you can," he tells her. "It's the pizza place tonight. And listen for the bell—if you're late, you're out. Winnings and cuts can be picked up at the bets counter after the fight. Good luck."

Starters. Relief swamps me.

"Thanks." She turns to leave. The name KYLIN glows from one cheek as she slips into the crowd.

I move up to the counter before I can chicken out. If it ends up that there are actually no answers to be found here, or if it's impossible for me to keep my promise to Rudy—I'm no boxer *or* wrestler—I'll just leave. No one will ever know.

"Ring name for the books?"

"Rudy."

I watch him write it down on a lined piece of paper. He puts the number thirty-eight in front of it.

Then he writes on my cheek.

I feel better with my ring name on it. No one seeing it would guess I don't know what I'm doing. A deception is as good as casting magic, and I don't even have to be in pain for it.

But now to get to the starter counter. *Don't forget*, the registration guy made a point of saying not just to Kylin but also to me. Which means it's probably important.

I find the bets counter before the starters one. As much because I see it—the word BETS is written over the main menu of the noodle bar—as I hear it. Just as the guy at registration was calling loudly for fighters, *two* more men from the bets counter shout out for wagers. They're standing in front of the restaurant, their voices rising above the crowd. Behind the counter, three people are frantically taking bets.

"Spectators, get your bets in now for tonight's match!"

"Place your win here! Fifty fighters going tonight, so c'mon and get your picks in!"

"Minimum bet is five marks, and you got your choice of status- or technique-style wagers!"

Gamblers press close at the counter, hurrying to place their bets and calling them out over one another.

"Ten marks on Cheddar to be a bow-out!"

"Seventy-mark technique on Paddy to cast two skins!"

"Fifty marks on returning champion Finch to survive, and five on Clayton to be a knockout!"

"Twenty on Lil to survive, then twenty on Aimee to cast a blood!"

Cast two skins.

My ears pick up on the phrase the way speakers listening to a foreign language strain to catch words like their own. It's more proof there's magic involved in some way tonight. And while I don't understand any of the betting terms I just heard, something the registration guy said comes back:

Winnings and cuts can be picked up at the bets counter after the fight.

Winnings must mean fighters can place bets, too, maybe even on themselves. And cuts must mean if anyone bets on you, you get a portion of whatever they win.

Maybe tonight isn't just going to be about Shire and Rudy and uncovering secrets, I think as I leave the bets counter and continue searching for the starters one. Maybe I'll make some marks along the way. If I can figure out what I'm doing and make others believe it enough to lay bets on me.

One week before Saint Willow snaps.

My already-buzzing nerves wind up even tighter.

I spot a few other fighters in the crowd as I keep walking along the food court's restaurants. The white writing on their cheeks flickers and winks as I walk by, like stars do in a dark sky.

A guy in his twenties whose ring name is Wilson.

A balding Asian guy in his forties, and his ring name is Crawl.

A tall blonde, fair-skinned woman in her thirties—Aimee.

Who are you? How did you come to be here? Why do you fight? Did the ghosts of those you've failed chase you here? Promises you mean to keep? Marks? Cops and gangsters and families who don't see you?

I get to the pizza place a few minutes later. The word STARTERS is scribbled across the menu in white chalk. It's a woman behind the counter, looking bored. I keep a few steps back, remembering to be cautious again.

Instead of pizza slices, there are baskets of coins behind the glass of the display case. Square holed coins just like the black one I found with Rudy's note, but in shades of red, white, silver, and gold.

I peer around for Kylin, hoping she listened to the registration guy just like I did and is here. But there's no sign of her, and no else has gone up to the counter yet, either. I hesitate, not wanting to wait so long that it becomes too late to do whatever I'm supposed to be doing.

I glance up at the guy who's come up beside me—tall, dark hair, hazel eyes. He's around seventeen or eighteen and White, like Kylin.

"Are you in line to buy, or . . . ?" he asks me, trailing off.

The seriousness of his navy button-up shirt is saved by the perfect way it fits. His tone is friendly enough, but his expression says he's in a hurry. His cheeks are bare. So either he hasn't registered to enter yet or he's not a fighter.

"No, go ahead," I say. In my head I'm already calling him Navy. "Sorry, I'm still . . . deciding."

Navy's eyes slide to my cheek, and he nods and moves up to the counter. I can hear him from where I'm standing, so I just wait, listening.

"Hey, seven of each," he tells the woman. He sets marks down on the counter. "You need a ring name from me before selling or anything?"

"It's fine, I still remember you from last year's tournament," she says. "Need another key just in case?"

Tournament.

The word and all its implications echo loudly in my head—so much for simply showing up at midnight and somehow getting all my answers. I should know it's never that simple. If it were, then I wouldn't be casting illegal magic while lying to my parents, avoiding a gangster's henchman, and running from a suspicious cop, all because I'm trying to save the family legacy.

And Navy was around last year. Had he been a fighter? I wonder how much I can get him to share about the whole thing while pretending I know exactly what he's talking about.

"Nope, no more keys needed, just the ring ones," he says to her now.

She takes out seven coins of each color—all but the black—and sets them down on the counter. "That's two hundred and eighty marks."

Navy nods, places his marks on the counter, and slides the colored coins into his hand. "Should all be there, thanks."

So the black starters are *key* starters, while the colored starters are *ring* ones. And while the key starters are reusable—I cast on both the mall door and the elevator using the same black coin—the ring starters aren't, considering how many Navy bought.

I get the black ones being called keys, since they got me into this place. But as for ring starters, I'm still lost. I wonder if it's connected to us choosing ring *names*. If it is, then us being fighters explains a lot—we must have to use the starters in a ring of some kind. But in a ring for . . . a match? A match consisting of . . . what, exactly?

I guess I'll find out soon enough. The registration guy said that the fight starts once fifty fighters are registered—I'm number thirty-eight, so that means there are twelve more fighters to go.

It hits me then—I don't have any marks. After Jihen found me this afternoon, I had to pay him what I made casting magic for Coral's mind wipe. I haven't had another buyer since.

My heart sinks, and I start to dig my hand into my jeans pocket to check anyway. Now I do regret chucking that last mark at Jihen's head, no matter how pettily satisfying it felt in its childishness.

Navy pauses slightly as he passes me.

Uncertainty flashes across his face as he takes in whatever he sees on mine. His eyes flicker toward the crowd before coming back, and he slows down to an actual stop. I can practically hear him stifle his impatience as he forces himself to be polite.

Don't bother, I almost feel like saying out loud. *Seems like we're only going to be fighting each other anyway—I bet it's better for us to not even meet.*

"You lose something? You seem kind of distracted."

I shake my head. "No, it's okay."

"I could help you look if you think it might be nearby or something . . ."

His hope that I turn him down is so obvious I bite back my own impatience, then a wave of embarrassment comes. It makes me think of Rudy and how he was always so reluctant with whatever I asked of him.

"I didn't lose anything, I just—"

I break off when my fingers hit the bulk of a folded-up wad in my pocket. Marks. But where did I—?

Rudy's wallet, that's where. Now it comes back to me. Checking his wallet for accidental paper trails, then taking his marks because he would have wanted me to . . .

I take them out and count—two hundred. Not too far off from Navy, who just spent two hundred and eighty and seems to know what he's doing.

I smile to let him know he can leave. "I thought I left all my marks at home, that's all. Thanks for offering to help, though."

His return smile is tentative. "Well, good thing you didn't actually leave them, then. Probably wouldn't get too far tonight without any ring starters."

"Definitely lucky. I don't think this is the kind of place that would let me buy on credit, either."

He laughs, and the sound of it is genuine, with a hint of rust in it that tells me he doesn't laugh like this a lot, and I'm not sure what it means that I don't feel very bad that I'm keeping him. I like how he doesn't seem like he's dying to get away anymore.

Since he really doesn't seem like the tattling type, I decide to take the risk and hint at how little I know. "Now I guess I need to decide what ring starters to buy."

"Oh." He drops his gaze to his new ring starters, still loose in his hand. He gives me a look that says he'd almost forgotten why he was here in the first place, and wariness slides into his eyes. And I can tell the second where he might have considered saying more slips away, if it was ever there at all. His expression goes tight, like I've secretly pulled magic on him to make him talk.

"You'll get your strategy down soon," he says. "All fighters do."

"You're right, they do. I'm sure I'll figure it out, too."

Navy nods and moves away, stuffing colored coins into his pocket. "See you."

I almost call out "Good luck!" as he disappears into the crowd, but think about how that might sound sarcastic when presumably we're going to be fighting each other.

Unless we're not. He had no ring name on his face. And I don't know the rules for this tournament yet. I assumed only fighters could buy ring starters here, but maybe that's not true. And the woman saying she recognized him from last year could mean almost anything.

I approach the starter counter, even though I'm still unsure of what to buy. But I can't wait any longer—what if I run out of time?

The woman behind the counter is still bored-looking. "What would you like?"

"Do you . . . have recommendations?" I know how inane the question is as soon as I ask it. Like I'm asking about a dinner special. I could just do as Navy did and buy some of each.

But if he's not a fighter here—or maybe not one any longer—maybe there's a reason for that.

The woman slowly lifts both eyebrows. "Say again?"

I sense the red climbing up my neck. "I mean, do fighters usually buy one kind of starter more than the other?"

She shakes her head. "Fighters buy what they buy. I really can't say much more about ring starters than that."

"Okay, thanks." It does make sense that she has to stay impartial and not have any suggestions. It wouldn't be fair if she had favorites and still had to work with every single fighter.

I stare at the baskets of coins, thinking fast, knowing I'm

supposed to *know* how ring starters work. The woman's gaze is unmoving from my face, and I wonder what she sees. I'm worried about being kicked out for sneaking in, but what if I'm not thinking dark enough? I could be a spy. Or working for a Scout. Something happening to me would send a definite message to cops hunting down certain kinds of magic.

One of the spectators I overheard placing a bet put marks on whether a fighter would cast skin spells. Which means it's reasonable to assume that each coin is just a different kind of starter. And that they work with this third kind of magic that I don't yet understand, the same kind of magic that worked with the black key.

Four colors—red, white, gold, and silver—for four different kinds of spells—skin, bone, blood, and breath. I'm afraid to ask which color coin stands for which spell, so I'm just going to have to guess.

"Five of each kind, please," I say, hoping my voice doesn't shake. Her eyes are still probing, and I want to get away. I'm buying some of each as Navy did anyway, despite doubts about mimicking his strategy if he's not a fighter. If Rudy would have had a different method, I'll never know.

"Need another key?" the woman asks.

Navy didn't buy another ring key, so I'm assuming I won't need another one, either. "No, just the ring starters, thanks."

She sets the pile of coins down on the counter. "Five of each, for a total of twenty ring starters. That'll be two hundred marks even."

I hand over every single mark of Rudy's, and the gesture feels very final somehow. It lands somewhere in my stomach and sits there like a cramp. The gravity of the moment presses hard—passing over this last thing of Rudy's is like losing my last tangible grasp on Shire's secret life.

I slide the starters off the counter and stuff them into the pocket of my jeans, not wanting to mix them up with my usual ones in my starter bag. I know the rules of full magic and of leftover magic, but not the ones of this magic and its specific starters. A quick escape in an emergency wouldn't be so quick if I grab a starter that doesn't work.

I'm sure that they must be getting pretty close to fifty fighters by now. So I duck inside the food court's washroom, remembering to listen for the bell that says the fight's starting—*if you're late, you're out*. Only one of the five stalls is occupied, and I hop into a free one.

I'm about to flush when the sound of quiet retching comes from the other stall.

I wait, holding my breath, unsure of what to do. Ignore? Ask?

"Um, you okay?" I finally call out.

There's a long pause. "Yeah, I must just be nervous."

Another fighter. She does sound nervous, her voice thin. And young. I peek down to see her shoes from beneath the stall.

Rose-gold sneakers, their canvas properly scuffed up. They're cute, even if they're not my style. But she's definitely more a kid than a grown-up.

"I'm nervous, too," I tell her, trying to make her feel better. It's the truth anyway.

"You're also fighting tonight?"

"Yes, and I have no real clue what I'm doing," I let myself admit. I probably should be more careful. But since Shire died, there's been a lot I can't talk about with anyone—using full magic might be the biggest thing—but there's also all the stuff I keep from my parents. I can add killing Rudy to that list, too. And now, in this bathroom stall where no one can see me, I sense some of those secrets coming way too close to the surface, the ways they make me feel wanting to come out. "I'm still trying to figure out what I signed up for."

"Maybe I'll just cast a shield spell so I don't die, and wait everyone else out." Her laugh is tinged with hysteria. "Exciting, right?"

Die.

A chill washes over me.

The tile floor swims, and I brace my shoulder against the side of the stall. *Rudy, you couldn't have known, right? Couldn't you have just made plans for a midnight date?*

"I'd do a shield spell, too," I finally manage just for something to say. Though I'm not sure what she means.

"Well, right now I don't even care about winning," the other fighter says. "I just want to make it to the next round."

Her secrets are just like mine, threatening to bubble over. Would she be saying any of this if she could see me? It'd be like her handing me her fighter's psyche on a silver platter with the permission to take it apart.

Want to exchange secrets? I'm nearly tempted to call out. *You tell me what kind of fight this is supposed to be, and I'll tell you I don't belong here. Deal?*

But all I say is "Good luck." I don't really know how I mean it— not sarcastically, just as I wouldn't have meant it that way when I nearly said it earlier to Navy. Maybe I do want her to stick around during this tournament. Or maybe it's her secrets I'm wishing her luck with. I understand secrets right now more than I do this whole fighter thing, that's for sure.

"Thanks," she says. "You, too."

She flushes and the stall door opens.

I let her go without trying to see who she is. Which likely says something about *my* fighter's psyche, too.

Out in the food court, a loud bell rings.

THIRTEEN

I rush out of the washroom, my heart drumming high into my throat. My nerves are raw, too close to the surface of my skin. I wind my way into the crowd, heading toward the center of the food court. The expectancy in the air from just moments ago has gone sharp, vibrant, and my blood runs faster along with it. Excitement, fear, a kind of thrill that I don't fully understand but that's formed anyway—I feel everything.

The crowd is splitting up. Spectators go to line the walls and edges of the food court, cheering and clapping exactly the way crowds at events always end up doing. The tables and chairs being pushed to the sides make sense now, with people standing on them to see us.

I stand with the rest of the fighters in the middle of the floor, being seen, waiting for whatever's supposed to come next. I look at them, and terms like *bow-out* and *knockout* and *shield spell* run wild in my brain.

Some of them are alone, like I am.

And some of them aren't. A red-haired woman in a bright yellow silk dress fusses over a fighter whose ring name is Luan. He's taller than anyone else on the floor and has an artist's well-muscled hands, and I have no idea if either is an advantage or disadvantage here—you can't judge magic by its caster. The smallest person can cast the most powerful full magic, just like a physically clumsy person can have the most spell control.

I watch them and think that they are lovers. But then the woman ties a pink silk ribbon around his upper arm, shakes his hand, and leaves, and I realize it's something different. Boxers and wrestlers sometimes have managers, investors who make sure they get the right training and support—I guess fighters here have backers, too. Maybe Rudy was coming here to be someone else's.

The floor continues to thin. Soon there will only be fifty of us here in the middle.

There's Wilson, and Crawl, and Aimee. There's a fighter named Doll who's either got a condition that curves her back, or she's an Ivor who's managed to hide from the Scouts so far, her condition not dire enough that she needs to stop casting altogether. There's Robson, whose smirk doesn't hide the anxiety in his eyes. And more names, all flashing bright and white until they form a jumble in my head.

I spot Kylin, the fighter I listened to entering the tournament. She sounded so sure of herself and her expression says she still is. Her eyes are the same chestnut as her hair, and their gaze cool as she stares straight ahead, uncaring of everyone else still streaming away. I size her up, going from head to toe, and freeze.

She's wearing rose-gold sneakers.

Oh.

By the time I'm able to meet her eyes, she's already watching me. Her face says she peeked in the washroom to see my shoes, too. Another *oh*.

I'm debating if I should go over and say something—though what, I'm not sure, and she looks stunned enough that I can't predict what might happen. Then I see Navy.

His cheek is still blank. Not a fighter. But he's with a guy who *is*. He's about my age, blond to Navy's dark hair, green eyes instead of hazel. His gaze is flat and unfeeling, while Navy's has only been careful, wary. But they look enough alike anyway that I bet they're related—brothers, half brothers, maybe cousins. Shire and I were so different, but beneath everything our bones were the same. We shared the same kind of magic, if not its control.

The fighter's ring name is Finch.

I struggle to think back to where I heard that name tonight.

Fifty marks on returning champion Finch to survive...

So *he's* why Navy was around last year, and why Navy's back again. Not for himself. The woman at the counter remembering him being around last year's tournament also makes sense now—Navy wasn't memorable as a fighter, he was the champion's backer.

Navy ties a blue-striped ribbon around Finch's upper arm, gives him a light punch on the shoulder, and leaves. Finch doesn't bother to watch him go but instead turns to take in the crowd, like he's expecting a reaction. Demanding it.

They remember him. There are cheers of his name, a rise in the level of applause. I wonder how many people have bet on him tonight, how many marks are riding on him.

Beneath the coldness, his eyes are empty, and a chill runs along my skin.

Ghosts or promises or marks—but what if a fighter chooses to be here for no reason at all? Would they be the kindest because they have nothing to lose? Or the cruelest because of the same?

Soon the trickling away from the middle of the floor ceases and there's no one left but us.

Fifty fighters.

The food court slowly falls silent, the final throat clearing and bit of applause fading into echoes.

In one far corner of the crowd, a man stands up and begins to make his way toward us.

His suit is a dark slate-gray, sharp and classy. As he nears, I see the black plum blossom print on his tie, a paler gray handkerchief in the jacket breast pocket. He's in his forties, and he wears his dark hair slicked back from high cheekbones. Bright teal eyes take the time to meet each of ours in turn. It's a single glance that tells me everything I need to know: Whoever he is, he's the most powerful person in the room.

He reaches the middle of the floor and comes to a stop.

"Once, before the world banished full magic, it was full magic that helped create legends." His voice is a low rumble, too soft to reach everyone's ears. But somehow it does anyway, and his words hold the entire room rapt.

"Fifty competitors and a contest of skills," he continues. "Who would be the last caster standing? Who would be the strongest, fastest, most cunning? Who could fight honorably more than not? The ancient Tournament of Casters is why we still know legends such as Amani the Strong, Horvath the Fast, and Kelton the Clever. It's why we know Etana the Cruel, who *chose* dishonor in killing in order to win."

The power I saw in his eyes—it's the same kind that lines his words, threads through his voice.

"When the age of full magic came to an end, so did the tournament. For hundreds of years, no more contests of full magic were held. No more legends were created. Only leftover magic was permitted." Teal sweeps the crowd. "My name is Embry Rush, and as the Speaker of the Guild of Now, I'm here to welcome you to this year's Tournament of Casters."

Loud applause breaks out, but I remain unmoving, stiff with disbelief.

Nothing about this makes sense.

There's no such thing as the Guild of Now. There was only ever the Guild of Then. After the last of the original seven casters died, the Guild as it was died with them.

As for a Tournament of Casters, yes, once it *did* exist, and during the years that it did, legends *were* made of some of its champions. The Guild of Then created the tournament as a challenge and celebration of full magic, and every year casters from all over the world would gather together and battle one another to test their skills.

The first tournament took place nearly two thousand years ago, halfway across the world in the now-flooded Kan Desert of Barra. Some years saw the entry of less than honorable casters—every kid in school learned about Etana the Cruel—but whoever the champion and wherever the chosen location, the theme of showcasing full magic remained the same.

Just as Embry said, the Tournament of Casters hasn't taken place for a long time. After full magic was banned, the age of leftover magic took over and anything to do with full magic came to an end. And there's a very good reason for that. Fifty casters casting magic against one another over the course of a single tournament would shatter the earth into about a million pieces.

I watch Embry with narrowed eyes, not sure what to think at all. I'd thought him powerful, but I might have just mistaken it for madness.

He waits for the crowd to quiet. He hasn't smiled despite the applause. The directness in his gaze nearly convinces me he's sane.

"The rules of the tournament are still simple. Survive, and you move on to the next round. Don't get knocked out, and you move on. Don't request a bow-out, and you move on.

"And though full magic has changed so the tournament can't run as it once did, we've made it as close as possible. We'll be casting full magic—a diversion spell—around the fighting rings so no Scouts will be able to find us. The Guild's magic will help contain your magic to within the ring—damage to the earth will be minimized. Our magic will also strengthen your bodies as you fight, so pain and injury will be slowed.

"There will be a fight every night, for a total of four, including the championship. The last caster standing will be crowned champion, the winner of two hundred thousand marks, and eligible for membership in the Guild of Now. To become a modern great."

Now Embry does smile, and it turns him from powerful to charming, from frightening to merely intimidating. The change is disarming for how sincere it seems. I almost wonder if I'm wrong about him being dangerous.

I look for Kylin to see her reaction, but I can't see her. I *do* catch sight of Finch, and the raw hunger on his face is startling, almost hard to look at.

So now I know what he's fighting for anyway—not just for two hundred thousand marks but to also become a member of the Guild of Now. To become a modern great.

"Of course, while every member must be a champion, not every champion will become a member," Embry continues. "We use the tournament to help us determine who might be a fit for the Guild—who will be great, as it were. It's not just about how much magic you can draw, but how you control it, how you use it, how you *don't* use it. New membership is determined by a majority vote, and because we maintain a strict seven-member standing, only when a current member chooses to leave is a new one considered and put to the vote.

"It doesn't need to be said, but as Speaker of the Guild, I will say it anyway: Outside of fights, the tournament doesn't exist. If you decide to reveal us, you will experience the full magic of seven very powerful casters turned against you. And I can guarantee it will not be a particularly pleasurable experience."

I very nearly glance around, wondering where the rest of the Guild *is*. If Embry is just one of its seven members, shouldn't there be six more of him around, all of them casting all their magic to keep the tournament running?

But then I realize how they *are* here, even if I can't see them. The Guild is the *tournament* itself, its own nebulous cloud of the very magic that has put it together. The Guild is in the floating light bulbs, in every single ring starter, in the air, maybe even as parts of

Embry himself. They are everywhere here. To be a fighter in the tournament is for the Guild to always be close.

I shuffle a bit on my feet, not sure if I'm more creeped out or impressed.

Now Embry's smile does disappear, and his teal eyes go back to reminding me of his power. What is he when he's not a member of a secret and powerful guild of casters? A lawyer? A con man? A gangster like Saint Willow?

"The original Kan Desert is long gone now, flooded over," he says. "But as the original greats once brought their tournament there, then so will we."

FOURTEEN

The world changes and I'm standing in sand.

The floor of the food court is now an endless stretch of dunes, of swirls of dusty clay. The ceiling's turned into a sky of blue that no longer happens over Lotusland. There's already grit in my mouth, coating my teeth. The air is dry and hot.

The Kan Desert.

It hasn't existed for over a thousand years.

I bend down and touch the sand, letting it run over my fingers and get stuck beneath my nails. It covers my sneakers, the trickle of it brown and dusty through the laces. A sudden thirst prickles my tongue, and I'm parched, desperate for water. My throat hurts for real.

Embry's power is a palpable thing—I felt it myself. But each of the seven members of the Guild of Now must be just as powerful, their full magic working together to convince not just one mind of a lie but hundreds of minds, all at once. How else to explain full magic that doesn't hurt its creators? Magic held together with a level of control that doesn't split the earth but turns it into its toy?

If my own full magic is a red fire, then that of this tournament is like all fires put together. It is magic of another time. When we didn't have to pretend.

I stand up on trembling legs and peer out at the cheering crowd. A chill passes through me despite the desert heat. Reality wavers, and I know I'm slipping—who am I? A caster pretending to be someone else, sneaking around the back alleys of this city to keep surviving? Or a caster who really believes she can become a new great, about to measure her magic against that of others?

The food court tables and chairs are gone, the outer ring of them now upswept piles of sand. Spectators sit on their tops the same way crows perch on power lines. They're shouting down at us from above, cheering and calling out our names. I don't have to see their eyes to know they want to see full magic. To see us fight with it. It's in the air like an electric charge, a storm about to break. What had been anticipation in the food court has become a thirst out here in the desert.

I suddenly feel very small within the vastness of the Guild's magic, inside this tournament that is beyond a contest. In reality, this building should be hanging in tatters. This ancient part of earth should never again exist before anyone's eyes.

But I rub sand from my fingers.

Rudy, you should be the one seeing this. I'm sorry to have taken it away.

"The tournament's full magic is a closed system," Embry says. "Only the Guild's key starters will give you access to the fighting locations. Only our ring starters—red for blood, white for bone, gold for skin, silver for breath—and the elements taken directly from within the fighting rings will work as starters. As the world once was, you can cast full magic here and not die, just as the world won't die."

Embry turns and heads out toward the crowd. Desert kicks up at his feet.

Five seconds later he stops and looks back, like he's forgotten to say something. Everyone goes quiet, waiting.

"The opening round will be a ten-minute free-for-all—whoever remains standing at its end will move on to the next round." He squints teal eyes against the bright sun as he moves away. "Those ten minutes start now. Good luck."

In the blazing hot desert, time freezes. Fighters around me go absolutely still. I don't even breathe because I forget how to.

Just . . . fight?

Just . . . start?

It's the caster whose ring name is Aimee who wakes up first.

She bends down and scrapes sand into her palm. She turns to the fighter next to her—his cheek is emblazoned with his ring name of Morton—and casts, her finger a blur.

An eight-pointed star and a bone spell. Full magic.

Morton lifts off upward and back. Like his entire rib cage is taking off and dragging him along. Three long airborne seconds later and fifteen feet away he lands with a dull thud. Sand flies up in a cloud around him. His groan of pain comes through it.

We all stare at Aimee. She stares back, just as shocked. She drags her hand to her nose.

There's a single long smear of blood on her finger. No more comes.

No one speaks as we all wait for a sound, a sign. What part of the landscape is going to crack?

But the desert remains unchanged.

Then someone shouts, another fighter casts, and Aimee doubles over as though she's been kicked. Two seconds later everything is chaos as fighters turn on one another. Through all the frenzy, I'm vaguely aware of searching for Finch. To keep track of his bright blond hair and unfeeling eyes and the danger he is as the reigning champion. For a second, Navy and his perfectly fitted shirt appear in my mind, and I think of how he's somewhere up in the sand, watching.

Whoever Finch is to you, you'd understand why I'm going to have to try beating him, right?

The chaos deepens. Casters are yelling, falling, throwing magic at one another to prove their own is the best. Someone is pinned to the ground by some spell I can't see, and he slams his hand down on the ground three times.

"Bow out!" his lips bellow. "Bow out!" A second later he turns into a statue, a marble form still lying on the ground.

No, something else has turned him into a statue, I realize. He's been turned by the Guild of Now that is all around us in its nowhere-yet-everywhere form, watching for fighters who are eliminated and putting them on hold until the end of the match.

I can't seem to move. Everything around me unfolds, and it's like I'm watching a movie. This isn't happening right here, it only appears to be.

Sort these, Aza. Rudy in my head, saying what he always said to me when he set me to work in his apothecary. *Think of a good system. First things first, then work outward from there.*

I drop to a crouch, mind whirring as I peer low across the sand. The same way I peered low in a washroom stall to see rose-gold sneakers, to hear another competitor's secret to survival.

Maybe I'll just cast a shield spell so I don't die, and wait everyone else out.

Shield spell.

Because first things first.

I dig at the ring starters in my pants pocket. My fingers are clumsy, already sweating, and I swear out loud. I'm still glad I kept the starters out of my starter bag, but I'm not so sure about being able to get to them fast while they're in my pocket.

And I swear out loud once more for Embry and his Guild of Now—if anything from a fighting ring can be used as a starter, why build a ring that is nothing but an endless field of sand?

Finally I'm able to yank my hand free.

In my palm, flashes of white and silver.

I stuff the white coin back into my pocket.

How many points to cast a shield spell and keep it going? Too many, and it'll weaken any other spells I cast; too few, and someone else's magic will break through.

Everything's a jumble, so I let caution win. I draw a seven-pointed star, drop the silver coin into my palm, and puff a breath onto it. I imagine an impenetrable layer of red fire wrapping itself around my body, as cool and safe as flowers, jasmine and wisteria.

The air around me bends, goes wavy, like a just-invisible cocoon—an invisible suit of armor. The bodies of other casters blur the way hot pavement blurs. I'm standing on sand that appears half-liquid. The sound of the desert goes muffled and gauzy.

I let the spent silver starter slip from my hand and brace myself for the pain of casting to smash into my bones. Only when the wave of it comes, goes, and then doesn't come back, do I remember: Casting here won't hurt as badly.

But then a *different* pain comes. A dozen punches all coming at once.

I let out a strangled half scream.

The image of red fire slips away as I slam forward onto my stomach. Pain drives down on my arms and legs and back, and my mouth kisses the desert.

Shock reverberates as I struggle to turn my head, spitting out sand and trying to absorb the truth:

I'm going to have to get way better at holding on to a shield spell.

The desert around me is a swelling tide of noise, cheers and applause and heckling from the crowd, fighters yelling and screaming.

I move my eyes and there's a guy two feet away—thin, pale, watching me. His cheek says his ring name is Teller. His hand is still in a fist, clutching the starter for the spell he just cast on me.

I don't have to see the starter to know that it's a gold coin. Good for a skin spell, an impact one on my muscles to break my concentration so I'd drop my protection spell.

Teller grimaces as his hand lifts to his temple.

Headache.

The price he has to pay for having cast that nine-point spell.

The invisible hammers of my own pain start to pull back, and my thoughts rush together as I slowly lurch off the ground. My fingers grapple at sand.

Casting nine points would normally take me half a day to sleep off. I'm guessing it'd be about the same for Teller. These are the most general rules of full magic, of the spells we cast and how much they cost.

But not here. And not for this headache, which will only be a glimmer, the pain of it just as brief.

Before I can waste time deciding how long I actually have, I pick up the sand I've scrabbled together with my fingers. Different skin spells I can choose to cast flash across my brain.

I can make his muscles go numb or knot them up. I can turn his headache blinding.

Or I can simply cast to kill. Only here in this fighting ring, with its made-up rules that don't punish me for knowing full magic, is this chance possible. And I want to win this tournament, don't I? What do I care about being dishonorable and not getting voted into the Guild, when all I want is the two hundred thousand marks? How would honor help me figure out things about Rudy and Shire and payback?

Can you ever be sure you're using magic and it's not using you?

My father's words as we sat at the table in the teahouse earlier tonight, the kindest ones he knows for telling me he doesn't trust me.

I cast before Teller has recovered, while still a bit breathless, with sweat dripping down my face.

A palmful of sand, and he's clutching at his eyes. A thin shard of agony ripples down my spine.

Another palmful, and the desert around Teller rises in a cloud. It circles his head, a mass of swirling sand.

I dig out a second silver ring starter from my pocket. I cast, and my shield spell comes back. I draw six points this time, paint up cool red fire and rhododendrons and chrysanthemums in my mind.

I stagger, unsteady; blood drips from my nose, once, twice, three times. The desert pales, turns gray, before righting itself.

The sound of the crowd changes, a surge of cheers and applause the way an incoming tide surges. I wipe my face and turn to see what's happening. Bright blond hair glints beneath the sun, the wave of a blue-striped ribbon. It's Finch, being impressive. I catch a glimpse of his face, and it's back to the way it was before he gave away his longing for the Guild, stony and unreadable. He cuts his way through fighters, and I look elsewhere around the desert.

Casters have fallen.

There are thirty of us left, maybe thirty-five. Eliminated fighters are sprawled all over, marble statues tipped on their sides. Spilled blood lies in dark, coppery swaths across the sand. The air smells of fire and smoke as earth is drained more of its magic, a well visited by too many buckets. I taste salt and metal on my lips.

It's too easy to imagine this fake world being on fire for real. A single fighter here could do it with one spell, if the Guild's magic wasn't so protective. No wonder the earth took back our magic when we couldn't learn limits. It must have been able to see itself being set on fire, too.

Teller's tripped out of that swirl of sand I cast around him and is stumbling in my direction.

My hand's still in my pocket as he goes flying through the air.

The fighter who cast the punch on him is a woman with the ring name of Nola. She's in sand up to her ankles, having snuck up on him while he was still coiled up and more than half-blind.

He crashes to the ground.

Nola pushes up her glasses with a light brown finger, draws another star on her palm, and begins to cast. She casts over and over again, her hands a blur as she draws, blows on her palm, repeats. Each punch of air pushes Teller deeper into the desert, until he's nearly entirely buried.

Finally she stops. She's gone ashen beneath her complexion, breathing hard. She leans over and retches.

Teller doesn't move at all. Knockout.

A second later, he is a marble statue, held in the invisible arms of the Guild until it's over.

I jerk a starter out of my pocket. It's red, good for a blood spell. I'm about to cast on Nola when another fighter finds me first.

I know this because I can't breathe.

A ringing sound fills my ears and time shrinks. My eye sockets start to burn. It could be a skin spell on my lungs so they don't work, on the part of my brain that tells those lungs how to work, manipulation of my air itself with a breath spell, but what does it matter when I can't breathe, *I can't breathe*—

It's Kylin.

Her eyes stay locked on my face as I strangle. They shimmer like they're damp, like she's sorry. Gray fog swims across mine, turning the desert into stormy sea. My heart is bursting.

You know my secret, her gaze says. She swipes at her eyes. *I have to do this.*

And because I still can't breathe, I picture the blood spell I know will save me. I picture my hand on a spigot, turning it to full blast, and cast.

Kylin begins to bleed—from her mouth, nose, eyes, ears. Breath whooshes back into my lungs, and I'm gasping, coughing, crying as the pain pounds at me like a dozen fists.

The desert sand begins to turn black at her feet. She begins to gurgle, the sound too much like my own still-jagged breathing.

The crowd is louder than ever. The sound smashes into the roar of the casters around us, still fighting. My mind is at war.

I should save her. A counterspell will do it.

I should eliminate her. Because only one of us is going to win in the end, and she knows one of my secrets, too.

The smell of the air has turned salty. Kylin's clutching at her neck, and her bloody eyes bulge. Her rose-gold shoes have turned maroon. Shoes for a kid.

I swear to myself, drag out a new red starter, and cast.

She falls to her knees, heaving in huge breaths.

I drop the red coin, and the desert swallows it up.

The blow comes without warning. A slam to the side of my head so that I see a blur of colors and taste blood. Before I can fall, I'm twisting through the air. My back smashes hard into the desert floor so that sand arcs up in sheets.

I can't even gasp for breath. Overhead, the sky is such a bright crystalline blue, it almost hurts to look at it. Sand floats back down, and for a second, it's like being buried.

He appears through the clouds of tan and gray, the fighter taller than anyone else in the desert, with the perfect hands of an artist. Luan's skin has gone as pale as milk where it's not covered in bruises or blood. There's enough desperation in his eyes that I know he's completely dangerous. His silk ribbon hangs from his arm, sodden with blood.

He's holding a starter in his fist. I can't see the color, can't predict the spell.

He opens up his palm, about to draw.

I roll over before I feel how much my body hurts. I scratch at dirt as I go and drag myself to my feet, finally able to gasp now. I draw and my mind reaches for red fire. I draw and imagine it filling my veins and making me more than I am, powering up muscles until they are simply power contained. I draw until my arm is lightning and its cracking is in my mind, stinking and smoking and alive.

Rudy, controlling magic is like sorting, putting everything in its place.

But sometimes it's also just like another way you said it might be.

About not overthinking it, about just letting go.

I stagger to my feet and face Luan. I start running at him, and surprise widens his eyes when I don't stop—magic has never needed contact.

I cast right as I slam my fist directly into his face.

Full magic meets bone and surges through. He soars through the air and lands twenty feet away. Sand halos up around him. He doesn't move.

Knockout.

The crowd shouts. It's a waterfall of noise, crashing down. Faces go in and out of focus.

It finally sinks in that they're cheering for *me*.

I turn in a jagged circle in the middle of the desert. Pain is a knife that cuts through my middle, and I half hunch over as I keep turning. I'm searching for the next caster to fight, the next fighter I have to knock out. I'll let it happen without thought, let it be borne on nothing but impulse. I won't fight what just wants to be. *What I am.*

I want to say dread fills me at the idea of having to cast, and it does. But there's a sick anticipation, too, because casting full magic is what we do.

The taste of the blood that coats my teeth makes my stomach roll; it makes me thirsty.

Can you ever be sure you're using magic and it's not using you?

What if I don't care to tell the difference anymore?

Then a bell rings across the desert.

The first round of the tournament is over.

FIFTEEN

There are twenty-one of us left.

I observe the others without trying to be obvious.

I bet they're all doing the same thing.

Beneath a fake desert sun, while standing in sand turned black with our blood, we're shy again with one another.

There's Nola, wiping her glasses on her shirt and squinting at nothing in particular.

The twenty-something-year-old guy named Wilson, his grin huge and delighted.

Kylin, still covered in blood. Who won't meet my eyes. Who stares down at her ruined rose-gold sneakers.

Only Finch doesn't hide how he's observing. I sense his green eyes on the side of my face and wonder what he saw, if anything, of my fighting tonight. I wonder if Navy saw me fight and if he'll tell his fighter about it. And I wonder what Navy's real name might be, something that should be weird to think about right now if I weren't so desperate for normal things to think about.

Twenty-one.

I feel like a giant bruise. The pain from casting that last spell has already begun to fade, but I still hurt all over, from fighting and falling and being thrown. Adrenaline that kept me pumped during the fight is leaving me as quickly as it came, and now it all hits me at once—how it's long past midnight, how I just hurt a bunch of strangers with magic, how I'm still alive despite everything.

The crowd is still perched high on the sand above us. They won't stop cheering and clapping and the sounds of both hurt my ears.

I make out one chant:

Rudy the First!

It's not Rudy the Amazing, but it's also not Rudy the Dishonorable. I'd hate to be Rudy the Killer.

And then the Kan Desert is gone and we're standing in the middle of the mall food court again. The room is all floating light bulbs instead of a blazing yellow sun, a ceiling instead of the kind of blue sky the world hasn't seen for decades. The dunes are once more just tables and chairs. The sand's gone and the tile floor is back; used-up ring starters lie all over it the way coins do in the bottom of a wishing fountain.

Eliminated fighters are waking up, no longer marble. They get to their feet and head into the crowd, mere spectators now. Teller, Aimee, Crawl, Luan, others with ring names I can't remember. No caster was killed in the desert tonight.

One fight down, three more to go.

Embry is crossing the food court floor and heading toward us.

"Congratulations, everyone," he says. "And now we have twenty-one."

Wilson lifts an arm and hollers. His eyes flash with triumph, sweat glistening on his brown skin. "And soon it'll just be me."

The crowd whoops and whistles.

Embry's teal eyes glint. "You're confident."

"I'm a programmer. Built to always be thinking outside the box. It'll be easy." Wilson taps his temple with a finger.

The corner of Embry's mouth twitches. The reveal reminds me how he can easily be as charming as frightening, a desert made real with magic in order to fool.

"I beat a programmer one year to become champion," he says.

There's another whoop from the crowd. Wilson slowly lowers his arm.

Embry faces us, expression already back to veiled and cool. I bet that's how he looked when he fought, before his days in the Guild. I wonder why he stopped. If the memories of his fights are good memories or ones he dodges.

"The second round of the tournament will take place tomorrow at midnight, 1212 Thorn Avenue. Third floor. The third round the night after, and then the final the night after that. The Tournament of Casters *is* a test, and tests that are easy test nothing at all, so feel free to withdraw now if you think you're only going to withdraw later.

"If you move on but then miss a fight, you will unfortunately be eliminated from this year's tournament. A final thought for you to consider in the meantime: However well you think you fought tonight in the Kan Desert, you'll have to find a way to be even better, each and every night. On the night of the final, the fighter who wins will be the one who didn't only get better, but figured out the way to become the best."

Then he leaves, slipping away as smoothly as oil moves over heat. The crowd cheers some more before dispersing throughout the food court like bees leaving a hive. Most of the spectators head toward the bets counter, picking up whatever they've made tonight before leaving. Some linger close by, as if they're getting something by staying near those of us who cast as we did without dying.

When one of them pulls out a notebook and a pen for autographs, I turn and head toward the bets counter. Chances are small that anyone would have placed any bets on me. But it can't hurt to check. I have no marks left, and if Jihen finds me while I'm still empty-handed, Leafton might only be the first of our suppliers to mysteriously stop working with my parents.

But hoping for others to bet on me so I can eke out marks is one thing—winning the two hundred thousand marks as champion is another. Only one of them is under my control, so that's what I'll focus on.

The floor is still really crowded, but there's a sense of the night being over, and exhaustion tells me I need to get home and sleep. Just as before, the crowd in front of the bets counter is the thickest and loudest. Behind the counter, the three clerks who were taking those bets earlier are now checking spectators' bet receipts against the fight results.

I stay at the far side of the group, unsure. I don't have a receipt because I'm not a spectator and I didn't place any bets, but didn't the guy at registration say fighters got a cut of whatever winnings they brought in?

Soon I've shuffled my way to the counter. "Anything for Rudy?" I gesture toward my cheek. "Fighter number thirty-eight if you need to check the register."

The clerk has about half a dozen binders open in front of her. She pulls one over and flips through its papers.

"Oh, here you are. It's your first tournament."

I nod. Something like hope rises, though I know it's stupid. Maybe if the tournament allows betting *during* a fight, I have a chance of earning some marks. I started off okay with Teller, and then there was me not killing Kylin, and finally Luan at the very end.

The woman checks even more binders, and just when I'm sure there's nothing, she nods and checks off some columns. She reaches for an envelope from a box set below the counter and holds it out. "Fighter thirty-eight."

Stunned, I take the envelope from her. Inside are fifty marks. It's not much, but it's also not nothing. And someone—maybe *someones*—actually bet on me.

She reads my continued shock as disappointment. "I saw you fight, dear. I'll be shocked if dozens more bets aren't placed on you next round."

I smile and stuff the envelope into my starter bag. "Thanks."

I turn to go, weaving through the still-clustered crowd to get to the elevator, when I spot her.

The red-haired woman in the yellow silk dress, the one who was Luan's backer. Luan's tree height and strong hands meant little when it came to casting magic. My fist still stings from the punch, a tenderness in the knuckles that has less to do with the pain of having cast the magic for it than just smashing bone against bone.

Seeing the woman makes me think of another backer, and for a second I glance around for signs of Navy. Finch is last year's champion—it means a lot of spectators are betting on him. Navy, as his backer, would be here, picking up his winnings.

But he's nowhere to be seen. And it's just as well because neither is Finch, and the memory of Finch's delving eyes is something I can do without.

The woman in silk nears the bets counter, stopping to talk to one of the men who are calling out for spectators and their receipts.

I slip back toward the edge of the crowd and watch.

"Hello, Hugo," she says. "I'm here for my fighter's winnings."

He nods. "Just give me and Jack a few minutes, Piper, and we'll get you your marks. Not sure if it'll make you feel better that only a few spectators wagered on him getting knocked out tonight."

She arches a brow. "It doesn't."

"Sorry for the tough night."

"Yes, well, there will be other fighters." She opens up her evening bag, but instead of taking out a starter, she's checking her hair in a compact. "At least I'm saved from having to fund ring starters now—until I find someone new, anyway. Maybe next time I'll choose a fighter with a bit more flair. Luan was just so *conservative*."

I wait until Hugo's turned back to the crowd before approaching her. I'm too tired to be timid. I want to stop worrying about having marks for ring starters. And I don't think I'll get another chance as good as this.

"I'm the fighter who eliminated yours," I blurt out. There's no real good way of saying it. "And I'm looking for a backer."

SIXTEEN

Piper slowly drops her compact back into her purse. Her gray-eyed gaze goes to my cheek. The letters of Rudy's name must still be legible because I watch her eyes scan them.

"Ah, yes, the fighter who knocked out Luan from the tournament." Her tone is practically breezy. "Rudy the First for a physical punch, something the tournament's never seen before."

"I'm—"

"If you're about to say you're sorry, then you don't need a backer, as you won't last long enough to make it worth their marks."

The back of my neck gets hot. I don't regret beating Luan, but it's true I was about to say it.

"It seemed like the right thing to say," I mutter.

"Maybe anywhere else, but not at a tournament where you have to beat forty-nine others." Piper smooths a painted nail, oozing cool aggression much like the way Embry oozes power. "Backers can't have their fighters be sorry about winning. Poor investments, if so."

Her tone is still light, but it doesn't hide how she's grown annoyed. With Luan leaving her without a fighter, yes, but just as much with me for talking to her about it.

"I'll be your new fighter," I say. "Since Luan's been knocked out."

"Unfortunately, I'm not looking to back another fighter yet. I'll need at least one more round to watch and decide. You'll have to ask someone else."

I have no one else to ask. And one more round is one more round where I can't be sure I'll have marks to buy more starters.

"You'll be spending the tournament just watching other backers get rich," I say. "Not the greatest business tactic."

Piper's gaze sharpens. Her smile is nearly amused. "And I'll want to back you, since you're the one who knocked out Luan."

"I need a backer and you need a fighter."

"Backers only *need* fighters as long as they enjoy having a stake in the tournament," she says. "Now, why do you *need* a backer? You did well enough tonight. A lot of fighters never even consider it."

"I want to win those two hundred thousand marks. But first I need marks to buy starters."

"Piper," Hugo calls out, "got your fighter's winnings sorted here at the counter. Ready for you whenever you want to grab them."

Piper ignores him and keeps her eyes on me. Beneath them I feel like an insect pinned to a board. I can sense her coming to a decision the way I sense pain comes for magic.

"That's also unfortunate, but it doesn't change how I'll want to watch you fight once more before deciding. Come find me after the next round—*if* you survive it."

She steps away and heads toward the bets counter.

"You saw me fight tonight," I call out after her. My voice is thin and hoarse. The desperation in there hurts my throat. "I thought you wanted flair."

Piper slows down but keeps going.

"You *know* why I'm Rudy the First," I say.

I'm thinking it's too late when Piper stops. She speaks over her shoulder.

"The Mothery, Textile Sector, tomorrow. We'll talk."

"Wait—I—what?" But Piper ignores me and keeps moving. I swear she's laughing at my being so shocked. My pulse is fast and jittery, like I've been running. Or maybe it's real hope and it's just that I'm no longer used to it.

I want to wait for her to finish so I can talk to her again. What if I heard wrong? What if she's just kidding? What if—?

"Hey. Rudy."

I spin on my heel, nearly crashing into her, she's standing so close behind me.

Kylin.

"Sorry," I say to her when my mind goes blank for something more meaningful. *I'm sorry I nearly killed you, but I only did it because you tried first.* "I didn't see you there."

She frowns, but it's a thoughtful one, as though she's measuring me up. There's no sign of the confident caster I watched register as a fighter, but she's also not the one who couldn't meet my eyes afterward.

"Can we talk really quick somewhere?" She glances around. Her shirtfront is stiff with drying blood, and her rose-gold sneakers have been ruined forever. "Not here."

Suspicion comes. I make myself see the kid she is—thirteen, maybe fourteen—beneath the blood still on her face, the white ink of her ring name clinging to her cheek.

I wait for a group of casters to walk by before saying, "I think it's against the rules for fighters to talk." I'm making it up, but I don't want to say any more to her than I already have. Casting battle magic at someone is easier if you don't know them.

"There's no rule about not talking or Embry would have said it," Kylin argues.

"It's still not a good idea." I start to move away. So much for thinking I might wait for Piper.

"Just two minutes. I promise I won't try to kill you again."

I wish I could hate her or something, when really I just wish I'd been as gutsy a few years ago. Maybe I would have been able to convince my parents to let me help out earlier. Maybe then Saint Willow wouldn't be the problem he is now. Maybe Shire would still be alive, still here being my older sister.

"Two minutes," I mutter. "And if you try anything—"

"Why would I, now that you'd expect it?"

"Is that your fighting strategy, then? Just catching casters off guard?"

She shrugs with both shoulders. The gesture makes her seem even younger. "So can we go somewhere, then?"

"Where?"

She half smiles. "The washroom?"

Kylin twists shut the main lock using full magic. The pain from casting leaves her pale and trembling, tired-looking. The Guild's protection spell must have ended with the match. She should be saving her magic for tomorrow, but if she hasn't figured this out yet, she's not going to hear it from me. I'll be fighting her tomorrow, and I need all the advantages I can get.

I've already figured out I won't be able to cast myself clean before getting home, just as I won't be able to cast myself to heal, either. Casting more full magic now would just add even more pain.

More than that, I know casting full magic outside the fighting ring over the next three days isn't going to be a smart move at all. Not only would I be using up full magic when I should be saving it for fighting, but any pain from casting that magic will then come with me to the ring.

I'll have to turn away buyers, something I've never done before.

Saint Willow, Jihen, my family's debt—their shadows loom that much larger in my mind.

"Okay," Kylin starts, taking a deep breath, "I just wanted to talk to you about what I said before. About not caring about winning. You kind of said something like that, too, remember?"

"I didn't, I only said I was nervous. But okay, what about it?"

"I didn't mean it. Obviously. That's why I tried so hard to knock you out of the tournament."

I lift a brow. "That's an interesting way of saying you tried to kill me."

"I was trying to make you pass out."

Kylin does her best to look sorry when we both know she's lying. I know it because I've pulled the same trick before on Shire. My stomach clenches—I don't want to see myself in Kylin, to be that age again. It makes me think of Shire, being a big sister.

"You could have done it a dozen other ways," I say, trying to sound as cold as possible, "ways that wouldn't involve trying to kill me."

"I could have. I didn't. I'll choose better next time."

"What's the point of this conversation again?"

"See, what I said was stupid, and I really regret it now. So can we make a pact? For us to both forget what each of us said and not use it against each other during the tournament?"

"You know we might still end up having to fight each other, right? If we're the last two left, I'll still try to beat you."

Kylin nods. "But for now, let's pretend we never said that stuff. I kind of need to if I want to believe I can do this."

I'm pretty sure this moment might never happen again in the history of the tournament. How this might even be the very first— two fighters agreeing together to pretend to be brave.

Of course, I could always just say no.

I glance up at my reflection. My eyes are lined with purple, and a sheen of dried blood covers most of my skin—my clothes are unrecognizable. No, *I'm* unrecognizable.

Is this what being a fighter instead of just a caster means? To have to become someone else entirely? I drop my eyes, not liking this face of full magic that feels like a stranger's.

I use my finger and some spit to wipe the blood off my face and neck, then turn back to Kylin.

"Fine, we're making a pact. This doesn't mean we're friends or anything." *Don't make me care about having to save you again.* "We're both still going after the same thing."

"Thank you. For stopping out there, by the way." She attempts a smirk. "I guess it was the least you could do after ruining my lucky shoes."

"How lucky can they be, then?"

Kylin snorts and casts the door unlocked. The thick metal of the lock twists back into its original shape.

I move to leave, deciding to make a point of avoiding her over the rest of the tournament. I can't make friends while at this tournament. Not when enemies are easier to cast magic on.

"I'm going to need more than luck to beat Finch, anyway," Kylin says as I take another step. She sounds tired *and* miserable now. "Maybe it was beginner's luck—I still don't like how he won last year. But he must really want to be in the Guild, and unless you win, you won't even be considered."

Impatience ebbs and flows. I want to remind her, *You said two minutes, time's up, this conversation is over.*

Is this how Shire felt each time I pushed her? When I clung a little too hard, or for a little too long? And her eyes couldn't hide her frustration—the way I wanted too much?

"Still, he won," I say. "He must have been the strongest."

Kylin does that double-shoulder shrug again. "I was just a spectator last year, so maybe it's different when you're only watching. But he wasn't the favorite. When he won, I was really shocked. I think he cheated somehow."

I glance over at the washroom door and half wish for someone to come in. Then I could leave and not feel bad.

"I think a lot of people were shocked. This fighter named Shire was the favorite and—"

My head swivels. My heart begins to pound hard enough that it hurts. "Shire?"

Kylin nods. "She was the favorite all the way to the final round. But then Finch killed her during their final battle. That's how he won."

SEVENTEEN

There's a roar in my ears. It wants to drown out Kylin's words, but they're in my head all the same. I can't unhear them.

Shire didn't die casting banished magic for marks. She died while fighting in this tournament.

No.

She didn't *die*. Finch *killed* her.

This is the payback that Rudy was talking about. To do this one last thing for Shire and enter the tournament so he could fight Finch for killing her. He was dying and didn't tell me, maybe hating the idea of taking me down with him as much as my possibly ruining his chances.

Maybe he even meant to kill Finch in return.

I'll never be sure how far he meant to go. You have to really know someone to make that kind of guess, and that wasn't Rudy and me. I don't think we were even really friends. Not the way he and Shire had been.

And of the three, who is left now?

I shut my eyes as the room spins. The past presses close, full of all the moments that kept me in the dark. Rudy and Shire spun them to keep me safe, and yet—

How far can *I* go?

"What's the matter?"

I peek out and Kylin's face is close, searching mine. "You look like you're going to be sick."

"I— Do you remember if Shire had a backer?"

"Yeah. A guy. But I can't remember his name."

"Was it—?"

Kylin freezes. It's almost comical watching the realization hit as her eyes land on the letters on my cheek and get huge. But only almost, because nothing about this is exactly funny. "Rudy," she whispers.

I shudder. So it's all really true. I guess it's never easy having ghosts change on you, when there's already too little of them left behind. "Shire was my sister."

Kylin's eyes might pop out of her head soon. *"What?"*

"We knew she died casting full magic, but just not how."

"Wow. Wow. *Wow.*"

I silently will her to not say another wow. If I hear another *wow*, I might just scream.

"She deserved to win, you know."

My pulse trips as I stare at Kylin, a sharper, even uglier dread now swirling in my stomach.

I think he cheated somehow.

"She was better than he was," Kylin continues. "But then—"

"You said you think Finch cheated?" Shire losing fairly is one thing. She would have known the risks of the tournament, going back for each round the way she did. Even Finch going all Etana the Cruel on her and killing just to win is completely fair— dishonorable, but fair—because Shire would have known that that was a possibility, too.

But Etana never cheated when she fought. During the years she was champion, she at least killed her opponents in clean combat.

Something in my tone must scare Kylin, because she pales and rears back a bit on the counter.

"I don't really know if he cheated or not," she says. "Killing isn't cheating according to the rules, but it's just—I was so shocked when he actually won and—"

"But that's what you said. *You said he cheated.* And I don't mean killing, but cheating in some other way, then. Is that possible?"

Kylin just stares at me. She's still pale, still backed away from me, but now something on her face says she feels sorry for me.

"The thing is," Kylin says, "even if Finch *had* used a gathered spell—which aren't against the rules, either, just like killing isn't—what can you do about it now?" The door opens and two women come in and Kylin snaps her mouth shut.

I run from the washroom, needing to escape.

A gathered spell?

The food court is much emptier now—a clock on the wall says it's two in the morning—as I dart across. The registration area and starter counter are deserted, and even the bets counter has calmed down.

Is all of the Guild of Now needed to run the magic for this part? It's a question for Embry I'll never be able to ask, because who am I but one more fighter in a long string of them? *Or is it only during the actual fights that all of you have to work together so the whole place doesn't snap in half? How strong are each of you on your own? Did any of you do as Etana the Cruel did to become champion? Do any of you remember my sister?*

I nearly fumble my key starter to the ground as I cast for the elevator to take me back to street level.

Gathered spells.

What was Kylin talking about? It's like trying to catch the wind, the way I'm having to learn about the tournament even as I'm in it.

The elevator comes and soon I'm outside. I take all the wrong streets and the Meat Sector smells raw and bloody as I head toward Tea. Or maybe it's just the tournament I'm still smelling, carrying it home with me on my skin. I'm wide awake now, the late hour meaningless as bits and pieces of the night swirl in my head, trying to form themselves into something I understand.

If Shire had won a year ago, everything would be different now.

Two hundred thousand marks would have paid off all of Wu Teas's debts. Saint Willow would have left us alone. Jihen would be off shaking down someone else. The cop who's probably already moved on from watching the apothecary to watching me—he would have no reason to be around at all.

Shire would be alive.

My parents would be happy.

Something in my chest wrenches.

Even if Finch did *cheat and used a gathered spell or something, what can you do about it now?*

The question keeps me moving fast despite still hurting from the fight. My bruises ache with each stop, and the soreness of my bones is a feverish hum within my skin. The idea of fighting tomorrow while feeling anything like this fills me with dread. Because what if everyone else won't have to? How do I know they're not all better at healing, even?

I shove my smog mask on and head west, cutting through the sectors of the city—Spice, Tower, Government. The streets glisten from a recent rain, as wet as the Kan Desert was dry, such that it burns. My lungs burn, my sore body shouts, and my mind continues to race as I run.

Time winds back.

It was nearly a year ago, an hour before midnight.

I checked the time again on my bedside table and listened. The sounds in the kitchen were soft enough that I knew it would be Shire, being careful to not wake up our parents. They agreed a long time ago to let Shire cast in order to keep Wu Teas alive, but it existed for them as an unhealing sore, a thorn they could never fully extract. Shire always did her best to help them forget. She did what she could so that her marks entered the teahouse without notice and then left nearly the same way—silent payments for the banks, the suppliers, to Saint Willow and the dark web of his business.

There was the sound of a drawer being shut, then the bang of a cupboard door. I heard Shire saying something to herself, over what she was doing as she prepared to leave for a job.

Too restless to lie still anymore, I climbed out of bed. Not bothering to change out of my old T-shirt that I wore for pajamas, I slipped on jeans and grabbed a light jacket from the floor. I looked at my starter bag that I'd placed on my desk, hesitating, then picked it up and slung it over my shoulder. I left my bedroom and headed down the hall.

Maybe tonight would finally be it. I would be able to convince my sister to let me go along and watch her cast full magic. I would watch and learn and then I could help, too. I was more than old enough, and not getting to learn with Rudy wouldn't matter so much if it just meant getting to learn from Shire.

Hope brimmed in me like hunger as I turned into the kitchen.

My sister was at the island. She was concentrating hard enough that she didn't hear me come in. Only half the lamps were turned on, and the light of them skimmed off her face.

"What are you doing?" I asked in a loud whisper, going over to see. Whatever it was, it must have been something beyond leftover magic, something important that needed full. Shire had learned to be careful about casting anyway, but on days she had a job, she was especially so—never do more than needed. This was something special.

She swept away the tangle of metal before I could see. The lot of it fell into her starter bag that she held on her lap. "Nothing much, just fixing something," she whispered back. "What are you doing up, Aza?"

"I couldn't sleep. And I heard you in here, getting ready to go."

Shire's gaze fell to my jeans, the jacket I held, the starter bag at my shoulder I would leave behind if promising just to watch made any difference.

Her dark eyes flashed with irritation. Over the years her patience with me had slowly faded, worn thin by my unchanging insistence, the little sister who kept asking for the one thing she couldn't have.

"You know you can't come," Shire said. "How many times do you have to keep trying?"

"If I stop asking, it's always going to be a no."

"Stop asking because it's always going to be a no."

"C'mon, I'll stay out of your way." I slung my starter bag around so it hung from my back, out of easy reach. "Your buyer won't even see me."

"And what if it was a Scout who saw? Then it'd be the both of us in trouble."

"You've never been caught all these years. And Mom and Dad would never know, either—why would I say anything?"

"It's more than Mom and Dad, it's—" Shire zipped shut her starter bag. "I have to go. I'll be back soon."

It was true that our parents hadn't been Shire's main argument for a long time. Now that I was fifteen, I could keep a secret as well as anyone. And though I wasn't nearly as good at controlling my full magic as Shire was with hers, I was definitely better than I had been at the beginning—so how would I get even better unless I practiced when I could?

A part of me was also sure that *Shire* herself could help convince my parents to let me help. How with the two of us making marks together, Wu Teas would never have to be in trouble again. Shire would stop being in danger from casting. The honor of our family's legacy would be safe.

But then, I couldn't tell *what* it was exactly that kept Shire from letting me go. It seemed like she didn't want me to go for her *own* reasons. Not because she was worried about me getting hurt or accidentally killing off a species or a forest somewhere, or because of our parents and all their forever worrying, but because she wanted to keep being the one who did it all. The one who could be trusted.

Resentment swelled until there wasn't room for anything else.

"There's always going to be buyers in Lotusland looking to buy real magic, you know," I said. "Maybe one day they'll be able to come to me. And you and Mom and Dad won't be able to stop me from casting."

"Oh, Aza." Shire got to her feet, telling me she was done.

"I'm serious. I only need one buyer, and then it's word of mouth. Just how you did it. It can't be that hard."

She looked at me, her expression exasperated. "I trained with Rudy for years, and then there were more months where I cast for almost nothing because I messed up more than I didn't. It *can* be that hard."

"I'm not stupid." I clutched my jacket close even though we were still indoors.

"I'm not saying you are. I'm saying that learning how to control your magic by casting on those who think you already know is reckless." Shire walked past me as she left our cramped kitchen and headed toward the front of the teahouse.

I hated hearing her call me that. *Reckless.* It was one of the words our parents often used to describe me. She knew I would argue with them over it. She'd always taken my side.

My throat was tight, my eyes gone all hot and stinging as I stared at her. It was like she was someone new, not the sister who'd always said she had faith in me.

You can't be scared of your own magic. It's full magic. It's rare, just like mine.

I can't control it.

One day, you will.

"You're just like Mom and Dad, you know," I said. "Not trusting me."

Shire's expression went hard. The low lamplight of the teahouse at night deepened her scar and turned it full of shadow.

"I *do* trust you," she said. "But you have to trust me, too. And you can't come with me for this, okay?"

Then she left, going off to save us the way she'd been doing for years. But she never came back. She died that night, and now I know how.

EIGHTEEN

The loud rush of a train thundering overhead on steel tracks brings me back to the present, and I'm in the Tea Sector again, just a few blocks from home. The same late-night tea cafés and teatini bars I passed earlier are still open, even with dawn not too far off. Nothing looks any different, only hours have passed since then, but the world stays tilted on its axis, knocked over that way by my discoveries of the tournament and how Shire really died.

I tug my starter bag closer to my chest, the one that was once hers.

After she died, my parents let me take whatever I wanted of hers. And I knew Shire would have wanted me to, because she'd shared everything with me when she'd been alive, so why would that change after she was gone? A week after her funeral, I'd stepped into her room and stood there in the doorway, looking around with a heart turned into fire in my chest. I felt a grief that was too huge to escape, so it became a part of me, burrowing into my bones and knitting itself into my muscles, coloring every single word I might ever speak from then on.

I was sure that nothing was real.

The last conversation I had with Shire couldn't have been an argument. Rudy couldn't have called the teahouse at dawn to say she'd cast too much full magic and had lost control of it. My parents couldn't have spoken about full magic with such poison in their voices that they almost

made me feel like poison, too. They couldn't have spent the next days
whispering together at night over the state of the teahouse, never asking
me if I was willing to help in any way.

It wasn't until I touched her starter bag left on her bed that I finally accepted she was really gone, her absence final. I felt it like someone had sucked all the air out of the room, out of my lungs so that I was just a dried-up shell—now that the person I used to follow behind was gone, the wind would just blow me away, wouldn't it?

This bag held the items that started Shire's magic, and it'd just been *left on her bed.* Discarded there like any unimportant shirt or pair of socks. *The starter bag was Shire's connection to her magic and she would never need it again.*

My eyes stung as I picked it up, knowing instantly I wanted nothing else of hers, needed nothing. My own starter bag was stained dark gray canvas, nothing special. I bought it because it went with everything in my wardrobe. But Shire's was the yellow of chrysanthemums, of emperors and empresses, and the shiny silk moved like liquid gold. It suited my sister, who always dressed like she had better things to do than pay off a gangster.

But now, walking this last part home, I wonder if I missed something in her room. Something I wouldn't have guessed about because how could I have known? Tonight, fighting and using ring starters, I found out for myself how impractical it would be to use a starter bag in battle, my pockets not much better.

Kylin said Shire had been the best. Shire, who never jumped into anything the way I did, who spent months training and then practicing in order to be exceptional.

That last night had been the final fight, the one for the championship. She'd been fixing something on the table. Something she'd rushed to hide to keep me safe. All her life, Shire had only ever hidden one big thing from me, and that was how she was really using her magic.

My nerves prickle with the lightness of discovery.

It's all a guess, but it also feels very right. Like *I'm* making a new connection to Shire, even if she's gone. She had to keep everything about being a fighter a secret when she was alive, but now that I'm a fighter, too, she's finally able to share. Distant laughter from the teatini bar I pass drifts over but I don't entirely hear it, and it's starting to drizzle again but I barely notice. Shire's never coming back, but I have these pieces of her now that I never had before, pieces I think she's giving me herself.

Shire, maybe I was wrong to think I didn't need anything else of yours. Maybe I'll see if I can find a tangle of metal in your room.

When I reach the block of the teahouse, I duck into the alley that runs behind it and squeeze my way through our fence of snowball bushes. I fold my mask back into my pocket, walk up to my bedroom window, and yank.

It doesn't open.

My mother, exasperated, locking it from the inside.

"Damn it," I whisper before yawning hugely. I dig out my key to the teahouse from my back pocket. Exhausted, I half walk, half limp my way around the side of the building, every part of me craving sleep.

Golden light flows out from the front window of the teahouse.

I slow down, then climb the steps to the door.

Confusion dances with the murkiness of my brain as I work the lock with clumsy fingers. Could my parents be waiting up for me, discovering me gone and thinking I'm coming back from handling a late-night package for Saint Willow? Even so, why would they be waiting in the dining room instead of our regular kitchen? The kitchen is where my mother has her television and *Liar's Lair* for her to disappear into, where my father chooses to drown in paperwork.

I open the door, and there's a man sitting at the back table. He has a cup of tea in front of him. For a second I see my father, with his parental intuition somehow knowing that I'm hurt from fighting and wanting to cast leftover magic to help.

But then my father lifts his head and it's Jihen.

NINETEEN

My blood runs cold. My heartbeat pounds in my fingertips, wrists, behind my eyes, as I struggle to make sense of Jihen being here, in this place that's too good for him. The scents of too many gentle things like red fire–dried leaves and smoky green fields aren't supposed to make room for anything else.

I shouldn't be surprised, though. I of all people understand the reasons for staying unpredictable. And hadn't I done this same thing to Rudy? Breaking into the apothecary and waiting for him to arrive? If he felt as I do now, invaded and vulnerable, no wonder he was always particularly livid those days. Shame flows now, and I let it.

"A late night for you, Aza," Jihen says, "and a rough one by the looks of it." His gaze crawls over my face and the bruises and the blood on my clothes. He makes a sound of disapproval. "You teenagers, always so confusing with the things you do. Like wild animals, like gnau neng. Dare I ask for details?"

"It's none of your business." There is no explanation that would work. Not that I owe him one anyway. Anger begins to boil up.

"Delicious tea." Jihen sniffs from his cup. "I can see why you're so determined to keep the family business alive."

"How did you get in here?" Jihen's leftover magic can't have broken open the lock. And now an absurd sense of betrayal begins to creep in—he *agreed* to never show at the teahouse again. I've been paying each time he finds me, haven't I?

"The simplest way, Aza." He holds up a key. "Saint Willow doesn't like it when things get unnecessarily complicated."

They have a key. Of course they do. I forgot that Saint Willow and his family technically own nearly every piece of land in the sector, so it makes sense that they also maintain access. It's a given so obvious that no one actually talks about it anymore—if you are here, it's because Saint Willow allows you to be. Our home isn't really ours because it's really his. It's Jihen's. It's any of his henchmen's.

This place being off-limits is just one more illusion I've let myself be fooled by.

"We had a deal," I say. "I pay you directly, and you stay away from the teahouse. How is that complicated?"

Jihen sips at his tea. Seeing his thick fingers gripped around one of our most delicately designed cups makes my stomach roll. He was in our kitchen. He was in my *room*, locking the window to make sure I came in through the front. My stomach rolls harder.

"Well, beauty, here's the problem. You're *not* paying—not the way you promised you would and definitely not the way Saint Willow needs you to."

His voice is louder than it needs to be, and I think he's doing it on purpose. I force myself to keep from glancing down the hallway that leads to my family's apartment, willing my parents to stay asleep.

"I *did* pay you today, and I'm sorry it wasn't enough. I told you that. But I can't just cast more marks into my pocket."

While it's not impossible to cast an object into something else, it *is* nearly so to keep it from changing back. Same for casting objects into reality and making them stay that way. It took the

Guild combining all its power together to re-create the Kan Desert, and even then, all that sand had still been more illusion than real. I don't have that type of spell, and neither did Shire. Of course, a thief like Jihen would want to take full advantage of being able to pull marks from the air.

"Now wouldn't that be nice? Full magic my way and everything's fixed." Jihen's smile is mocking. "Know anyone I can tell the boss about?"

My throat goes dry—why did I have to mention full magic to Jihen of all people? His boss would collect full magic casters the way a child collects toys if he could. I hope my face gives away nothing. "Would we be having this conversation if I knew someone who had real magic?"

"Perhaps one day, then." Jihen slurps from his cup. "We can always dream, can't we?"

"So just tell Saint Willow exactly what I told you—that I can't pay what I don't have. I'll have more the next time I see you."

"Beauty—"

A bitter helplessness surges, coats the back of my mouth. "Don't call me that, remember?"

"—you don't think the first thing I told the boss was that you just didn't have it? I was walking in there with a pathetic amount of marks—of course I had to explain how it wasn't me doing a bad job, a job Saint Willow says even a beebee could do." He lifts his palm and casts, picking up his cup. "I hate cold tea."

A waft of the freshly heated tea tickles my nose. It's our Content blend. I've never liked it.

"What do you want, Jihen?"

"Where is the teahouse's till money?" Now his voice has softened, and it stirs the hair on the back of my neck. "The day's sales. Boss sent me here for them. Consider it interest on your frequently late payments."

Panic is a vise around my ribs, squeezing. I picture where my parents always keep the day's sales, in the safe in the family kitchen.

"I— You can't. That's for everything else we have to pay—bills, suppliers, insurance, rent to the company that *Saint Willow owns*."

"Ah, but there's one less supplier to worry about now, yes? If you like, we can look into getting rid of more contracts for you. Anything to help remind you to pay your debt of honor marks as soon as possible."

The vise tightens. I can barely breathe as the name *Leafton* floats across my mind. "Saint Willow can't do that."

But of course he can. Saint Willow can cut Wu Teas off from companies one by one in Lotusland just to see how hard he can push, how far we'll bend. How I'll do almost anything to save us.

"The day's sales, Aza."

I make Jihen wait outside the teahouse, just in case my parents wake up. I walk over to the safe inside the deep cupboard in the kitchen and open it with shaking fingers and a heart full of hate. The number of marks I take from it fills my stomach with a real nausea as I step outside and shove the envelope at him.

Jihen takes it from me with a small, smug grin. "Much appreciated, beauty."

I go back inside, lock the door. Exhausted or not, it takes me until morning before I can fall asleep.

TWENTY

I'm still stiff when I wake up the next afternoon—sleep didn't do as much as I hoped. Worry nags at me as I get dressed. How will I feel by the time I get inside tonight's fighting ring? How will the *other* fighters be feeling?

When I open up my starter bag to see what needs replenishing, I go still. My thoughts race as I dig the tiny glass jar out from the pebbles and leaves and other starters I always keep in my bag.

Having Rudy's healing meds would change everything. I wouldn't be walking into each fight still hurting from having to use my magic. Shire must have used the same method, since the pills were hers.

But the bottle is empty. I took the last pill after casting for Coral's mind wipe. I meant to get more from Rudy yesterday when I visited the apothecary, but given that he died during my visit, asking for a refill slipped from my mind.

I decide I'll have to break into the apothecary. I'll have to use full magic to do it, but then I'll at least have medicine afterward to help with the pain from casting. I'll go today, before heading for the Mothery to convince Piper I'm worthy of being her fighter.

I cross the hall to Shire's room.

It's been a year and my parents have left it mostly untouched. Other than using it to store the odd bit of supplies, they rarely come in. Shire's room is just like family meals out in the teahouse dining room—too painful still for them to consider.

Maybe it doesn't help that I've let them forget. Maybe I should remind them that Shire wasn't the only one who liked those family dinners.

I check her bookshelf first, then her trunk, before finding it in the pull-out drawer of her desk.

The tangle of metal isn't as random as my glimpse of it that final night made me think. It's actually a lot like one of those octopus-style key holders, with a flat disk as its main body and then half a dozen small loops coming out from along its edges where you would attach your keys. There's a sturdy clip at the top of the disk for attaching it to something, which I think is what Shire might have been adjusting when I caught her with it in the kitchen.

The small loops are spring-ring ones. A single hard tug and—

Then I get it. How it works and why Shire must have made this to give herself an advantage in the ring.

I take out the ring starters from my pocket—I transferred them there from last night's still-ruined jeans—and lay them out on Shire's desk. A smattering of square coins—red, white, silver, gold.

I pick up a red coin and slide it onto one of the small loops through its center hole. After a second of debate I attach the clip to one of the belt loops on my pants. I test my theory, giving the red coin a single hard tug as though I'm in a fighting ring right now, needing a starter without wasting even a second.

The red coin drops smoothly into my palm.

Shire, you really were the best, weren't you? The favorite, there in the ring and here at home, too. But now I think it's my turn to try, and I think you're helping me try. I feel the ghost of you and I hope it'll be enough.

I detach the holder and slip on the rest of the ring starters, making sure I know where each different color rests on my hip. I spend the rest of the afternoon practicing reaching for starters and yanking them free until the motion is mindless, until I grab whatever I need entirely by feel, and in a fraction of a second. It's the repetition of Rudy's sorting exercises in his apothecary all over again. Then I unclip the whole thing and place it securely in my starter bag. Slinging the bag across my shoulder, I head for the kitchen, starving because it's long past lunch.

The kitchen is empty, the island top wiped clean. My parents are in the tea shop, and their voices as they serve customers float back down the hall, along with the scents of fresh tea and pastries.

There's a covered plate on the island, though—wedges of scallion pancake, sides of fruit recently ripened courtesy of leftover magic, a teacup with water and a selection of tea bags next to it. Like they know I haven't slept enough and food is still one of the ways they can speak to me.

My eyes go to the deep cupboard beside the fridge. The safe inside hasn't been touched since I opened it for Jihen in the middle of the night. My parents won't open it until closing tonight, which is when they'll add today's sales to it. At the end of the week, they'll use the saved-up marks to pay off our family's long-running suppliers, business partnerships as old as the sector we live in.

I take the fifty marks from last night out of my starter bag and slip them into the safe. The amount isn't nearly enough to cover what I took to pay Jihen, but I just have to hope my parents won't

150

notice anything is missing until the end of the week. That's when they'll take it all out to make their payments. By then, I'll have hopefully replaced everything with more winnings from bets getting put on me during the tournament. Getting Piper to agree to back me is a huge part of replacing the marks. Of course, winning two hundred thousand marks is also another part of the solution.

Pressure swells in my chest as I lock up the safe. I can't let my parents notice anything at all. It's not my having to pay Jihen that will throw them, but my doing it the way I did. Why would I need to give him marks from the safe when they believe I'm working down our debt as Saint Willow's courier?

My head spins over my own web of lies. The shadows between its spirals are like traps—one wrong move and I'll be falling. The family legacy will tumble down behind me.

I cast leftover magic and the water in my cup heats. I cast the television on so I can stop thinking for a few moments about all the ways I can mess up.

It's just the news, recaps of the city since early this morning. I'm only half paying attention as I tear open a bag of our Energizing blend to steep and start in on the food.

I nearly choke on a bite of pancake when I actually start listening to the news report.

At dawn, a huge sinkhole opened up in the Meat Sector. Measuring fifty feet across in both directions and nearly forty deep, it took out an entire intersection between major streets. No one was injured when it happened because all the adjacent businesses were still closed for the night. Though there's some structural damage to some of the nearby buildings that will take weeks to fix, the one that suffered the most damage—a nearby underground mall that was completely crushed—was already set to be demolished in two weeks, luckily enough.

I could try believing it's just a coincidence. Every day, somewhere in the world, something falls apart or is destroyed or dies out. Not because someone's currently casting full magic, but because too many someones did so a long time ago, and the earth's still paying for it. A quake. A freak wildfire. A tsunami. Lotusland isn't saved from any of that.

But the underground mall—I can still feel the sand of the Kan Desert between my fingers—is too much to ignore.

A knot of dread sits in my stomach.

I helped do this. The Guild of Now's magic is powerful, but it can't turn earth back to being unbroken. Last night's fight, fifty of us, just casting full magic as though we'd been reborn into casters of old, as though no consequences existed. No price for magic.

And just like that, I realize I should have known.

Because just about a year ago, didn't the same thing happen? A series of disasters, memorable because they were all located within the borders of the city, each one the breakthrough damage from the battles of last year's tournament.

First, a minor quake in the Paper Sector. Then a landslide in the High Shore Mountains that wiped out a bunch of houses in the north end of Spice. The unexplained overnight death of hundreds of crows in Culture, their raven corpses scattered throughout the streets like spilled coal.

Then finally another quake, this one in the Tower Sector. It leveled an apartment building. People died.

They were the cost of Shire and Finch fighting on the roof of that building in the final tournament battle—those people, that wedge of earth. They paid for the Guild of Now insisting on casting full magic just as the Guild of Then once got to. *Shire* paid.

But how has Finch paid? How has Embry paid, or any of the other members of the new guild? I thought entering the tournament—winning it—would fix all my problems. And maybe it will, still. But who's going to pay *my* cost?

I put on my smog mask and leave the kitchen. I slip out of the teahouse, glad that my father is serving a customer at the till and that my mother is putting together a tray of tea and cakes for one of the tables. So that they're too busy to see me leave, guilt ablaze all over me like I'm fire itself.

TWENTY-ONE

It's late afternoon as I head toward the Tobacco Sector, half looking out for Jihen as I make my way out of Tea. Going to Rudy's apothecary means more healing meds and getting to fight unhurt, while Piper's in Textile means getting to fight in the first place. But Tobacco is closer, with no backtracking, and midnight isn't that far away.

I wish it were the other way around. It shouldn't make sense to have to go back to the place where Rudy died. Where I left him lying on the floor, cold and alone.

The scents of fire and ash thicken the deeper I get into the sector, and soon there are the barest hints of camphor and mint in the air—the apothecary is close. I wait at the corner for the light to change, shifting on my legs, unable to keep still. It's starting to rain and I wipe my wet face. The need to hurry presses, an ache of its own kind. A mantra plays itself over and over in my head: *healing meds—Piper's shop—tonight's location, healing meds—Piper's shop—tonight's location, healing meds—Piper's—*

"Aza Wu?"

My heart trips in my chest, and it's like the world slows down as I look up and see the cop standing in front of me.

Rudy's cop. Baseball Cap.

I haven't thought about him all day. In between the loss of the till money and getting ready for round two, the possibility of the cop finally showing up to ask about Shire slipped through.

My own foolishness keeps me speechless as he waits for me to respond.

Baseball Cap is younger than I first thought, late twenties max. He must be new to being a cop, which explains the doggedness *and* the carelessness. Maybe I should have called him Puppy instead of Baseball Cap.

"Are you Aza Wu?"

I don't want to be, not to you. "Why?"

He gestures to his silver armband, now in full view, to show he's a cop. "My name is Cormac." Then he smiles, blue eyes crinkling at the corners, and the smile is so earnest and proud that in some bizarre parallel world I might even *want* to help him. "Well, not just police, but a Scout, actually."

The world slows down even more. My stomach crawls into my throat and sits there, a fist. "Oh?"

He nods. His intent to help the city—no, the *world*—beams from him. He shines like a little kid who's just cast his first leftover magic.

I shiver and it's not from the cold rain. A Scout. Right here, within arm's reach. A destroyer of full magic casters, someone who makes his living hunting down people like me.

"So, you're Aza Wu, aren't you?" He gestures to his chin. "Mind taking off your mask for a second? I have your picture on file."

I slowly slip off my smog mask. "File?" I'm only capable of useless answers because the word *Scout* is blaring too loudly in my head and swallowing everything else up.

"Yes, the file on your sister, Shire. I've been meaning to come and talk to you and your parents, actually. About Shire's death last year and some discrepancies . . ."

His voice fades, becomes a hollow rush.

Parents. Questions about Shire. *Discrepancies.*

I've been worried about this scenario ever since seeing Baseball Cap, ever since Rudy mentioned it with his dying breath.

But hearing the cop say it now fills me with fresh dread.

He *can't* question my parents about Shire and the details of how she died. He can't question my parents, *period*. They loved Shire and they love me, but they also hate full magic, and that conflict would spill from their faces like tea from a cracked pot.

The secret of my magic suddenly feels newly raw, a fresh wound.

"What do you mean by discrepancies?" I finally manage. "We saw the medical report. It explained everything."

Cormac shakes his head. The rain's coming down harder and the shoulders of his jacket are starting to darken. "As it turns out, the medical report *is* the problem. The medical examiner who signed off on it had been under investigation for falsifying reports. After he disappeared two weeks ago, investigators looked closely at all the reports he's *ever* signed off on; your sister's is just one of them that has turned up with issues that need to be resolved. Now I'm just following procedure and trying to reach those who can tell me more about how Shire died. I've already spoken to a Rudy Shen—him being the one to find her—but he was surprisingly unhelpful. Unfortunately he's also just passed away, so . . ."

For a second I can't decide if I should already know that Rudy's dead. I don't think I should because it was just yesterday and his ties to us on record should look thin. But I also know I'm no actor. "I . . . heard. He had a weak heart. He—it was just a matter of time."

"Oh, so you already know?"

I nod.

"I'm sorry. I wasn't sure how well your family knew him, or if he'd been friends with just Shire . . ."

His voice trails off, waiting for me to add more, but I just nod again. He doesn't need more than what's already in the file—Rudy was there that night, present when Shire fell. The rain pours.

"Well, I'd like to come speak to you and your parents together as soon as possible," he says. "Perhaps tonight?"

"Why you?" I hope my voice isn't as shaky as I feel. "Why a Scout on this? A medical report with holes—shouldn't that just be reviewed by Lotusland's coroner system or something like that?"

"Typically, yes. But certain wounds don't match up with how she died, and *how* they don't match up—well, it was decided the file should be passed on to a different depart—" Cormac's gaze seems to sharpen as he watches my face and he frowns. "I'm sorry, but I really do need to speak to your parents about this, so if tonight sounds—"

"Wait. There's—" My hands clench. If only I could cast full magic right now. Just rip from his mind the existence of Shire's report, Shire herself. Rip from his mind who *he* even is—I've already cast into his mind once before, why not again?

But he's a *Scout*. If I tried anything in front of him, he would stop me before I could even grab a starter from my bag. And then there's the tournament tonight—casting a mind wipe so close to starting time would leave me useless. Goodbye, chance at two hundred thousand marks.

"There's something I think you need to know about Shire that might change your mind about this investigation," I tell him.

I have no clue what I'm saying. The words are meaningless as they spill from my mouth. All I know is I have to say *something* to stop him from going to see my parents. My mind whirls even as it goes blank, telling me I'm making a mistake.

Cormac's face lights up. Boyish eagerness flows even as his eyes stay sharp. "Tell me over coffee? I know a good breakfast-all-day diner just down the street."

TWENTY-TWO

We get seated at the same window table I saw Cormac at last time. Through the rain, Rudy's apothecary across the street is a blur of glass and stone. The blinds of the windows of the shop are pulled, probably by whoever discovered Rudy's body. There's no sign on the door to say why the shop's closed and I wonder what's going to happen to it. Rudy never talked about family, and I never felt like asking, and maybe that's another difference between Shire and me. Because I bet she would have asked.

The healing meds that I still need inside seem very far away.

"So you have information about Shire you think I should know?"

I watch Cormac stir sugar into his coffee and my own stomach churns. The smells wafting from his loaded plate aren't helping. I pick at my dry toast, needing something to keep me from throwing up.

"I have information," I say, starting my act now. "But I need a guarantee before I tell you."

"A guarantee?" His brows pull together slightly. "I don't know if I can do that. Not if it keeps me from doing my job."

"This information will *help* you do your job. The guarantee is actually for me—so I can do mine."

You *have a job to do with this?* I read the question in his puzzled gaze. "What's the guarantee you need?"

"This stays between us for now. So you can't go to your bosses and you can't talk to my parents. You asking about Shire is just going to upset them, and they won't be able to help you anyway because they don't know anything else but what they were told last year by the medical examiner."

"I'm listening. I can't promise anything, but—"

"No, it's the guarantee or nothing. Go to your higher-ups and my whole setup's collapsed. Talk to my parents, who won't be able to help you, and I won't help after that, either. So I won't talk without the guarantee. It's the only way."

Cormac smiles. That there's as much sympathy in it as condescension reminds me how new he is to this job—Scouts are supposed to be ruthless in their casework.

"Look, I know this is your sister we're talking about and that you're only trying to help, but this is now official Scout business."

"And you're a new Scout, trying to make an impression," I say. "Trying to clear up an old case before the full year hits and it gets filed against your department's annual performance. How is it going to look later when it ends up you just ignored someone who offered to practically spoon-feed you your answers?"

He takes a sip of coffee. "Tell me how working with you is going to get me what I want."

"This obviously goes deeper than clearing up some discrepancies on a medical report, doesn't it?"

"Yes. The discrepancies are just the symptoms of a bigger problem. We think the medical examiner has connections to full magic, whether he was getting paid to cover for casters of full magic or was a caster of it himself."

Goose bumps lift. His suspicions fill the air between us at the table, as strongly as if he'd said them out loud anyway.

That Rudy and Shire had something to do with full magic, too.

"Rudy and Shire had nothing to do with full magic." My fingers spin my glass of orange juice, over and over again. Nerves prickle in my throat so that I have to clear it. "But if you're looking to take down some full magic casters, the information I have might be the lead you need."

Cormac leans forward, waiting. All around us diners are eating, the sound of cutlery on plates almost surreally normal.

"First the guarantee," I say.

He exhales. Ten seconds later: "Fine. This stays between us, for now. So talk."

I take a small bite of toast and chew slowly, working myself up to being able to meet his eyes. My web of lies trembles with me struggling to stay balanced on top of it, as I begin to weave it more tightly.

"Rudy and Shire were both undercover cops," I begin, lowering my voice. "*Undercover* undercover—only Rudy's immediate boss knew. Rudy had been undercover for years, secretly working on growing intel about the gangs that run Lotusland."

Cormac's mouth twists the slightest at this. A single glance at his face and I get the skepticism. He's new to being a cop, still full of bravado, still learning how things really work around the city. He's likely based in a sector where its gang keeps a lower-key profile than Saint Willow does in Tea, than Earl Kingston does in Tobacco. A sector like Tower or Culture, one that's filled with more people who look like him than people who look like me.

And it's people who look like me who first formed the city's dozen sectors into empires to run as their own. Which means families like mine are the ones who best understand how the city's gangs work, the sectors that are still mostly ours where a certain kind of culture is unspoken truth. My parents and I have never disputed the payment of honor marks, but people like Cormac probably half doubt they actually exist.

"Two years ago, information started going the wrong way," I continue, "with one of the gangs gathering *cop* intel. Rudy figured out the gang must have planted a mole in the cops. So Rudy enlisted Shire to be *his* mole, planting her as a member to uncover from the inside who the gang's mole was."

Cormac is rapt. "Which gang?"

"Saint Willow's."

He barely reacts to the name, which is what I'd been more or less expecting. To someone like Cormac, it's just another easy stereotype, the idea of what a gang is. A faceless entity he doesn't understand should scare him, but he's too cocky for his own good.

"Okay, go on," he says.

"Then last year, Shire was killed. Rudy got the medical examiner to sign off on the altered medical report to hide how she died, to make it seem like she'd just fallen off that building. And not mention what had happened before that, so it wouldn't break her cover. But he believed it was the gang's mole in the cops who had her killed up there. That it was only a matter of time before he was also found out."

"And so he was."

I nod. "Yesterday."

The Scout sits back in the booth and looks at me for a long minute. "So let's say I believe that Rudy and Shire had nothing to do with full magic. How they just had the bad luck of choosing a medical examiner sloppy enough to give away his own corruption, whether it's through magic or not. How is this information going to lead me to casters I can *take down*?"

"I've been secretly working as an informant with Rudy since Shire died, trying to figure out who the mole is in Saint Willow's gang. Now that they've killed Rudy, too, I can't just leave it. It means they knew he was close, which makes me close. People with information about the gangs—they aren't as tight-lipped around someone who looks like me as they are with someone who looks like *you*. I still have my leads, good ones that aren't just about the mole, but about potentially much more."

"Casters of full magic."

"Yes. We think the gang may have been using one to clean up their messes."

"A full-magic *hitman*?" Cormac sounds alarmed.

I nod. "But you can't get involved now or everything I've worked on is going to fall apart. Try to get to Saint Willow on your own and they'll make sure you never see light again. So I need more time before you can move in. After I get the mole, then you can have your casters. Deal?"

Cormac's eyes glow with the need to do what's right, to do his best as a Scout. Whatever he might see in mine, I hope it's not the truth.

He asks, "How much time do you need?"

"A month." I'll know in a week if I've saved Wu Teas from Saint

163

Willow or sunk us. If I've saved us, then this ridiculous lie I've just laid out to get rid of Cormac might actually work out for me. Our debt to Saint Willow will be paid. A cop poking around Saint Willow's gang won't be enough for them to kill him; even Saint Willow will think twice about starting a war with the Scouts, but his influence will be able to scare Cormac off for good.

And if I *can't* pull this off, I might still have enough time afterward to figure out another way to get rid of him.

"No way," he says, frowning. "I can't buy a month's time from the department. I can try pushing for . . . let's say a week. But that's all I can do. After that, I'll have to go back to procedure, talk to your parents, see if they can come up with leads of their own once they know what Shire had really been up to."

A week. Of course it has to be a week.

"Fine," I say, while my head screams that it's not enough.

"I'll find a motel close to the teahouse—the department will expect that."

"You can't let my parents see you," I remind him in a rush, hating the panic that leaks into my voice. *Just stay away from them, you damn Scout.* "Your guarantee, remember?"

"They won't see me. But I'll have to make a show of tracking you, even if actually I'm giving you room to work."

I nod, though the idea leaves me cold all over. Two people tailing me, one of them a gangster and the other a Scout—and somehow I'm supposed to make it to a secret tournament where I'll be fighting with illegal magic without tipping anyone off.

I chug some of my orange juice, feeling light-headed.

"Can I admit to being a bit blindsided by Shire and Rudy

working undercover this whole time?" Cormac shakes his head, thoughtful. "All of that just comes from nowhere—I really had no clue."

Maybe if you'd ever seen a Pearl of the Orient drama called Liar's Lair, I think, *you would have recognized the plot.*

But I was counting on Cormac's not knowing a story full of people as Chinese as the city's gangs, a story as Chinese as the person who's telling it to him.

"One week, Aza." He holds up his coffee mug in some kind of toast. "Here's to taking down some casters."

I lift up my glass, smile weakly, and will myself to not throw up.

TWENTY-THREE

I escape a minute later with the excuse of having to help out at the teahouse. I pull my mask back on and take off at a run once I'm out of sight of the diner, trying not to think about the healing meds I can't get to, how I feel like my web has me more trapped now than anything else.

The rain has stopped by the time I get to Textile. Some sectors in the city are noted for their smells, but some leave their mark on the eyes, and Textile is one of these. Windows of shops grow colorful and lustrous with their bolts of fabric on display, posed mannequins dressed in suits and gowns. My mother has to come here whenever the shop needs new napkins or place mats. But before, she would send Shire, who would then take me, and the two of us would study the windows for hours.

Today, though, I see none of this. The Mothery is in the middle of the sector, and as I weave my way through the streets to get there, all that's on my mind is convincing Piper to be my backer. It helps that the sun is already low, so that it flashes off the windows and hurts my eyes if I'm not careful. Midnight, getting closer.

Piper is beginning to feel essential. One, I need a steady flow of marks for ring starters, to get to fight. Two, I need the answers to the secrets that haunt me, and Piper could be a key. Did she back a fighter last year? Did she see Finch kill Shire? Could she know if he cheated? And three—well, it'd be nice to have one person on my side. Everyone else in the tournament I've spoken to is off-limits. Kylin's just a kid and a part of me is drawn to protecting her, but she's also a competitor. Navy is the champion's backer. Embry is Embry.

The Mothery's window display is beautiful—wide spools of silk in different shades of blue are stacked in the back to imitate a sky of old, while spools of silk in shades of brown and green line the floor to create a healthy earth. Tinier spools of gold and silver are inserted randomly in between all the blue of the sky, for stars.

I head inside and a bell over the door dings. The shop is basically the window display, only bigger. More bolts of silk along the walls, cabinets here and there with shelves stuffed with panels of color. The place smells how it looks, like roses and perfume and dust.

Piper is helping two customers choose between patterns, and I wait for them to leave, doing my best to not run my hands over every single inch of silk I see.

Then it's just Piper and me. She shuts the door, casts leftover magic to flip over the sign on the window to say CLOSED. She makes no move to lock the door, and I wonder why she's assuming no one's going to try to come in anyway.

Maybe it's because no one trying to uncover secrets would ever guess they could be in a place full of silk. Or maybe the customers around here really would stop at the sign. But mostly I think it's just Piper. How if someone came in, she'd only have to give them a single pointed look to make them leave again. Piper is someone you cross at your own risk.

I take in her sleek pantsuit and perfect makeup as she approaches and barely keep from pushing back my still-wet-from-rain hair in response. The look in her eyes as she scans me is a reminder that I'm just business, a potential investment. How I need her more than she needs me. How neither of us is in this for friends.

"Rudy the First," she says. Her gaze goes to my casting arm, the palm of my hand. I think of how Coral did the same thing, as if potential can be judged by sight. "I've been thinking all day about that move you pulled on Luan."

"Because you want flair."

She smiles. "If you're going to fight, you might as well do it in style."

"You invited me here so we could talk about you maybe being my backer."

"Do you know what it means to have a backer?"

I nod. "You give me marks for ring starters, and if I become champion, you get a percent of the pot."

"Wrong."

I peer up at her, surprised. "What do you mean?"

"Having a backer means you're representing that backer and yourself." She circles me, all gloss and hair and silk, just as intimidating as Embry. "It means that backer's put their marks and their faith in you. Having a backer means showing everyone they know how to pick a winner. *Having a backer means they trust you to know how to use your magic and not for your magic to use you.*"

The age-old question for all of us casters of full magic. We carry it with us as surely as we carry the magic itself, one never without the other.

"I know how to use my magic," I say.

"I don't doubt that you think that. But if you're going to represent me, I need to know what you represent. What honor means to you. What *dishonor* means."

I blink away the sting of tears. It catches me so off guard that it takes me a second to be able to speak. Ghosts are swirling around me, and I don't know if I want to reach out for them or ask them to leave me alone.

But this might be my best chance to win Piper over.

"My sister, Shire, was the fighter Finch killed last year," I say.

She goes still. Her gaze is nearly soft now as she looks more carefully at me. "You're Shire's sister? Yes, your faces—they're the same, deep down. Shire was very good."

"But I'll have to be better."

"To beat Finch? Yes."

"I have to do what Shire couldn't."

"Finch is a merciless fighter, his hunger for victory boundless. Like Etana the Cruel. We must respect him as a fighter if not as a caster, yes?"

I nod. "What do you know about his backer?"

"His older brother, Oliver. Who often looks like he'd rather be anywhere else than ringside, but I suppose Finch is family, and family can complicate things."

My throat has gone tight. "Family can definitely."

And his name is Oliver. It's nicer than Navy.

So he backs his brother but doesn't fight. He might not even *like* fighting. I wonder if they're brothers in full magic, the way Shire and I were sisters. I'm reminded that I've never seen Oliver cast either way.

"Family might be especially hard for those two," Piper says, interrupting my thoughts. "It's just them on their own, running the Salt Lick over in the Spice Sector."

"What happened to their parents?"

"All I know is that they're gone."

It means Finch fights with ghosts behind him, too. How fresh are they? Do they have anything to do with him being in the tournament in the first place?

"Do you think Finch cheated last year to win?" I ask. "If Shire was the favorite all along?"

Piper taps her lips with a finger. "Cheat? It's hard to cheat in a tournament with so few technical rules. Perhaps you're thinking about bending the rules rather than breaking them. Because there's still honor in doing what must be done to survive, even if such ways are ugly."

"Ugly?"

Her lipsticked mouth curls into a smile. "Survival and ugliness are often one and the same, and as a fighter, you need to remember that."

I try not to shudder. For all her beauty and soft silks, Piper is as barbed as wire.

"Okay, so if it's still honorable to fight ugly when it comes to survival," I say, "then it becomes dishonorable when it's no longer about survival. Ugly versus dirty."

"Very generally speaking, yes."

"So do you think Finch fought dirty last year to win?"

Piper smooths another nail. "I suppose it's possible. A lot of things are made possible with full magic, depending on the caster—their capacity, control, intent—"

"What about gathered spells?"

Her expression stiffens. "Careful, Rudy. The line between honor and dishonor can shift, yes, but never more so than with spells some believe should never have existed in the first place."

I flush. "I just want to know what they are. How they started."

"Back in the days of the Guild of Then, members began to experiment with spells. They wanted to create ones for effects normal full magic wouldn't do. But these man-made spells ended up calling for full magic that was beyond what was found in the earth, and so they ended badly, with casters dying or falling ill and never recovering. So the Guild stopped experimenting and that was that." She lifts an arched brow. "But no full magic is limited by form—once it learns the shape of a spell, it never truly forgets it. So that ghosts of those spells are always just lying around, waiting to be discovered and formed again."

"And these are gathered spells?"

"Gathered spells are what remain of those experiments. Some casters—gatherers are what they're called now—began to view magic as a toy at their disposal, and so re-formed certain man-made spells back into being. And instead of dying as a cost for these gathered spells, casters have to pay a great price in other ways."

I picture it. These spells that are as formless as my magic, but instead of red amorphous clouds, they are invisible vapors, floating around lost in the ether, before someone else's cloud of magic comes and finds them.

"Can you give me an example of a gathered spell?" I ask.

"Bringing the dead back to life. Snuffing out the sun. Time looping. The price is perhaps another caster's life. Their mind. Their *magic*." Piper lifts her other arched brow even higher. "Need I go on?"

"No, it's okay." No wonder the Guild of Then tried to destroy such spells. There's a madness in them that makes the earth slowly falling apart day by day seem almost kind.

Corpses can be made to breathe again, but the intangibles that make up who that person *is* in terms of their mind are gone forever.

Snuffing out the sun is, in general, not a great idea.

Time loops are dangerous because they play with reality.

And to lose your magic . . . It comes dangerously close to losing yourself. A person might not be their magic, but if their magic isn't them, then what is it? What part of you has been lost, sent into that ether, waiting to be found or taken?

"I don't know how you'd find out if Finch used a gathered spell anyway," Piper says. "He would likely never admit outright the price he must have paid for it. You *could* cast a reveal spell, I suppose, though I doubt he would ever give you the chance to try."

Shire, if you could do it all over again, would you use a gathered spell if it meant living? How far would you go to stay alive, to win? Would you let magic use you instead of you using it?

It takes a moment before I notice Piper has stopped talking. She's measuring me up like I'm one of her bolts of silk, and she's deciding the best way to cut me, to hang me up for display.

"You really are determined to succeed where your sister could not. Revenge can be a dangerous motive, but it's also an honorable one." Her gray eyes flash, their lashes coated into tiny feathers. "I will be your backer, Rudy the First, if you'll be my fighter."

Relief, trepidation, a sense of things falling into place—my stomach's churning even as I smile. "My real name is Aza, but I'll stay Rudy for the tournament."

"Aza. All right. I'll save that for after you win, then. Tonight, come find me before the fight, and I'll give you marks to buy your ring starters." She reaches for a bolt of cream silk, the fabric of it shot through with pink and red peony blossoms. "Now, for the armband you'll wear to show that you're fighting on behalf of the Mothery."

She smiles and presses a folded ribbon of silk into my hand. "I'll find you at midnight. Don't be late."

TWENTY-FOUR

I make my way to the Flower Sector in the dark, winding through alleys and taking small detours. It's not likely that Jihen and Cormac are on me this far out of Tea, but I'm still annoyed by having been caught off guard by both. I curse them from beneath my mask. All the other fighters are going to be sneaking around tonight, too, but none of them have to also keep shaking off a gang enforcer and Scout.

Inside my starter bag, the empty glass jar of healing meds clanks softly against stones and twigs. One more thing I still need to get done. Tonight, then, after the fight, and I curse Cormac again for showing up as he did.

Thorn Avenue is on the east end so that I have to navigate through the entirety of the neighborhood to get there. But the night air is sweet with the scent of roses and lavender, and sidewalks are carpeted with fallen blossoms. Baskets of blooms decorate every corner, and if a shop isn't a flower one, it's selling herbs or grasses or small potted trees.

I pass the sector's display cage hanging from a lamppost, and someone's taken the trouble to wind green vines around the metal bars. Scouts wouldn't normally allow the vines—the Ivor inside could turn the vines into whips or another weapon of some kind—but this one is bent nearly in half, too wrecked to want to cast anymore.

The address of the fighting ring turns out to be an apartment building. It's a low-rise, and it's old, the banisters full of rust, the siding warped, moss on the dipped roof. And clearly abandoned, with the weeds that make up the lawn knee-high and the adjacent carport a long and empty stretch of cracked cement.

It's a place at its end, just as the mall was. It must be easier for the Guild to maintain its magic over dead things. To not have to work against the will of something living.

I cross the street and head toward the front entrance. Roses leave my nose as the scent of spent firecrackers takes over. Closer now, the soot stains on the walls show themselves, and some of the windows are shattered inside their buckled frames.

Fire is what chased everyone away. The yellow and blue kinds, not the gentle red of our teahouse.

I find the black coin—the key starter—and cast on the lock. The pain is a minor twinge in my bones as the metal of the bolt retracts.

The lobby is small and smells of age and mildew and rotting wood. Through the broken windows, moonlight leaks in and reveals the blackened floral carpeting, the warped paintings on the walls. The water used to put out the fire lingers as a cool dampness in the air.

But there's the faint echo of voices. The walls and ceiling are full of small tremors, reverberating with the presence of the tournament two floors above.

I cast on the elevator using the black coin. Just as with the mall, the power being already cut here makes no difference, either, and the Guild's tournament magic sets the motor running. I press the button for the third floor and fall back against the side of the elevator.

My nervousness climbs just as the elevator does. It's almost harder walking in to fight now that I know what to expect. Or maybe it's just that I know what's expected of me. I know everything that can be lost now if I screw up.

How can I repeat what still feels like a fluke? What if every spell I've ever cast was never a sure thing, my control over them only perceived? What if seeing Finch makes it hard for me to see that line between honor and dishonor?

I shove my mask away, take a deep breath as the elevator doors open, and step out into the mouths of apartments that no longer exist. Yellow and blue fire were hungriest here, so that the Guild chose it to be the location of tonight's fighting ring—easiest to fill what is no longer there.

The third floor is a cavernous shell, its space full of high, shadowed corners and thick support beams charred along their edges. All its inner walls are gone, with only broken wooden framing and pipes to mark where they were. Its ceiling is missing, too—peering upward is to see a floating darkness, then the hint of the fourth floor's ceiling. Random furniture the fire didn't get to is pushed up against the outer walls, remnants of those who once lived here—a stained couch, mattresses, an old-fashioned console. Light glows down from the dozen or so bulbs that hover in the air. That light wasn't visible from the ground, I remember—the Guild's magic, woven to hide even the smallest parts of the tournament from the outside.

Just as with the food court, the entire space is crowded with casters. There's a table set up on the left side of the room, and some-one's scrawled the word REGISTRATION on the wall behind it in thick white letters. The starter counter is at the far wall, while the bets counter is on my right. Here again the casters are the loudest and most anxious, pushing at one another to get their bets in on time.

"Twenty-mark technique on Wilson to cast five bone spells, five-mark status on Nola to survive!"

"Hundred marks on Finch to survive!" An image of Finch flashes, his eyes cold green glass. I've already noticed his face in Oliver's—has he seen Shire's in mine?

"Seventy marks on Pav to request a bow-out!"

"Fifteen marks on Rudy to survive!"

More gamblers betting on me.

A surge of pride leaves my face warm, even as fresh fear is a trickle in my stomach. I want this, and I need the marks collected with each bet. But expectations are also weights, and they're piling up now, breathing down my neck—faith, revenge, escape.

"Rudy."

I turn to see Piper swiftly crossing the floor. She's changed into a green silk dress, her purse a mass of sequins and beads hanging near her hip. Her red hair is coiled into a sleek crown on top of her head.

She takes out marks from her purse and hands them over to me. "Two hundred for your ring starters. Are you ready?"

I slide the wad into my pocket. "I think so?"

She purses her glossed-over lips. "Try again."

"I mean, yes, I'm more than ready. Absolutely. I'll out-flair every-one in this room."

"Well, you'll never out-flair *me*, but the other twenty fighters are fair game."

I take out the folded silk ribbon from my starter bag. "Should I put this on now?"

"As good a time as any. Let me help."

She winds the ribbon around my upper arm, snugly enough so that it doesn't move when I do. Silk peony blossom print shimmers as I move my arm beneath the lights. The weight of expectation grows another degree.

Piper squeezes my arm through the band. "There will be many bets placed on you this match, so don't forget to go by the bets counter afterward to claim your winnings."

I nod, flush a bit. "I already heard a gambler bet on me. To survive."

"Then don't let them down, or me." Her tone isn't unfeeling, but it reminds me how the tournament is a business to her and nothing personal. After all, just this time yesterday it was Luan who was wearing the Mothery's silk band. Has a *backer* ever walked away from their fighter, if another becomes a better investment?

A final squeeze of my arm and Piper heads off.

I go to the registration table first. It's the same clerk as last time, and after he makes a check beside my ring name on the clipboard, he writes RUDY on my cheek. Just as I'm about to turn to leave, he stops me.

"Hold up, you'll need one of these, too." He holds out a small box with a hole in its top for me to draw from.

I pull out a white sticker with the number 15 on it. "What's this?"

"I find out with the rest of you. But for now, you're supposed to put it on your sleeve."

I slap it on and move over to the starter counter. I use the marks Piper gave me and buy twenty ring starters, five of each. The process makes me think of Oliver, and I find myself half searching the crowd for a tall guy with wary eyes and a shirt that fits too perfectly, the brother of the fighter who killed my sister.

But I don't see him, and I stop looking altogether after noticing how many others are watching *me*. Is this a taste of what it's like for Finch? Everyone wanting a bit of you just to feel that much closer to magic the way it once was, without cost and done freely? Most are careful to look elsewhere as soon as I meet their gaze, but one guy—earrings, a strangely rounded beard—can't seem to. His eyes stay on mine, his thirst for magic of old palpable, and because he reminds me of last night's autograph seekers, I quickly move away.

It takes me a few minutes to find the washroom. The original apartment ones were all destroyed in the fire, so the Guild of Now had to cast up another. I follow an arrow through a winding maze of half-broken walls until I get to a barricaded area with two doors. Behind the door to the women's washroom is an exact replica of the washroom from the food court.

I duck into a stall and take out Shire's key holder from my starter bag. I slide on all my new ring starters, combining them with the ones I have left over from last night's fight. The key holder is heavy, reassuring. I attach it to my belt loop, step out of the stall, and crash into the person standing there.

It doesn't surprise me at all that it's Kylin.

She's grinning, back to the confident kid caster I first saw yesterday, her bright chestnut braid swinging over her shoulder.

I should be dismayed that she's clearly ready to fight, but instead I'm relieved she's no longer so nervous. The feeling irritates me, and I stride by roughly.

"What is it with you and washrooms?" I mutter.

"Recognized your shoes," she says as she follows me to the sinks. "From beneath the stall."

"Then I'm changing them for next time."

"I wanted to see if you were okay," she says as she climbs onto the counter. "About your sister. And about Finch, seeing him today."

I stare at my reflection and tell myself I don't see fear there. "I'm fine."

"That's good." Kylin points to her sneakers. They have a sunflower print all over them. "New lucky sneakers."

"No, it's not good that I'm fine." Why does Kylin have to be such a kid? It'd be easier to remember how she almost killed me if she didn't keep talking about lucky sneakers, or asking me if I'm okay. "At least, not to you. You shouldn't want me fine—we're competitors."

"So I've got a new pact for you." She tilts her head as she sees my cheek. "Also, what's your real name if it's not Rudy?"

"I'm Rudy here. And no more pacts—we're not friends."

"But maybe we're not enemies, either. Not really. Not kill-you enemies, just competition enemies, and that's different. We can even enter again next year, if we wanted to."

But I wouldn't, because it'd be too late then.

As for the rest, I glare at her while I wash my hands. "We both tried to kill each other yesterday; what are you talking about?"

"That was *before* our first pact. Which is why I'm asking you to make another one with me."

I say nothing as I dry my hands on my pants. The sticker on her sleeve says 6.

"Let's make a pact that we'll avoid each other in the ring," she says. "We'll just go for everyone else. Maybe it'll even just be us two by the end."

Something flares in me. An ache, when I haven't even cast.

Her words, her wish—I might have said the same thing to Shire. And my stomach hurts because I'm no longer sure what she might have said. Yes, because she always said yes to me. But also no, because the tournament was hers, a secret she'd decided to keep.

"You're forgetting about Finch," I say to Kylin. "Eliminating him won't be so easy."

"I don't think he'll kill in this tournament. The Guild won't vote him in if he keeps doing it, once they have an opening."

"What if he uses another gathered spell?"

"That was just a guess about him using one last year." One of her double-shoulder shrugs. "If he did, he would have had to pay something huge. And also, I guess that means he's still been able to hide it."

A bell rings.

Back outside, spectators have pushed themselves to the outer edges of the room that is now the third floor. Kylin and I walk into the center where the rest of the fighters already are. Twenty-one of us left, standing in a loose circle.

The dimensions of the apartment building are smaller than the food court's were, and the noise level has folded in on itself, waves of sound lapping over one another and growing. Cheers and yells and clapping, a smattering of heckling boos. I make out names: *Pav* and *Rudy* and *Finch*.

I scan the fighters around me and wonder how much better they are tonight than last. Nola has new glasses, and she's wearing the number 4 on her sleeve. Wilson is number 14, his wide grin telling us all how happy he is to be here. Pav is number 13. He looks Chinese, around thirty, with pretty bird tattoos all over his arms and a panicked look in his eyes. Kylin is staring straight ahead, as she did last time, and for a second I regret not agreeing to her pact, if only because it couldn't have hurt. At least, not at first.

And Finch. Number 5 on his T-shirt sleeve, blond hair and celery eyes. There's the shine of a blue-striped ribbon from his arm, showing how Oliver and the family business of the Salt Lick are behind him.

I don't know how long I'm staring at Finch for before he notices and turns. His expression remains unchanged as his gaze meets mine—if he recognizes Shire in me, he doesn't show it. It only makes him colder, how simple his purpose is. He is here only for the challenge of his magic, the weighing and measuring and testing of it, and we are merely the ways he is proving to the Guild that he can be a great.

Shire was better, and in his way.

What are you hiding, Finch? How did you beat her?

I drag my eyes away and there's Oliver in the crowd, just behind Finch. The shape of their bones is an echo of each other's, and they're both tall with wide shoulders. That they're brothers is clear. And if their parents are gone and it's just the two of them, they must be close, too.

I wonder how deep the similarities go, how strong the bond. *Oliver, what kind of magic do you have? Could you ever kill with it?*

A dull, thudding fury grips me—why did it have to be Oliver who I noticed? I *liked* his rusty laugh, his reined-in impatience. I liked the guarded wariness in his eyes that said he cared too much. Why can't someone else back Finch? What is Oliver still helping him hide?

Oliver catches me watching him then, his gaze flickering over, and I know my stare is stony before I pointedly look away.

The sound of the crowd changes, gains an edge of excitement that is as sharp as hunger. I feel it in my own throat, the need for magic. My casting arm twinges as Embry appears and makes his way toward the center of the room.

Then I blink and the burnt-out shell of a building around us is gone.

TWENTY-FIVE

Gone is the singed carpeted floor, and instead we're standing on smooth, sun-beaten pavement. The four outer walls of the old apartment building—soot-stained, broken through with piping and wiring—are now the curved walls of a circular temple. The walls are of a polished green brick, dotted through with bricks of gold and pearl and with cutout windows of painted glass. Fat gold pillars line the courtyard, and covered staircases wind upward toward balconies. Huge potted ginger plants sit on these, full of thick green branches and fat dangling vines. Three tiers of sloped jade tiles make up the temple's roof; massive dragons carved out of pearl perch on their peaks and hang off their edges.

I've only ever seen an ancient Zinaese temple in history books. The ancient land of Zina still stands on the other side of the Pacifik, but is filled now only with the relics of these temples, with ruins of once-great palaces and courtyards. The last one fell more than a thousand years ago.

And yet.

I peer upward, at the sky that is more than vivid with pinks and plums, at the strings of glowing lanterns that crisscross for miles over the length of the temple's inner courtyard. Our shadows are blurs on the pavement, softened by the dusk light. Spectators fill the spaces between the pillars, and their faces are ovals, equally blurred by distance.

The air blows across my skin, as soft as velvet, smelling of ginger; if I stick out my tongue, I know the taste of the plant would stick. How much of that taste is the Guild? Their ethereal magic *is* this world, wrapping around us as it weaves together an existence that no longer is.

I've never felt less like I was dreaming; nothing has ever seemed more real.

"When the first Tournament of Casters took place two thousand years ago," Embry says as he moves closer to us, "it was a test of skill. Three hundred years later came the first battle of caster *families*. It was still a test of skill, but even more so one of teamwork."

His voice is that smooth low rumble again, the one that worms into your brain and makes you question your own magic—*Do I deserve to be here? How do I measure up?* He's in another sleek suit, this one of deepest midnight blue, and his tie is a stark contrasting white with an elegant raised rose print.

He glances around, as though unable to keep from admiring the Guild's work. *His* work.

"This is Jayde Temple," he says, "one of the most revered temples in ancient Zina on account of the royalty who once lived there— emperors and empresses, their families and their servants. It's said the royals were so indulgent with their full magic that the grounds of the temple stayed warm year-round. How even in deep winter, snow would melt feet before it hit the earth. Today only ruins remain, but before it fell, Jayde Temple was also the site of that first battle between families. Two great lineages of casters clashing right here, spilling blood and magic."

His words stir up images in my brain. Standing in the middle of this re-created world, it's easy to picture the royalty that once filled this place, the grand lives they would have led. Back when casting full magic was celebrated, done out in the open. When no one had to hide their power because everyone had the same kind. People in silks and velvets drinking Wu teas while they pulled power from the earth, casting it to do whatever they wanted it to do. How the only challenge they faced were other casters, racing up to the temple walls with fire in their veins and stars drawn on their palms.

"You each wear a number on your sleeve," Embry says, "a number you chose at random. Numbers one, two, and three, please stand here." He gestures to his right.

Three fighters move over: a teenaged boy with the ring name of Hurley, a woman in her twenties named Lia, and a guy in his fifties with a cigarette jammed between his lips whose name is Oscar.

"Numbers four, five, and six, please stand here." Embry gestures to a spot not too far from the first.

This is Nola, Finch, and Kylin. Kylin's expression is just as cool as Finch's as they move to stand together, giving away no sign that she ever mentioned the idea of Finch being a cheater.

Soon we're standing in seven groups of three. We circle Embry like we're numbers around a clock face.

I study the other two people in my group, just as they study me in return.

Number 13 is Pav. Up close the worry in his eyes is underlined by purple bags of sleeplessness, and his hands are shaking. His regret over entering this tournament comes off him in waves. Or maybe it's just pain from fighting last night, or from whatever casting he does outside of here. I don't know if it makes any difference when it comes to needing him to fight.

Number 14 is Wilson. While Pav reeks of terror, Wilson's excitement burns like a fever. He's built smaller than I first thought, is all tightly coiled energy and barely reined-in swagger. But he's bought into that swagger, believes absolutely in his own capacity for magic and control over it. I'll have to make myself believe it, too—that it's better to be on his side for this fight than not.

"Fighters, this is your team for tonight's battle," Embry says. "If one of you falls, all three of you do. So, please take a moment to introduce yourselves to one another."

There's an awkward kind of shuffling among us. We're supposed to knock each other out, not become allies. I think of Kylin and Finch being in the same group and can't deny I'm relieved—I'm not ready for her to be eliminated just yet, and her getting stuck with Finch means her chances of moving on are better than they were.

Wilson just shakes his head as he faces Pav and me. His grin is dismissive. "Let's not bother with the niceties. After this match we move on, and I'll just have to get back to thinking of how I'm going to eliminate you two anyway."

Pav's shoulders slump slightly. "Not the greatest attitude to have for this, kid."

Wilson scowls at the *kid*. "Casting magic is casting magic. Being nice isn't going to help us."

"Doesn't hurt anything, either."

"That's where you're wrong. Everyone knows it's easier to knock out a stranger than a friend."

"I agree with that," I say. "But not for this match. You heard Embry. Tonight's about teamwork if we're going to move on to the next round. And teamwork's easier if we can at least pretend to be friends."

"I *am* pretending," Wilson says. "I haven't complained yet about being stuck on a team with 'Pav the Coward.' I heard the crowd. I know why they call you that. Hiding is boring."

Pav's face goes red. "Casting shield and invisibility spells is a type of strategy. Sorry if it's not one you agree with."

"You're both wrong," I blurt out. "Pav, what you're doing *is* boring. Wilson, that doesn't mean Pav might not be smarter than all of us put together. But we still have to figure out a strategy we can all agree on."

Pav's expression is one of near betrayal. "I can cast other spells, too. I just don't use them as often."

"I'll believe that when I see it," Wilson says, far from impressed. He turns to me. "Fine, I'll be friendly, but none of us are *friends*."

I nod. "We're not, but you better learn fast to care about helping Pav and me stay alive."

"All right, now that everyone's made nice," Embry says as we all turn to face him, "let's move on to the next step."

He flashes a deck of cards so that the cards fan out evenly from his hands.

The gesture's oddly theatrical. It makes me think of pretend casting, the stuff of fake magic shows and staged spells. Which *is* a good trick for Embry, I suppose, considering he's a member of the Guild of Now and the Guild likely knows more about magic than anyone else here.

He walks from group to group, holding out the cards. "One per team, please."

Lia draws for her team.

"What is this?" She flips her team's card over and over again. Its front is blank.

So is the card Finch's team is holding.

More teams draw. Their cards are all blank, too.

Pav's the one who takes our card for us. He flips it over. The front side is completely blank, just like everyone else's.

"Look again," Embry says, the remainder of the deck somehow now gone from his hands.

Pav flips our card again.

The front is no longer blank. Now there's a drawing of a bright silver coin on it.

Silver for breath.

"The card your team holds is the kind of spell your team will be casting tonight." Embry pauses for effect. "The *only* kind of spell."

Wilson's grin turns into a grimace.

And dread fills me at the abrupt dimming of his glee—because it can only mean one thing.

Pav, seeing my face fall or whatever it does to show my sense of doom, turns frantically from me to Wilson and back again. "What is it?"

"It's his weakness," I whisper.

Pav's mouth forms a perfect O of dismay.

Even the strongest casters of full magic can have a weakness, whether it's obvious or hidden. Just having a preference for certain spells can be a weakness, because it leaves you rusty with others. If

Wilson's weak in breath spells, he might not be able to do much more than just protect himself with a shield spell. He won't be able to cast attack spells. No air punches. No heat or fire. Under these circumstances, he might as well have no magic at all.

Now Pav's the one with the scowl, and he turns it on Wilson. "No wonder you're hating on my casting shield and invisibility spells. It's because you're weak in them."

"*Weak* is a strong word."

"You *can* cast a basic shield, right?" I ask, no longer sure. Wilson made fun of Pav for casting his shields, but what if he's been covering up this whole time how he can't cast even that?

"Yeah, of course," he says. "I made sure my shield was good so I could focus on getting great with bone spells."

Pav snorts. "So *that's* why I thought I heard them call you 'Wilson the Boner.'"

Wilson looks toward the ground.

"*Really* useful for this round, all those bone spells you're so great at. Thanks so much."

Wilson flings his arms out wide. "Hey, as if any of us had an idea this was coming. Any other kind of match and *you'd* be the one—"

"We're going to have to deal with it," I snap in a whisper, nearly feeling bad for Wilson except for the very real fact that he might now get me eliminated. But a team, spell restrictions—I didn't expect those tonight, either. "Pav, we'll just have to cover for him."

My brain is frantic. I run down all the breath spells that would be useful in the fighting ring. Rudy would say it's just one more form of sorting, what fits and what doesn't. Shield, air punches, fever, fire, swelling, breathing . . .

"A team is only as strong as its weakest member," Embry says now. He moves closer toward the line of gold pillars, where he means to watch us fight ourselves away. "Just like a fighter is only as strong as their greatest weakness. To be truly great, a caster must know how to balance their magic.

"You'll fight until two teams remain." He scans his teal eyes over us. The weight of his gaze is like static electricity in the air, a storm over a temple from ancient times. "Starting now."

TWENTY-SIX

It is the sliver of space between heartbeats. The seconds between *breath in* and *breath out* within your lungs.

That's how long it is before the entire courtyard is full of cast magic.

"Shield spells!" I yell as I yank free a silver coin. First things first, which means surviving long enough to at least figure out what to do next.

Wilson and Pav cast, and we back into a loose circle, each of us facing outward. Invisible armor turns the lines of the temple blurry, the carved dragons on the roof into unnamable creatures. A twinge of pain from casting passes through me.

Around us in the courtyard, the other six teams are already at it. Figures are barely more than streaks of color and motion. A bright smear of blond is Finch, a swish of a brown braid is Kylin. There are flashes of light—the low sun, glinting off Nola's glasses. There are muffled yells, dull smacks. The crowd roars and cheers from the perimeter of the courtyard.

"What do we do?" Pav asks. His voice wobbles through my shield. "We can't just stay here!"

"Wilson, you do," I say. If he can't help us, then we can't let him hurt us, either. "Stay low and just keep casting shield spells, got it?"

He sputters, indignant. "What, you want me to just stay out of the way the whole time?"

"Ye—"

An explosion sends me sprawling backward. I hit the pavement with a thud. My head pounds like a drum, its beats painful enough that I can't hold together my shield spell. I'm dimly aware of Wilson nearby, calling my name.

I drag my eyes over to the fighter who cast that skin spell on me. It's number 7, a fighter named Bess. She's older, like she works in an office otherwise. She's moving closer, her eyes huge and wild. Her palm is out—she's about to cast again.

My hand's reaching for a starter when a blur of motion crosses in front of me. It's Pav, channeling Wilson at his most exultant. He charges toward Bess as he casts, a sketching of a star, a silver coin dropping from his hand. His long yell is a war cry and it sends a chill along my skin. It bounces off the distant temple walls like the clanging of swords.

Bess drops to her knees, her hands at her throat. Her skin begins to turn blue, the tint spreading outward from her mouth.

So much blue.

It can't just be manipulation of her breathing, then. Pav must have cast magic to change her oxygen, to make it become something else that she's now breathing in. The effect is fast, harsh, telling of both its spell's potency and cost. A twelve- or thirteen-pointed star, at least. And even though we're here in the tournament and the Guild helps lessen our pain from casting, it's still a pretty big hit to put on yourself right at the beginning of a fight, especially when you've already cast for a shield.

Pav, don't get carried away!

Now Bess goes even more frantic. Her fingers scrabble at her neck. Her eyes bulge.

Someone's cast a *second* spell on her, layered on top of Pav's.

I whirl around. Wilson is crouched behind me, pale and trembling as he drops the just-spent silver coin to the pavement. It joins one already there, the starter he used for his shield spell.

"What are you doing?" I shout at him over the roar of the crowd. "Pav's spell is enough!" You can't choke someone when they already can't breathe; any second now Bess would have declared herself a bow-out. Why is Wilson depleting his magic for nothing, especially if he's already weak in breath spells? He's only supposed to be casting shield spells on himself to stay in the fight. To keep Pav and me in the fight with him.

Wilson wheezes, sneers. "You sure about that?"

I spin back around. He's right. Instead of being eliminated and encased in marble, Bess is whooping in huge breaths, palms braced on the pavement. She's managed to outlast *both* breath spells, and now they're wearing off at exactly the same time.

My team has only wasted magic. Wilson is more liability than weapon. And Pav's gone off, charging ahead with his war cry.

I swear under my breath and cast another shield spell. A long shiver of pain as the world shimmers, and my mind's whirling, trying to think, as I toss the spent coin and take in the rest of the courtyard.

On the other side, Kylin, Finch, and Nola are working as a team. They stand shoulder to shoulder as they break up the pavement. Finch is burying a fighter with slabs of stone. It's the teenager, Hurley. A second later, Hurley turns into marble, declared a knockout by the Guild. Two more fighters across the courtyard tip over, also transformed into marble—Hurley's teammates, Lia and Oscar, automatically eliminated in turn.

One team down.

If someone like Finch can figure out teamwork, why can't we? Frustration bites and my thoughts are chaos. How to work *with* Pav and Wilson instead of against? Complement, not clash?

Beside Finch, Nola casts, and rocks fall like rain. Fighters are yelling, dodging. Kylin's using chunks of pavement as huge fists, sending them through the air and knocking fighters to the ground.

Bess, back on her feet, gets hit by one and goes down. She's marble. Behind her, two figures fall over, become marble as well.

A flare of pride—unwanted, dangerous, but here anyway— flashes through me. *Good for you, Kylin.* Five teams left, fifteen fighters.

But then, through the dust and rock, I catch how she's smiling hugely at me, and my heart sinks even as it twists. She knocked out Bess for me. We don't have a pact, but she's acting like we do. Like we're in this together.

"No," I whisper.

I stumble back a step, like she's cast magic to hurt instead of save.

I can't owe Kylin a single thing. Not here, not when I can only care about me. Sure, I would have done the same thing for Shire if she were here, but Shire's gone, and I'm the only one left now. The only one who can avenge her.

A new awareness rolls across the courtyard as the other fighters finally realize what just happened. Kylin's smile was a beam, so that my whispered protest might have been as loud as a scream.

Her coming to help me has marked out my team as the weakest. An easy target.

My vision begins to flicker wildly; black creeps in on its edges. It's the full magic of other fighters, trying to pry apart my shield spell. The smell of fire is everywhere, used-up magic smoldering in the air. The pavement's painted red in swaths, and hunks of stone are flying in every direction. The crowd's a distant wave of cheering and hollering.

Pavement careens into my chest, and my shield of air trembles. Something behind my ribs cracks. My shield trembles harder, goes thin.

Then pain explodes in my head. I can taste it, a wave of copper that stings my tongue. I fall low to the ground in a crouch and my already-weakened shield spell trickles away.

I tear free a silver starter from my holder. Fear swims as blood spurts from my nose, begins to drip from my mouth. My heartbeat roars as the blood in my veins is ordered to stream from me.

The scene takes on a haze of red as I lift my head and look for the fighter out to bleed me dry.

She's hunched down between two pillars. *Freya* is scrawled across her cheek. Her casting arm is out, its palm ready to be drawn on again. Her mouth works as she stares at me with huge eyes. *I'm sorry, I have no choice, I have to—*

I cast.

Wind gathers and spins a loosed ginger tree branch through the air. It pierces Freya's thigh and she topples. She slaps the ground three times and turns to marble. The vague thought comes about whether or not fighters still feel pain after the Guild's changed them, but it disappears as my own pain stabs through me. I fall back, my breathing loud and jagged as I slowly stop bleeding.

One more team down. Twelve fighters left.

A shout. Pav, yelling in my direction, the birds on his arms flying with him. He's no longer exultant, no longer triumphant with his war cry. Instead panic is all over his face, gold-hued skin bleached pale.

"It's Wilson it's Wilson it's—!"

I drag myself to standing, dread cold lumps of ice in my blood.

Wilson's on his feet, staggering and stumbling as he struggles to fend off nearby fighters. They swarm close, six of them, Wilson their choice of prey. They smell weakness the way a gang of vultures will stick close to the nearly dead, knowing it's just a matter of time.

Wilson's shield spell is almost gone as he keeps fighting. He's shaking with the effort, pain in every line of his body as he casts. He is unrecognizable from the Wilson who dared to banter with Embry about winning it all.

My mouth is dry as my hands dig at my starters, as my eyes hurriedly scan the courtyard. Six fighters on Wilson—so where's Kylin's team? Where are Finch and Nola? Kylin might not want to help take down my team, but Finch, who kills, would. Nola, who punched Teller into elimination, would. So where are they?

Pav's helping Wilson already, casting on the six as they approach. One fighter flies backward, a gust pushing him away, but he gets up as soon as he lands. Pav's growing weaker, too.

Panic climbs, is a crescendo in my blood.

There are too many of them. Too many at once for Pav and me to try to fight off and have Wilson still be standing by the end of it. If only there were more of *us*, more of—

My breath catches.

I have seconds to decide. Be reckless or not. Break the rules of only using silver starters or not.

Then Pav's falling, and I choose.

I go to grab at the key holder on my hip. My mind is a storm as Piper's words fill it.

Perhaps you're thinking about simply bending the rules rather than breaking them. Because there's still honor in doing what must be done to survive, even if such ways are ugly.

I draw. Not just a star to fit my palm, but with points that reach my fingertips, that travel to my wrist. So many points, so much magic. An endless red fire in my brain that screams for escape. My body burns, my casting arm and its palm a whole torch.

I yank ring starters from the key holder at my hip. A mess of all four colors, too many to count right now—red for blood, white for bone, silver for breath, gold for skin. My breathing's rough in my throat, my pulse a thrum along my skin.

I drop the coins into my palm.

Magic tumbles from me, a huge bloom of red that I barely just hold back. I stoke it and direct it, begin to shape it with the will of my mind.

I choose a shape I know well.

Azas come to stand around me. Clones of my own skin, bones, breath, and blood. I'm all over the courtyard.

Not more of us, then, but more of me.

There's the roar of the crowd as they shout their approval. The noise is a wall, tumbling across the courtyard. They know I've broken the rules, but they can't help but be entertained at the spectacle.

The pain builds. Splinters of it drive deep into my bones.

With trembling hands I tear a silver coin from my key holder. A dozen other Azas tear one off theirs.

We cast as one.

Air extinguishes itself from the lungs of the fighters zeroing in on Wilson and Pav. Their hands go to their necks, then slam on the ground. *Bow-out.*

The crowd bellows. It's my name—*Ruuudy*—and the noise wants to tear my head apart.

One by one the other Azas begin to disappear as my spell fades. I count the fighters still in the courtyard with eyes that hurt as I move them. Copper fills my mouth again.

Wilson and Pav and me. One team.

Finch and Nola and Kylin reappear from wherever they went—team number two.

The fight's over.

Six of us left.

The last thing I see is Finch, his green eyes narrowed as he finally takes real notice of me.

I black out.

I die.

TWENTY-SEVEN

I come back to life inside Jayde Temple.

It's a round room, with a sunken center. The walls are covered with white paper that has the sheen of pearls. Stained glass windows are painted with dragons and flowers. The floor is all polished tile—jade, emerald, and gold. Gold lanterns hang from the ceiling.

I'm sitting at a table in the sunken area. There's a bouquet of jasmine flowers on it, so that the whole place smells of them.

Across from me sits Embry.

Being two feet away instead of across a fighting ring makes him no easier to read. His odd teal eyes are like chips of polished glass, reflective instead of revealing. His expression is neutral as he watches me. All traces of whatever charm he once showed are gone while the power remains.

I stare at my hands, at the room, back at Embry again. None of this can be real if I—

"You just *almost* died. The Guild's magic over the tournament was just enough to save you."

My mind goes blank. I say the only thing I can say even though it feels more than inadequate. "Thank you."

"I'm to offer you tea. Would you like some?"

There are no pots or cups in sight, but I nod anyway, understanding. I might not be able to cast marks into existence, but

Embry's a member of the Guild. He could probably do it while half-asleep.

He takes a jasmine flower from the bouquet and places it on the table. It becomes a pot full of hot tea. Two more flowers laid down and they become cups.

I'd expected it, but I'm still stunned. Not at the proof of such magic, but because Embry's hands hadn't moved to cast.

"You didn't do this," I say, growing confused.

"I didn't have to because someone else in the Guild did. We are always here somewhere, in some part of the tournament." He smiles, but it's still not warm. "Without form, like full magic itself."

I have to force myself from glancing around the room, searching for hints of vague, indefinable clouds over our heads.

He pours tea for the both of us. Only after he sets the pot back down does he speak again.

"You broke the rules with the casting of that clone spell. You cast outside your team's assigned starter."

"I did break the rules . . . but only kind of."

"How only 'kind of'?"

"I only used other starters when I cast the clone spell. For spells on the other fighters, I only cast using silver ones."

He narrows his eyes just the slightest bit.

"Even my clones only used silver ones," I press.

"True. Though all those clones would have never been cast in the first place if you hadn't broken the rules."

I take a sip of tea, trying not to wither beneath his stare. "It's okay, I already know you're letting me stay in the tournament."

Now he laughs. "Oh?"

I nod. "You haven't met with any of the other eliminated fighters after a match."

"None of the other eliminated fighters have done what you did." Some of his power peels back, revealing more of his charm. I let myself relax a tiny bit.

"I know I broke the rules." I scrub at dried blood on my arm. There are bruises all over and every single muscle hurts from fighting. I think of doing this again tomorrow, and my mind goes to the empty medicine jar in my starter bag. "But I had to. My team was in trouble."

"Having a reason doesn't change how you still broke the rules. However, given the theme of tonight's match, the Guild eventually voted to allow you and your team to move on to the next round. It was clear you only cast that spell in the name of teamwork, covering for your team's weakness as you did. And as you said, you still only *fought* using silver starters, even each of your clones—the casting of which, I must admit, some of us enjoyed watching very much."

Relief has me slumping slightly. "Thank you."

"But honorable move or not, you'll still have to pay for breaking the rules." His teal eyes stay on mine. "A caveat for the Guild's generosity."

I begin to unwind Piper's silk ribbon from around my arm so I don't have to look at him.

"The tournament has always been about being a show of full magic, a display of skill. It's why the Guild has never banned any specific spell—not when the real world already restricts too much of our magic. But this also means we're responsible for keeping the tournament and its effects under control. Your spell called for too much magic, and our diversion spell was tested. We cannot afford to slip."

I nod, folding up the ribbon with fingers gone cold and stuffing it into my starter bag. The crowd loved the spell, and Piper wanted flair, but I nearly died in casting it. How might the earth now have to pay? My mind skitters away from the thought.

"To keep you from trying anything like it again—and any other caster who might now be considering something similar—the Guild has decided that for the remainder of the tournament, we will no longer use our magic to help you survive the cost of casting."

"You can't do that." Panic unfurls, filling me. "Please." I'll feel everything, while everyone else will feel close to nothing. A punch to them would be an explosion for me. There's no way I can win now.

"It is a punishment that suits the crime," Embry says. "Of course, you don't have to accept our decision. In which case, you can enter again next year. It's up to you."

The panic turns into a fist. My grasp on the tournament—on answers, saving my family, my promise to Rudy—begins to slip. The two hundred thousand marks feel like they're drifting even further out of reach.

But what choice do I have? If I don't agree, the Guild will kick me out of the tournament anyway.

"Fine," I say. "I accept the decision."

"Good. And we want to make clear to you, no more second chances. Another rule broken and you *will* be eliminated from the tournament."

His tone doesn't give away if he cares or not. And I'm not sure why it suddenly matters but it does. Maybe because he and his Guild accept a killer like Finch as their champion, while my saving Wilson has only put me in danger of elimination.

"You said the Guild voted on us moving on or being eliminated," I say. "How many members wanted us out?" I imagine them, a group of seven greats, sitting around and weighing Finch's skill against his cruelty. How many of them might vote in someone like him? How far can Finch go and still be considered?

"It was close—hence the caveat." Embry drinks tea. "As the tie-breaker, I had to come up with something to tip the scales."

"Thank you." My resentment that he decided I would be in pain isn't fair, so I push it away. "Why didn't you vote the other way?"

"As I said, the Tournament of Casters has always been a show. I enjoyed your fist spell from the last match, and then the clones tonight."

"But . . . sometimes fighters die. For a *show*. That doesn't bother you?"

"Not as much as you think it should." His eyes grow sharp. "Leftover magic is for its casters to cast, just as full magic is ours. And while it runs in our veins, death from it does, too, and that is the cost—that is how, whether we like it or not, the world has created us to be now. Those who enter know that death is a possibility, and so we don't prevent it. But it's on us to ensure the tournament stays a secret, and that nobody gets caught. That is why you breaking the rules and calling for too much magic has a penalty—while killing does not."

I blink and the inside of the temple disappears from around us.

Gone are the papered walls and jade brick and dragon-painted windows. Instead of a teapot and cups on a table, dried petals are scattered on the floor at our knees. The scent of jasmine is replaced with ones of smoke and fire, the last traces of a past inferno, of spent magic. We're back inside the burnt-out shell of the apartment building on Thorn Avenue.

"Before I forget." Embry hands over some marks. I count them. There's five hundred, way more than I've ever earned from a job. Way more than a *bunch* of jobs, even. "You weren't able to get to the bets counter after the fight tonight to collect your winnings. You should celebrate—that's a very impressive amount for having only fought twice. You have left an impression."

I tuck the marks into my pocket, wishing I wasn't so pleased that *he* seems pleased. But more than that, this means I can replace the marks I had to take out of the safe for Jihen. My parents can still keep thinking everything is fine when it comes to the teahouse and Saint Willow.

"You also missed my announcement of tomorrow night's location." Embry hands me a small card as he gets to his feet. There's an address scrawled on it. "Midnight, as always."

5040 Helvetica

I tuck the card into my starter bag and get up, too. I hurt all over from fighting, and I think of Rudy's apothecary. More than ever I need to get more healing meds.

"Thank you for the tea," I say, "even if you weren't the one who cast it."

"I didn't cast it because I no longer cast. I fought in five tournaments—they took their toll."

Shock has me gaping. "You're an Ivor?"

He nods. "Bones of glass. I can't cast without shattering apart, even with the Guild's help. The other members cast the magic for the fighting rings, and I am the tournament Speaker. It is the arrangement we came to after I . . . changed."

"But—the playing cards tonight. They were blank and then—"

"The Guild as a whole."

"And tournament magic."

"Yes."

My thoughts run together, threaten to tangle. How many of us might go Ivor over the years because of this tournament? The amount of magic I did tonight alone could have easily tipped me over, because the Guild's magic can only do so much, and Embry is proof of that. For so long I've pushed to the back of my mind the chances of one day ending up an Ivor. Pushed it back so deep that tonight, I was staring the possibility right in the face and didn't even realize it.

I wonder what Embry thinks when he sees a display caster hanging from a lamppost. If he thinks about how it could easily be him up there if not for his damage being hidden, or if he's so busy thinking about his guild's tournament that seeing an Ivor doesn't mean much at all.

I want to ask him about it, but I don't because I think he'll just give me the same answer. The one that somehow disappoints me, even though I don't think it's actually wrong. And I don't have a better one.

That it's just the cost of magic.

Then I nearly tell him I'll keep his secret about being an Ivor, but I also don't do this. Because he already knows I'll keep it. Spilling it would mean having to face the Guild, greats powerful enough to create whole worlds and then take them back apart.

"My name's really Aza," I decide to say instead. An exchange of secrets, I guess. "But I'm Rudy for the tournament."

He nods again. His smile is all charm now. "Good luck, then, Aza."

TWENTY-EIGHT

Once outside, I begin making my way out of the Flower Sector. I head toward Tobacco, moving as fast as I can despite being sore. If not for Cormac, I'd be going home instead of to Rudy's. But there's an upside to his delaying me—now that I know he's staying near the teahouse instead of staking out the apothecary, I'll at least be able to break into Rudy's place in peace.

Salty air blows in off the Pacifik, drifts through my mask, and lingers. It mixes there with the thickening scent of smoke as I enter the Tobacco Sector and get closer to Rudy's shop. The neighborhood is mostly quiet, with a bar and a club a block over still open, and of course the breakfast-all-day diner directly across the street.

There are no new signs or notices posted anywhere outside Shen Apothecary, nothing to let his loyal customers know what happened to him. Rudy would hate that—not only their not knowing, but also that they have to go anywhere else. The blinds remain pulled—briefly I wonder again who discovered Rudy's body, as I couldn't ask Cormac, and he never said—and I peer around their edges to look inside.

The shelves are still full of bottles of tonics and elixirs. Jars and tins fill cabinets. The soaps Rudy was checking are still all over the table, inventory the last thing he did for his shop.

Heat comes to my eyes. I'm not supposed to miss all those days of coming here and being unpaid help while Rudy gritted out bits of advice, but I do. He kept me at a distance because of Shire and the tournament, but I had something to do with that, too, already half-sure when I went to him for help that he was just another enemy. Like Saint Willow and Jihen were. And now there's Cormac. And Finch.

I go around the outside of the shop and get to the back door. I find a rock in my starter bag, brace for the pain, and cast.

Heat travels from my feet and into my hands, forms in my mind as a ball of red haze. I send it to the lock and untwist it. As soon as it's done, my skin cools down and I lean back against the door, waiting, half holding my breath. The pain comes in a wave, hammers on the bones of my arms and legs, and I wait it out, gritting my teeth.

When it finally passes, I stand up again on shaking legs and go inside.

Smells swirl thickly, medicinal, herbal, one of rosemary most of all. I think of the broken bottle when I found Rudy and try not to gag at the scent.

Too tired to even consider leftover magic, I slap at the wall with my hand, searching for the light switch in the dark, finally finding it and flicking it on.

Light fills the room. It looks the same as it always does, stuffed full of boxes and supplies and shelves. I glance down at the floor—it's been cleaned up of Rudy's blood, of the broken and spilled bottles. Everything is so clean and neat—looking at it, you'd never guess someone like Rudy had died here two days ago, a mess of banished magic, secrets, and lies.

I head out to the shop floor, using only the light flowing

out from the supply room to see by. In the dimness, I move slowly around the room, realizing I will likely never see the apothecary again the way it is. How if I ever do come back, the space likely won't be Rudy's anymore—someone else will have moved in, might be selling anything else; all the sights and smells will be different.

The thought fills me with sadness, like I'm finally saying a proper goodbye to the person who connected me to Shire in ways I wouldn't have been otherwise. It also fills me with guilt, because hadn't I kept pushing him for more? To show me the spell Shire had died casting, when such a spell never existed? I try to imagine how he must have felt, keeping that secret, and find that I can't.

I keep working, feeling half-numb. I neaten a basket of dried herbs and straighten a shelf of oils. I find a lone twenty-mark coin on the counter but the till is locked so I slip it into my pocket.

It takes me a bit to find the right healing meds on a shelf, but I eventually do, matching their labels to the one on my empty jar. I debate taking them all, but then I think of how it was bad paperwork that set Cormac toward Rudy—if someone's going to be checking inventory against what's actually on the shelf, a whole bunch of missing meds might set off alarm bells, too.

I take a single bottle, but then duck behind the counter—if I can find Rudy's inventory binder, it'd be easy enough to doctor it so the shop's not missing any healing meds at all. I open drawers and peek into skinny cubbyholes. Before I find his binder, though, I find a notebook, one with dog-eared edges that say he used it a lot. Like me, Rudy never carried around a digital planner, because our magic would kill them each time.

I flip it open. Most of the notebook is a calendar, with some blank pages in the back for notes. The days are filled in with initials and times, which are meaningless to me, so I skip ahead to the back pages. Rudy's writing is messy, but a lot of the notes seem to be about ideas for the shop, things like new formulas and research ideas.

I keep flipping, trying not to feel like Rudy would mind. He probably would. But maybe now that I'm in the tournament and know about his plans and what happened to Shire, he wouldn't mind *so* much. And if there's anything in here that could help me at all over the last two rounds—

Finch's name leaps up at me from a page.

My heart trips inside my chest, and I hurriedly turn the page back. My fingers are clumsy and it takes me longer than it should. And it's dim in here. Maybe I saw wrong.

But then I find the page.

Finch—gath. spell possible?
Oliver?
That was the cost??

Now my pulse is racing. My mouth's gone dry with the shock of what I've found.

Rudy *also* suspected Finch cheated to beat Shire. That Finch maybe used a gathered spell, just as Kylin mentioned.

And that Oliver is somehow involved.

I shouldn't be as surprised as I am. It makes sense that Oliver would be helping his brother hide how he cheated. Just as Piper said, family complicates things, and I of all people know that loyalty sometimes knows no bounds.

Finch longs so badly to be in the Guild of Now, too. If you need to win in the first place to be able to do that, then what does the cost matter *as long as you still win*?

I shut the notebook with trembling fingers, slide it back into its drawer, and turn to leave. All thoughts of doctoring the inventory binder have fled—given the potential of what I've just found, a few missing bottles of medicine really won't matter.

I return to the supply room and exit through the back door, making sure to turn off the light before casting the lock back. Once more pain comes, a slow wave of it that is a knife through my middle.

I yank down my mask, dry swallow a pill, yank the mask back up. I try to walk as steadily as I can down the alley. It's pouring out, the air smelling more of the sea than of smoke, and I'm tired and sore enough to decide to grab a train back to the Tea Sector. I pay for the ticket using the mark I found at Rudy's, saving me from having to use any of the ones I got from the bets counter.

The train's rocking motion and the sound of rain on the roof nearly lull me to sleep. But then the latest news comes on, scrolling across the screen over the doors. No one else on the train seems to pay attention—it's just the most recent addition to a long string of bad news for the earth—but I do because I know so much of it is my fault.

The report is that, as of the last hour, over two hundred fish have washed up on the northern shore of the Flower Sector. The fish are a heavily mutated strain of catfish, warped over the years from adapting to pollution of the Pacifik and Upper Inlet and one of the few kinds of fish still able to survive in local waters. City water authorities have no explanation so far for the sudden mass death of the school of fish, and admit the population might take years to fully recover, if ever.

I'm wide awake the rest of the train ride home.

TWENTY-NINE

My eyes are still bleary from lack of sleep as I head out of the teahouse the next day. The events of last night haven't stopped pulling at me, filling my brain at a low buzz that won't completely quiet.

I didn't think it would be easy advancing to the final of the tournament. I've always considered myself a long shot. That Shire got there is never so much a source of hope as it is one of discouragement—she spent years training to control her magic—she was the reliable and dependable daughter.

But still. As the first rounds passed, I began to believe it was possible. That maybe it wasn't such a wild idea, getting to the final.

And now here I am, fighting for the rest of the tournament without the Guild's protection. They'll cover the cost of my magic when it comes to the earth, but not to me.

I might really die fighting for marks.

Just like Shire did.

For a second, the idea of walking away from the whole thing washes over me. Sure, my parents will lose the teahouse and a family legacy that goes back hundreds of years, but at least not both their daughters. Rudy's dead and can't care about my breaking my promise. Shire's dead, too, and just as Embry said, everyone who enters the tournament enters knowing they could die.

But all those reasons—they're also the same ones why I *can't* quit. My parents and everything they've worked for. Rudy, who might still be alive if not for me. Shire, who didn't know she'd be fighting someone dirty.

Finch, Oliver, the puzzle of Rudy's notebook and what was written inside—I know all of that will keep eating at me. It will never leave me alone until I find out what all of it means.

I cross the street in the direction of the Textile Sector. For the Mothery, and Piper.

I dreamed last night that she had dropped me as her fighter. I'd broken the rules and my chances at winning were slim—why would she continue to back me? The possibility left me shaky enough—on top of fighting vulnerable, the last thing I need is having to go back to worrying about marks for ring starters—that I knew I had to go see her in person and convince her she hasn't made a mistake. So I told my parents I was going to work and slipped out.

My web of lies, still being spun.

And then I stop cold.

Jihen.

He's sitting at one of the sidewalk tables of the café down the street. He's branched out this time with his striped suit, but his sneakers are as glaringly white as ever.

I start to reverse direction before he can see me, but it's too late. He's already getting up, throwing marks down on the table for his bill before he rounds the gate and heads toward me.

Always tempted to use magic to get away from him, my hand nearly goes to my starter bag. The healing meds I took last night worked—though slowly, making me wonder if I'm getting too used to them—and I woke up this morning without pain, despite having barely slept.

But I'm fighting tonight, and now without the Guild's protection. And I've actually got marks on me, a few left over after replacing the rest in the teahouse's safe last night. I might as well pay him and get him off my back again for a bit.

"Aza, good morning, shall we walk?" He takes my arm and guides me along the road.

"I guess so?" I try to throw off his hand, but his grip is irritatingly strong today. The thicker-than-usual undertone of ownership in it makes me uneasy. I glance over at him as we walk. "I have marks for Saint Willow. Let go of my arm and I'll give them to you for him. And then you can leave and do whatever it is that you guys do when you're not robbing or killing people."

His hand squeezes. "You can't rob those who owe you. And we only kill when we have to send a message. Messages are important. They let others know what is expected of them." Another squeeze and I regret not casting magic to get away after all.

We're not too close to the teahouse, but close enough that I'm uncomfortable. I turn a corner in the opposite direction, trying to get Jihen farther away from my parents.

"Here." I pull out the marks from my pocket. "There's more than there was last time—just take it." I brace myself for another round of Jihen making threats because it's still not enough. It *is* more, but never has it been enough.

Instead of counting the marks, though, Jihen stuffs them into a pocket. He gives me his greasy smile that's somehow a little too predatory today. That earlier uneasiness comes back, and I wonder if I've missed something.

He pulls me closer. He whispers into my ear words that turn my blood cold: "*I know you're a caster of full magic.*"

I stumble. His grip tightens and still we walk. I'm only dimly aware of the world that's fading in and out. The rain-damp sidewalk recedes. Shops and other casters go silent. The scents of tea and leaves lingering inside my mask fade. There are only his fingers that dig into my arm, keeping me from running away.

"You're wrong," I finally manage. My voice is thin and thready. "I only know leftover magic. Like everyone else."

"Let me tell you how I found out, Aza. You and I and everyone else in the sector know that Saint Willow sometimes has a . . . hard time keeping any full magic casters on. My boss loves full magic, but maybe a bit too much, and casters get scared off, yes?"

I just shake my head.

"Well, sometimes, being such a distant cousin in the Saint Willow enterprise has its benefits. People stop *seeing* you. They forget who you are. They think *the boss* has forgotten you. So when one of those casters used full magic for a memory wipe on Saint Willow and everyone else important in order to escape, *they forgot me.* And I let them. I let them because one hand washes the other. I let them have their freedom, and they give me a window into your world, Aza. Casters like you will be the end of the earth one day, but I also know there is power in information that others don't have. And so this caster and I—we're still friends, Diego and me. I have full magic right in my back pocket and *Saint Willow has no clue.*"

My heart is beating thickly in my throat, in my ears. Still we walk. I'm only half listening, my mind whirring with different spells to get away. But we're out in the open, in sight of the street, traffic, other people. And Jihen knows this.

"And Diego," he says, "it turns out he's a fan of this underground tournament. All full magic casters, all battling one another for big marks. He tells me about this one fighter with the ring name of Rudy who caught everyone's eye during the opening match."

There's a roar in my ears now. I picture Jihen sitting at the table in the teahouse that night, looking at all the blood still on me, his mild tsk of disapproval.

"So when Diego offers to sneak me in to last night's match, how could I refuse?" Jihen grins. "I missed seeing you up close, but Diego saw you. Do you remember him? Earrings, beard like a bird's nest hanging off his chin?"

I only shake my head again, despite knowing exactly who he's talking about. The guy who couldn't stop staring at me before the round.

"Well, the clones blew me away, beauty. Like a bunch of gorgeous dolls, you were. So many leng goong-doi."

I rear back, desperate for escape. But there is nowhere to go. Jihen pulls me closer.

"Of course, I *should* tell my boss. Then you, Aza Wu, would be Saint Willow's newest full magic caster. And if you didn't work out, there would be a tournament full of others to pick from. For my discovery, I would become the most important cousin in the family. I might even be promoted to something beyond debt squeezer. But then I got to thinking, why share? What if *I* would like a full magic caster? To have such terrible yet fascinating power for my own use?"

It takes a second to process. "You want me to work for you?"

Jihen nods. "You won't have to deal with Saint Willow's tantrums, and I'll have my own personal caster to cast me spells as I need. Do we have a deal?"

My head's spinning. Jihen or Saint Willow—it's like having to choose either getting eaten by a shark or a slow death by drowning. "I can't."

"*Or* the teahouse pays. There are so many ways it could pay. More honor marks. More suppliers cut off. And your parents— they won't want me back on the premises, will they?"

"Stop."

"Or imagine a Scout at the door. How many customers do you think your family's teahouse would get once it's out that their kid is a full magic caster? The despair your parents would feel, losing not only their remaining daughter but also their livelihood, this family legacy they've held on to all this time."

I twist free of his arm, feeling sick, needing to breathe. "Fine, I'll do it."

Another greasy grin slides across his face. "And a cut of the tournament prize, if you win."

Fury explodes at the pettiness of this last demand. How it's just one more thing on top of everything else, when he's already got way too much on me. "Say that again, and I'll go straight to Saint Willow about Diego. He'll drown you in the Sturgeon River the same way Earl Kingston did *his* cousin for keeping secrets."

Jihen's features twist. "You wouldn't dare, you brat."

"I would. So?"

He mutters something in Chinese too quietly for me to catch.

"What's money anyway, when I get a sweet caster of my own, right?"

"Right." I exhale. "I'm leaving now. Don't fol—"

The sight of my parents coming up the street freezes me before I can even take a step.

Why are they here instead of at the teahouse? Panic is a buzz in my head as I scramble for a cover. Where exactly did I say I was going this morning? *Did* I say anything specific? I can't remember.

"Ah, such timing," Jihen says softly. "Should we say hello to your loving fou-mou?"

I rip open my starter bag. "Walk away before they see you, or I'll cast."

"Not so fast. You want to cast something terrible on me, I can tell. But I'd be suffering and so would you. The pain of casting, yes?"

My parents are closer now. They see us. My stomach drops.

"Here's the first of my requests, beauty," Jihen says. "Consider this my test of your agreement, and you can save yourself. And you'll be saving your parents as well—small talk can be dangerous with all these secrets floating around."

Fury claws. *"Tell me."*

"A small accident or distraction right here on the sidewalk. And I'll leave."

I do it before I can think about it. How I'm now casting on orders from *Jihen*. My fingers shake as I pick up a water capsule. I cast, my hands low to my sides. Heat fills me. I stare at the pool of water that's still puddled on a nearby overhead awning and send it flying.

Everyone on the sidewalk gets drenched. There are cries of dismay and the shop owner emerges, confused. Behind it all there are my parents' faces, ovals of surprise as they take in the strange spill.

Through the headache that begins to circle my skull, Jihen's smug voice is at my side: "I'll be sure to give your marks to Saint Willow, Aza. Now don't go disappearing on me. I'll be in touch soon."

I start walking before he can say anything else. My head pounds, and the gray of the sky is too bright. I find my parents and hope my face looks normal. I'm kicking myself for making up a ridiculous lie that's now come true—I'm working for Jihen for real.

"Why aren't you guys at the teahouse?" I glance at the mess on the sidewalk and try not to feel guilty. Nobody got hurt, but soon some part of the earth will pay, however minor.

"Tomorrow is a bank holiday," my mother says from behind her smog mask, "so we're making payments today."

I forgot about the holiday. And tomorrow is Friday, and Friday the teahouse opens late on account of my parents going around the city and paying suppliers and distributors. I only replaced the rest of the missing marks in the safe last night after getting back from the apothecary. The close call sends a shiver through me.

"Aza, did we see Jihen with you?" My father is squinting over the heads of the casters on the sidewalk.

I nearly nod but for the pain. "I had to meet up with him to get instructions for a package I have to deliver." Such bland words—instructions, package, deliver—I use to describe working for a gang. It keeps my parents from remembering Jihen's intimidating tactics when he was squeezing them. It keeps them from wondering if I could be doing the same thing, their reckless daughter who might not understand full magic but who must know to be careful while working for Saint Willow.

"I have to go now," I tell them, "but I'll be home for dinner." I still need to get to the Mothery. To get to Piper and try to convince her she needs to stay as my backer.

"Can you wait for an hour or so, Aza?"

I glance at my mother, curious.

"There's a café down the block—we could all eat some lunch before you have to go?" Her smile is almost surprised. As though she asked before she knew she was going to. And maybe she did. The three of us haven't eaten a lunch together anywhere since before Shire died. Between her ghost and full magic and the teahouse, it's been hard to find room to fit together.

I want to point out that we shouldn't be spending marks on lunch. How the teahouse might be late to open if they don't get back now.

So my answer surprises me just as much. "Lunch would be nice."

THIRTY

It takes until dessert for things to not feel so strange. Without my mother's television to watch or my father's paperwork to read, we only have one another, and there is the awkward shuffling at first that happens when you're eating with strangers.

My headache's gone, at least.

My mother watched as I took the healing meds at the table, her eyes on me the whole time. At first I wondered if she was going to ask me about them, which would have been easy enough to lie about. But then it hit me that she might recognize the bottle or label as being the same as the one Shire had in her room and dread washed over me.

But it was about something else altogether.

"That was Shire's bag," she said, her eyes on it.

I nodded. I ran my hand over the yellow silk. Threads had begun to spring up from it, and there were some thin patches. A tiny hole had opened up near the top corner that leftover magic could probably fix except that I hadn't gotten to it yet.

"It's getting worn," my mother added.

"I know. But it's still usable."

"You should fix that hole before you lose something."

"I will."

Then the waiter came over and we were choosing between pasta and sandwiches and salad, and whether we wanted dessert. I'd been about to protest the price of dessert—the hole of Leafton's contract cancellation was still fresh on everyone's minds—but something on my father's face stopped me. It said we all needed this as much as wanted it.

My mother sniffs her tea now. She makes a face.

"I keep telling you to just order the coffee like I do." My father casts and the spoon in his mug stirs.

"It's research."

He sends me an exasperated look, and I have to smile. My mother has made it a habit over the years to always try the teas of others just to proclaim Wu ones are better. This, at least, has not changed.

The silence that follows isn't wholly uncomfortable. I eat cake and stare out the window and feel nearly half-normal. My mother casts, and the service bell on the wall rings; when the waiter comes, she tells them the tea is off and orders coffee. My father studies the menu like there's some code to decipher, something he could apply to the teahouse's to bring back the customers.

A text comes through on his cell and he frowns.

"It's an office out in the Spice Sector," he tells us. "Some of our statements just got delivered to them by mistake. They can redeliver, but their courier is behind—with the bank holiday tomorrow, we won't get these statements until Monday."

"Can they wait?" My mother nods her thanks as the waiter brings her coffee.

"Well, I'm supposed to meet Yun tonight over them. I've already confirmed the meeting. I'd hate to change it now."

Yun's one of the guys in our distribution system. Trying to fit in a meeting with him is tough because he's always juggling so many different companies.

My mother sighs, tired despite the coffee.

"I can go pick them up for you," I blurt out.

Because Oliver and Finch's family store is in the Spice Sector.

And while I don't think I'll get the chance to cast magic on either Finch or Oliver to get to the truth, maybe just observing their shop for a bit will tell me something. Having a legit reason for being in their neighborhood is too good of a cover to waste. My conversation with Piper will have to wait.

"I'll bring the statements home when I get back for dinner," I tell my parents.

My father's not convinced. He doesn't want me to get in trouble with Jihen or Saint Willow. "Don't you have to get to work?"

I nod and finish my cake in a rush. I *have* to go to Spice now—the need to try to uncover Finch's secret burns as hot as magic does, even if I have no idea yet what I'm actually going to do. "This won't take long. Here, write the address of the office down for me?"

"Well, thanks, Aza." My father writes on the napkin and hands it over. "Much appreciated—you know Yun's schedule."

"I do." I fold it into my starter bag, slip on my smog mask, and start to get up.

"Wait a second," my mother says. "One more thing before you go."

I stop.

She rips off some of her napkin—leftover magic—and casts.

The hole in my bag disappears, the tiny threads around its edge made to knot together.

"Thank you," I say. I can't explain the ache in my throat. Maybe because she still bothered to fix it, when it's just me using it now.

She hands me some marks. "For the train there and back—it's raining again. And don't be late for dinner."

I get to my feet and head for the door. My eye catches on a figure outside the window, standing on the sidewalk, clearly waiting for someone.

Cormac.

THIRTY-ONE

I falter for a second, confused. I'm supposed to get a week. A week where he thinks I'm getting information together to help him bring down casters of full magic, while really I'm just stalling before I can present him to Saint Willow as a cop to be dealt with.

One glance at his face says I don't have a week anymore.

I push open the door and rush out of the café.

"What are you doing here?" I hiss at him, too on edge to be glad that he never went inside looking for me. I *should* have just wiped Shire's file from his memory. Then I wouldn't have to be dealing with him on top of everything else. "You guaranteed you'd stay away from my parents."

He looks almost sheepish. "I'm sorry, I had no choice. I had to find you."

"Just—let's get away from here so they don't see us when they leave."

I head away from the café and the teahouse, but also keep eastward, toward Spice. The rain's coming down steadily, little pins of ice like darts in my skin.

Cormac follows me step for step, as determined as ever. "Listen, I can't get you that week you want. You're going to have to give me something on Saint Willow and his gang before that."

"Why? What happened?"

A flush reddens his face beneath his baseball cap. "This is my first assignment. I'm not getting much leeway."

I almost feel sorry for him, except that he'll lock me up in a second if he ever finds out I'm a full magic caster.

"That's not my problem," I tell him, still walking. "Go back and say you need a week."

He grabs my arm, right where Jihen grabbed it, reminding me he's a *Scout*, not just the inexperienced and overeager cop he comes across as. We do a parody of a casual stroll over toward the mouth of an alley where he drops my arm.

"*Today*, Aza. I already feel foolish that this case rests on unconfirmed informant testimony from a teenager. I need to know what you know." Cormac's mouth is in a hard line. The tone of finality in his voice chills me. "I need something from you *today*, or I'll have to move on and question your parents."

The chill deepens. "Today?"

He nods.

My mind goes blank. I've already told him everything I meant to, the whole part of the plot of *Liar's Lair* that matters. I've got nothing else because he was supposed to give me a goddamn week.

"I can't," I whisper. "I don't have anything concrete. I need more time."

"You said you and Rudy had leads, good ones, ones that will get me full magic casters. You've been working on these leads together since Shire died, right?"

I'm numb. Fear's locked up my throat.

"It's been *a year*, Aza. You've got to be lying about not having anything concrete. My stalling is the only reason why a team of

Scouts aren't talking to your parents right now, do you know that? And I can't give you any more time."

I shudder at the picture that comes. Scouts towering over my parents, who never asked for their daughters to be born with full magic. "You guaranteed you'd leave my parents out of this."

"But I never promised other Scouts would. Just like I never promised you the week, only that I would try. Believe me, I want to leave your parents out of this, too. But you're going to have to give me something."

"You know I want to find out who killed Rudy and Shire as much as you want your casters. Why would I be lying?"

Cormac's blue eyes go all glinty and sharp. It won't be long before he looks like this all the time—a Scout through and through. "Who was that guy you were talking to earlier today? Ugly suit with too-big stripes, even uglier white sneakers."

Jihen.

Panic flutters. Of course he knows about Jihen. When Cormac said he'd be tracking me for show, I knew that still meant the physical act of tracking. He wouldn't be able to help seeing Jihen. It explains how he knew to find me at the café, too.

But maybe if he'd gotten that week, neither of those things would have mattered.

"Aza? Who was that guy? Is he one of your leads?"

My mind leaps on this. "Yes, okay? But I'm still working on things. You can't move in on this yet!"

"Okay, give me a name. Can you at least do that? I'll go back with it and buy you more time."

I look at him. His eagerness to destroy casters like me bakes off him like a fever, the cost of a dream. I want to hate him, but I understand him too much.

I lower my voice. "His name is Milo Kingston."

"Who's that?"

"I was telling you about Saint Willow's gang before, remember?"

"Yes. How Rudy had planted Shire as a mole to figure out who Saint Willow's mole in the police was. And that it was Saint Willow's mole who ended up killing Rudy and Shire."

I nod. "Okay, there's actually a second gang involved. A rival gang of Saint Willow's. Earl Kingston's gang."

Cormac just narrows his eyes. "You're kidding me."

"I'm not. It looks like Saint Willow was contracting out some of his dirty work to the other gangs. That way it becomes nearly untraceable. And Milo Kingston is my access guy to *Earl* Kingston, who I need to bring down Saint Willow."

He sighs. "So the name is Milo Kingston?"

"Yes."

"And all of this will help me get my casters?"

"Yes."

"I just—this is sudden, Aza."

"You just saw Milo Kingston yourself, didn't you?"

If he keeps doubting me, I'll have to figure out some way to cast some belief on him. Except the pain of using a spell like that would be immense. The healing meds work, but only sometimes. And with my new punishment in the tournament, I really can't afford to go in already weakened.

Cormac stares at me for a good long minute. My new lie feels too clumsy, the lie that's now threatening to make all the others spill over. What if he's heard the rumor about Earl Kingston killing his cousin and matches it up with the name Milo Kingston?

Believe me. Just believe this one last lie.

"I'll let you know what comes next," Cormac finally says before walking away.

THIRTY-TWO

I grab a train to get to the Spice Sector, but it breaks down halfway there. I don't mind getting out to walk the rest of the way, though, even with the rain—I still need to think of how I might figure out Finch's secret.

Twenty minutes later, the area greets me with its pungent air, thick with the scent of peppers and herbs and salts that sting my nose through my mask. The first place I go is the office to pick up the Wu Teas statements.

"Here you go." One of the security guards at the front desk hands over an envelope. "The company apologizes for the inconvenience."

"It's okay." I take the envelope and place it in my starter bag. Another security guard at the desk has his cell switched to the local news, and even though I can't hear it, I can see the screen well enough. Across the street from the café where my parents and I ate lunch, a large crevasse opened up on the sidewalk. No one was seriously hurt, though a biker fell in and had to be rescued.

Sorry, random biker.

I speak to the first security guard. "I forgot my cell so I'm wondering—would you be able to look up an address for me?"

The Salt Lick is in the north end of the sector. I make my way over, the High Shore Mountains peeking through buildings and smog like faint smears of gray-green. The Upper Inlet that lines the sector's northern shore isn't visible from here, but it's not hard to picture its dark brown waters where mostly strange things live now. Earl Kingston drowned his mutinous cousin in the Sturgeon River that cuts through the city itself, but Milo Kingston could have easily met his end in the Upper Inlet.

Milo Kingston.

I go from thinking it was a stroke of genius to add him to my story to believing I'm going to pay for being so stupid. I was so lost for what to tell Cormac that when he mentioned seeing Jihen, my mind leapt to it.

But my reasoning is this—things really can't get much worse. Cormac can only buy me so much more time. I'm fighting in a tournament I now have almost no chance of winning. Even winning won't solve everything, now that Jihen knows I can cast full magic. What's one more lie about a dead gangster?

Despite all this, I still have to do everything I can to win those two hundred thousand marks for my parents. If I can just do that, I'll be saving the teahouse. I might still be in Jihen's clutches afterward, but Saint Willow would be off my parents' backs, our family legacy still intact.

Shire must have felt this same way. Must have felt such desperation to save us that it drove her toward the risk of the tournament.

We have more in common than full magic, Shire, I'd say to her now. *We would have understood this part of each other, too.*

We even have Finch in common. He stood in the way of her winning and now he stands in mine. Not just as my biggest obstacle to winning the tournament, but to my getting the truth, and payback. And if he killed Shire to beat her, then who's to say he won't kill again?

I stand on the corner of the block the Salt Lick's on, debating about going inside or not. I almost want to convince myself there's a rule about fighters talking to each other outside the ring. But as Kylin pointed out, if there was, Embry would have said something that first night.

I walk over, my pulse skipping, and peer into the front window of the shop.

There's pale wood shelving everywhere, silver canisters and tins and jars. Barrels sit on bleached wood flooring, little taps jutting out of their sides.

Oliver's helping a customer weigh out something from one of those barrels.

There's no sign of Finch.

I can't deny I'm more relieved than disappointed. It's one thing to face him in the fighting ring, with both of us surrounded by other fighters and the crowd and Embry's watchful gaze. But this is Finch's territory, his place in the city, and to confront him here is like walking into a minefield. That I even thought about trying to break into his mind to search out what he wants to hide now seems beyond foolish.

But Oliver—he's no fighter. Finch's secrets are also his. And nothing's shown me he can cast full magic. Which is what he needs if he wants to fight off a reveal spell.

I fold my mask away, yank the door open, and go inside.

Oliver looks up at the sound and goes absolutely still when he sees me. His hazel eyes go from friendly to wary, even chilly. It takes the customer asking him something to break him from that stillness, but even after he returns to what he was doing, there's a stiffness to him that is clearly from my being here.

I made him laugh when we first met, and he helped me as much as he could being another fighter's backer. But the last time we saw each other, I was glaring at him from the fighting ring. And I broke the rules during last night's fight. He doesn't know if I've been kicked out of the tournament or not. As far as he knows, I'm still his brother's competition.

The last customer leaves, and it's just him and me.

Oliver's expression says I'm wholly unwelcome. He goes over and locks the door by hand. He pulls the shade down over the front window, also by hand.

So far, still no sign of full magic. But nothing that says he's not a caster of it, either.

Should I cast now? Just catch him off guard enough to give me time to find *some* answers in his mind?

He comes back. "You shouldn't be here."

The skin at my neck warms. The leap—from fighting his brother to fighting *him*—feels too big to make. "I, um, want to buy some salt."

He blinks. "You want to buy salt."

"You sell salt, don't you?" My face is warm now, too—I'm *buying salt* instead of casting a skin spell. "This place *is* called the Salt Lick."

"Um, okay." He glances around. "Take your pick."

I point to one of the other barrels, hoping the place isn't just full of overpriced gourmet salt. I only have the marks for the train ride back to the Tea Sector. "Would you recommend that one?"

We both move over. The sign says it's a lemon salt inside the barrel. "Here, hold out your hand," Oliver says. "Right here beneath the tap."

I should just cast. While he's not in protective-older-brother mode but helpful-shop-owner mode, wanting to help *me*. It would be so easy. Just cast and look into his eyes and dive in.

I hold out my open hand, he gives the tap a quarter turn, and a bunch of crystals fall out onto my palm. I try one. "It tastes like salty lemon candy," I say, unable to keep from smiling.

"Sounds about right." He fills a tiny paper sack with it. "On the house."

"Oh. Thanks." I tuck it into my starter bag. My heart's going too fast, and the nerves in my system are all standing at attention. What is supposed to come next when you're about to use magic to invade someone's brain? Make more small talk to throw him off?

If he's stiff with me now when I'm just any other fighter, I can't imagine how he might be if he ever finds out how we're connected through Shire and Finch. He might just snap in half with the awkwardness.

"So are you still in the tournament?"

My skin gets hot again. "Yes. Sorry, I guess? If it means anything, Embry says the vote was close."

Oliver shrugs. "It's the Guild's decision. You don't have to say sorry."

"The other fighters won't be happy about it." Well, Kylin won't mind. And Wilson and Pav won't mind, either. But all the ones

I eliminated will, once they find out. "And I'm sure your brother, Finch, would've been happier to have one less person to battle."

He sweeps salt from his hands. His eyes are still wary. "How do you know Finch is my brother?"

"He's the current champion and you're his backer. Some things just become common tournament knowledge. Even beginners hear most of it after a while."

I pull out the napkin where my father wrote the address for the office and finish wiping salt from my palm. I keep the napkin in my hand.

"I wouldn't have guessed the families of fighters would be very interesting to hear about," Oliver says.

I nearly ask him about his parents, but I stop. So much of Oliver is closed off, and I'm already going to be prying too much. I scan his face, taking in the angles and hollows.

"You and Finch look alike, if no one's ever told you that. The bones beneath. That's another reason why I know you're brothers."

Oliver doesn't move, just lets me keep looking at him. His hazel eyes go to roam my face in turn. Something curls in my stomach, this flicker of heat.

I turn away and slowly glance around the shop, forcing my thoughts back toward the reveal spell. The two of us are still alone—if I'm going to do this, it'd be better to do it before Finch comes back.

"Where is Finch, by the way?" I ask, hoping my voice sounds normal. I drag my gaze from shelf to shelf, thinking fast. My heart's thudding hard, and there's a low rush deep in my ears.

"Out."

I nod, though the answer tells me little about how much time I might have. From Oliver's tone, I'm not going to find out much else, either, no matter how I might prod for details.

I circle closer to where he's still standing, blood racing in my veins. I already feel warm, like my magic is breaking through all on its own. I keep my hands low and draw a spell star.

If he's only got leftover magic, this will be simple.

But if he's got full, then this might get messy.

First, magic to hold him still. Catching him by surprise and hoping for a delayed reaction will only go so far, so I'll have to cast *a lot* of magic to make that hold last. By the time he can break free, I'll already be deep into my reveal spell and uncovering the answers I need. I'll be in pain, but so will Oliver, and that should let me get away.

What did your brother do to my sister?

"Your face—"

I swivel at Oliver's voice, the star already drawn on my palm.

He's pale, shocked, staring at me with eyes gone dark.

"Last year, the fighter Finch beat"—his hand goes up to his own cheek—"you look just like her." The bones beneath.

I rip in two the napkin still in my hand. I drop one half and cast around the other. Heat climbs and there's fire behind my eyes, in my palm.

Oliver goes so still, it's like I've taken his breath as well as his muscles. But there is fear in his eyes as he stares at me, a sharp anger at what I'm doing.

I toss the spent napkin half across the room and bend down,

scrambling for the half I haven't used. My breath coming fast, I grab it and cast.

Seventeen points.

Tonight, in the ring, I'm sure I'll regret this.

In my mind, the red nebulous cloud of my magic dances, waves. I taste salt and smoke and heat; my eyes feel hot. Pain from casting the skin spell comes then, an ache in the form of a wave that rolls throughout me. Heat becomes an inferno. It wraps around my heart and fills it. The world shimmers at its edges, everything I see set to a boil. My pulse is a drum beating wildly in my throat.

I meet Oliver's eyes and will my magic into his brain. Through his skull and then along the coils of his mind, the turns and twists there full of the trees that stand for time, memories, emotions. All of which make Oliver who he is.

And am stunned by what I see. There are memories that stick out from the landscape of Oliver's mind like stars against the night, like scars dug into skin. Not because he's making me see them but because they are still so much of everything *he* can see. I push the red haze of my magic closer to them, dimly aware of how outside my mind—outside Oliver's—we're still in the middle of the shop, unmoving. Out there, time passes in seconds, but in his mind, my magic stretches it long and thin.

Three memories. Each of them is a huge tree, and each has been charred by fire. The landscape around each is blasted fine and bare, like fallout from explosions, from events that still sound. Each tree is still smoking because in Oliver's life, each memory lives on, continuing to haunt. He has nothing but guilt, these memories that have taken over the landscape of who he is. In here, in this world of his mind, guilt is an endless smog.

I will my magic closer, toward the first tree. As I near it, faces form in the smoke it sends out. The magic of my reveal spell knows these are his parents, and so I know. I know his parents died in a car accident when he was a kid, that Oliver was angry and used magic to call them back and it went all wrong, that Finch has never forgiven him for it.

My magic drifts away, moves close to the second memory. As I get closer, my reveal spell makes its tree shape change. It becomes an arm reaching for the sky. The branches are its fingers.

The meaning slams into me like a fist.

Shock tears me away and I fall from his mind. In the shop I crash to the floor, gasping as fresh agony from casting comes. Instead of heat, a cold steely pain fills my chest, the silver lake of it as still as death. Pain takes the form of spears and they jab at my skull from all directions. I lean to the side and retch, but nothing comes up.

"A spell star with seventeen points," Oliver says softly. "All for a reveal spell. I hope it was worth it."

Ever so slowly I turn my head. He's sitting on the floor, his expression more exhausted than anything. There's no pain there because he didn't cast anything to counter my spell. Not because he chose not to but because he *couldn't*.

He has no magic. I wondered if he had real magic like his brother, but Oliver hasn't any magic at all. Not even leftover.

He's lost it.

No. Not lost.

He *gave it away.*

I yank open my starter bag and fumble for the jar of healing meds. I swallow two pills and stagger to my feet. I hope I'm wrong about them being less effective for me, but what can I do about that now?

You gave up magic. You gave up you.

"Why?" I ask Oliver.

"You're going to need another reveal spell for that," he says, getting up, too. "And casting again right now will kill you. I don't have to still be a caster of full magic to see that."

That third memory, the one I missed—that's the answer.

But my chance is gone now. Oliver won't let me catch him off guard again.

I *felt* it, while in his mind—the guilt that drove a decision. Guilt that blends into but isn't the same as the guilt he feels over his parents.

The room spins.

"You gave it up for your brother," I whisper. Piper was absolutely right when she said family can complicate things. *Why do you blame yourself for your parents' car accident, Oliver?* "For him to win *a tournament.*"

He goes even paler than before. His eyes are hollow. He looks like he's been gut-punched. "You should go now."

I need to remember that it was Finch who killed Shire, how hundreds of casters saw it happen. How it wasn't Oliver. But being here with him right now, having been in his mind and breathing in that smog of his guilt, the fact feels slippery, thin.

"How did Finch beat Shire last year?" My voice is ragged. "How did you help?"

"You shouldn't be here."

He said those same words to me when I came in. Like he knew I was here to take something, and he had so little left to give.

Oliver walks over and slowly unlocks the door. And he does it by hand, just like before. I know now it's because he has to. Just like he had to before, too.

I leave.

THIRTY-THREE

After I dragged myself home from the Salt Lick—I don't really remember much of the trip; a walk to a Spice Sector train station through a white haze of pain, falling into dreamless bits of sleep on the train, then a few more blocks of walking where each step felt like another bone breaking—I crawled into bed and fell asleep.

By the time I wake up, it's nine in the evening. And though my head still hurts, and there's an ache in my bones I don't like, I know I'm not going to die. I'll be able to fight. I eat my warmed-up dinner at the island in our kitchen. My mother sits beside me and watches one of her dramas, while my father and Yun have their meeting out in the dining room of the teahouse.

I know my parents know. How I must have cast full magic to need to heal that way. But my mother only tsked that I'd slept through dinner, and my father cast leftover magic to heat up my tea. So that feels like something. It feels like a lot, actually. It feels like so much that sometimes it even blots out what I wasn't able to sleep away.

Helvetica Street is in the Paper Sector, east of Tea, and at eleven I head out of the teahouse.

I watch for signs of Jihen and Cormac to see if they're following me, but there's nothing. Still, I'm careful to keep checking, and only after I leave the Tea Sector and am well within Textile do I let myself stop taking roundabouts. As I walk, every once in a while I'll shake my starter bag just to hear the rattling of the healing meds inside their glass jar. I'll need them tonight if I have any chance of making it home after getting through this next battle. My magic can once again hurt me for real.

My thoughts come back to Oliver and the gaping hole that is his magic. The absence of the thing that is so much *him*. He paid such a terrible price, and for what? To somehow help his brother destroy us?

But . . . what if *Oliver* didn't know, either? What if all that guilt I sensed is because of something he wishes he could have stopped? I know guilt, too. Wanting fire to dance and Shire's scar, hounding Rudy until he died—even if I didn't mean either of those to happen, I'll never stop feeling bad about them. Just like however Oliver came to give up his magic, it would change him forever. His parents' dying would have also altered his path.

My thoughts chase me forward, and soon I reach Paper. The sector is just east of Textile, and the changeover is like going from an oil painting to a watercolor. Bright hues turn into cream and grays. Bookstores replace fabric ones, and print shops replace tailor houses. Kiosks are on every corner, selling newspapers and magazines.

The location of tonight's fighting ring is the sector's—and therefore Lotusland's—oldest library. It's been shut down for years, a shadow of the past.

Whoever built the library was an admirer of ancient Xulaian architecture, and so the structure is a replica of the famous Vigo Baths halfway across the world in Xulai. It's been scaled down a lot, but the library still takes up a whole city block. It's a huge circular building with a roof that's made up of a series of connected glass domes and painted archways. The ceilings inside are thirty feet high, and dozens of rooms all flow into one another. The original baths were sorted by water temperature, from sweltering to icy.

At a quarter to midnight, I cross the street to get to the main entrance. At the door, shoving my mask into my back pocket, I glance around to make sure I'm alone, and I am—this part of Paper is quiet at night anyway, made even more so with this whole block being dead for so long. No longer protected by the Guild's magic, I brace myself as I cast with my key starter.

Heat stings, becomes an ache wrung into my bones just as water is wrung out of rags. The lock twists open with a *click*. Pain still swirling beneath my skin, I pull at the door and step inside.

A small foyer that is dark and empty, marble floors stretching out in front of me and leading to a pair of large inner doors.

I open them, and the sight I see is fast becoming a familiar one.

It's the library's main room, and a crowd fills it, all the way to the corners and spilling out into side corridors. Everyone is walking in all directions and talking in loud voices and yelling out to one another. Oversized bulbs bob in midair and fill the room with light.

All the books are gone now and all the shelves are thick with dust. The huge stone pillars inside that held up the roof are still there, though the roof's glass domes shattered a long time ago. Signs of the quakes that have hit the area over the years show in the deep cracks across the frescoes that cover the walls, in the marble floor that lifts and dips.

The registration area's set up on the left side of the room, and the starter counter is on the right. The library's checkout area in the middle is now the bets counter. Hugo and Jack are calling for bets, both raising their voices to be heard over the noise of the crowd.

I can't help but look for Oliver. To see his face and figure out what comes next. I can't tell if he's my enemy, or if I even want him to be my enemy. His height makes him hard to miss, though, so I know he's not here yet. Or if he is, he's somewhere else in the building, likely reliving this afternoon just like I am. Reliving losing his magic, too. The memory has never died out for him, but I'm pretty sure I just gave it new life, something that leaves me torn between guilt and satisfaction.

I also look for signs of Piper. I still haven't seen her since I broke the rules last night, my plans to find her earlier today interrupted by my decision to go to the Salt Lick instead. Oliver ended up answering a lot of the questions I might have asked her, but I still need to find out if she means to keep backing me. If she does, then I need marks to buy starters. And if she doesn't—well, then that's *two* disadvantages I'll have to fight with.

But I can't see her yet, so I head over to the registration area. As I weave through the mass of casters, my ears pick out my name— pick out *Rudy's*—and I get snippets of what it might be like to be in the audience instead of in the fighting ring:

I've got five hundred marks on Rudy to survive, no way she'll top the clone spell.

I still think Finch will win.

I still think she and her team should have been eliminated since she broke the rules.

I like how Rudy's done something unique each time.

She doesn't cast enough blood or bone spells and I bet it's because she's weak that way, less control over those—

I frown as I keep walking, trying not to be irritated and to remember that the spectators don't know me outside of the tournament. They don't know anything about what's happened this past week, this past year, my entire lifetime.

Still, the word *weak* digs in like a splinter. The words *less control*. I don't want to be that caster anymore, when once I wondered if I'd ever be anything but.

At the registration area, I get my name written on my face, and then make my way over to the starter counter. A headache threatens, the last of the pain from the spell I cast to get inside. I'm beginning to worry about not finding Piper in time when I finally spot her in the crowd. She's also looking for me, and we both head toward each other.

Right before I reach her, my stomach drops. This really could be it for me. As far as I'll ever get in the tournament. Without Piper's support, I'll have nothing working for me, only too much against.

But I want to show everyone she knows how to pick a winner.

"Piper, I'm really sorry about the clone stunt," I blurt out before she can say anything. "Embry's already given me hell for it, if that makes a difference. And even though I'm stuck having to fight without the Guild's protection, I promise I'll fight through the pain."

Piper sighs. "Are you done?" She's in a cream silk tuxedo, her purse a slip of black velvet. Her hair is a pile of red amassed on top of her head.

"Yes?"

"Good. I'm not dropping you as my fighter. You broke the rules, but for a good reason. Just don't do it again."

I release a deep breath, wholly relieved. "I won't. I can't, or I'm definitely out for good."

She smiles. "You broke the rules with flair, at least."

"I was lucky."

"Luck is a part of a lot of things, some more than others." She opens up her purse and gives me two hundred marks. She helps me tie on my silk armband, smoothing it out with enough care that for a second I want to tell her about Oliver's magic. I want to ask her about the loss of such magic and if she could ever imagine it.

But the discovery feels too raw still. It's not even my memory, but the sight of it lingers in my own mind, like I touched someone else's wound and am now also stained with its blood. And I can't explain why it feels nearly like a betrayal, telling anyone about Oliver without knowing the whole story. Maybe because it makes him look worse and that doesn't feel right. Why couldn't it have been Finch alone?

Then Piper is wishing me luck and leaving, saving me from having to think any more about Oliver at all.

I go over to the starters table and buy my ring starters, rashly deciding on a few extra red and white because I can't stop hearing *weak*.

I follow dusty plaques bolted to the walls of one of the corridors leading out of the main room and find the washroom. Inside one of the stalls, I take out the key holder from my starter bag, slip on my new ring starters, and attach the whole thing to my belt loop.

Someone comes into the washroom. They go into the stall next to me.

I sigh and peek down.

Sunflower-printed sneakers.

THIRTY-FOUR

I sigh again, get up, flush, and leave the stall. I pause outside Kylin's stall, then knock.

"Okay," I say to the door, "why are you following me?"

She flushes and emerges. The letters of her name on her cheek seem exceptionally big tonight, as though she's smaller than I remember or she asked for the guy to write it that way. I'm betting on the latter.

"It's a public washroom," she says, washing her hands in the sink beside me, then sitting up on the counter the way she always does. "But, yeah, I was following you. I didn't see you after the second round. Are you okay?"

"Still in the tournament, no thanks to you."

Her mouth drops open. "I *helped* you."

"You *drew* attention to us is what you did. You made us look weak by helping. We never made a pact, Kylin. You have to stop imagining we're in this together because we're not, at all."

She snaps her mouth shut, but she can't hide how upset she is with what I said. It shows in the sheen in her eyes, the way she tugs at her braid the way a little kid does.

"Actually, I wanted to ask you again about making one," she says. "We really should, now that there's just six of us and we both have a good chance of making it to the final. It really could be me and you tomorrow, fighting for the championship."

I dry my hands on my pants, almost envious of her ability to dare to believe so easily. To simply want and not worry about paying for that want. Or, at least, to not worry so much it keeps you from wanting at all.

I give her a look. "I can kill you tonight, you know, and you're asking me to be in a pact with you?"

"Except you wouldn't, because you're not Finch. And with two fighters moving on, I say we have a better chance if we stick up for each other."

"Kylin, even if we make a pact and it works and we do move on, it'll just make fighting each other tomorrow harder. There's only ever going to be one winner." To be honest, I already think it's too late for us to stay strangers. Having to fight Kylin would no longer be as easy as it once might have been. I shut the door on her, but somehow she snuck in anyhow. Or maybe I let her in and just told myself I didn't. But I can't tell her this. It'd be just like her to use it against me, to say since it's already too late, we might as well make that pact. I know this because I would have said the same thing to Shire.

She scowls, then grins. "How about a pact to gang up on Finch together? That might be a good idea, too."

Oh. Now I'm hesitating.

She leaps. "C'mon, how could it hurt? And he's the champion—he's going to be the hardest out of everyone. We might as well try. We cast invisibility spells last round to wait out the fighters teaming up on you. I didn't want to see you eliminated with all the teams ganging up on you because it seemed unfair, and I told Finch that. So his idea was that we sit back by hiding to let the other teams cancel each other out. It worked really well!"

A chill runs along my arms. Kylin showed Finch a weakness and it's me. "You can't trust Finch. You can't trust me. You can't trust anyone but yourself, Kylin."

She frowns. "I don't trust him. And I do trust myself."

Nothing about not trusting me, and I glare at the back of her head in the mirror. She's nothing but a distraction, really. I look at her and see how I can fail out there in a fighting ring because I have to think of someone other than myself. Shire was thinking of our parents and me and everything the teahouse stands for, but all of that was in her head only, and still she died. I've already got revenge and ghosts and the weight of Saint Willow in mine—I don't need a real live Kylin right in the fighting ring with me as something else to worry about.

"So what do you think?" she asks. "About a pact?"

"This tournament isn't for pacts." I stare at my reflection, at the letters on my cheek, and tell myself that's all I can be right now. The ring name of a fighter.

Kylin sighs. "Okay, but maybe we can be friends after the tournament. I can come visit you, wherever you are in the city."

I try to smile at her. "Okay, sure."

Though I'm not certain at all. I think this tournament will never leave me entirely once it's over, whether I win it or not. I think maybe seeing Kylin outside of a fighting ring will only make me think of Shire and how much I miss having a sister. Or of Rudy and what happened, of Oliver and Finch and secrets of lost magic and gathered spells.

Or . . . maybe seeing Kylin will help me *stop* missing having a sister so much.

A bell clangs.

Kylin hops off the counter. "Good luck, Rudy—but only until we have to fight each other."

I have to laugh. "Now you're learning."

She's nearly out the door before I call her back.

"My real name's Aza, okay? Since you asked last time."

"Cool." She smiles like we made some kind of pact after all, and I follow her out of the washroom, down the corridor, and back into the main room of the library.

Spectators have pushed themselves out toward the walls. Kylin and I go to stand in the center where it's clear. Wilson, Pav, and Nola are here, too.

And Finch, who's already watching me by the time my eyes get to him. The blue-striped ribbon representing the Salt Lick is wrapped around his upper arm. His gaze is flat and direct and tells me I made a mistake in making him notice me. For a second, I think it's because Oliver told him what happened, what I know. But then I remember his glare at the end of the last match, when I cast the clone spell.

Whichever the reason, he makes sure to let me know I'm the fighter he'll be going after tonight. Whether I'm the sister of the fighter he killed who now wants revenge, or the fighter who put on a bigger display than he did last round, it makes no difference to him. I'm the fighter standing in his way of the championship, of the Guild. Of being a great.

A cold vise that's shaped like a fist squeezes my heart and I look away. For all that Finch is a killer, he's also a winner, and I long for my head and heart to be as clear as his. That they not be so crowded with faces and questions.

I keep myself from looking for Oliver, knowing he's here.

Then Embry strolls in from one of the corridors. He's in a suit of dark maroon silk this time, the shade so dark it's nearly black. He's paired it with a shirt and tie of the brightest poppy red, his tie a print of orchids. There's little sign of the caster who talked to me about his glass bones and not being able to cast anymore. Again I think of Oliver and just wish tonight's fight would start already.

Embry's teal eyes are back to being more watchful than welcoming. The crowd shuffles and falls quiet.

He walks up to us in the middle of the room. Six of us left. It seems like so few, and at the same time, too many.

He flashes out six playing cards, front side down. "Pick a card, please." His low rumble of a voice echoes off stone and marble.

I'm beginning to think I wouldn't mind too much never seeing a deck of cards again.

Finch is first. He holds his card up. It has a single number on it. Number 1.

Nola's next. Her card's a 3.

Wilson chooses. It's a 2.

I choose. 3.

Pav chooses. 1.

Kylin's last. She's a 2.

Embry walks over to one side so that he's standing with the spectators.

"In ancient Xulai," he says, "the most powerful didn't go to pubs or bars to hang out, they went to the Vigo Baths. The greats were known to stay for days at a time, drinking and bathing and *frolicking*."

Someone hollers, "Even the greats had to do it!"

Laughter is a ripple through the crowd.

Embry smiles. "Sometimes it's easy to forget how the original seven greats were human, just like everyone else. They loved, they fought, and they hated. Eighteen hundred years ago, Max the Deceiver cast a love spell on Otta the Swift to win her from Valery the Bleeder. And so Valery challenged Max to a duel. Right here, in the famous Vigo Baths."

The Guild of Now—wherever and whatever they are in here, as specks of dust in the air, as winks of light in their bulbs—casts.

A millennium and a half winds back in time.

And we're in baths across the sea.

THIRTY-FIVE

The lower half of my body is on fire, and I peer down, terrified of what I'm going to see.

Steaming-hot water comes up to my chest. I'm standing in a sunken stone bath that's bigger than any of the city public pools. And it's much bigger than the main room of the library in the Paper Sector. I hadn't realized just *how* much it'd been scaled down as a replica.

Only the fighters are in the water, and we're all spaced out from one another, twenty feet apart. The spectators are crowded onto the marble platform that wraps around the entire rectangular bath. They're already cheering, a reverberation of noise that bounces off ancient stone and washes back over us.

For a second, I think of Jihen, of Diego. Whether they're watching me from the crowd right now, parts of another world bleeding into this one. But it's impossible to try to make them out, and maybe it's better that I can't tell. I wasn't bluffing about going to Saint Willow to blow Jihen's secret if he didn't leave me alone about the tournament, but it doesn't mean I want to do it, either. The idea of purposely seeking out Saint Willow chills me.

I peer up at the glass dome that is this part of the ceiling. It's the biggest one of the baths, and through it, the night sky is beautiful. The moon is full and silver, the kind of moon Lotusland will never see again. There are stars, too, a spill of diamonds onto velvet—the city will never see these, either. Pearly light floods down and into the bath and mixes with the flickering amber glow coming from the torches sticking out of the walls.

"So can we get out of this oversized hot tub already?"

It's Wilson, way over on my right, kicking at the water. He looks oddly uncertain, dark skin flushed and without a sign of his typical swagger. His voice is a hollow echo as it rolls across the vastness of the bath. Behind him is Kylin. She's staring up at the sky just as I had, her expression dreamy and distracted, and I want to yell at her to wake up.

"What's the matter, can't swim?"

I turn my head at the taunt. It's Nola, standing behind me and at the opposite end of the bath.

"Did I say that?" Wilson's voice is churlish. "I highly doubt we're here to swim, genius."

But I hear it in his voice. The heat's already getting to him. The water seems to get even hotter as the thought crosses my mind. I take a step along the stone bottom. My legs are sluggish. My *brain* feels sluggish.

"'Nek' means *hot* in ancient Xulaese," Embry says. He's standing on the thick stone edge of the bath so that he's looming over us. "'Sui' means *water* and 'fwong' means *room*. Nek sui fwong. This is the hot water bath, right here. It's built to fit up to five hundred bathers at a time. The water temperature is a consistent one hundred and nine degrees Fahrenheit. The average bather will begin overheating within five minutes."

"And you want us to battle in *this*?" Nola frowns and wipes sweat from her forehead. She takes off her eyeglasses and shoves them into the back pocket of her jeans. "What if we get heatstroke before the fight's done?"

Embry's teal eyes are the same shade of the water but without the warmth. "Then make sure the other fighter gets it first."

Finch is off to my left. His laugh is low, a dark and dry and somehow *knowing* chuckle that slips into my ear. Despite the heat—it's an envelope around me, already pressing too close, nearly smothering—I shiver. The laugh is the first sound I've ever heard Finch make during the tournament.

Pav is behind him. Caught between silver and golden light, his complexion is nearly green. His panic spills from him, a kind of fever on its own to mix with the heat of the water. Invisibility spells are virtually useless if there's any kind of liquid or rain involved, since it shapes around your form and gives away where you are. Which means he's mostly left with just shield spells, his other go-to. And every single fighter here—and likely most of the audience as well—knows it.

Who will it be tonight, Pav? Pav the Coward or Pav the Brave?

And I'm Rudy the First. The audience wants me to be like that again, expects me to entertain and surprise them—I sense their demand like a pull from all sides of the room.

I'm hot. Dizziness creeps close, circles me like predator to prey. My pulse thuds hard enough that I *feel* the great drum of it, deep in my ears. It pounds at my wrists, along my neck. The strain of dread pulls at me just as the audience does, and I am thin from it, about to snap. I long for winter and ice and the luxury of casting a chill spell through the water.

Embry hops down from the edge of the bath to stand on the marble floor of the room. "There are six of you. Three duels, three winners, and your direct opponent is the fighter who's drawn the same number as you. *Go.*"

For an entire heartbeat my mind goes blank.

Number?

Then it comes to me, a headlight behind my eyelids:

3.

Another heartbeat.

Your direct opponent is the fighter who's drawn the same number as you.

Who, though? I can't remem—

Another heartbeat.

Nola drew the other 3.

She's behind me in the water.

Another heartbeat.

I take a deep breath and duck beneath the water's surface.

The bath is liquid fire. It engulfs me in clouds of seething, swirling jets of bubbles. The world in my ears dials down—to the thump of my own pulse, low muffled shouts, the churning of the water all around me.

Everyone else is now thrashing around, too. They're digging through wet clothes for their starters, fighting the weight of the water as they move because it's become another enemy in the ring.

I twist around in the water so that I'm facing the back of the bath. So I'm coming at Nola and she's coming at me. Only her jean-clad legs are visible from down here—she's still standing up, ten feet ahead and getting closer. Through the frenzy of churning liquid, her hand turns into a light brown blur at her side. She's reaching for a starter.

Staying beneath the water's surface, I yank a silver coin from the key holder on my belt loop. The skin of my face burns; my *eyeballs* burn. My chest is starting to tighten, lungs getting heavier and heavier with the instinct to breathe.

Did Shire's eyes feel like this when she died? Did she see fire from the outside as well as the inside, more of it than she'd ever seen before? Was fire the last thing she saw, felt?

A wave of nausea hits me, the same kind that comes when I've been in the sun for too long. If I don't stand up soon and cool off, I'll pass out. I'll drown.

But I stay beneath the surface. I draw and cast. Shield. I'm already hot enough that I barely feel the fresh heat of magic climb through the stone bottom of the pool and into my veins. The water against my skin *morphs*, forms a kind of skin on its own.

Then the pain of casting comes. And it's pain the way casting magic always hurts outside the tournament—whole and deep, alive with its own pulse. It jolts through me, an ache that travels from head to toe.

Dread goes off in my mind like an alarm. I've gotten too used to the Guild's protection. This fight—I'm going to suffer.

I tear off another silver starter and cast again. Air.

Fresh oxygen propels into my bloodstream. The pressure in my chest goes from explosive to bearable, the urge to take another breath beaten back. A hard ache clangs through my skull at the casting, and it lingers, deep claws sinking in. I am nearly compelled to cast again right away, just to get a bit more breath, a bit more fighting time. But I need to save magic for attacking, to think about the cost of casting that's going to pile up fast without the Guild's protection.

Nola's already down in the water with me. She's dunked herself beneath the surface, too. I see a silver coin drop through the water as she turns to face me—has she just cast a shield on herself? A second passes, and when I feel nothing, I know she must have.

I drag my hand to my hip, reaching for a new starter.

But Nola's already got one in hand. She casts first, faster than me.

A punch.

She's good with them. I should have remembered Teller, being driven into the sand. But I didn't, so when the giant invisible fist crashes into my stomach, the impact catches me flat out. My shield spell falls apart. I'm driven backward through the hot water, my legs a numb blur of darkness through pale blue. There's a single wild second where I can't figure out who the legs belong to.

I'm still moving backward through the baths as I fumble a white starter from my key holder. My hands are slow, clumsy—the word *heatstroke* flashes across my brain. Across from me Nola's going for another starter, too, her hands moving just as sluggishly through the water.

I'm faster this time. I draw, I cast. A thick, undulating ripple of pain spreads outward from my spine like thorns along a branch.

Her hand falls from her pocket. Her entire body goes limp, as limp as I've cast her bones to go. Her eyes are flashes of panic.

My lungs are burning again. There's a high-pitched ringing in my ears. I need to breathe.

I yank off another starter, gold this time. There's a body on the bottom of the bath, gone to marble in the chaos of the water. The world wavers, flickers gray, and my chest has become a tightly wound bundle of agony—*I need air.*

I draw. I cast.

The panic in Nola's eyes becomes a flood as her airway tightens. Her arms give a single useless twitch at her sides, their bones still too soft for her to move.

Pain floods me, a storm inside my body the way the pool is one outside. It's the cost of casting, building faster and higher, threatening to break. I push back, imagine I'm a dam. My lungs are spilling fire. I'm about to black out.

Nola has already begun to drown, unconscious and sinking.

Knockout.

I grab her by the arm—she's deadweight, and terror that I'm too late stabs me like a dagger—and stumble to my feet on the bottom of the bath. I drag her face free of the water.

Cool air comes and I'm drinking in huge gulps of it. Nola's draped over my arm, still out. I draw another spell star and tear at another gold starter. I cast, despite knowing how it's going to hurt.

Nola coughs as her airway opens back up and air rushes in. Between gasps, she asks, "Why are you saving me?"

"Because." I'm still gasping, too. Agony is a swollen, knotted fist in my skull. "I've already beaten you."

THIRTY-SIX

Finch, Kylin, and me.

We're the last.

The three of us are still standing in the bath. The crowd around us is on their feet, cheering and clapping. The sounds of our names come at me as shouts and yells, and the ring of noise encircles me, presses close, makes me feel like I'm drowning again. My heart is loud in my ears, beating in a wild rhythm that matches my still-hungry breathing, the jagged pain that fills my head.

Shut up.

I want to beg. How all their noise *hurts*. But the crowd keeps cheering.

Shut up!

My eyes scan faces, desperate to see Piper, Embry, even Oliver. Anyone I know who's talked to me and can remind me I'm still someone else, someone outside this fighting ring. To remind me I'm Aza Wu and how I exist outside these terrible ancient baths.

But I see only strangers. Just those who came to see magic, and if that magic has a cost, then they will accept that, too. Because we're casters of a banished magic and this is our world now.

I drop my eyes to the side of the room, hating everyone here.

Pav is out of his marble state, sitting stunned on the stone floor. It was him at the bottom of the pool. Eliminated by Finch. No surprise there.

Wilson and Nola sit near Pav, equally hunched in defeat. They're still soaked and water drips off them back onto the floor.

I begin walking out, needing to get out, to get away. Water has never been heavier as it drags at my legs. The pain of casting that final breath spell to save Nola is still alive inside my head, has become one with my bones and muscles. Bruises form all over my body. I long for sleep, for recovery time.

Behind me, the water stirs again as Finch and Kylin follow.

Then Embry's at the front of the crowd again, and everyone falls silent, confused. He's supposed to have left by now, already back with the rest of the Guild somewhere. His disappearing at the end of a fight marks the end of that round.

I stop moving. So do Finch and Kylin.

What now?

My brain's like taffy in the sun as it struggles to recall the ending of the story of Valery the Bleeder, Max the Deceiver, and Otta the Swift. Did I ever learn it in school? Who won between Valery and Max? What happened to Otta? How did those three greats declare their battle done?

"You see, Valery thought he'd defeated Max," Embry says. "But Max was known as the Deceiver for a reason. He'd cast magic within magic—if Valery ever broke the spell that made Otta love Max, Otta would turn on Valery. And so the battle continued, this time with three."

The water in the bath turns icy. The bath shrinks, becomes half the size it was, turns into a rough oval.

"Here in the lungh sui fwong is where they fought," Embry continues. "The *cold* baths."

The glass dome disappears. A massive painted arch takes its place. I get a glimpse of painted figures before the last of the silver moon fades from my eyes and only dim torchlight flickers from the walls.

Embry says, "Only two casters will be moving on tonight."

Kylin moves first. She draws and grabs at the surface of the bath. Casts.

Freezing water climbs in a wave and slams down. Again. The waves fill the air with their roar. It's the sound of the world's coldest beach.

I'm knocked from my feet. Knives of ice pierce me all over as my side skids along the bottom of the bath. Stone scrapes and pulls at the silk tied around my arm. I hurl my weight to one side, trying to grab hold. Water dives into my nose and mouth.

The waves keep coming. I can't see anything past them. I cough out ice water. I'm still scrambling for a starter with nearly frozen fingers when I slam into the side of the tub.

Stone tears my knuckles open and the water around my hand streams red. There's no pain, though, since my hands are so cold. The crowd's shouting, loving the full magic that has turned the baths into a storm at sea. *Kyyylin*, they scream.

But she's made a mistake in her rush to cast first, in casting for repeated waves. It's too wide of a spell with not enough of a focus. She should have cast only with enough magic to affect Finch and me. Now her magic will be slow to recharge, on top of her already hurting. More than anyone else, I could have reminded her to cast with caution.

The waves build beyond her control—higher, faster. A second

later, and all three of us are dragged under, and the world is nothing but blue and ice and struggling to breathe.

Oh, Kylin.

A wave crests, breaks, crests again. Through the water still rushing at my ears, I hear the crowd, cheering.

Finally, I surface all the way, and I look over for Kylin and Finch.

They're across the bath. She's in retreat, one arm bent at an
unnatural angle—Finch must have cast a spell to break it. And
she's too pale, the icy cold working its way through her.

He looms over her, about to cast again. Kylin's on the verge of
elimination and he knows it. One more spell, a final dose of magic,
and he'll be in the final round.

Dread comes in a flood. It makes me as cold on the inside as I am
on the outside. The water's a roar and the crowd is shouting and
I'm trying to get to my feet.

Is this what it was like for Shire? Had she already been backing
away, and still Finch had come?

A new wave of water builds.

I yank off a gold starter. My fingers are icicles, thick and unbend-
ing as I force them to draw. I cast.

Against the icy water, the heat that climbs my legs is excruciating. It burns upward and into my veins, a red fire billowing in my
mind.

Finch flies backward. My magic drives him through the water.
He hits the edge of the stone tub with a deep thud.

The crowd erupts. *Rudy, Rudy, Rudy—*

Pain is a sheet of lightning behind my eyes.

The icy wave crashes down.

I claw at my starters from beneath the water. I tear off another gold coin. The wave flattens and Finch is still in the water, trying to stand up. I cast again, unable to care about the lightning still shooting across my brain, how there will be more now.

He falls back into the water as his muscles seize, exactly as I meant them to.

The coldness that had been dread filling me now feels darker, sharper, *sweeter*. Control has never felt so close, my magic never so touchable. When more lightning flashes behind my eyes, I barely blink. I can only think about destroying Finch.

Because that fine line between honor and dishonor—I can't stop it from shifting.

I toss away the gold coin and grab a white one. I cast.

Finch has dragged himself up to lean against the edge of the bath, and he screams as his bones shatter.

I stagger my way through the water. Kylin's waves are fading, her spell run out. She hasn't moved, is still standing in the bath. She's shivering even harder than I am, still cradling her crooked arm. Just behind her, Finch is still slumped against the stone tub, frozen by pain as much as he is by the water. His eyes are wide and stunned—he's never looked more vulnerable.

When I reach them both, I loom over Finch the same way he loomed over Kylin. One more spell and he's out. New pain of my own comes, as pointed as knives in my guts.

I'd meant for it to go full circle, for me to beat him in the final. I'd meant to poke around in his brain and find out answers for all my questions. But what does it matter, if I still beat him? If he still dies for killing Shire, for nearly killing Kylin?

The audience is one huge roar, amplified by all the marble and stone. I can't tell if they're cheering more for me or for Finch. A part of me wishes I could tell. That maybe if I could hear chants of Rudy the First and nothing else, then I wouldn't need to do this. But everything's happening so fast, and magic is just a different kind of roar in my blood, urging me on.

I draw, then tear free a silver coin.

The line shifts and shifts and shifts.

I cast.

Finch becomes an inferno. I burn him from the inside out—for all the water around him, it can't stop what it can't touch. I watch him burn and wonder why my heart stays frozen. Why I don't feel satisfied when this is supposed to be payback.

The sound of the crowd changes, turns slightly uneasy. I'm not supposed to be like Finch, who can live with the cost of magic. I'm supposed to be all about the show, here to entertain.

"You've surprised them."

Kylin says this. But her voice is Finch's. She grins, and it's with Finch's green eyes.

My mouth goes dry, and I blink.

Because it's Finch standing where Kylin was. Or where I was *made* to think Kylin was.

It's not Finch in the water, burning away. It's Kylin.

"A disguise spell," Finch says softly. There's venom in his voice, stinging my skin.

The crowd realizes what's happened and their cheers are thunderous. The swell of the noise rolls through me, and I want to be sick for all the longing I hear in the audience.

Shire, did they cheer like this when it was you? And there I was at home, furious with you for leaving me behind.

I'm numb. Ice is everywhere and everything. Kylin's body slips beneath the surface of the water and a sob wrenches free from my throat. She was about to eliminate Finch and I stopped her. Because of his spell. And now—

No. No. I'm sorry, Kylin.

"I knew who you were as soon as I saw you."

I turn to face Finch, his broken arm still at an angle. "How?"

"I never forget a fighter I beat. Each of you, just helping me get where I want to go. And you look like her, especially when you're casting."

The bones beneath.

I shudder. "Why the trick?"

"The Guild's watching—they like a show, too." Now he smiles, and it chills me the way all the ancient cold baths in the world never could. "And Kylin was weak. She didn't want to fight you— she thought you were *friends*. She showed me that herself last round, and that was her mistake. Now it's just me and you, tomorrow night. Let the best caster win."

THIRTY-SEVEN

I run while the crowd's still loud.

The Guild's magic unweaves even as I crash my way toward the entrance. The cold baths and arched ceiling and fat stone pillars disappear as I shove my way through casters. Contact hurts, each part of me bruised and aching, but I keep going. Eighteen hundred years pass as the library's main room comes back with its empty bookshelves and cracked-open frescoed walls. People turn and stare and I can't meet anyone's eye. Blood trickles from my nose, and a low roar fills my ears.

Maybe we can be friends after the tournament. I can come visit you, wherever you are in the city.

I push open the doors and rush outside into the night. Sunflower-print sneakers chase me down the street, the swish of a braid. I'm crying, my chest burning, the fire there nothing but a weak echo of the one I lit up inside Kylin.

Why didn't I agree to that pact? Why couldn't I have just done that for her? Kylin might be alive then, and Finch eliminated, and none of this would be happening.

I'm sorry, Kylin, I never meant to leave you behind!

There's no full silver moon to be seen out here. No stars because they never stop hiding. I run beneath a smog-covered sky as the last remnants of an older time fall away, left in my wake like lint picked from my clothing. Goodbye, all you dueling greats, all of you who made magic a game, you who created the Tournament of Casters in the first place. Dropped newsprint lies silently across pavement and murky light billows from the streetlamps.

If a Scout found me now, one look and they would know me for the caster that I am. I feel stained all over with full magic, with the terrible things it can do.

I keep running, then slow to an awkward limp, out of breath, my tears and drying blood thin smears on my cheeks. Casting has cost me tonight, and I feel all its claws still inside me, still scratching and digging. I lift my hand toward my starter bag, but then drop it. Hurt, Aza. You deserve to.

"Rudy."

I swivel at the voice.

It's Oliver, coming up behind me. He's breathing fast, too, running to catch up. In my need to get away from the library, I didn't think to check if anyone would follow me. I guess killing Kylin has distracted me from the basics. The faces of Jihen and Cormac and my parents swarm me and my eyes get teary again.

I turn around and start walking fast. A confused kind of anger fills me. I want to hate him but I can't forget those burned-out memories of his, the absence of his magic that's so gaping its edges have touched me, too.

"Go away, Oliver," I call back. "Go congratulate your brother."

"Wait—"

"I can't."

He runs faster and then he's at my shoulder. "One minute, okay? Here, I collected your winnings from the bets counter."

I stop and take the marks. There are a lot, even more than what

I got last time. It feels like blood money with Kylin dying tonight, and a queasiness in my stomach rolls and rolls.

"You should put those away before you lose them," Oliver says, watching my expression. I can tell *he* can tell that I've been crying.

I stuff the marks into my pocket and start walking again. I drag on my smog mask, wanting to hide as much as I can. He follows me. "I just tried to kill your brother. Why do you want to talk to me?"

He doesn't say anything right away. Then a soft: "I'm still working on that."

"You can go do that on your own, you know."

"What he did in there, tricking you like that—I'm sorry."

My heart pinches and pulls. "He killed her. He didn't have to." I'm no longer sure if I'm talking about Kylin or Shire.

"I'm sorry," he says again.

The simple apology hurts more than if he'd defended Finch, and I can't tell if he means Kylin or Shire, either.

I push back because fighting with him is easier than hurting. "I'm not going to say I'm sorry about that reveal spell I did on you."

"I know."

"Why don't you just tell me how he cheated? There's nothing I can do about it now anyway. But I need to know."

He ignores me. "Why didn't your reveal spell show you?"

"Because. It ended too early." *Because I was too shocked about your magic to keep it going any longer.* It would have told me. Why didn't I hold on?

"So how do you know he cheated?" Oliver's tone is careful, like he doesn't want to set me off any more than he already has.

"I didn't. Not at first. But then pieces started coming together.

272

And then tonight, finding out about your magic—" I glare point-edly at him. Or *lack* of magic. Even the lack of leftover magic, when everyone has that.

"And I'm his brother, so my lack of magic has something to do with it."

A catch in his voice finally lets me stop walking and face him. He stops, too.

That earlier hollowness is still in his eyes. He looks haunted and uncomfortable and like he's wishing he could be anywhere else. Chasing me down this way—I had thought maybe he was doing it because he wanted to, not because he felt he had to. It makes me feel stupid, not seeing this until now.

"What else did your magic see in my mind?" His eyes have gone dark, more brown than hazel.

"Your parents," I say. "The car accident. How you blame your-self. You cast magic and something happened. Finch has never forgiven you."

A muscle works in his throat. "I was twelve. I'd been arguing with my parents, and then they had to leave for a party. But I . . . wasn't done arguing. So I cast myself into their heads as they were driv-ing. I distracted them. They died listening to me yell at them."

A new pinch forms in my heart. "I'm sorry. I—the last time I talked to Shire, we argued, too."

He nods. His eyes say he's sorry in return. "And it changed Finch. I went from being a big brother to the person who took away his family because I couldn't control my magic. So we used to be friends and now we're not. It made him hate full magic just like it made him hate me. In his own twisted way, winning this

273

tournament, getting into the Guild, I think it's him proving he's stronger than magic, if that makes sense. Becoming a great is his ultimate way of beating magic at its own game."

Against my will, a small twinge of understanding *does* come. The things you hate the most are the things that are loudest in your head, so that you can't hear anything else. Because they are also the things you fear the most. I'm still scared of having no control, and so I hate the idea of being that way.

But as much as I can get this aspect of why Finch is so messed up, I'll also never forget what he's done. Shire never coming home again, his smile tonight as he revealed himself as Kylin—I'll never forgive him.

Oliver exhales. "Okay, so there's a reason why I'm out here. Why I came looking for you. I want to make a deal with you."

My chest goes hollow. *So can we make a pact?* "What kind of deal?"

"If I tell you how Finch cheated, will you promise not to fight him tomorrow night?"

I blink. "You mean just . . . walk away from the tournament?"

He nods.

All the reasons why that's impossible—from the marks to my promise to Rudy—push close, wrapping around me so I can barely breathe through them. I was always going to fight if I could, whether I found out the truth about last year or not.

"I can't walk away now," I say to Oliver. "I need to win this as much as your brother wants in on the Guild."

His expression turns grim. "And if he kills you? Like he killed your sister and Kylin?"

I try not to shiver. "I have to think I won't let him. It's a contest and I've made it this far. And his arm is broken, which works in my favor." I can't decide if I'm more insulted that Oliver thinks I'm going to lose or happy that he's trying to save me.

"You and I both know he'll have it healed by morning," Oliver says, "if he hasn't already."

Then I'm staring at him, realizing something, and almost hate myself for having to say it. "But now you *have* to tell me. Because if you don't, and it could have helped me beat him, and he kills me anyway . . ."

He's beyond grim now. "Then how could I live with myself?"

"Well, *could* you?"

Oliver swears. His expression clouds over. "You have to promise you won't kill him, then. Beat him, but that'll have to be enough."

Enough as payback for Shire, he means. Can any payback ever be enough? She's gone and I'll never get her back. I could have all the full magic in the world and I could cast until I died, but it'd still never be enough. While Finch lives on, killing other casters, trying to become a great.

"I could just cast another reveal spell on you, you know," I say.

Oliver shakes his head. "No way. You caught me by surprise last time. And even if you *could* cast without me catching you, you're way too wiped out from tonight's fight to handle casting another seventeen-pointer now. So either promise or you'll never know."

He's got me and he knows it. I haven't even told him about how the Guild's punishing me for the rest of the tournament and he's got me. Frustration is a knot in my stomach, pulling tighter and tighter.

If I agree . . . I'll still beat Finch. I'll still win. I'll still be taking away what he wants the most, and that'll have to be enough. I think Shire would want it to be. Would want her reckless sister being sensible in this.

"Okay, I promise," I finally say.

THIRTY-EIGHT

Oliver holds up his casting arm.

"I owed him," he says quietly. "That's what he said after I killed our parents with my magic. For years, he shut me out, never letting me be his brother again. But last year, for the tournament, he asked if the Salt Lick would sponsor him—if I would sponsor him. So I said yes. I thought it would bring us closer together, help fix us. But after he began to doubt he could beat your sister, he came to me, again. And he said he'd forgive me, if I gave him one thing."

"Your magic." In the thickening night smog, his face is full of shadows. I can barely see the shapes of shops and outlines of roofs behind its haze. Tendrils of it curl through the streetlamps' patches of light, and the city seems covered with a layer of gauze. I taste it on my tongue—exhaust, metal, dirt.

"He went to meet a gatherer," Oliver says. "And the gatherer had a spell Finch wanted. Time loop. But for a price."

My stomach curls just like the smog does. "The price of magic for a time loop? That's hardly equal. It makes no sense."

"It does when it's not his magic he's offering up." He gives me an empty smile.

"And so you did it," I say. "Because you owed him." *And Finch is your brother. And maybe . . . I would have done the same for my sister, too.* There are probably a million different ways family can complicate things.

Oliver nods. His expression is bleak, as pale as it was in his shop when he realized who I was. "All the winnings I get as his backer, I put right back into the Salt Lick. And since my parents, I've barely used magic anyway. If this got me my brother back, it would be more than worth the price. I didn't find out until it was too late how Finch really meant to use it. I never thought he'd kill your sister. Just that he'd use it to win."

I make myself ask. "What did he do?"

"He used the time loop on himself to see how the final round between him and Shire would go. He saw exactly how she would beat him."

The world sways and I think I'm going to throw up. "So Finch would have known all of Shire's spells ahead of time. He could have had all his counterspells ready. He could have beat her easily and let her walk away. *But he still decided to kill her.*"

Oliver nods, looking about as sick as I feel. "I'm sorry, Rudy. If I'd known, I would have never given him my magic."

Rage floods me. It's too late for all of that now. *Sorry* doesn't matter. All that matters is tomorrow's fight. "Where can I find a gatherer, Oliver?"

"Only Finch knows. I didn't go with him."

Something crosses his face and I know he's holding back.

"The deal is you tell me how he cheated," I say. "This is still part of it. Tell me the rest."

"You promised," he says.

"I never said what I would or wouldn't do with whatever you told me. I said I wouldn't kill Finch."

"Rudy, I—"

"My name is Aza, Oliver. Now tell me."

I watch him explore the name in his mind, see him wonder why I told him.

"I don't know where you can find a gatherer, and that's the truth," he says finally. "But I can tell you how you can find out. I can tell you who this one worked for."

I wait. The city's smog drifts between us, and for a second, he disappears on me before appearing again.

"Saint Willow," he says. "Tea Sector's gang leader."

THIRTY-NINE

I stumble back a step, like Oliver's just cast a huge spell on me.

Saint Willow, who obsesses over full magic because he can't cast it. Who has to settle for a semblance of it because he'll never truly know the real thing, has to accept that he'll only ever control ugly man-made spells and nothing more.

"Where's the fight tomorrow?" I ask Oliver. I left the library too soon, trying to escape from what I'd done.

"979 Discord Road."

I commit the address to memory, turn, and begin to run. I'm still hurting all over from fighting, but the ache is buried beneath the ache in my chest about Kylin. There's a buzz in my head, a low thrum in my veins.

"Where are you going? Ru—Aza, *wait*."

"I have to go!" I call back over my shoulder. I need to think about what comes next, and it can't be with Oliver. He clouds up my feelings and it's all too easy to forget why I'm here. What I want. What needs to be done. "Tomorrow, the fight—I'll see you then!"

"You promised, remember?" His voice comes through smog, turns smoky-sounding. I already can't see him. "You can't kill him!"

I call back again. "I know!"

I mean that as assurance, even as a tiny dark pit deep inside my chest says otherwise. To know that Finch could have let Shire go and didn't. That he used Kylin and me to put on a show for the

Guild. Fury stokes that pit into a blaze of hate. And it's hate that I don't want to control. To just be reckless and let it explode. Because then Finch would get what he deserves, while I'd still win everything.

But for a promise. For a *pact*. I made it with Oliver, but it's Kylin I keep hearing in my head, and how I said no, how she helped me anyway, and now she's gone.

Well, there are spells for things worse than death.

Soon, the smog is so thick that I can no longer see far in front of me, and I have to slow to a careful walk. My hand disappears into the gray, so dense that I can't see the bruises marking my skin in this huge bloom of pollution. I glance around, and the light from streetlamps has dimmed down to almost nothing. Sector streets are nearly pitch-black. Fear is like tendrils of the fog, weaving their way into my brain.

It hits me that this is because of the tournament. This blanket of dirt and exhaust is because of our fight tonight in the ancient baths. We did this.

By the time I limp to the edge of Tea—my joints on fire—the smog has only gotten thicker, just inches of visibility all around. Until it clears, there's no way Jihen and Cormac will be able to tail me.

My mind is still circling over everything that's happened in the last few hours—the last few days—as I turn into the alley that lines the back of the teahouse. I feel for branches of the snowball bushes that make up our fence and pull them to the side, preparing to squeeze through. Petals shake free, disappear into the smog as they fall.

The blade emerges from the dark and presses against my throat.

Shock is like a blow to the head, and I'm frozen with it. My mouth goes dry, and whatever I was thinking about instantly vanishes.

"You're one of the Wus, aren't you."

The voice is thick and rough and comes from right beside me. I don't recognize it. My heart is lodged inside my throat, a drum stuck pounding.

He nudges the blade against my neck. In the smog, he's nothing but a voice and disembodied weapon. "Yes or no," he grunts.

"Who's asking?" I let my hand drift toward my starter bag. In the smog, he won't even see. I can cast and—

"Hands up, don't even think about casting." I wince as he slowly tilts the blade back and forth against my skin. "I've got metal right here in my hand as a starter if I want, so who do you think is going to cast faster?"

I don't know if he means leftover magic, but it doesn't matter because he's likely right. He probably would be faster. And the knife isn't making me want to test him.

I raise both arms.

"I've been assigned the whole night to get answers, girly," the guy says. "Maybe we can go inside the teahouse and wait there."

The memory of Jihen inside while I dreaded the possibility of my parents walking in—I shudder and say, "Yes, I'm a Wu."

"Of Wu Teas?"

"Who wants to know?"

"Earl Kingston sent me. You know Earl Kingston?"

My mind spins. *Cormac.* He's talked.

"Yes, Earl Kingston from the Tobacco Sector," I say.

"Here's the deal. We're getting whispers of a city cop asking about one of our own, a guy named Milo Kingston. And the whispers are that the girl whose family runs this teahouse here is the one who's talking to the cop about Milo."

Anger slithers in and leaves me cold. The scents of smog and snowball bush petals swirl together and make my stomach clench. *Cormac, you fool.*

"I never talked to the cop about anyone named Milo Kingston." I grasp for words and hope they're believable. "I was on shift at the teahouse when he came in and met up with another guy. I was their server, I overheard the name Milo Kingston."

"So why are the whispers that you were the one talking to the cop?"

"I don't know." My voice shakes. From the knife at my neck, from having to make up another workable lie when I want to be all lied out. "Maybe it came from the other guy. Maybe he got scared that someone would remember him talking to a cop about Milo Kingston."

"Who's the other guy?" His voice comes from within the smog. He pushes the knife even harder against my neck. The skin there stings, and I know I'm bleeding.

I almost answer with *I don't know* again. But then I realize a name would have the benefit of keeping Earl Kingston and his men busier sniffing around a dead end.

"The cop called the other guy Diego." It's the first name that comes to mind, and now his face, his earrings and wild nest of a beard. The full magic caster who stays far away from the Tea Sector because of Saint Willow, a friend to Jihen and someone Earl

Kingston and his guys will likely never circle back to because he has no connection to anything at all. "He was doing most of the talking, if that means anything."

"Maybe, maybe. I'll pass it on. We'll ask the cop about it."

Trepidation dances on my skin. "You guys are going to talk to the cop?"

The knife lifts from my neck. "Girly, we've had Cormac for hours. Lucky for you, we've doubted every single word out of his mouth. Now we'll go see what this Diego has to say."

He disappears into the smog.

I squeeze my way through the snowball bushes and climb into my bedroom window. My pulse skids around in my veins, a loosed animal running scared, even as everything else shuts down, beyond exhausted. I tear off my mask and fall into bed. I'm asleep within a minute.

Faces chase me in dreams. Oliver's, Finch's, Kylin's, Cormac's.

And a face that stays veiled, like the earth with its smog. I know it's Saint Willow's even if I've never seen him before. His power over the Tea Sector comes as much from the mystery as it does from the long legacy of his family name.

If you need him, you're out of luck unless he also needs you.

FORTY

It's breakfast and the smog still hasn't lifted.

On the news they're calling it the Summer Souper, and it's the main thing everyone in the city is talking about. While it's thickest over Lotusland proper, it extends out over the Pacifik in the west, past the High Shore Mountains in the north, over the blighted lands in the east where nothing grows anymore, and spreads south into the last of the pink woods. No trains are running, and not much is open. We're all supposed to stay inside for as long as the smog lasts. Having so few customers in the teahouse finally feels acceptable.

Environmentalists can't pinpoint a single reason for it, so they're saying it's a whole bunch of things—factories, cars, the combination of years' worth of buildup of pollutants running into perfectly windless conditions. None come close to the truth.

My father is out on the teahouse floor, doing inventory. My mother casts at the stove to start eggs and toast. I sit at the island in the kitchen with her, now only half watching the news because no one can predict when the smog is going to end, my heart tightening like a turning screw with each passing moment that I can't go outside.

I need to find Jihen. Only through him can I get close to finding a gatherer of magic. My promise to Oliver to not kill Finch tonight is only that—to not kill him. Anything else, though . . .

That tiny dark pit deep inside my chest stings and grows.

Around it, the rest of my body continues to hurt. Last night's fight is still with me. All my bones and muscles are wound up tight, a taut fist of pain. I opened my starter bag this morning only to find that the jar of healing meds wasn't waterproof. As I fought in the baths with my bag submerged, the healing meds dissolved. I found nothing but a dried white film.

Whatever pain I'm still in when it comes to the final round of the tournament, I'll also be fighting with.

But . . . maybe this is the way it should be. Because daring to think about Kylin hurts even more, makes even the worst bruises and aches seem almost easy. There's a question that keeps circling my brain, too, relentless and awful, and it's this: If not for my need for revenge, would have I been able to see through Finch's trick?

Not that it matters, in the end. Because tricked or not, I'm still the one who cast the spell that killed her. So for Kylin as much as anyone, I can't let Finch win.

My mother brings over breakfast. I'm trying to make room for the food around this new physical agony, around that tiny dark pit of rage nestled within it, when she passes me a slim package.

Inside is a new starter bag.

It's made out of rich red silk, with a vivid floral print. I recognize all the different blossoms—jasmine, wisteria, rhododendrons, chrysanthemums. I'm transported to all the mornings I spent in the workroom with Shire, building gentle red fires together over the fireplace.

I run my hand over the bag. The softness of the silk is a balm against the skin of my fingers, against the knuckles that now wear scabs from having been dragged across ancient stone of ancient baths last night.

"What's this for?" I ask as I glance up at my mother. "It's pretty." And it is. Not as plain as I might have picked, but not as fancy as Shire would have. Something in between.

"Your sister's old bag is getting so worn. Your father and I thought you could use a new one."

I look down at Shire's bag. I have it close by as always, at my elbow on the island—my connection to her magic.

"You didn't have to do that," I say to my mother. My throat's gone tight. My parents do not shop outside of buying things for the teahouse. "I can just start being better about fixing Shire's bag."

"You can do that and save this for later, then. I think Shire would say the print suits you." Her smile says the worry she has carried for me since I was eight and made magic explode is starting to change.

I pick up the bag. Red silk flows. "I think she'd say that, too."

The smog finally begins to lift at noon, and I leave the teahouse, telling my parents I'm late for work. Through my mask, the air still tastes too strongly of exhaust, and there's an odd yellow light to the sky, but otherwise the earth has righted itself once more from us casting banished magic. I finish adjusting my new starter bag over my shoulder and start walking, making sure I'm easily seen.

I'm careful to stay within the sector, and especially within the blocks closest to the teahouse. It's where Jihen has always found me, and where he most expects me to be. But I have never *wanted* to be tracked down by him before. And today, he has something I need instead of the other way around. I need him to find me.

I don't think about Cormac tailing me because he's gone—unless I find a way to free him from Earl Kingston of the Tobacco Sector, I might never see him again. His higher-ups know what case he's been working on, so his disappearance will eventually lead them to me.

Jihen finds me in thirty minutes. I glimpse his black suit and white sneakers out of the corner of my eye and pretend I don't see him. I turn into an alley that cuts a block in half, both of its sides lined with back doorways, knowing he'll follow. I duck into one of them and wait for him to pass. Nerves turn my pulse fast and my hands are clenched into fists.

He walks past, his sneakers the whitest things in the world against the damp gray stones of the alley. He's glancing around as he moves, wondering where I've gone.

"Jihen," I call out.

He turns to face me, and approaches. His expression is annoyed. "I've been looking for you. I have another request, a casting one." His fingers reach out to grab my upper arm.

I cast around the small rock I'm already holding in my palm, the starter that sits in the center of the spell star I drew as he walked by.

A nine-pointed star and a bone spell.

Jihen's body locks up mid-step. My magic, holding still his legs and arms.

His face contorts. Amazement comes first—*Aza, have we not*

worked together so well until now?—then fury—*you'll be answering to Saint Willow for this!*

Good.

"What are you doing?" Jihen's voice is a slither of a hiss.

"I need you to bring me to a gatherer of magic."

His surprise is real. Real enough that he forgets to try to hide it. "What are you talking about?"

Pressure that is the headache from casting the bone spell begins to grow behind my eyes. I swallow thickly and force myself to look through it. "Gatherers, the ones who put together old man-made spells. They work for Saint Willow, for your gang."

His muscles work in his neck as he strains to move. "I have no idea—"

"I have a lot more rock starters in my bag, Jihen. I can break every bone in your body right here, one by one." It's more a bluff than not—I don't want to use more magic because I don't want more pain. And I can't forget that I no longer have healing meds. "So take me there, now."

He sneers, but it doesn't hide the confusion in his eyes. "*Now* your family's teahouse will suffer. *Now* you can be scared for your parents."

It clicks. He really doesn't know. Saint Willow has kept this from him. Jihen might be blood, but distant blood, and only good enough to squeeze marks from small family-run businesses. No wonder Jihen keeps Diego and his discovery of the tournament for his own secrets—they are his way of rising up past his current situation.

Family, always complicating things.

"Then bring me to Saint Willow," I say.

More surprise, and just as real. Casters know to stay out of the gang's way, and that means following the rules and lying low. "Why would I do that?"

I take another rock from my bag. I don't want to do it—already there are unsheathed knives clashing around inside my skull, and I have to fight tonight—but I'm too close now.

I draw, cast.

Jihen's baby finger snaps.

There's a gurgle of a scream low in his throat.

"Because he'll be able to tell me how to find it. So will you take me to him, or do we need to keep doing this?" Daggers are swinging around with the knives now, and I feel each and every one of their points.

"Stop," he says. "I'll take you. But you're going to see—whatever you've been hearing about these gatherers is wrong. There's no such thing. And now I'll be paying a visit to your family's teahouse."

"Do that and I'll tell your boss not just about your secret of Diego but about the entire tournament." Jihen's already told me he's keeping its existence from Saint Willow. And obviously Finch never said what he was using his gathered spell for, or Saint Willow would already know about the tournament through him. "What do you think is going to happen once Saint Willow knows? He'll take it away from you. It'll be his, just like the Tea Sector is his."

Jihen's lips work. Like he's reasoning silently to himself and still can't keep from mouthing the words. How Saint Willow would react learning that Jihen has kept something from him.

"Fine." Jihen flexes his arms, my bone spell now wearing off, and cradles his broken pinky. His glare is resentful and touched with still-stunned betrayal. "Let's go."

We turn out of the alley and walk down the street. Two minutes later, a fire truck blasts by, its sirens wailing. Jihen doesn't make the connection. But *I* do. As the sound of the siren fades, I try not to think about what part of the world my magic just broke, killed, destroyed.

FORTY-ONE

Saint Willow's headquarters are on the south side of the sector, right at the edge of the city. As Jihen drives, I get the occasional glimpse of the pink woods beyond, land cast hundreds of years ago to always grow trees that pretty shade.

The south part of the sector is heavy in supply shops and corporate offices. But just when I think I'm going to have to cast again to make Jihen turn back—which I really don't want to do with no healing meds—he pulls up to a tiny building and cuts the engine.

The place looks closed, a run-down, thin rectangle of dusty brick and dirty glass. The front window has its blinds pulled, and the door is just solid wood. Only the small sign with faded red block printing that's nailed above the door tells me what this place is: DIM SUM.

"Don't talk to anyone in there until I say you can," Jihen says. "You wouldn't be the first caster who thinks they're special enough to approach us only to not walk away again."

He gets out of the car.

I do the same, pretending that fear hasn't collected into a lump of ice that's sitting in my stomach. I follow him to the door, slipping off my mask and tucking it into my back pocket. "You're telling me a dim sum restaurant is Saint Willow's headquarters."

"It is today. Maybe it won't be this time next year, or maybe it won't be tomorrow."

He pulls open the door. Dim amber lighting, the tinkling of an old piano, and fragrant smoke waft out, symbols of a family legacy even older than that of Wu Teas. I step in behind Jihen.

The walls are papered over in gold, and the carpet is deep red with yellow lotus flowers. Five round black wooden tables with matching chairs are crowded into the room. Someone's playing the piano at the far end of the restaurant, their shoulders arched over the keys as notes are plunked into existence. The air is thick enough with smoke that I think of last night's smog, and a thin gray haze turns the already low lighting even lower. Different scents come: perfume, cigarettes, tea, smoked meat.

A woman and two men are seated at the table in the middle.

Jihen heads over and I stay near. My heart is pumping too close to the surface of my chest, wanting to leap out. I stare at the two guys and try to guess which one is Saint Willow. The one with the sleeves of his white business shirt casually rolled up as he drinks tea around the cigarette hanging from his mouth? Or the one still in his jacket and tie, tea and a bowl of rice at his elbow as he lays down a card on the pile on the table. They're playing War. The woman sits between them, dressed in green silk and reading a book, tea also in front of her.

All three glance up to watch as we approach.

It's the woman Jihen speaks to.

"Saint, this is Aza Wu. Her family runs Wu Teas. They're one of the families I've been collecting honor marks from on your behalf."

This is Saint Willow. A woman. My mind spins back to past conversations, trying to see how I missed this, why I assumed the leader of a gang would have to be a man. Jihen himself contributed to it, never correcting me. I guess even Jihen knows about mystery adding power.

Saint Willow slowly sets her book down on the table and her eyes lock on mine. They are darker than mine, and even harder to read than Embry's. Reflex makes me want to look away, but I sense that would be a mistake, so I just stare back.

"And why is she here?" Her voice is as soft as the silk of her blouse, hiding how she's made of steel. Her glossy black hair tumbles down to her waist.

"She . . . needs to know how to find a gatherer of magic."

I watch her eyes as Jihen says this—they don't change at all. Her gaze still on mine, she says, "Luna and Seb, mind going to the kitchen and seeing if they need any help?"

The two guys get up and walk away.

"Sit down, Jihen," she says as soon as they are gone from the room. Her tone is light but Jihen being in trouble is obvious. I slowly exhale as he pulls out a chair and Saint Willow turns her eyes on her cousin. "*Why* again have you brought her here?"

"She needs a gatherer," Jihen says. "I told her there's no such thing."

"So she just asked nicely?"

His mouth flaps. He doesn't want to admit I gave him no choice. More, he doesn't want to reveal I'm a caster of full magic. It would mean the loss of a toy.

"I cast full magic on him and made him bring me," I say to Saint Willow. In the background, piano notes rise into the air, heavy and somber.

Jihen glares at me, and I remember I wasn't supposed to talk until he said it was okay.

"It doesn't matter anyway because there's no such person," he says. "Or I would have known about them."

But Saint Willow isn't listening. Her eyes have come back to me. Now I *can* read them, and I shiver at the gleam of hunger there for my magic. It reminds me of the hunger Finch has for the Guild, something stoked by his *hate* of magic.

She gestures to a chair. *Sit.*

I do.

"Aza Wu," she says, "of *the* Wu Teas, your family's name once recognized by royals. Did you know at one point, more people in the world drank Wu Teas than every other brand combined? Incredible."

I can't tell if she meant for me to feel the barbs in that. "That was a long time ago."

"My ancestors once helped *your* ancestors settle here, hundreds of years ago. And now here we are, meeting each other, descendants of those ancestors. I'm the one who's had to assign a squeezer to get your family to pay what is owed mine, yet *you're* the one who's a caster of full magic."

"I'm here to make a deal with you," I say before she can get another dig in. "Bring me to a gatherer, wipe my family's debt, and I'll work for you as a caster."

Jihen sits up. He shoots me an indignant look and his mouth flaps open again. But then he snaps it shut. He can't reveal I already promised to be his caster because that would be admitting he's kept me a secret. And he's probably heard the story about Milo

Kingston and the Sturgeon River, about how it was family who put him in there.

Saint Willow's gleam of hunger sharpens. "Why do you want to find a gatherer?"

Now Jihen gives her a hurt look. "So they're really a thing? Why didn't you tell me, Saint?"

Irritation crosses the gang leader's face as she looks at her cousin. "You know what you need to know to do your job for this family."

The piano notes change, become lively and quick.

Saint Willow turns back to me. Her smile is elegant. "Cast full magic right now and we can talk."

"What do you want me to do?" I ask.

"Something to convince me you're not wasting my time."

I draw, grab one of the chopsticks still laid over the bowl of rice, and cast.

Heat flows through the lotus-printed carpet and into my shoes, up into my hands, and into my mind. I gather the red cloud that forms in there and direct it toward Jihen. I make the muscles of his legs move so that he's forced to stand.

He glares at me, scowls. "Stop it, Aza."

I push my magic and he jerks backward. His chair crashes to the ground. I make Jihen's legs start walking toward the kitchen. He's fighting me—his motions are awkward, uneven, his steps more shuffles—but still I push.

"Aza!" He starts swearing in Chinese. His face is red, sweating. "Don't think you won't pay—!"

He disappears into the kitchen, I let the magic slip away, and pain swamps. It's a massive punch to the middle, a wave of invisible gnashing teeth that I feel everywhere.

Saint Willow sits back and watches me grimace.

"Tell me," she says, "why a gatherer?"

"I want to buy a gathered spell," I say, my jaw clenched.

"What for?"

"It has nothing to do with you."

She frowns. "How did you know to come find me to ask?"

"You don't need to know that, either." The piano is still playing. I don't recognize the melody. Back to somber notes anyway. "So do we have a deal?"

"It's not that simple. The caster who finds these spells has developed the ability to pull together lost magic. It's no easy task, and these spells are not for just anyone to buy. Not even casters of full magic."

There's a note of dismissal in her voice—of near boredom—and whether she means it or not, desperation still chills me. What if she decides she's heard enough and forces me to leave? Then what?

"I guess you're right," I say, making sure to sigh a bit. "If you have access to those kinds of casters—to actual gatherers—why would you even need just a caster of full magic like me working for you?"

It's a huge risk, my pretending to not care if I leave empty-handed. But knowing what I know of Saint Willow, I think there's something she hates even more than suspecting her time is being wasted. And that's letting an easy opportunity slip away.

The elegant smile returns. That predatory gleam to own. "Ah, but gatherers can only do that—gather together the magic needed to re-create gathered spells. I still need a caster of full magic to cast those spells, as well as to cast more common ones."

"So maybe I'm the one here with something to offer, and not you." I widen my eyes just the slightest. "Not that I blame you for wanting to feel close to full magic by spelling gathered spells. Not if it's the only way."

Her smile tightens. "And yet, who has come to who, and why?"

She has me there. The pianist is still playing, though more quietly now. It's the only way I can tell the minutes are passing. With the covered windows, low lamplight, and curls of smoke that hang suspended in the air, late evening never leaves this room.

"Do we have a deal, then?" I ask again. Oliver pops into my head, but I push him away—simply considering a gathered spell isn't breaking my promise. But then it's Embry, wishing me luck, and Piper, telling me to prove she's picked a winner, and Kylin, making a face as she talks about cheating, and their faces are harder to push away.

Saint Willow nods, as authoritative as Embry can be. "We have a deal *except* for erasing your family's debt of honor marks. That is family business that goes much deeper than either one of us. You and your magic are just for me. You cast as I request, and I'll get you to a gatherer."

I nod back. "But no more visits to the teahouse. Leave my parents out of this." Disappointment claws, but I'm also not surprised. "So where is a gatherer?"

"Nima," she calls out, "will you come over here, please?"

The piano falls silent. The pianist stands up and heads over. It's a girl about the same age as me, and as soon as our gazes meet, I know she's an Ivor.

The color of her eyes is orange.

I rub mine, wondering if I'm seeing wrong.

"No, Nima really does have orange eyes," Saint Willow says, sounding amused. "She wears contacts when necessary, otherwise Scouts would have found her by now. Also, she is mine, which is another reason why she hasn't been found yet."

Mine. Like Nima is her pet. Like the way some Scouts keep Ivors as pets. Doesn't she own me just the same now?

"Aza, this is Nima," she says. "My gatherer of magic. Nima, this is Aza, and she would like to buy a spell from us."

Nima frowns as she comes to stand by the table. She's wearing a necklace of midnight-blue beads. Her orange eyes scan my face. "I don't know if you can handle a gathered spell."

I bristle. "Can you get me what I need?"

"That depends, what kind of spell do you—?"

Not here, I make my eyes flash.

Her orange ones slide just the slightest bit in the direction of Saint Willow before sliding back, and I can tell she understands I have secrets. But how could she not, considering what she does?

"Nine p.m.," she says, "the lounge at the Tea Chest Hotel."

FORTY-TWO

I head home, my walk stiff and careful.

Luna and Seb said Jihen had stalked off somewhere from the restaurant kitchen to sulk, and so after I was done with Nima, I left the dim sum restaurant by foot. I didn't mind not having Jihen drive me back. I was spared from him yelling at me for deserting him and bringing my magic over to Saint Willow, his whining about his broken finger and about his cousin keeping secrets from him. It left me time to wonder how I could escape Saint Willow just like Diego did, without leaving my parents in danger. I pictured all the ways Earl Kingston and his men were likely promising careless Cormac pain if he didn't give them information he didn't have.

I think about gathered spells and the match tonight and how I might fight.

I think of the ways I want Finch punished and how I might be willing to pay.

Can you ever be sure you're using magic and it's not using you?

I'm about to cross the street when I see a group of Scouts on the far corner. There are three of them, and they're preparing to rehang a display cage from a nearby lamppost. It's the changing of the Ivors, that time of the week when display casters are switched up.

Not wanting to get close, I stay on my side of the street to pass. I tug my mask up higher over my nose. Fear is the cold sweat that pops up all over me as I keep walking, not wanting to look at the Scouts but having to all the same, the way prey does as it's slipping past a predator. Only the most experienced and strongest of Scouts get to do the changing of the Ivors. Cormac is a Scout, but he's a Scout in the way a flower's thorns start out soft, still to be hardened with time.

Two of the Scouts climb up on stepladders to lift the cage up to the lamppost, while the third stays on the sidewalk, keeping watch over the milling crowd of curious people. His face tilts upward as he says something to one of the other Scouts and shock makes me stumble.

Embry.

The sight of his teal eyes is unmistakable.

What? How? *Why?*

The crowd jostling its way past makes me realize I'm just standing and staring. So I start walking again, still trying to understand. The world is back to being off-kilter.

What does it mean when a caster of full magic is also an undercover Scout? More, when he's a member of the most powerful group of casters *and* a Scout? I made up that story for Cormac about cops going undercover and how full magic casters were involved because I never thought anything like it could be true.

But I should have known better, because secrets—they surround me.

Rudy and Shire. Oliver and Finch. The tournament and how it only half exists, its own secrets of gatherers and gathered spells held within it. Full magic *itself* is a secret, buried away even as we keep casting. I can touch my casting arm and know it's real, but what is real when you're always having to hide?

Soon enough I'm nearly back home. Last night I didn't worry about Jihen and Cormac because of the smog. This time, I don't worry because Jihen's still off licking his wounds, and Cormac's probably being threatened with a burial in the empty vastness of the blighted lands right this minute.

Back in the teahouse, I set my alarm to wake up in time for dinner and go to sleep, wanting to heal.

The Tea Chest is in the central area of the Tea Sector, so not that far from the teahouse. It's one of the city's oldest boutique hotels, its concrete frame surviving quake after quake and somehow staying mostly intact. People flock to experience its themed rooms—the decor of each inspired by a kind of tea—the Marquess Blue room is gray and cream velvets, the Sparrow satins in shades of cinnamon and apples. There's even a Wu Teas room, which is as yellow as ever, the color of royalty.

I forgot there was a piano in the lounge of the Tea Chest. Or maybe I just never noticed. But now, walking through the lobby, there is the plunking of keys and I follow them.

Nima's there, playing. It's another song that I don't know. There are about a dozen people scattered around the sunken couches, a couple more at the bar. We're on the ground floor, and the window reflects back the lamps of the lounge. There's no view to miss anyway, just the side of the building next door, the smoggy gray night sky.

She looks up as soon as I walk in—she's been expecting me. She's wearing blue contacts. I cross the room, wondering if she has different colors, depending on the occasion.

She slides over on the bench even as her fingers never leave the keys. *Sit.*

I sit down beside her, stiff.

"So tell me," she says, "what spell do you want?" The melody is slow and liquid, hiding our conversation from the others in the lounge.

I only hesitate for a second.

"I want to take someone's magic away," I say.

"That's a pricey spell."

"What will it cost me?"

She keeps playing. "*Your* magic."

A chill rolls throughout me. Instinctively I pull my casting arm close. "Magic for magic."

She nods. "Is that acceptable to you?"

Yes. No. Both words stick in my throat. Shire wouldn't want me to, but she's gone and I'm still here, hating how Finch took her away. Is this how Oliver felt when he was told the price of being a brother? Love but also hate?

Finally I nod, and that tiny dark pit that's in my chest stirs.

"Then listen," she says softly. "Not a star, but a spiral, twenty revolutions, no more, no less. And the appropriate starter, of course, there on the music rack."

A midnight-blue bead sits on the piano where sheet music might sit. Nima wore a necklace of them just hours ago.

I pick up the gathered spell starter. "It's plastic."

"It's *essence*. Ether. Or the most tangible forms of such intangibles anyway, collected and re-formed."

Ghosts of spells lying around, waiting to be picked up again, spells that need twisted magic.

I close my fist around the bead.

"But I've already told Saint Willow I'll be her caster," I say, suddenly realizing. The relief of an escape would be bigger, but my mind is too full of the immediate—this ugly magic now in my hand, the tournament tonight.

"The price of the spell is the price of the spell." Nima switches up the song, picks a more fast-tempo one. "I'll tell her myself."

There's a note of satisfaction in her voice, but her profile remains unchanging.

"You don't want me working for her," I say, confused. "Why?"

"Do you think you're the first full magic caster she's found and had work for her? While she runs them into the ground, who do you think is there, trying to keep her under control?" Nima's fingers fly over the keys. "So that the world doesn't explode?"

I think of Saint Willow's face when I told her I was a caster of full magic. The gleam of hunger in her eyes, equal to Finch's for the Guild. Finch, who terrifies me.

"I'm doing you a favor." Nima turns her concealed eyes my way. "I wasn't always an Ivor, you know."

I grab a train out to the Electronics Sector. It's east of Tea, on the opposite end of Lotusland. The ride takes thirty minutes and I spend each and every one of them full of doubt. My casting arm twinges—phantom pain, as though my magic is already gone. How much will my arm hurt when my magic is gone for real? Does Oliver's still?

Neon lights are shining in through the train windows, and I get off at the stop closest to the address. But Discord Road is still blocks away, and so I walk down streets lit up with electronic signs and ads. Night is when the sector comes to life—a lot of its shops and arcades don't even open until after dusk—and the sidewalks are crowded. Everyone's loud. The blue bead hangs from the key holder at my hip, ether at its heaviest.

When I arrive at the abandoned warehouse, I cast open the lock using my key starter. There's a thrum in my bones, the echo of it a deep ache. Slipping off my mask, I pull open the door and step inside.

The warehouse is vast, the size of a ball field, one with a concrete floor, concrete walls, and a soaring ceiling instead of a sky. The front half of the space is still and quiet, while the second half is full of spectators and light and noise.

I walk toward this second half, and it's like walking into the surf and still trying to breathe. The tournament reaches for me and pulls me in and then I'm in the light.

Noise crashes into and rings off the warehouse walls; there's the sound of my name, of Finch's, of applause and anticipation and a hunger for a world that is long dead. The overhead orbs glow, cast into life by the Guild one more time for the year. I hear Hugo and Jack yelling for final bets, either Finch or me, because there can only be one winner.

Can a heart pound so hard that it bursts? My veins feel too full, magic threatening to spill over. Fear is the taste of silver in my mouth.

And yet, that tiny dark pit in my chest begins to bloom.

I weave my way to the starter counter—there is no registration area now that it's the final—and wait there for Piper. I know she's probably looking for me, too, the fighter she's put her faith in and shouldn't have.

She's here the next minute. Her silk gown tonight is gold, her purse a wisp of brighter yellow.

"Rudy." Her voice is brusque even as her expression stays soft. "I'm sorry about what happened." *Finch is a merciless fighter, his hunger for victory boundless.* "How are you feeling about tonight?"

I take a deep breath. "I'm ready." *I'm sorry.*

She helps me tie on my ribbon, gives me my marks, wishes me luck. Her words are a blur, but I smell her perfume, and in there she is my mother, she is my father, she is Shire and Rudy and Kylin.

The bell rings, the crowd rushes out like the tide, and then it's just Finch and me in the middle of the light.

His eyes are as cold as the Pacifik in winter. His arm is no longer broken, healed by magic. Another spell, some other cost, a pattern that can never be broken.

Chants of our names fill the air and I shiver. I'm half looking for Oliver in the crowd when the world changes.

FORTY-THREE

I'm standing on the slope of a long, jagged embankment. It's angled steeply enough that I have to brace my feet against the ground to keep from slipping backward. The sky's a dome of blue-gray clouds and it's pouring rain, sheets of it hard on my skin, turning the ground into mud.

The mud's blue.

It smells of flowers.

I look down.

A hundred feet below, there's a line of shrub, then a wide rushing river. Its surface churns and foams as rain crashes inward.

Dread is trickling into my stomach and there's Finch, twenty feet away from me, also standing with his feet braced in the embankment. I adjust mine even as I notice him because I'm already starting to slip.

That river down below...

"These are the Painter's Cliffs of ancient Rinra."

Embry's voice comes from the top of the embankment. I peer upward as rain streams into my eyes.

He stands there, the crowd a thick mass of color behind him, their cheers drowned out by the rain. His suit is black tonight, the shoulders gone even darker with wet, his tie the green of jade. The world is so overly blue that it tints his eyes, changes them from teal to cerulean.

Nima's orange Ivored eyes flash across my mind. I think of Embry telling me about his bones of glass. And then of Embry out there in the sector, his teal eyes as bright as gems as he helped keep an Ivor entrapped.

Who are you, Embry of the Guild of Now?

"The blue of the ground comes from a form of lichen that grows just beneath the surface," he says. Once more, his low voice shouldn't be heard above the rain, but it is. He crouches down and picks up blue mud, examines it in his palm. "These cliffs are gone now, and this lichen extinct. But when both existed fifteen hundred years ago, painters would travel here and try to capture the sensation of the sky melting into the ground, of the ground climbing into the sky. Some succeeded, and some failed, but each painted with passion.

"Just as it was when the greats fought here. And many greats did, because to win in this place was to conquer another world. Where natural phenomena stopped making sense. Where the sky was the ground and vice versa."

The Guild, their *essence* all around, casts.

A creaking sound comes from deep inside the earth.

The blue-gray sky shifts, begins to tilt over. As if the horizon has become some kind of stationary axis and the outer surface of the world wants to spin around it.

My stomach spins with it, and I clench my teeth against a wave of dizziness.

The *ground* shifts now, right along with the sky. It follows the same tilt, so now the sphere of the earth is spinning around the axis of the horizon.

I fall to a crouch as the ground keeps curving around. Some of it's instinct, getting low—if you're going to fall, you won't have as far to go—and some of it's because I'm still dizzy.

But getting low to the ground is useless here. If the earth is going to be completely upended, I'm going to fall no matter what.

Everyone's going to fall.

The entire river's going to spill out.

And then we're all upside down.

But my shoes stay planted in the mud. Only the heaviness of my blood slowly collecting in my head tells me I'm upside down. *Or* that somehow I'm still standing up even as I'm hanging from my feet from the top of the world, an impossible that is now somehow possible. The scents of wet soil and flowers—*lichen*—waft up my nose.

"Let me guess," I call out over the creaking of the earth, over the thunder of the rain, "the sky's the ground and the ground's the sky?"

Embry nods. "Gravity still applies, of course." He gestures upward toward the blue ground. "Mostly."

Finch points down at how the blue mud is making him slip. "It's 'mostly' no help with the rain."

The rain that is now coming from below us, landing at our feet above our heads.

Still crouched, I slip another inch. My mouth goes dry as I glance at the river. I look at the thin line of trees that's keeping the embankment from sliding into the water.

There's that, at least.

It might have to be everything.

All my thoughts have become snarled. Everything I know to be true is now half a lie. There's gravity, but I can still stand upside down. The sky's moving and it's not the clouds making it look that way.

Embry's smile is wry as the world spins back to upright again. "Do you think the greats ever said, let's wait for better weather before we fight?"

"Maybe." I flick mud off one of my shoes with my hand. "If they didn't want to end up in the river."

"And if they embraced the river as part of the fight?"

I glare up at him. I can't shake the dizziness from this world he's built. And I'm still tired of water from yesterday's ancient baths.

"So here we are," he says. "There are two of you left, but only one will win. You can choose how you fight, or you can let your magic choose for you, but either way, only one fighter will remain standing. Good luck."

Embry gets up, turns around, and disappears behind the lip of the embankment.

FORTY-FOUR

There's still mud in my palm from cleaning off my shoe.

It's a head start, two seconds.

I flick my eyes toward Finch. My heart's a knot in my chest. Head start or not, I should cast a shield spell. That's always first.

But.

I draw, close my palm, and cast.

Heat blasts upward from the mud at my feet and drives itself into my veins.

The red cloud of my magic blooms wide in my mind. I make it tear the mud thin beneath his feet. His green eyes flash and then his feet plunge through and he disappears into the hole in the ground.

The crowd roars. It's the sound of my name. The noise is rapturous, washing over me just as the rain does. *Rudy.*

My bones are on fire from the casting, like magic's spilled over and is burning them up. I ignore the pain. I claw at more mud. I draw and cast again, and my magic piles mud on top of Finch. I flick blue from my fingers, draw on my palm, and yank a gold starter from the key holder. I cast again, and my magic directs Finch's blood to thin. My head is starting to pound; the pain in my bones is now agony.

The crowd bellows. My pulse flies, and magic is red and hot and seething through my veins. Agony sharpens, goes as pointed as knives.

I drop the used-up gold coin into the mud. My fingers are trembling, wet with rain. I lift them to the blue bead starter.

I have just seconds. He's bleeding and hurt, buried down there beneath the mud. But I know he's also already fumbling for his starters, preparing to cast on me. But still, I can take his magic right now, and it'll all be over.

Or, I *don't* take his magic.

I can just eliminate him. Just cast a simple spell to close his airway, or one to change his oxygen into something else. Either way, he'll be knocked out and I win.

I could even kill him, except for a pact. That damn pact.

But . . . this is my chance to hurt him beyond anything else. Without magic he'll never fight again, just like he'll never be voted into the Guild. Embry can no longer cast, but he Ivored after he was already in.

And the price is only *me*.

Indecision is a roar in my mind. I don't know, but I need to *be sure*—

An invisible kick knocks me backward. I hit the ground with a thud, and the pounding that's still in my head soars.

I look over. Finch is free. Through the rain and mud there are flashes of his face, of his green eyes as he pushes at mud. There's the sound of the crowd—bellows of his name, heightened cheering, *Fiiiiinch!*—and applause for his magic strokes the land of the Painter's Cliffs, just the way a brush does over canvas.

Dizziness swarms. Desperation to get away is suddenly

everything—*I can't think!*—and panic licks as hot as fire. My hand shakes as I rip off a silver starter. I draw and cast—shield.

The air around me bends, shapes over me as a protective cocoon. When the cost of the spell comes, it's a series of internal punches that leaves me out of breath, even more panicked.

Not good. I have to slow down. The effects of casting are piling up fast.

I begin to struggle up the embankment, the blood pooling in my face as the world keeps spinning. The ground up there can't be sloped, right? There the mud would only be messy instead of dangerous. If I can just get on even ground, the Guild can wheel the earth around as much as they want and I won't be so dizzy. If I can just get up there, I'll know if I'm ready to cast my magic away. My shoes slide in blue mud and the river below (above?) foams. Rain lashes downward.

I twist, looking for Finch, reaching for a starter, when every muscle in my body freezes. My shield shatters. Pain slaps at me all over, and I utter a single useless gasp as I fall face-first into the mud.

Blue liquid stings my nose, gets shoved into my mouth. A vise cranks tight around my chest and breathing becomes impossible.

The vise cranks harder.

Then I'm flung sideways across the ground, an invisible force reverberating along my ribs as I skid along. Blue mud curls over me in a wave and splashes back down, coating me. To one side, the river flashes, a wild stream of yet more blue.

For a second, nothing makes sense. Finch can kill me right here. But instead he just casts his magic as an impact spell. A strong one, but that's it. Not even enough to knock me out.

Suddenly I get it.

He's going for show tonight. He wants to win the Guild over completely, the Guild who loves style and skill most of all.

I'm whooping for breath, coughing mud and rain from my mouth. I drag myself to my knees. Finch approaches, a figure against all the blue that has become the world. The ground shifts, and my stomach swims.

Is this it, then? The end?

"You almost killed me," he says. His voice is stunned, almost betrayed. But he's also short of breath, holding his side. Casting is costing him, too.

I turn my head and look him in the eye. He's a sight, covered in blood where he's not blue.

"You should have never asked Oliver to give up his magic for you," I say.

Another impact spell, and I'm blasted along the embankment. No, *down* the embankment—toward the rushing river. Pain explodes in my head. I try to grab for some kind of hold as mud grinds into my teeth, but my hands only flail at the ground. The thin line of shrub is ten feet away, maybe even less.

I get to my knees again. There's mud in my palm. I draw, I cast. No reaction. Finch didn't feel it all. He's cast a shield spell.

"He owed me," he says. "And he didn't deserve to keep it. He let it ruin everything."

The cost of casting skewers through me anyway, a thin line of agony that makes me utter a low scream even as I scrabble for mud and cast again. Fresh heat fills my legs, chest, hands, mind. I form the red cloud of my magic into a knife and push it into Finch's head.

He stumbles, shield spell shattered.

"How's the headache?" My words are thick and clotted with mud, strained with fatigue and pain. My own headache blooms, and I nearly retch. A wild buzzing grows in my ears, promising me the end is so close, that I'm nearly there. I grab at more mud and cast again, suddenly unable to care how much it hurts, I just want him done.

Finch grabs the sides of his head even as agony slams into mine. Through tearing eyes, I watch him bend over and gag. His fingers clutch at the ground.

I stagger to my feet. The earth turns and turns, past the halfway mark now. Blood begins to leave my face and head—we're no longer standing upside down. The sky twirls and nausea rises. I smell soil and flowers and fire, the scent of cast magic. Rain pelts.

An invisible fist meets the side of my face. I rocket back. My shoes skid through mud as I struggle for balance, my arms out. My hands smash into branches, leaves—I'm at the line of scrub. The river just behind it roars for me.

I reach for the key holder at my hip. I grab the blue bead and tear it free. Magic pounds in my veins, is a red fire in my mind, and I see Shire in there, helping me build it. Rudy and Kylin are in there, too, stoking the flames.

My eyes fill.

Am I really doing this?

Magic for revenge?

Finch is gasping. His gaze is all ice. "I could have let her live, you know that? But magic isn't fair. It never will be."

Then he casts around the mud in his hand.

A blow. It sends me slamming back into the trees. I scream as a branch pierces my shoulder from behind. Fire lights up my casting arm, turns into a white ball of agony to spear my brain.

The roar of the crowd swells.

I keep my arm across my chest, pinned there because to hold it any other way hurts even worse. The tip of the branch sticks out of my front like a giant thorn. The world and the sky and my stomach all spin.

Finch is bent over, struggling to stand up.

"She begged," he says. "She knew what I meant to do and she *begged*."

Rage floods, as hot as pain, as hot as magic.

I drag my other arm up. Still clutching the blue bead in my fist, I begin to draw on the palm of my casting arm with a shaking finger.

He staggers close now, his face pale with pain, still half-bent with it. He grins at me and reaches down for a final scoop of blue. The rain pours down.

"I just laughed," he says.

The tiny dark pit in my chest explodes.

I drop the blue bead into the middle of my spell spiral.

I cast.

FORTY-FIVE

Magic is never lost.

Lost is too gentle a word.

We never lose it the way we might lose a mark, or a shirt, or a word that stays forever on the edge of our lips.

Magic, it turns out, is *taken*.

It is ripped from us like the removal of an organ, the cutting out of a tongue. It is the excising of the part of our brains that stands for language, one of the ways we communicate. In Oliver's mind I saw it as a burned-down tree, because magic is fire, alive and vital and hot. All that's left afterward is ruin.

I watch Finch change, a part of who he is extinguished like the snuffing out of a candle. A shadow crosses him the way a cloud would have once crossed the hidden sun, and for a long second, every part of him *dims*. When he comes back, the only thing he has left of his magic is the memory of it, a smoking tree in the landscape of his life.

I'll never see it for myself, because my magic is also gone. As I watched it be taken from Finch, he watched it be taken from me, and now his eyes are dull with disbelief. The pain I see in them now is phantom pain, the pain of absence.

"No." He backs away from me. He falls into the mud. "No."

I nod. But I can't talk because I'm crying. I clutch my torn shoulder and drop the used-up blue bead into the mud. I'm standing in the middle of a woven world, but the absence of my magic is as fresh as a new wound, raw and stinging and undeniable.

And magic is as real as blood, but is as formless as a dream—where is mine now? Taken, but to where? A burst nebulous cloud now in invisible pieces, lying around waiting to be collected, re-formed, *reused*?

I shudder. To have someone else take my magic, to take it for their own—

The noise of the crowd begins to break through the shock of what I've done. The earth and sky continue to spin, the river to foam—so much blue, forever in motion. There's no sign of Embry to signal the end of a round.

Because the tournament isn't over, I realize. The Guild still needs a clear-cut winner. One of us has to be knocked out by the other, or one of us has to bow out on our own. Or one of us can die.

Except neither of us are full magic casters anymore. Or casters at all. We are without magic, and neither of us belongs here. The crowd has no idea they are cheering for no ones.

Before I can do anything, Finch—he's still sitting in the mud—slams his hand three times into the blue mud.

Bow-out.

From his expression, he's as stunned by his surrender as I am. And there's delusion there, too. As though he won't believe his magic is really gone. That if the round will just end, he will feel his power again. That this tournament might be over for him, but he'll fight again in the next.

The crowd is yelling, shouting. The sound of it is like thunder rolling across the Painter's Cliffs. I hear my name, the word *champion* added to it.

Embry emerges from among all the casters. He stands in front and peers down at us from the top of the embankment. Everyone falls quiet until there's only the sound of the rain, of the rushing river. Finch is still sitting and staring down at the ground; I'm standing near him, my hand cradling my bad arm. Both of us are blue, soaking wet, miserable. The idea of pretending to celebrate makes me even dizzier.

"Everyone—the champion of this year's Tournament of Casters." Embry's smile is reserved, which it usually is anyway. But his eyes are too aware as they go from me to Finch, and I wonder if he knows. Then his gaze meets mine and I know he does. "Thank you for fighting as legends do, Rudy."

I am no legend.

I've won, but I am empty.

I shut my eyes and around me the world changes back.

From within the dark, the spinning of the earth and sky comes to a halt. The rain stops and the river goes still. The scents of wet soil and blue lichen fade away. And when I open my eyes again, the Painter's Cliffs of ancient Rinra are gone, and once more it's just the abandoned warehouse in the Electronics Sector.

Everyone's moving again. Casters start making their way toward the bets counter, wanting to pick up their winnings. I'm half-aware of Finch getting to his feet and slinking away. For a second I wonder if I should call him back—but to say what? Everything I could ever think to say—about Shire, about Kylin and Oliver—was all wrapped up in what I took from him, and the price I paid to make him listen. There's nothing left.

I follow him for two steps anyway, thinking about Oliver, wondering if there's anything left for me to say to *him*. How maybe I need to see him once more to know.

There shouldn't be. We only ever had Finch between us. And I think for the next little while, Finch is going to need his brother again. More than he's wanted to for years.

It's Piper who I see first. She's grinning as she walks over, so pleased with me for what I've done. *There's still honor in doing what must be done to survive, even if such ways are ugly.*

She shakes her head at seeing my shoulder. The branch is gone now, a part of the Guild's fighting ring. But the hole it left remains.

She takes a small swatch of silk from her purse, draws, and casts. Her leftover magic works on my shoulder, turns the throb that's deep inside into something closer to a thrum.

My eyes sting from the gesture. "Thanks. It feels better."

"Oh, we both know it's nothing, but it'll help a bit until you recover enough to cast again."

She doesn't know how that's impossible. Some wounds never close, never get filled back up. This is just the new tiny dark pit that's replaced the first.

"I'll go pick up your winnings from the bets counter now," she says, "and after the Guild gets you your two hundred thousand marks, we'll meet again for *my* cut of those winnings, Aza." Then she's gone in a swirl of gold silk.

The Guild.

Embry.

I search the crowd for signs of him, needing him for something that has nothing to do with collecting my marks. Dizziness creeps back as my eyes scan the room for bright teal ones. I shouldn't have waited this long, but—

"Rudy."

It's Oliver, headed toward me, coming out of the milling crowd.

It shouldn't matter that I'm seeing him again—that he cares enough to not blow my cover by calling me Rudy still, even though the tournament is officially over—but it does, and my pulse skips.

One look at him and I know he knows. Finch must have already found him and told him, then. Or maybe Oliver only had to glance at Finch to know. To recognize the touching down of that second of *dim* across his brother's face and know what it means.

"Why?" His voice is low, shattered. "You don't know what it's like..."

"Because." I take a shaky breath and push back my wet hair. "I wanted Finch to hurt for what he did, and I knew this would hurt him the most. He could never be in the Guild, Oliver."

"Okay, but... *your* magic—"

"It was the cost. I paid it because I was willing to. And that's not really the same thing as wanting to, is it?"

His gaze burns and then he nods. I know his parents are now on his mind, and it's not what I meant, but I can't change how he thinks about that. I don't think it's for me to change.

"You know where to find me," he says, "if you ever need me." *To ask what it's been like. To be able to hold the world in your hand and then have it all be gone.* "I won't mind."

"Thanks. Maybe. I'm—do you know Wu Teas? It's in the Tea Sector. So that's where I'll be. Aza Wu. If you need."

He nods and turns away to find his brother. And my heart is still pounding as I go to search for Embry again.

Only because he's been looking for me as well does he let himself be found. He might never be able to cast again, but it's undeniable that he still has some kind of power. Beneath all the damage, some of that magic still remains in his veins, forever a part of him.

He crosses the warehouse, an envelope in his hand. He hands it over when we meet.

"Is it still Rudy, or is it Aza now?"

I take the envelope. It's thick with marks, both paper and coin. After Piper gets her cut, the rest will pay off our standing debt of honor marks to Saint Willow's family. I stuff the envelope into my starter bag that will no longer need to hold starters. "It's Aza."

"I'm unsure if I should congratulate you on winning the tournament, given the cost."

The back of my neck gets hot. "It's okay, I really don't want you to."

"You really didn't need a gathered spell to win." He sounds almost disappointed in me. As though how I fought in the first three rounds made him think I was capable of more. Something different, something better. And maybe I was. But now I'll never know.

"It wasn't about winning the tournament as much as it was about taking something from Finch."

"Because of your sister and what happened last year."

I stare at him, startled. "You remember Shire?"

"Yes. You look a lot like her, so I suspected. And I'm sorry she lost the way she did, just as I'm sorry Finch won the way *he* did.

We discouraged him from using a gathered spell during this tournament, after what happened last year. If that was the only way he could win, there would be no place for him in the Guild."

So Embry knew about Finch using a gathered spell.

I want to be mad about his being okay with this, about how the tournament runs on cruelty as much as it does on magic—and maybe cruelty and magic are two sides of the same coin anyway, just like magic and pain are. He would just say the same thing—how full magic has always had its cost.

"I would have voted against him becoming a member, Aza," Embry continues, "if and when a spot opened up. Most of the Guild would have."

I don't know what to say, or what he might want to hear from me. But I'm too tired to be mad, and I can't care anymore. I no longer have anything to do with the Guild or with the tournament or anything like that, now that I have no more magic. But Embry's power—for that I can't leave just yet.

So I only nod. And given what I need to ask, maybe it's for the best that Embry is now hoping for my understanding.

"I need your help." I speak quietly enough so none of the casters still close by will hear me. "I know you're a Scout. I saw you today, helping hang up a display cage."

For a second he's shocked enough that he can't speak. Then he simply says, "Oh?"

"I'm not—I don't want to ask *why* you're one—"

I take a half step back as his teal eyes go sharp enough to cut. I no longer have reason to be scared of any Scout, but a lifetime of built-in fear is hard to get over so fast.

"You mean why would a caster who helps runs a tournament based on full magic also be hunting down its casters and locking up his own kind?"

The back of my neck gets hot again. "Yes."

"For every Ivor I keep locked away and every caster I chase down, there are many more I'm able to overlook. We pay in many different ways for our magic, Aza."

I nod. He's right. We've always been paying. And I might not be a caster anymore, but that's just another way I paid for magic.

"What do you need my help for?" he asks.

"It's about another Scout, actually. He's new."

"Who?"

"His name is Cormac. He's been watching me."

"You've no more magic, Aza." Embry's tone is almost gentle. "He'll be assigned elsewhere soon enough."

I shake my head. "It's not that—not anymore anyway. But I had to get him in trouble with one of the city's gangs in order to escape."

"And?"

"Do you think you can go rescue him?"

I walk home, shoulder singing, all my bones and muscles throbbing and bruised. There's mud in my hair that's already smeared my smog mask, and the noise of the crowd lingers in my ears just as the scent of fifteen-hundred-year-old blue lichen won't fully leave my nose. The streets stay sleeping and dark as I head west, from the Electronics Sector through to Government and then on to Tea. It's not raining but the air still feels damp because it's Lotusland.

My mind is on none of these. It's too busy wrapped up around itself, around the memory of magic, when magic had been who I was and how I'm no longer that. So where does that leave me? Who can I be now, if not a caster?

When I get to the block of the teahouse, I don't bother turning the corner to get to the back alley. Now that Jihen no longer has any hold over me and Cormac is stuck with Earl Kingston until Embry finds him tomorrow, there's no reason to have to worry about being seen.

But I didn't know someone else was still looking.

Waiting at the front entrance of the teahouse are Saint Willow and Nima.

Fear prickles along my entire body.

Nima must have told Saint Willow about my magic. I knew she would, but not when. And now the gang leader is here to make me pay.

"What are you doing here?" My voice is thin in the night. It's starting to rain again, a fine drizzle that sits on my hair.

Saint Willow smiles her elegant smile. "I just wanted to make sure you haven't forgotten about our deal, Aza. I lead you to a gatherer and you cast magic for me."

I glance at Nima, confused. But her eyes don't meet mine, and she's pale around her mask.

"The price of the spell," I say to Saint Willow, "was my magic. I can't cast for you even if I wanted to."

She opens her hand.

In her palm is a blue bead.

More fear comes, full lashes of it.

"I don't need another spell," I say. "Spells are useless to me without magic."

"Nima, explain, please," Saint Willow says.

"This starter is for full magic," Nima says. "You'll have magic again."

My stomach lurches. "That's impossible. You can't get your magic back once it's been taken. It . . . *scatters*. Like—"

Ether. *Essence*.

"It's true, it's likely not *your* magic," Nima says. "But it's still *full* magic, collected and re-formed. It'll be nearly the same thing."

"Consider yourself lucky, Aza." Saint Willow's smile gains a bitter edge. "Full magic can only be given to those who once held it."

I stare at them both, at the bead in Saint Willow's palm that lets her pretend. She longs so badly for full magic of her own, but having access to someone else's must do.

"I can't." I feel sick. To have *someone else* in your veins, in your *mind*—

Except I'd be a caster again. Under someone else's control, and with a stranger's magic, but . . .

"You can because we have a deal," Saint Willow says. "Don't make your parents pay for a cost that you agreed to."

We pay in many different ways for our magic, Aza.

I nod, numb inside now as cold rain falls.

The price, always to be paid.

"Okay," I say.

ACKNOWLEDGMENTS

All my thanks to these amazing and wonderful people:

My agent, Victoria Marini, who is a constant inspiration and forever encouraging. I'm so very fortunate to have you in my corner.

My editor, Matt Ringler, for trusting me with this story about a girl and underground magic. Your enthusiasm and sharp eye have been everything. Plus, you're pretty cool.

The fantastic team at Scholastic who helped make *Caster* into a real book—Shelly Romero, Maeve Norton, David Levithan, Josh Berlowitz, Rachel Feld, Shannon Pender, Tracy van Straaten, Amy Goppert, Alexis Lassiter, Yesenia Corporan, Celia Lee, the Scholastic Emerging Leaders, the IreadYA team, and the book clubs and book fairs.

For always being just an email or text away, great writer friends Ellen Oh, Gail Villanueva, Jess Huang, and Sangu Mandanna.

And, of course, family. Especially Jesse, Matthew, Gillian, Wendy, Mom, and Dad. Lots of love to you all of you.

ABOUT THE AUTHOR

Elsie Chapman grew up in Prince George, Canada, and has a degree in English literature from the University of British Columbia. She is the author of the YA novels *Dualed, Divided, Along the Indigo,* and *Caster* as well as the middle-grade novel *All the Ways Home,* and the co-editor of *A Thousand Beginnings and Endings* and *Hungry Hearts.* She currently lives in Tokyo, Japan, with her family. You can visit her online at elsiechapman.com.

Acknowledgments

I'd like to thank all of the writers who contributed to this book. I wasn't asking an easy thing of them when I solicited their creative work; instead, I was asking them to write toward the hurt, to wrestle with the ugly truths that plague us in this country. Each of the writers did just that, and they did so beautifully. My editor, Kathryn Belden, believed in this book before I could even articulate why I wanted to work on it. She edited this collection tirelessly. She makes me a better writer, and I am so grateful to work with her. Her assistant, David Lamb, ushered the book through the first round of edits, communicated with the contributors about contracts, and aided in copyedits. I'm thankful for Jennifer Lyons, my agent, who has always been my advocate. I am indebted to Scribner, who welcomed this book into their catalog and me into their coterie of writers. Finally, I'd like to remember the sage, fierce artist who inspired this book, James Baldwin. I hope our work makes you proud.

Contributors

CAROL ANDERSON is the Samuel Candler Dobbs Professor and chair of African American Studies at Emory University and the author of *White Rage: The Unspoken Truth of Our Racial Divide* and *Eyes Off the Prize: The United Nations and the African American Struggle for Human Rights, 1944–1955*, which was awarded the Myrna F. Bernath Book Award and the Gustavus Myers Outstanding Book Award and was selected as a finalist for the Truman Book Award and the W. E. B. Du Bois Book Award.

JERICHO BROWN has published two poetry collections, *Please* and *The New Testament*, and has been the recipient of the Whiting Writers' Award, the American Book Award, a fellowship at the Radcliffe Institute for Advanced Study, and a National Endowment for the Arts grant. He is an associate professor of English and creative writing at Emory University in Atlanta.

GARNETTE CADOGAN is editor-at-large of *Nonstop Metropolis: A New York City Atlas* (coedited by Rebecca Solnit and Joshua Jelly-Schapiro). He is currently a visiting fellow at the Institute for Advanced Studies in Culture at the

University of Virginia, and a visiting scholar at the Institute for Public Knowledge at New York University. He writes about culture and the arts for various publications, and is at work on a book about walking.

EDWIDGE DANTICAT, born in Haiti and raised in New York, has written both fiction and nonfiction for adults and children. Her memoir, *Brother, I'm Dying*, was awarded the National Book Critics Circle Award, and was finalist for the National Book Award, as was her short story collection *Krik? Krak!* She is a 2009 MacArthur Fellow.

RACHEL KAADZI GHANSAH is an essayist and critic whose writing has appeared in the *Believer, Rolling Stone*, the *Paris Review, Transition*, and elsewhere. She was a finalist for the National Magazine Award, and she is a contributing writer for the *New York Times Magazine*. Her first book, *The Explainers and Explorers*, examines twenty-first-century America within the context of what it means to be black, brave, and self-defined, and it will be published by Scribner in 2017.

MITCHELL S. JACKSON is the author of *The Residue Years*, which won the Ernest J. Gaines Award and was a finalist for the Center for Fiction's Flaherty-Dunnan First Novel Prize, the PEN/Hemingway Award for Debut Fiction, and the Hurston/Wright Legacy Award. He is a recipient of a Whiting Award and teaches writing at NYU, where he earned an MFA in creative writing.

HONORÉE FANONNE JEFFERS is a poet, fiction writer, and critic. She is the author of four books of poetry and is at work on her first novel. Her fifth poetry book, in progress, *The Age of Phillis*, imagines the life and times of the eighteenth-century poet Phillis Wheatley, the first (known) black woman to publish a book. The recipient of fellowships from the National Endowment for the Arts and the Witter Bynner Foundation through the Library of Congress, Jeffers is an elected member of the American Antiquarian Society, an organization to which fourteen U.S. presidents have been elected. She teaches at the University of Oklahoma.

KIMA JONES's work has appeared in *Guernica*, *NPR*, *PANK*, *Scratch Magazine*, and *The Rumpus*, and she has received fellowships from PEN Center USA, Yaddo, and the MacDowell Colony.

KIESE LAYMON is associate professor of English and Africana Studies at Vassar College and a recent Grisham Writer in Residence at the University of Mississippi. He is the author of the novel *Long Division*, which was selected as a best book of 2013 by *Buzzfeed*, *The Believer*, *Salon*, *Guernica*, *Library Journal*, and the *Chicago Tribune*, and an essay collection, *How to Slowly Kill Yourself and Others in America*. He is a columnist at *The Guardian*, and his forthcoming memoir, *Heavy*, will be published by Scribner.

DANIEL JOSÉ OLDER is the author of the Bone Street Rumba urban fantasy series (Roc Books, 2015 and 2016) and the

Young Adult novel *Shadowshaper* (Scholastic, 2015), which was shortlisted for the Kirkus Prize in Young Readers' Literature. He coedited the Locus and World Fantasy Award–nominated anthology *Long Hidden: Speculative Fiction from the Margins of History.* You can find Daniel's thoughts on writing, read dispatches from his decadelong career as an NYC paramedic, and hear his music at danieljoseolder.net and @djolder on Twitter.

Emily Raboteau is the author of *The Professor's Daughter: A Novel* and *Searching for Zion: The Quest for Home in the African Diaspora*, winner of the 2014 American Book Award and finalist for the Hurston Wright Legacy Award. Her distinctions include a Pushcart Prize, a literature fellowship from the National Endowment for the Arts, and the Chicago Tribune's Nelson Algren Award. She is a professor of English at the City College of New York, in Harlem, where she codirects the MFA program in creative writing. Her next novel is in the works.

Claudia Rankine is the author of five collections of poetry including *Citizen: An American Lyric*, which won the National Book Critics Circle Award for Poetry in 2015, the PEN/Open Book Award, the PEN Literary Award, and the NAACP Image Award, and was a finalist for the National Book Award. She lives in California, where she is the Aerol Arnold Professor of English at the University of Southern California.

CLINT SMITH is a National Science Foundation Graduate Research Fellow and a doctoral candidate in education at Harvard University. He was a 2014 National Poetry Slam champion and has two popular TED Talks, *The Danger of Silence* and *How to Raise a Black Son in America*. His poems and essays have appeared in *The New Yorker, The Guardian,* and *The American Literary Review.* He is the author of the poetry collection *Counting Descent.*

NATASHA TRETHEWEY is the author of four poetry collections, *Domestic Work, Bellocq's Ophelia; Native Guard* (which won the 2007 Pulitzer Prize) and *Thrall,* as well as a book of nonfiction, *Beyond Katrina: A Meditation on the Mississippi Gulf Coast.* Her column, "Poem," appears weekly in the *New York Times Magazine.* She teaches at Emory University as the Robert W. Woodruff Professor of English and creative writing and has served for two terms as the United States Poet Laureate (2012–14).

WENDY S. WALTERS is the author of *Multiply/Divide: On the American Real and Surreal; Troy, Michigan; Longer I Wait, More You Love Me;* and a chapbook, *Birds of Los Angeles.* She is associate professor of creative writing and literature at The New School.

ISABEL WILKERSON is the first African American woman to win a Pulitzer Prize in journalism, awarded for her coverage of the 1993 Midwestern floods and for her profile of a ten-year-old boy caring for his four siblings. She is the author of the *New York Times* bestseller *The Warmth of Other Suns*, which won the National Book Critics Circle Award for Nonfiction in 2010.

KEVIN YOUNG has edited five collections of poetry and published eight poetry collections of his own, including *For the Confederate Dead, Book of Hours*, and *Jelly Roll*, which was a finalist for the National Book Award for Poetry, as well as *Blue Laws: Selected and Uncollected Poems, 1995–2015*. He is also the author of *The Grey Album: On the Blackness of Blackness*, an encyclopedic nonfiction book examining through Jay Z's *The Black Album* and The Beatles's *The White Album* how African American culture *is* in many ways American culture, which won the Pen/Open Book Award and the Graywolf Press Nonfiction Prize and was a finalist for the National Book Critics Circle Award for Criticism.

Permissions

ABOUT THE EDITOR

Jesmyn Ward received her MFA from the University of Michigan and is currently an associate professor of creative writing at Tulane University. She is the author of the novels *Where the Line Bleeds* and *Salvage the Bones*, which won the 2011 National Book Award and was a finalist for the New York Public Library Young Lions Fiction Award and the Dayton Literary Peace Prize. She is also the author of the memoir *Men We Reaped*, which was a finalist for the National Book Critics Circle Award and the Hurston/ Wright Legacy Award and won the Chicago Tribune Heartland Prize and the Media for a Just Society Award.

them, brown and black bodies living with "certain uncertainty," to use Frantz Fanon's words, black bodies fleeing oppression, persecution, and poverty, wherever they are.

"You think your pain and your heartbreak are unprecedented in the history of the world, but then you read," James Baldwin wrote. Or you see. Or you weep. Or you pray. Or you speak. Or you write. Or you fight so that one day everyone will be able to walk the earth as though they, to use Baldwin's words, have "a right to be here." May that day come, Mira and Leila, when you can finally claim those crowns of yours and put them on your heads. When that day of jubilee finally arrives, all of us will be there with you, walking, heads held high, crowns a-glitter, because we do have a right to be here.

*children will be the last who experience all this. And please
do live your best lives and achieve your full potential. Love
deeply. Be joyful. In Jubilee, Mom.*

To my draft of this letter, I often add snippets of Baldwin.

"I tell you this because I love you and please don't you
ever forget it," Baldwin reminded his James. "Know whence
you came. If you know whence you came, there is no limit
to where you can go."

"The world is before you," I want to tell my daughters,
"and you need not take it or leave it as it was when you
came in."

I want to look happily forward. I want to be optimistic.
I want to have a dream. I want to live in jubilee. I want my
daughters to feel that they have the power to at least try
to change things, even in a world that resists change with
more strength than they have. I want to tell them they can
overcome everything, if they are courageous, resilient, and
brave. Paradoxically, I also want to tell them their crowns
have already been bought and paid for and that all they have
to do is put them on their heads. But the world keeps tripping me up. My certainty keeps flailing.

So I took them to the border, the one between Haiti and
the Dominican Republic, where hundreds of refugees were
living, or rather existing. There they saw and helped comfort men, women, and children who look like them, but are
stateless, babies with not even a bedsheet between them and
a dirt floor, young people who may not be killed by bullets
but by the much slower assault of disease.

"These are all our causes," I tried to both tell and show

born in a society which spelled out with brutal clarity, and in as many ways as possible that you were a worthless human being."

That same letter could have been written to a long roster of dead young men and women, whose dungeons shook, but whose chains did not completely fall off. Among these very young people are Oscar Grant, Aiyana Stanley-Jones, Rekia Boyd, Kimani Gray, Renisha McBride, Trayvon Martin, Michael Bell, Tamir Rice, Michael Brown, Sandra Bland, and counting. It's sad to imagine what these young people's letters from their loved ones may have said. Had their favorite uncle notified them that they could qualify for refugee status within their own country? Did their mother or father, grandmother or grandfather warn them to not walk in white neighborhoods, to, impossibly, avoid police officers, to never play in a public park, to stay away from neighborhood watchmen, to never go to a neighbor's house, even if to seek help from danger?

I am still, in my own mind, drafting a "My Dungeon Shook" letter to my daughters. It often begins like this. *Dear Mira and Leila, I've put off writing this letter to you for as long as I can, but I don't think I can put it off any longer. Please know that there will be times when some people might be hostile or even violent to you for reasons that have nothing to do with your beauty, your humor, or your grace, but only your race and the color of your skin. Please don't let this restrict your freedom, break your spirit, or kill your joy. And if possible do everything you can to change the world so that your generation of brown and black men, women, and*

To think, I remember telling my husband, our daughters will never know a world in which the president of their country has not been black. Indeed, as we watched President Obama's inaugural speech, my oldest daughter was shocked that no woman had ever been president of the United States. That day, the world ahead for my girls seemed full of greater possibility—if not endless possibilities, then at least greater than those for generations past. Many more doors suddenly seemed open to my girls, and the "joyous daybreak" evoked by Martin Luther King, Jr., in his "I Have a Dream" speech, a kind of jubilee, seemed to have emerged. However, it quickly became clear that this one man was not going to take all of us with him into the postracial promised land. Or that he even had full access to it. Constant talk of "wanting him to fail" was racially tinged, as were the "birther" investigations, and the bigoted commentaries and jokes by both elected officials and ordinary folk. One of the most consistent attacks against the president, was that, like my husband and myself, he was born elsewhere and was not *really* American.

Like Barack Obama's father, many of us had brought our black bodies to America from somewhere else. Some of us, like the president, were the children of such people. We are people who need to have two different talks with our black offspring: one about why we're here and the other about why it's not always a promised land for people who look like us.

In his own version of "The Talk," James Baldwin wrote to his nephew James in "My Dungeon Shook," "You were ous nature of citizenship here: that we too are prey, and that those who have been in this country for generations—walking, living, loving in the same skin we're in—they too can suddenly become refugees.

Parents are often too nervous to broach difficult subjects with their children. Love. Sex. Death. Race. But some parents are forced to have these conversations early. Too early. A broken heart might lead to questions we'd rather not answer, as might an inappropriate gesture, the death of a loved one, or the murder of a stranger.

Each time a black person is killed in a manner that's clearly racially motivated, either by a police officer or a vigilante civilian, I ask myself if the time has come for me to talk to my daughters about Abner Louima and the long list of dead that have come since. My daughters have met Abner, but I have never told them about his past, even though his past is a future they might have to face.

Why don't I tell them? My decision is about more than avoiding a difficult conversation. The truth is, I do not want my daughters to grow up as I did, terrified of the country and the world they live in. But is it irresponsible of me to not alert them to the potentially life-altering, or even life-ending horrors they might face as young black women?

The night President Barack Obama was first elected (would he too qualify for refugee status?), my oldest daughter was three and I was in the last weeks of my pregnancy with my second. When President Obama was inaugurated for the first time, I was cradling both my little girls in my arms.

other unarmed black bodies, with nowhere to go for refuge, find themselves in the path of yet another police officer's or armed vigilante's gun.

When it was announced that Darren Wilson would not be indicted for the killing of Michael Brown, I kept thinking of Abner Louima, whose assault took place when Michael Brown was just eighteen months old. Abner and I have known each other for years. Both our families have attended the same Creole-speaking church for decades, so I called him to hear his thoughts about Michael Brown's killer going free. If anyone could understand all those broken hearts, all the rage, all the desperation, the yearning for justice, what it is to be a member of a seemingly marooned and persecuted group, I thought, he would.

Abner Louima, unlike Michael Brown, had survived. He went on with his life, moved from New York City to south Florida, started businesses. He has a daughter and two sons. One son was eighteen years old when we spoke, the same age Michael Brown was when he died.

How does he feel, I asked him, each time he hears that yet another black person was killed or nearly killed by police?

"It reminds me that our lives mean nothing," he replied.

We are in America because our lives meant nothing to those in power in the countries where we came from. Yet we come here to realize that our lives also mean nothing here. Some of us try to distance ourselves from this reality, thinking that because we are another type of "other"—immigrants, migrants, refugees—this is not our problem, nor one we can solve. But ultimately we realize the precarithe wooden handle of a toilet plunger or a broom inside a precinct bathroom. After Abner, there was Amadou Diallo, a Guinean immigrant, who was hit by nineteen of the forty-one bullets aimed at him as he retrieved his wallet from his pocket. Then there was Patrick Dorismond, the U.S.-born child of Haitian immigrants, who died trying to convince undercover cops that he was not a drug dealer.

These are only a few among the cases from my era that made the news. There was also sixty-six-year-old Eleanor Bumpurs, who, thirteen years before Abner's assault, was killed by police with a twelve-gauge shotgun inside her own apartment. I have no doubt there were many others. We marched for all of them in the Louima/Diallo/Dorismond decade. We carried signs and chanted "No Justice! No Peace!" and "Whose Streets? Our Streets!" even while fearing the latter would never be true. The streets belonged to the people with the uniforms and the guns. The streets were never ours. Our sons and brothers, fathers and uncles, our mothers and sisters, daughters and nieces, our neighbors were, and still are, prey.

My father, a Brooklyn cab driver, used to half joke that police did not beat him up because, at sixty-five years old, he was too skinny and too old, and not worth the effort. Every now and then, when he was randomly stopped by a police officer and deigned to ask why, rather than a beating, he would be given a handful of unwarranted traffic citations that would wipe out a few weeks' hard-earned wages. Today, one might generously refer to such acts as micro-aggressions. That is, until they turn major and deadly, until and early '80s, the violence was overtly political. Government detractors were dragged out of their homes, imprisoned, beaten, or killed. Sometimes their bodies were left out in the streets, in the hot sun, for extended periods, to intimidate neighbors.

In New York, the violence seemed a bit more subtle, though no less pervasive. When I started riding the city bus to high school, I observed that a muffled radio message from an annoyed bus driver—about someone talking too loud or not having the right fare—was all it took to make the police rush in, drag a young man off the bus, and beat him into submission on the sidewalk. There were no cell phone cameras back then to record such abuse, and most of us were too terrified to demand a badge number.

Besides, many of us had fled our countries as exiles, migrants, and refugees just to escape this kind of military or police aggression; we knew how deadly a confrontation with an armed and uniformed authoritarian figure could be. Still, every now and then a fellow traveler would summon his or her courage and, dodging the swaying baton, or screaming from a distance, would yell some variation of "Stop it! This is a child! A child!"

Of course, not all of the police's victims were children. Abner Louima, a family friend, was thirty years old when he was mistaken for someone who had punched a police officer outside a Brooklyn nightclub, on August 9, 1997, sixteen years to the day before Michael Brown was killed. Abner was arrested, beaten with fists, as well as with police radios, flashlights, and nightsticks, and then sexually assaulted with migrated from the rural south to urban centers in the northern United States for more than half a century during the Great Migration were often referred to as refugees, as were those people internally displaced by Hurricane Katrina.

Having now visited many refugee and displacement camps, the label "refugee" at first seemed an extreme designation to assign to citizens of one of the richest countries in the world, especially if it is assigned on a singular basis to those who are black. Still, compared to the relative wealth of the rest of the society, a particularly run-down Brooklyn public housing project where a childhood friend used to live had all the earmarks of a refugee camp. It occupied one of the least desirable parts of town and provided only the most basic necessities. A nearby dilapidated school, where I attended junior high, could have easily been on the edge of that refugee settlement, where the primary daily task was to keep the children occupied, rather than engaged and learning. Aside from a few overly devoted teachers, we were often on our own. We, immigrant blacks and African Americans alike, were treated by those who housed us, and were in charge of schooling us, as though we were members of a group in transit. The message we always heard from those who were meant to protect us: that we should either die or go somewhere else. This is the experience of a refugee.

I have seen state abuses up close, both in Haiti, where I was born under a ruthless dictatorship, and in New York, where I migrated to a working-class and predominantly African, African American, and Caribbean neighborhood in Brooklyn at the age of twelve. In the Haiti of the 1970s consideration by the priest and nuns who were giving out the only food available to the camp dwellers, but the food would always run out before they could get to everyone.

A few days after leaving Haiti and returning to the United States, I read a Michael Brown anniversary opinion piece in *The Washington Post* written by Raha Jorjani, an immigration attorney and law professor. In her essay, Jorjani argues that African Americans living in the United States could easily qualify as refugees. Citing many recent cases of police brutality and killings of unarmed black men, women, and children, she wrote:

> Suppose a client walked into my office and told me that police officers in his country had choked a man to death over a petty crime. Suppose he said police fatally shot another man in the back as he ran away. That they arrested a woman during a traffic stop and placed her in jail, where she died three days later. That a 12-year-old boy in his country was shot and killed by the police as he played in the park.
>
> Suppose he told me that all of those victims were from the same ethnic community—a community whose members fear being harmed, tortured or killed by police or prison guards. And that this is true in cities and towns across his nation. At that point, as an immigration lawyer, I'd tell him he had a strong claim for asylum protection under U.S. law.

This is not the first time that the idea of African Americans as internal or external refugees has been floated or applied. The six-million-plus African Americans who

Message to My Daughters

EDWIDGE DANTICAT

Soon after the one-year anniversary of the fatal shooting of Michael Brown by the Ferguson police officer Darren Wilson, I was in Haiti, at the southernmost end of the country's border with the Dominican Republic, where hundreds of Haitian refugees had either been deported or driven out of the Dominican Republic by intimidation or threats. Many of these men and women had very little warning that they were going to be picked up or chased away and most of them had fled with nothing but the clothes on their backs.

It was a bright sunny day, but the air was thick with dust. As some friends and I walked through the makeshift resettlement camps on the Haitian side of the border, in a place called Pak Kado, it felt as though we, along with the residents of the camps, were floating through clouds. Around us were lean-tos made of cardboard boxes and sheets. Dust-covered children walked around looking dazed even while playing with pebbles that stood in for marbles, or while flying plastic bags as kites. Elderly people stood on the edge of food and clothes distribution lines, some too weak to wade into the crowd. Later the elderly, along with pregnant women and the disabled, would be given special *despair*, you told me weeks later when I said I didn't know how to write this essay. And in that I saw a miracle: your own journey, your own revolution, unraveling beside me and mine and also separate, a whole country and sea away. You chose hope, and the night is quiet and I write while you sleep—and this moment with all its weight and responsibility, this turning point in the world and our lives, is ours, and these words are for you.

—D

nals, and late-night phone calls. The revolution wasn't televised—there we saw only burning cars and concerned pundits—but it was live-tweeted. And while my own revolution took place on the page and in the streets, yours was a much more personal one, profound and earthshaking in its own, very different, way. I watched you stand at the crossroads of despair, Nastassian. Watched fear wash over you, and uncertainty. As that ache detonated again and again, I know the temptation to shut down entirely loomed large. We arrived at Manley Airport in Kingston to return to New York, checked our bags and emptied our pockets into the plastic bins, took off shoes and belts and were patted down and X-rayed and then whisked up an escalator to the waiting area. Kingston was a distant smattering of lights across the bay and home seemed a long way off for both of us. Sandra Bland's face stared out from the television as broadcasters wondered through their phony cheer about her last moments on earth, languishing in that Texas jail cell. International travel is a closed circuit—once you're in flight, there's no turning back and then you're vomited directly into the hands of U.S. immigration officials, passport control, customs, sniffing dogs, and the forever fallout of 9/11. And even if you have nothing to hide, and we had nothing to hide, it feels like the cold machinery of the state closing around your neck. I thought about all the times I'd been "randomly" searched and quelled my own anxiety and turned to you, wondering if you would be freaking out, but you met me with a smile.

Tell them how their mother landed on hope amidst all the

media and the long-pent-up feeling that no social movement in recent memory has done anything but tiptoe toward justice. You can't tiptoe toward justice. You can't walk up to the door all polite and knock once or twice, hoping someone's home. Justice is a door that, when closed, must be kicked in. "No state," Baldwin wrote, "has been able to foresee or prevent the day when their most ruined and abject accomplice—or most expensively dressed prostitute—will growl, 'This far and no further.'" And maybe that day is more like a series of days, the whole year of protest that erupted between now and then, a culminating mass of days and nights, bodies laying down in intersections, symphony halls, strip malls, superhighways across this country, stopping traffic and business-as-usual, declaring by their very presence: "No further," and again, "No further."

I texted you updates as we marched: "Still safe and things are mostly calm. We've taken Columbus Circle. Helicopters overhead but cops can't seem to keep up with us or figure out where we're going next." They couldn't figure out where we were going next because we had no idea where we'd go next. We spun in an impossible, unruly snake through Midtown, spilled out into the streets and then the bridges and throughways. One night we shut down the Manhattan Bridge and pushed deep into Crown Heights, an army of flashing blue lights at our backs. With no coordination, no grant dictating our steps or signs, no leader, we marched in lockstep with hundreds of thousands of protestors across the United States and then the globe, and the simple, resonating demand that black lives matter nization, that a successful armed struggle proceeds to out-administer the adversary and not out-fight him." Ahmed is concerned with victory, which is to say, survival.

It's been a year since Officer Darren Wilson shot Michael Brown dead in the streets of Ferguson. (I was in an airport that day, too, waiting for a flight to Cuba and watching Twitter explode with tweets from the scene of the murder. You texted me then and many times since, that you weren't so sure about coming to a country that could do this to its people, a country that went out of its way to destroy black life.) It's been a year of politicians stumbling to declare that all lives matter and reinstill the illusion of justice to the justice system. It's been a year in which police took more than three hundred black lives as protestors shut down bridges and highways across the country to remind the world that those lives matter.

I spent my twenties with a healthy distrust of the word *revolution*. When I was a kid, it was ancient American history or what *Star Wars* characters did—something heroic and distant. But I'm the son of a survivor of how wrong revolutions can go, the nephew of a revolutionary turned counterrevolutionary turned political prisoner. And these days, you're more likely to see *revolution* on a car ad than anywhere meaningful. Words mean things, we say again and again, but overuse and abuse can wear those meanings down, render them pale parodies of what they once were. And revolution, it seemed, had long since lost its meaning.

The Ferguson uprising changed that. The movement for black lives spread from city to city, spurned on by social

This Far: Notes on Love and Revolution

DANIEL JOSÉ OLDER

August 2015

Dear Nastassian:

You told me to write this essay to our future children, but I'm writing to you instead. You said to tell them about how their mom worried, how she wasn't sure if it was a good idea bringing black life into a world that doesn't value it, but that she landed on hope amidst all the despair. *Tell them*, you said, *about why their father does the work he does, what kind of world you hope to help build for them.*

And I will, love, I will. But this moment right now—the night is quiet and I write while you sleep—this moment with all its weight and responsibility, this turning point in the world and our lives, is ours, and these words are for you.

Three weeks ago we rode through the midnight streets of Kingston, Jamaica, past shacks and gas stations, jerk chicken cookouts and quicky motels, to the airport and this new life together. Our Twitter feeds and the national news were filled with updates on Sandra Bland, the latest black life destroyed while in police custody, the most recent name to become a hashtag. Every time her deathlike mugshot flashed across the screen I felt an ache detonate in me. It's an ache many of us have become intimate with over the past year, as the hard work of protesters brings light to each new state-sanctioned murder. It recedes and then returns, compounded by the tragedy of how familiar it feels to mourn a stranger.

In college, I scribbled a quote from Eqbal Ahmad in the back of my notebook: ". . . this out-administration occurs when you identify the primary contradiction of your adversary and expose that contradiction . . . to the world at large." Ahmad wrote those words in reference to global struggles against empire, and trapped as I was just then, and probably always will be, in some wordy labyrinth between the future and past, the sentence settled somewhere in my brain and caught fire.

In a way, these words infer the same conclusion as the other quotes I'd copied around it: that art is a creator and a destroyer and no less a player in the great stage of the world than politics or violence. "It is in the nexus of representation, words, and space," Michel Foucault wrote, "that the destiny of peoples is silently formed." Or the Syrian poet Nizar Qabbani: "Our deliverance is in drawing with words."

But Mr. Ahmad dispenses with the formality of arguing the power of representation, and jumps directly into strategy. Unlike so many of the texts we read in college, this passage is not concerned with making people comfortable or rehashing basic truths that are deemed controversial only because they agitate overprotected egos. "I argued that armed struggle," Eqbal Ahmad writes at the beginning of that paragraph, "is less about arms and more about orgawas a collective howl, it echoed through the streets and out across the world: "This far and no further."

It's that hunger that I was trying to understand back in college when I jotted that quote down. It felt like tracing along the clues of a murder mystery: something was wrong. I couldn't identify the crime, but I was aware of it, inside of me and in the whole world around me, and both were deeply connected. That's why Eqbal Ahmad's idea about primary contradiction tattooed itself on my brain. I knew from very early on that I was an artist, that art was my own form of medicine, both for myself and the world: a tool that could create or destroy. And I knew I profited from the crime—as a straight cis man, a Latino who isn't black, a citizen of this great disastrous nation. And I knew I suffered from this crime with no name, too, that it robbed everyone in its grasp of humanity and self, made us tools and killers and liars and suicides. There were so many myths to unravel, even just within my own heart, my own head, but mythology was something I could understand. There were myths that were lies and myths made from truth, and often the falsest ones were the most plausible and the truest filled with dragons and gods. Every journey is a crisis, a turning point, a shedding of myths, and mine began with the gnawing certainty that something did not add up. And in a way, this journey never ends, but in another sense, it ends where all great roads lead: to the discovery of voice.

This year, the desperate hunger born from so much mourning found its collective voice. It happened in the streets, but it also happened across the Internet, in jourlaid bare the twin lies of American equality and exception-alism. Even on the left, even in this age of exposed racial rifts, politicians still say with a straight face that this coun-try was founded on principles of equality. Words mean things, we say again and again, but actions mean much more, and still as a nation, we worship the very slave own-ers who gave legal precedence to the notion of percentages of human beings. We scream *equality* and *freedom* while unabashedly modeling our actions on the fathers of geno-cide. The only way to rationalize this most American of contradictions is to devalue the lives of the slaughtered, as was done then, so it must be now, and so apologists remind us that those were the times, and they didn't know bet-ter, and on and on. But if those lives matter now then they mattered then, and the clapback stretches through history, unraveling all the creation myths this country has always held most sacred, toppling our many false idols and clean-ing out our profaned temples.

There was a terrible hunger revealed in that ongoing funeral procession. So many showed up because so many must mourn, the trauma of bearing witness etched across the streets of America. And collective mourning became collective resistance, and the hunger born from so much witnessing and so little action over the years was the hunger to rebel. Revolution has sounded, as Tracy Chapman once sang, like a whisper. I heard it in my own writing on equal-ity in publishing, demanding more than just reform, more than just diversity. Heard it in my friends and loved ones' quiet ferocity as we talked into the night. But suddenly it

what you must carry—tome of memory,
its random blank pages. On the dock

where you board the boat for Ship Island
someone will take your picture:

the photograph—who you were—
will be waiting when you return.

Theories of Time and Space

NATASHA TRETHEWEY

You can get there from here, though
there's no going home.

Everywhere you go will be somewhere
you've never been. Try this:

head south on Mississippi 49, one-
by-one mile markers ticking off

another minute of your life. Follow this
to its natural conclusion—dead end

at the coast, the pier at Gulfport where
rigging of shrimp boats are loose stitches

in a sky threatening rain. Cross over
the man-made beach, twenty-six miles of sand

dumped on the mangrove swamp—buried
terrain of the past. Bring only

PART III

JUBILEE

my granddad came home early from work and spotted me sitting on that park bench with a girl whose name I couldn't name now if you paid me, but whose face I will never forget. By sitting I mean that I was leaned into her ear whispering the sweet nothings I hoped would lead to her knickknacks. She and I had not been in the house, though, so I was miffed when my granddad stopped his Buick in the alley and furied over to us. "Hey, Dad, this is—" and before I could finish, he barked, "What did I tell you?! What did I tell you about this?!" and slapped the sound of a firework out of my cheek. He breathed over me for a moment or two and stomped back to his idling ride and meandered it into the garage. The girl's mouth was agape when I got up the courage to look at her. You should go, I said. She shook her head yes. You should go now, I said, and she rose and headed up the alley. She and I never spoke another word to each other after that day. These years later, I realize it was a testament to how much I love my granddad that it never dawned on me to curse him under my breath or consider running away like I damn sure would've if instead it was my DNA dad who'd struck me. Pretty sure I never snuck another girl into the basement either—which spells mission accomplished for Sam Jackson, Jr., excuse me, mission accomplished for Dad.

philosophy, and ethics. If you're looking for the lasting influence of TJ's composite, you need look no further than the ideals and language of the most important document in American history. The list of presidents who built composites also includes Gerald Ford (GF)—he was born Leslie King, Jr.—whose mother, Dorothy, divorced his biological father, Leslie King, Sr., on the grounds of "extreme cruelty" when her son was five months old. GF's biological father was the son of the millionaire businessman Charles Henry King, but that didn't stop him from bolting out of state (so much for broke pockets being the impetus for a deadbeat dad) and, as rumor had it, colluding with his father to skirt alimony and child-support judgments. Lucky for baby GF that Dorothy met Gerald Ford, Sr., a couple of years later. Ford Sr. wasn't no slouch. He became a successful businessman, was a church vestryman, a Mason, and later a local politician. He married Dorothy, adopted her young son, christened him a junior, and was, in GF's words, "kind, fair, and firm." Ford Sr. and Dorothy, who had three more boys together, didn't mention to GF that Ford Sr. was not his biological father. GF didn't find that out until his biological father showed up at his high school job. But years and years later, in a letter GF dictated from the Oval Office, you can see how that visit did little to change his mind about his beloved composite: "I loved and was guided in life by the only father I ever had—Gerald R. Ford Sr. There was never any longing on my part to seek family outside of the one in which I was raised with such love, tenderness, and happiness."

4. When my cousin-brother Jesse's mother was murdered, he went to live with my great-grandparents for a time, but when he hit the first grade, he moved in with my granddad and lived with him until he became a legal adult. My granddad parenting Jesse is yet another hashmark in the ledger of why he deserves my love, respect, and admiration.

5. The backstory: this occurred after I'd been caught on occasion with naked to half-naked girls in my basement bedroom. The scene: my granddad's house sits beside an alley, and there's a park bench at the opening of the alley. The action: this particular day

title of Most Controversial of all presidential composites: a liber-
tine, ex-journalist, poet, and Communist associate named Frank
Marshall Davis, a man who became especially infamous during
BO's first campaign when conspiracy theorists claimed Davis was
his biological father. The truth, though, as confirmed by BO in
his memoir, is that Davis helped shape his views on racial identity, race relations, and social justice. Davis was a part of BO's life
but for a handful of years, but I'm calling him a composite for
his impact. For example, though this next point may be a stretch
(then again, so was a black man being elected the leader of the
free world), remnants of Davis's radical thought can be found in
the socialist-leaning legislation that is Obama Care. From the last
to the first. George Washington (GW) lost his father, Augustine
(Augustine's people called him Gus), when he was eleven. From
that point, GW's older half-brother Lawrence Washington became
his surrogate father. Answer me this: What would America look
like if GW hadn't followed Lawrence into the military and politics (Lawrence fought in the War of Jenkins Ear and was later
elected to Virginia's House of Burgesses)? Lawrence christened
the Mount Vernon estate (or should we call it a plantation?), and
GW paid homage to his beloved older brother when it was in his
sole possession by hanging only his portrait in his study. GW and
BO are notable for being the first and last, but the list between
them includes Thomas Jefferson (TJ), who lost his father at thirteen and found a mentor in the philosophy professor William
Small when he entered William and Mary College a few years later.
Smith fostered in TJ a great appreciation for diverse disciplines
and also a love of Enlightenment thinkers. He also introduced TJ
to the politician and law professor George Wythe—the man who
became TJ's unofficial political and cultural mentor—as much a
composite as any man was for the future president. How amazing
it must've been for an ambitious young TJ to sit around a sup-
per table discussing politics and culture with Small, Wythe, and
a governor. How fortunate TJ was to have been given the chance
to later study law (there were no law schools in colonial America)
with Wythe, and have that apprenticeship that included history,

love is not dictated by law or blood, that being a constant presence is as much a part of being a man as almost anything else, that what I want must be earned, that I can win and win I will, that there's hustle in my genes, that either I swim or drown and there is no one more important to that outcome than me.

Now here I am the father of two children, trying my all-out damnedest to mind the lessons of my beloved composite, all the while feeling encouraged by the fact I know they're rooting for me to best the job they did.

Thank. You. Pops.

• • •

1. Praise be to the gender politicians. By male and female I mean cisgendered male and female—the Latin prefix *cis* means "on the same side"—i.e., men and women whose gender identity is aligned with the gender they were assigned by birth.

2. For my DNA dad's sake, I must note that the absoluteness of his early absence is a point of dispute.

3. Obama (BO) is the latest exemplar—a total of twelve were either abandoned or lost their biological fathers when they were young—of a president whose life confirms how efficacious it is to compose a composite. It's damn near folklore now, how Barack Hussein Obama, Sr., had bounced on his wife and BO by the time he was a toddler, how his mother spent time in Seattle, remarried in Hawaii, took young BO to live with her new husband in Indonesia, but sent him back to the Aloha State to live with her parents around the time he entered the fifth grade. One of BO's composites thereafter, if nothing else for the fact that he assumed the role of his long-term primary caretaker until he went off to college, was his maternal grandfather Stanley Dunham (no shade to Stanley's wife's role in co-parenting her grandson). Stanley was also the one who introduced BO to the man who just might own the

Mitch Jackson was not about to get his MJ-esque dew wet nor—the extent of my swimming skills at the time was a hella-weak doggy paddle—was I about to risk my life. But my biological father flexed contrary designs by creeping up behind me and scooping me in the air and tossing me in the pool. He didn't flinch while I flailed and screamed and gulped mouthfuls of overchlorinated water. He said something to me that I can't remember but that my subconscious must've heard because soon I calmed and got my curly head above the surface, and stayed in the pool and had a damn good day frolicking with my father, brother, and sisters— aka the Johnsons. The message of that day took years to reveal itself to me: "Troubled water or not, you best learn to swim. 'Cause when your young-ass get to drowning, I may not be moved to rescue." That message, by the way, I now count as an act of stern beneficence.

Not one of the men I mentioned has existed in my life beyond the reach of critique. Oh yes, I comprehend flaws. But their foibles weren't the crux of what I used to build. I must say, too, that they were much more than mentors. Mentors teach you a skill. Fathers teach you to live. Your mentor's role can remain static. Your father's role must evolve. A mentor's direction might be free of deep feeling. A father's guidance must be rooted in love.

Who I am now is who I must be: a flawed human striving to live in a state of becoming. Along the way I've discovered a thing or more about myself: that who and how I for him. Because he knew that no matter what we did, we would need to learn how to hustle—to reimagine paths to success—that hustling was vital to young black boys, that without it we were destined to be failed black men. Though I never made hundreds of thousands nor had the misfortune of being the local drug kingpin, Uncle Henry's lecture and legacy helped convince me that I had hustle in my blood, and please believe me when I tell you, I've been a hustler ever since.

WESLEY

Ten—that's how old I was when I met my biological father. One of my most significant memories of him occurred not too long after when his wife, oldest son, two daughters, and I road-tripped to visit Disneyland, Sea World, and a few Californian family members. One of those relatives lived in an apartment complex with a pool—a pool! We all changed into swimming gear and headed out to the pool, where my dad and my brother and sisters began having a grand old time swimming and playing in the water and goading me to get in while I gallivanted *around* the pool and at most teased my foot in the shallow end once or twice. My trepidation was for good reason as this was circa '85, arguably the height of a certain highwater-pants and rhinestone-glove-wearing pop star, and I had a Jheri curl befitting a kid who claimed to certain credulous classmates that I was a not-so-distant cousin. Or let me put it like this: young uncle Henry titled, "Superman in Solitary: Oregon's Biggest Dope Dealer Tells All." The story details Uncle Henry's 1970s to mid-'80s evolution from car thief and pimp to drug kingpin. The article was straight-up inspiration, though, full disclosure, I didn't know Uncle Henry at all during the days of him hustling enough funds to buy a plane and Rolls-Royce. In fact, we spent almost no time together until right after I graduated high school, which was the summer I decided that being a devoted part-time dope dealer was the best present way for me to make a living. Keep in mind, this was decades past Uncle Henry's gilded heyday, well into the age of him being a shyster and ardent addict, and though I knew about his fall, I was beguiled by the lore, was hungry to profit from secrets I was sure he owned. So one day my older brother—a fellow neophyte dope dealer—and me tracked down Uncle Henry at the apartment of another uncle and pressed him for what in effect was a session of Drug Dealing 101. Uncle Henry, ever the capitalist, obliged us a lesson for a few shards of our dope. Can't recall everything he said, but one point will stick with me till I'm dust: "The fast nickel beats the slow twenty." My uncle went on to explain that while we waited forever for a twenty sale, we could've sold umpteen fives, which meant to me that what I dreamed of would not arrive in a windfall but would accrue one small sale at a time. It's easy to make the case that Uncle Henry was undermining my brother and me, but the way I see it, his advice had less to do with corrupting our youth or sabotaging our gleaming futures, and more to do with the munificence of exposing us to a maxim that had grand effect

BIG CHRIS

Far as I knew growing up my biological father was a ghost by the time I was born. By the time I was a year old, my mother had been heart-throbbed by a man named Big Chris. Big Chris was a recent parolee—bank robbery, what a dreamer!—and a neophyte/soon-to-be-prosperous pimp, but also a smart, witty, compassionate man whose jokes could give you stomachaches. My mother had two boys by Big Chris and stayed with him until just before I reached double digits. For years after he left, he would swing through trying to rekindle his and my mother's faded love or else connect with his boys, and without a doubt, whether Big Chris and my mom were an official couple or not, I was one of those boys. The man never treated me one bit different from the sons of his seed. The naysayers can knock how he hustled his bread and meat, but that don't change the fact that Big Chris was the one who showed me the value and impact of a father's love, that family often had nothing to do with genetics. This was a lesson he taught me in life and in death.

In September 2009, I got a call from Big Chris's daughter—my oldest sister—saying that he was sick and that I should fly out to Phoenix to see him. In the span of a few days, she went from prodding me to make it out soon, to imploring me to come ASAP if I wanted to see him alive. The next day I was on a flight, bracing for the worst and praying against it. My flight landed heartstroke hours later and while passengers were grabbing their bags, I turned on my cell phone to a fusillade of texts: from my mother, from my brothers, from my sister—all warning me Big Chris had died. My big sister picked me up from the airport, and tried to console me with Dad's near-to-last words: "I've got to hold on. I've got to hold on so I can see Mitch." The story didn't console me in the moment, but later, much later, when the grief begrudged me room to breathe, Dad's near-to-last words confirmed for me the bond that we'd shared, reaffirmed that I would forever be one of his boys, that our kinship was deeper than DNA.

SAM

My maternal grandfather, Sam Jackson, Jr., rose every day for thirty-plus years to go to the same job. He attends church every Sunday—and arrives on time all the time. He pays his bills and his tithes. He represents at neighborhood rallies and community meetings. He bought and has lived in the same house since the '70s, lived there with his wife until she died, lives there with a new wife now. Granddad or Dad, as I call him, rescued us—my mom and her boys—countless times with funds because the electric company put an apartment of ours on eclipse or the rent had somehow vamoosed out of my mom's purse. Granddad moved me into his house for my last two years of high school, this after I ran away from my biological father's house, after I'd made it clear to all concerned adults that I couldn't be trusted under the charge of my half-paralyzed great-grandmother. Me, Granddad, and my cousin-brother Jesse ate breakfast together in his kitchen damn near every weekday.[4] Granddad sat in the bleachers at my home and away high school hoop games and kept full stats. He chided me to mow the lawn and take out the trash and repaid me by spotting me the bucks I needed to hang with my homeboys on Friday nights. He never once bemoaned being my caretaker, as I imagined he had a right to, not even after he had to slap spit from me for the class-A house crime of sneaking girls into my basement bedroom.[5] Granddad has modeled what it means to be a stand-up dude, what it means to honor your commitments, what it means to shoulder your obligations and your burdens without gripe.

ANTHONY (ANT)

My maternal uncle Ant wore some version of a Jheri curl well past the great epoch of Jheri curls. Furthermore, Ant's held on to his almost-a-high-school-All-American story for generations, a legend I've heard told so often at family dinners, that sometimes I go ahead and tell it myself. Let Ant or me tell it, the judges clocked him at 9.7, 9.6, and 9.5 in the 100-yard sprint at a district track meet, but if they had given him an official time of 9.5 instead of 9.6, he "would've been an All-American that year."

Ant's story is a tendon to what happened to me in sixth grade, the only year I ever competed on a track team. That year, I'd taken second place in the district meet to a rival who had been putting a whooping on me all season. Ant attended that meet and was disappointed right along with me. He could've let me play a defeatist, but instead he took it upon himself to train me for the city championship, swooping me afternoons after school and teaching me to run on my toes and lean forward and lengthen my stride, drilling into my porous brain the idea that I could beat anyone as long as I used good form and believed. The championships rolled around a couple of weeks later and sure enough I was lined up against my rival in the 100-meter final. Pow! We took off and by midway through the race I was losing in slo-mo and heard my heart scream no, no, nooooooooooooo. Then by some kind of Prefontaine magic I heard Ant screaming, "REACH, nephew! REACH!" above all other voices, and reach I did on the way to winning the race with a slight cushion. You should have seen Ant afterward, rejoicing as if, at once, I'd won Olympic gold and salved his All-American wound. Thanks to Ant, I had my first taste of being a champion in public, of realizing that with assiduousness and self-confidence, my impossible was possible. For sure he was a father that day, one who'd pushed me to succeed where he'd failed, to be bolder, bigger, stronger, best.

HENRY

Somewhere in my random collection of family archives is a hubris-building copy of a news feature on my paternal being a male that I hope I have helped my son navigate in a way that only I could.[1]

This is my beating heart: boys need fathers.

Boys need fathers—period, exclamation point.

And if a boy is not blessed with a father or gifted with a dynamic stand-in then he must find ways to make one. He must identify the father*ish* men in his life, find what he needs from them, and compose one.

It is an act of necessity, and I should know. My mother was not far along into her nineteenth year when she had me by a man who lived no more than a bike ride away but was absent for my first decade of life.[2] To say I had no father, though, is a half-truth. To say my mother was my father would be a sentimental-ass lie. I had a father, and I had one because I made one. Or rather I composed a father from the men at hand, brothers who kept me long before Obama made it a project.[3]

There was my mother's long-term boyfriend Big Chris, my maternal grandfather Sam, my maternal uncle Anthony, my paternal uncle Henry, and at long last my biological father, Wesley. If you asked me to spell *father*, I could turn their names into one long-ass portmanteau.

Or I might just say "p-o-p-s."

Pops was a group of men who provided a loving example of what it would soon enough mean to be a man. Pops nurtured me. Bestowed me with his wisdom. Pushed me to nuance the way I saw the world. He inspired me to dream. He tended my harms. He made sure I knew it was in me to surpass him.

Composite Pops

MITCHELL S. JACKSON

How does a fatherless boy spell *father*?

One answer is in the video of a poet who monologues about a dream in which he's a child contestant in a spelling bee. For the win, he has to spell the word *father*. He proceeds to spell the word *m-o-t-h-e-r*. Then when the spellmaster says he's "incorrect," he launches into a rant about absentee fathers and womanizing men and maternal strength . . .

While plenty mothers in the world deserve the most huge hurrahs, what I want to say to this poet and other like minds is this: no matter how much we lambast men and high-note praise women, a woman maketh a father not.

Yes, ours is indeed a revolutionary era of gender fluidness and sexual equality and girls doubtless need dads too—I repeat: girls need their dads. No way no how no day would I try to diminish or worse negate the role of a dad in his daughter's life. No one, and that includes humans, saints, and extraterrestrials, could convince me that my princess's life would be better off without me in it. However, just as there are some aspects of being a female that my daughter's mother is more equipped to guide her through, there are aspects of

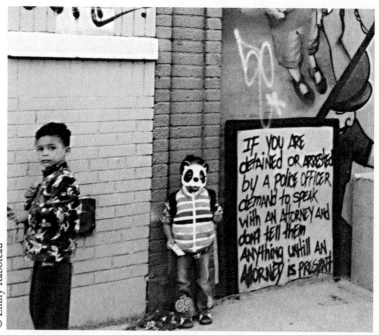

© Emily Raboteau

moving in circles and so I stopped to take stock of my pictures, scrolling backward. Though the style of each mural was distinct, the message was the same. Somebody loves you enough to try to keep you safe by informing you of your rights. The murals' insistence on those rights, which the citizens of our nation don't yet equally enjoy, reminded me that like the High Bridge, the Constitution is just another lofty infrastructure in need of rehabilitation. Such changes do occur, it seems. Were it not for the fact that I shot them in different locales, I felt I could craft a zoetrope of the passersby to show my children. The many walkers would appear unified as one—even if at times that walker was a woman or a man, or black, or brown, or old or young— advancing toward one steady goal. "Look how marvelous," I would say of the moving image. And if my children asked me where the walker was going, I would answer, "To the bridge."

rored the person in the mural who films a plainclothes police officer cuffing a man over the hood of a car. I had to wait over an hour to get this shot because a belligerent drunk pissing on the sidewalk refused to get out of the frame. Finally, he zipped up and drifted off beneath the Bruckner Expressway. Of all the neighborhoods I traversed, Hunts Point felt the roughest. On the long walk to the Point from the elevated 2 train through the red light district, I was surveyed with interest. I felt that if I wasn't mindful, someone down on his luck might succeed in snatching my phone. Yet I stayed planted by the mural, looking for something concrete.

The phone in the Hunts Point mural is almost as tall as the woman walking beneath it, its screen the approximate size of her handbag. In the screenshot we see repeated the nested image of the plainclothes police officer cuffing a man over the hood of the car. The dizzying effect of the mural is to put the viewer in the perspective of the photographer.

I have fallen into the mural or rather the mural has sucked me in. I am the third dimension; the watcher. I am the photographer with the phone in her hand. So, potentially, is the passerby, though in this context her posture is also a reminder that passivity has its cost. The woman is about to step out of my frame. For now she is caught, as in a web, by the shadows of power lines and trees. The text behind her echoes that of the first mural I shot on the streets of Washington Heights: "If you are detained or arrested by a police officer, demand to speak with an attorney and don't say anything until the attorney is present."

It was as if the text were on a loop. I'd begun to feel I was

© Emily Raboteau

Artist: Dasic Fernández. *Know Your Rights,* Hunts Point, Bronx, Barretto Street and Garrison Avenue, 2012. "You have the right to watch & film police activities." "If you are detained or arrested by a police officer, demand to speak with an attorney and don't say anything until attorney is present."

verdict in Los Angeles, and the Freddie Gray verdict in Baltimore, and the Michael Brown verdict in Ferguson, which reverberated across the country like so many waves of heat.

In New York, I remember the Ferguson protesters took to the streets chanting, "Whose streets? Our streets!" I myself was drawn to the vortex of 125th Street, where I shot pictures of the crowd swarming toward the Triborough Bridge. I paused there at the edge of my own reason sometime before midnight to return to my children, but the mob pushed on as far as the tollbooths on the Manhattan side, succeeding in shutting the bridge down. It felt so logical an impulse, to act unruly in the face of misrule. Yet this impulse is what the Bed-Stuy mural admonishes against.

Radio Raheem's fist is the focal point of the mural, adorned with its gold "LOVE" knuckleplate. The mural, dominated by the color red, cautions the viewer to "Stay calm and in control. Don't get into an argument . . . Don't resist, even if you believe you're innocent."

The man I photograph walking past the love punch wears paint-splattered work boots, a headcloth over his dreadlocks, and earphones. I wonder what he's listening to. Perhaps because he's distracted by his music, he's unaware that I've shot him with my phone.

So was the woman in the Bronx, where I took my sixth and final picture. She was too absorbed by the screen of her device to notice me, though if she looked my way, she would have seen that I too was operating my phone. My posture mir-

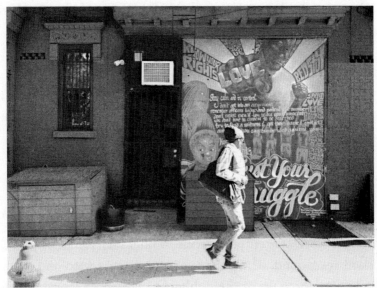

Artist: Trust Your Struggle (collective), *Trust Your Struggle,* Bedford Stuyvesant, Brooklyn, Marcus Garvey Boulevard and Macdonough Street, 2010. "Justice or Just Us." "LOVE/HATE." "Stay calm and in control. Don't get into an argument. Remember officer's badge and patrol car number. Don't resist, even if you believe you're innocent. You don't have to consent to be searched. Try to find a witness & get their name & contact. Anything you say can be used against you. Know Your Rights. Trust Your Struggle. Spread love. It's the Brooklyn way. Didn't pass the bar, but know a little bit; enough that you won't illegally search N.Y."

said, emphatically. "He's a jerk." We smiled at each other. She returned to her dispute and I went on my way.

"If you are HARASSED by police . . ." the Long Island City mural advises, ". . . take PICTURES of any INJURIES." Again, the mural is a backdrop to walking but this time, because it consists entirely of text, the message is even starker. A woman is about to cross the street. I don't know where she's going, or what she's looking at. She may be checking for oncoming traffic or reading the warning on the mural. Her braids swing across her back as her sneaker approaches the curb. My friend the writer Garnette Cadogan has said, "Walking is among the most dignified of human activities." But here, the woman's simple dignified act of walking, whether home from work or school, or to the bodega for a carton of milk, is erupted by the somber memo that hangs in the background. The public space feels contested and even traumatic because of the public art. The intersection looks hazardous, like something is about to hit her.

The fifth mural I shot was in Bedford-Stuyvesant, the swiftly gentrifying Brooklyn neighborhood made famous by Spike Lee's landmark film *Do the Right Thing*. In fact, the Bed-Stuy mural directly references that movie by depicting the character Radio Raheem. At the start of the movie, Radio Raheem blasts Public Enemy's "Fight the Power" from his boombox like a reveille. Near the movie's end, he's choked to death by a nightstick-wielding cop—a pivotal plot point that incites a riot, much like the uprisings that followed the Rodney King

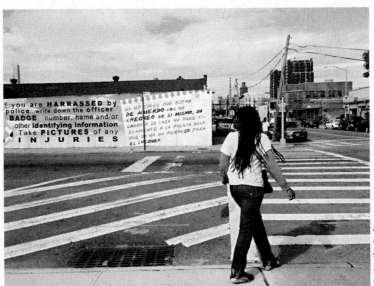

Artist: Dasic Fernández. *Know Your Rights,* Long Island City, Queens, Thirty-fifth Avenue and Twelfth Street, 2012. "If you are HARRASSED by police, write down the officer BADGE number, name and/or other identifying information. Take PICTURES of any INJURIES." "Ud no tiene que estar de aquerdo con un chequeo de si mismo, su carro o su casa. No pare físicamente a la policía. Diga que ud. no da permiso para el chequeo."

iPhone like mine for her thirteenth birthday. After peram-
bulating for a half an hour we finally located the mural in an
overgrown lot behind a chain-link fence. We'd had so many
false sightings at that point that I sensed it was part of the
girl's mental, rather than physical, landscape. It rose out of
the weeds in pastel shades like an enormous Easter egg. "I
love this one," she confessed. "It's so *big*."

As with the murals in Washington Heights and Harlem, the
text of the Bushwick mural exhorts the viewer to watch and
film police activities. This time the message is underscored by
a figure in the foreground who points to her enormous eye as
if to say, "Watch out. Keep your eyes open." A man directly
behind her uses his phone to film a police officer making an
arrest in the mural's background. The phone is configured as
a weapon for social change. The teenager that I photograph
walking past the mural is also on the phone. Though she
appears oblivious to the mural, she also appears, in the context
of my photo, to be wielding a tool. That is, the phone distracts
her from being present but she could also deploy its camera at
any moment to record what's happening on the street.

The fourth mural that I shot was painted on a corrugated fence
in Long Island City, Queens, across from the Ravenswood
housing projects. On my way through the projects I passed
a barefoot lady in a church hat pushing a stroller full of cans.
She was involved in a heated argument over a Metrocard
with a man invisible to me. In the middle of an invective she
stopped to tell me he was a lying thief. "I believe you," I

© Emily Raboteau

Artist: Dasic Fernández. *Know Your Rights*, Bushwick, Brook-lyn, Irving Avenue and Gates Avenue, 2011. "If you are harassed by police, write down the officer's badge number, name, and/or other identifying information. Get medical attention if you need it and take pictures of any injuries." "All students have the right to attend school in a safe, secure, non-threatening and respectful learning environment in which they are free from harassment." "No tenant can be evicted from their apartment without being taken to housing court." "Si ud. es detenido o arrestado por un policía, pida hablar con un abogado immediatamente. No diga nada hasta que tiene un abogado presente." "Owners are required by law to keep their buildings safe, well maintained and in good repair. If not, call 911."

unarmed black man shot forty-one times by police, and the assault of Abner Louima, who was sodomized by police with a broom handle in 1997, allegedly told to "Take that, nigger!" Liem said, "Our original goal was to highlight the systemic nature of police violence in communities of color. We've taken a proactive approach to empowerment that includes organizing neighborhood-based Cop Watch teams and outreach that uses public art as a means of education. It's about shifting culture and creating hope."

Maybe that's what I was scavenging for. Hope. I like how Emily Dickinson defined it—"the thing with feathers."

The third mural that I shot was in Bushwick, Brooklyn. I had difficulty finding it, in part because Bushwick is a neighborhood of murals but also because Liem had given me bum directions. I lost myself in the rainbow spectacle of street art. There was Nelson Mandela on a wall overlooking the parking lot of a White Castle, but where was the mural I sought? I asked a group of kids in Catholic school uniforms if they knew where I could find it. They all claimed to know the Know Your Rights mural, but none could give me an exact address. Either it was somewhere down Knickerbocker Avenue or else it was located in the opposite direction past three or four schoolyards and a car wash. In the end, one girl kindly volunteered to walk me there. She wore a purple backpack, braces on her teeth, and a gold name necklace that said coincidentally (or not) "Esperanza." Esperanza told me with excitement that she'd be getting an

Stop-and-frisk policing was implemented in New York as part of an increased trend of enforcement that began in response to rising crime and the crack cocaine epidemic of the 1980s and '90s. The technique disproportionately affects young men of color. (From 2004 through 2012, African Americans and Hispanics were subject to nearly 90 percent of the 4.4 million stop-and-frisk actions despite constituting only about half of the city's population.) In black and Latino neighborhoods like Harlem and Washington Heights, residents often view the police, a force ostensibly there to protect them, with mistrust and fear. In 2013, the year the Harlem mural was made, a federal court judged the use of stop-and-frisk tactics to be excessive and unconstitutional. Since then, their use has declined. Critics of reducing the practice predicted a rise in crime. Instead, overall crime has dropped. I would like to believe these statistics mean it's growing slightly safer for my children to walk.

Yul-san Liem, who works for one of the activist organizations that makes up People's Justice, explained to me that the murals were financed by the Center for Constitutional Rights. "Visual art communicates differently than the written or spoken word," she commented. "By creating Know Your Rights murals, we seek to bring important information directly to the streets where it is needed the most, and in a way that is memorable and visually striking."

People's Justice formed in 2007 in the wake of the NYPD killing of the unarmed black man Sean Bell the day before his wedding. "It wasn't an isolated incident," Liem lamented, recalling the 1999 killing of Amadou Diallo, the

© Emily Raboteau

Lead Artist: Sophia Dawson. *Know Your Rights,* Harlem, Upper Manhattan, 138th Street and Adam Clayton Powell Jr. Boulevard, 2013. "Write down the officer's badge #, name, and/or other identifying info." "Get medical attention if needed and take pictures of injuries." "You don't have to answer any questions from police. When they approach, say, 'Am I being detained, or am I free to go?' If they detain you, stay silent + demand a lawyer. A frisk is only a pat down. If police try to do more than that say loudly, 'I do not consent to this search.'" "You have the right to observe, photograph, record, and film police activity."

cruelty of the world. It was also a salve, to reclaim physical and psychic space. I wondered who had done it.

After some Internet sleuthing I discovered the painter was a Chilean artist who goes by the tag name Cekis, and that this mural was the first of several public artworks commissioned by a coalition of grassroots organizations called People's Justice for Community Control and Police Accountability. The other Know Your Rights murals were spread out across four of New York City's five boroughs (excluding Staten Island, where a great number of cops live) in poor neighborhoods most plagued by police misconduct. For the rest of that summer and into the fall, I photographed as many of them as I could, like a magpie collecting bright things for her nest.

The second mural I shot was in central Harlem.

As with the mural in Washington Heights, I chose to capture a passerby in the frame, to give a sense of scale but with the intent to preserve the subject's anonymity. Thrown against a sharp white background, the man in Harlem appears in silhouette, his beard like Thelonious Monk's, his shadow extending from his feet, and the shadow of the fire escape above him slanting down against the mural like the bars of a cage. A woman depicted in the mural's foreground holds a bullhorn to her mouth. A portion of the text reads, "Write down the officer's badge number, name, and/or other identifying info. You don't have to answer any questions from police." Her advice is specifically targeted to those at risk of being stopped and frisked.

I passed every weekday morning on the walk to the children's day care. A vision of tropical blues, it splashed out from the gritty gray surroundings, creating an illusion of depth. My eyes drank it in.

This mural operates like a comic strip in panels marrying image and text. In the first panel, a youngster is carded by a law enforcement official. In the second, a goateed man in a baseball cap is being handcuffed. In the third, a group of citizens stare evenly outward. One of them wears a look of disgust, and a T-shirt that says, "4th Amendment," a sly allusion to the part of our constitution that protects us against unreasonable search and seizure without probable cause. Another holds his cell phone aloft to record what is happening on the street. "You have the right to film and observe police activity," the mural states in Spanish, appropriate for a neighborhood where Spanish is the dominant language and where young men of color are regularly stopped and frisked by the police. In the lower left-hand corner the Miranda rights are paraphrased in English.

My first instinct was to take a picture of the mural so that I could carry it with me in my pocket. I was grateful for it, not only as a thing of beauty on the gallery of the street, but also as a kind of answer to the question that had been troubling us—how to inform our children about the harassment they might face. The mural struck me as an act of love for the people who would pass it by. I understood why it had been made, and why it had been made here in the hood next to a Laundromat as opposed to on Fifth Avenue next to Henri Bendel, Tiffany's, or Saks. It was armor against the

Artist: Nelson Rivas, aka Cekis. Washington Heights, Upper Manhattan, Wadsworth Avenue and 174th Street, 2009. "If you are detained or arrested by a police officer, demand to speak with an attorney and don't tell them anything until an attorney is present." "Ud. no tiene que estar de acuerdo con un chequeo de si mismo, su carro o su casa. No trate físicamente de parar la policía. Solo diga que ud. no da permiso para el chequeo. Tienes el derecho de no aceptarlo." "Ud. tiene el derecho de observar y filmar actividades policiales."

entrance to the bridge to make sure we appreciated the marvel of its rehabilitation. He was something of a history buff and spoke in a European accent—Greek, I think. He could recall when the bridge was shut down after falling into long decline, and the time before that when miscreants and vandals tossed projectiles over the guardrail into the polluted water below or at the traffic on the Harlem River Drive. Thanks to him, I know that the bridge was a feat of engineering originally modeled after a Roman aqueduct, siphoning water from Westchester County through pipes beneath its walkway into the city, enabling New Yorkers to enjoy their first indoor plumbing (including the flush toilet). The old man never thought he'd live to see the day when the High Bridge was back in business, and was proud that the citizen-led campaign to reopen it had succeeded. "This bridge changed everything," the old man said in wonderment, as if the relic was a truer paean to empire than the skyscrapers twinkling in the skyline far to the south of us— the Chrysler Building, the former Citicorp Center, and the spire of the Empire State. Dutifully, we paraded across to the Bronx. Maybe it was because I so admired the old man's perspective, attuned as it was to a less conspicuous wonder of the world, that on our return trip home I noticed a mural I could have sworn had not been there before.

"KNOW YOUR RIGHTS!" the mural trumpeted in capital letters. How had it escaped my attention? The artwork covered a brick wall abutting the twenty-four-hour Laundromat details and take notes," as well as, "Enjoy yourselves!" on their way out the door.

But for now, I carried our sweaty girl down 173rd Street on my back while my husband led our stubborn son by the hand. You know the thermometer's popping in Washington Heights when there aren't any Dominicans out on the sidewalks playing dominoes. Nobody had yet cranked open the fire hydrants. The heat knocked out the girl as if it were a club. The boy was in a rotten mood. He demanded a drink then rejected the water we'd packed. He whined that the walk was too long, then challenged our authority in a dozen other hectoring ways until we at last arrived at Highbridge Park. There he refused to descend the hundred stairs to the bridge by flinging himself onto the asphalt with his arms and legs bent in the style of a swastika, not five feet from a dead rat. The kid's defiance bothered us for all the usual reasons a parent should find it irksome, but also because if allowed to incubate in the ghetto where we live, that defiance could get him killed.

Our son was soon coaxed down the vertiginous stairs by the magical horn of an Amtrak train on the railway beneath the bridge. He has explained to me his fierce attraction to trains and boats and vehicles in general with irritation that I didn't already know the answer: "They take you somewhere else." That's just it. From the time your children begin walking, they are moving away from you. This is as it should be, even when you can't protect them from harm with anything but the inadequate outerwear of your love.

A sweet old man in seersucker shorts stopped us at the

shoot!" "White silence is violence," and most poignant to me as a mother, "Is my son next?"

"It's too *hot* and my legs are too small," our son protested on the way to the bridge.

The boy was right—it was hot and getting hotter. He was tall for four but still so little. When standing at our front door, his nose just cleared the height of the doorknob. He was the same size as the pair of boys depicted in a two-panel cartoon by Ben Sargent circulating widely on my Facebook feed that summer. Both panels depict a little boy at the threshold, on the verge of stepping outdoors. The drawings are nearly identical except that the first boy is white and the second, black. "I'm goin' out, Mom!" each boy calls to a mother outside of the frame. The white boy's mother simply replies, "Put on your jacket." But the other mother's instructions comprise so intricate, leery, and vexed a warning that her words obstruct the exit: "Put on your jacket, keep your hands in sight at all times, don't make any sudden moves, keep your mouth shut around police, don't run, don't wear a hoodie, don't give them an excuse to hurt you . . ." and so on until the text in her speech bubble blurs, as in a painting by Glenn Ligon. The cartoon is titled, "Still Two Americas."

I didn't wish to be her, the mother who needed to say, "Some people will read you as black and therefore X." Why should I be the fearful mother? Nor did I covet the white mother's casual regard. I wanted to be the mother who got to say to her children, "Keep your eyes open for interesting precisely, should be said? The boy was four then. The girl, just two.

The day was hot. En route to the bridge we felt no reprieve from the sun, just as we'd felt no relief from the pileup of bad news about blacks being murdered with impunity. When we learned of the terror at AME Emanuel in Charleston, we had not yet recovered from the unlawful death of Freddie Gray in Baltimore, nor the shooting of Mike Brown in Ferguson, nor the chokehold death of Eric Garner in Staten Island, nor the shooting of Trayvon Martin in Florida, nor the shooting of Tamir Rice in Cleveland, to name but a few triggers of civil unrest. We weren't surprised there were no indictments in these cases, sadly enough, but we were righteously indignant. The deaths seemed to be cascading in rapid succession, each one tripping a live wire, like the feet of Muybridge's galloping horse.

The picture we were getting, and not because it was growing worse, but because our technology now exposed it, was clear and mounting evidence of discriminatory systems that don't treat or protect our citizens equally, and escalating dissent was giving rise to a movement that insists what should be evident to everyone: Black Lives Matter. There were hashtag alerts for pop-up protests in malls, die-ins on roads, and other staged acts of civil disobedience such as disruptions of white people eating their brunch. Protesters against police brutality dusted off some slogans from the civil rights era, such as "No justice—no peace!" but others were au courant: "I can't breathe," "Hands up, don't

Know Your Rights!

EMILY RABOTEAU

On the Saturday after the Charleston church massacre wherein nine worshippers at one of the nation's oldest black churches were slaughtered during Bible study by a white gunman hoping to ignite a race war, we dragged our kids to the east side to walk them over New York City's oldest standing bridge. It seemed as good a way as any to kill a weekend afternoon. The High Bridge, which was built with much fanfare in the mid nineteenth century as part of the Croton Aqueduct system and as a promenade connecting Upper Manhattan to the Bronx over the Harlem River, had recently—and somewhat miraculously—reopened after forty-odd years of disuse. I say "miraculously" because the bridge was an infrastructure most of us had come to accept as blighted, even as some civic groups had coalesced to resurrect it. In the back of our minds that summer of 2015, as an uprising and its violent suppression raged in Missouri, was the problem of when and how to talk to our children about protecting themselves from the police.

At what age is such a conversation appropriate? By what age is it critical? How could it not be despairing? And what,

or young, man, woman, or child. There exists no equivalent reality for white Americans. We can distance ourselves from this fact until the next horrific killing, but we won't be able to outrun it. History's authority over us is not broken by maintaining a silence about its continued effects.

A sustained state of national mourning for black lives is called for in order to point to the undeniability of their devaluation. The hope is that recognition will break a momentum that laws haven't altered. Susie Jackson; Sharonda Coleman-Singleton; DePayne Middleton-Doctor; Ethel Lee Lance; the Rev. Daniel Lee Simmons, Sr.; the Rev. Clementa C. Pinckney; Cynthia Hurd; Tywanza Sanders; and Myra Thompson were murdered because they were black. It's extraordinary how ordinary our grief sits inside this fact. One friend said, "I am so afraid, every day." Her son's childhood feels impossible, because he will have to be—has to be—so much more careful. Our mourning, this mourning, is in time with our lives. There is no life outside of our reality here. Is this something that can be seen and known by parents of white children? This is the question that nags me. National mourning, as advocated by Black Lives Matter, is a mode of intervention and interruption that might itself be assimilated into the category of public annoyance. This is altogether possible; but also possible is the recognition that it's a lack of feeling for another that is our problem. Grief, then, for these deceased others might align some of us, for the first time, with the living.

after his death. Everyone could see what the police would have to explain away. The justice system wasn't able to do it, and a judge found probable cause to charge the officer who shot Rice with murder, while a grand jury declined to indict any of the officers involved. Meanwhile, for Samaria Rice, her unburied son's memory made her neighborhood unbearable.

Regardless of the wishes of these mothers—mothers of men like Brown, John Crawford III, or Eric Garner, and also mothers of women and girls like Rekia Boyd and Aiyana Stanley-Jones, each of whom was killed by the police—their children's deaths will remain within the public discourse. For those who believe the same behavior that got them killed if exhibited by a white man or boy would not have ended his life, the subsequent failure to indict or convict the police officers involved in these various cases requires that public mourning continue and remain present indefinitely. "I want to see a cop shoot a white unarmed teenager in the back," Toni Morrison said in April. She went on to say: "I want to see a white man convicted for raping a black woman. Then when you ask me, 'Is it over?' I will say yes." Morrison is right to suggest that this action would signal change, but the real change needs to be a rerouting of interior belief. It's an individual challenge that needs to happen before any action by a political justice system would signify true societal change.

The Charleston murders alerted us to the reality that a system so steeped in anti-black racism means that on any given day it can be open season on any black person—old him. This loss of control and authority might explain why after Brown's death, McSpadden was supposedly in the precarious position of accosting vendors selling T-shirts that demanded justice for Michael Brown that used her son's name. Not only were the procedures around her son's corpse out of her hands; his name had been commoditized and assimilated into our modes of capitalism.

Some of McSpadden's neighbors in Ferguson also wanted to create distance between themselves and the public life of Brown's death. They did not need a constant reminder of the ways black bodies don't matter to law enforcement officers in their neighborhood. By the request of the community, the original makeshift memorial — with flowers, pictures, notes, and teddy bears — was finally removed by Brown's father on what would have been his birthday and replaced by an official plaque installed on the sidewalk next to where Brown died. The permanent reminder can be engaged or stepped over, depending on the pedestrian's desires.

In order to be away from the site of the murder of her son, Tamir Rice, Samaria moved out of her Cleveland home and into a homeless shelter. (Her family eventually relocated her.) "The whole world has seen the same video like I've seen," she said about Tamir's being shot by a police officer. The video, which was played and replayed in the media, documented the two seconds it took the police to arrive and shoot; the two seconds that marked the end of her son's life and that became a document to be examined by everyone. It's possible this shared scrutiny explains why the police held his twelve-year-old body for six months refusal to move Michael Brown's body, perhaps unknowingly continued where Till's mother left off.

After Brown was shot six times, twice in the head, his body was left facedown in the street by the police officers. Whatever their reasoning, by not moving Brown's corpse for four hours after his shooting, the police made mourning his death part of what it meant to take in the details of his story. No one could consider the facts of Michael Brown's interaction with the Ferguson police officer Darren Wilson without also thinking of the bullet-riddled body bleeding on the asphalt. It would be a mistake to presume that everyone who saw the image mourned Brown, but once exposed to it, a person had to decide whether his dead black body mattered enough to be mourned. (Another option, of course, is that it becomes a spectacle for white pornography: the dead body as an object that satisfies an illicit desire. Perhaps this is where Dylann Storm Roof stepped in.)

Black Lives Matter, the movement founded by the activists Alicia Garza, Patrisse Cullors, and Opal Tometi, began with the premise that the incommensurable experience of systemic racism creates an unequal playing field. The American imagination has never been able to fully recover from its white-supremacist beginnings. Consequently, our laws and attitudes have been straining against the devaluation of the black body. Despite good intentions, the associations of blackness with inarticulate, bestial criminality persist beneath the appearance of white civility. This assumption both frames and determines our individual interactions and experiences as citizens.

The American tendency to normalize situations by centralizing whiteness was consciously or unconsciously demonstrated again when certain whites, like the president of Smith College, sought to alter the language of "Black Lives Matter" to "All Lives Matter." What on its surface was intended to be interpreted as a humanist move—"aren't we all just people here?"—didn't take into account a system inured to black corpses in our public spaces. When the judge in the Charleston bond hearing for Dylann Storm Roof called for support of Roof's family, it was also a subtle shift away from valuing the black body in our time of deep despair.

Anti-black racism is in the culture. It's in our laws, in our advertisements, in our friendships, in our segregated cities, in our schools, in our Congress, in our scientific experiments, in our language, on the Internet, in our bodies no matter our race, in our communities, and, perhaps most devastatingly, in our justice system. The unarmed, slain black bodies in public spaces turn grief into our everyday feeling that something is wrong everywhere and all the time, even if locally things appear normal. Having coffee, walking the dog, reading the paper, taking the elevator to the office, dropping the kids off at school: All of this good life is surrounded by the ambient feeling that at any given moment, a black person is being killed in the street or in his home by the armed hatred of a fellow American.

The Black Lives Matter movement can be read as an attempt to keep mourning an open dynamic in our culture because black lives exist in a state of precariousness. Mourning then bears both the vulnerability inherent in black lives and the instability regarding a future for those lives. Unlike earlier black-power movements that tried to fight or segregate for self-preservation, Black Lives Matter aligns with the dead, continues the mourning, and refuses the forgetting in front of all of us. If the Rev. Martin Luther King, Jr.'s civil rights movement made demands that altered the course of American lives and backed up those demands with the willingness to give up your life in service of your civil rights, with Black Lives Matter, a more internalized change is being asked for: recognition.

The truth, as I see it, is that if black men and women, black boys and girls, mattered, if we were seen as living, we would not be dying simply because whites don't like us. Our deaths inside a system of racism existed before we were born. The legacy of black bodies as property and subsequently three-fifths human continues to pollute the white imagination. To inhabit our citizenry fully, we have to not only understand this, but also grasp it. In the words of the playwright Lorraine Hansberry, "The problem is we have to find some way with these dialogues to show and to encourage the white liberal to stop being a liberal and become an American radical." And, as my friend the critic and poet Fred Moten has written: "I believe in the world and want to be in it. I want to be in it all the way to the end of it because I believe in another world and I want to be in that." This other world, that world, would presumably be one where black living matters. But we can't get there without fully recognizing what is here.

Dylann Storm Roof's unmediated hatred of black people; Black Lives Matter; citizens' videotaping the killings of blacks; the Ferguson Police Department leaving Brown's body in the street—all these actions support Mamie Till Mobley's belief that we need to see or hear the truth. We need the truth of how the bodies died to interrupt the course of normal life. But if keeping the dead at the forefront of our consciousness is crucial for our body politic, what of the families of the dead? How must it feel to a family member for the deceased to be more important as evidence than as an individual to be buried and laid to rest?

Michael Brown's mother, Lesley McSpadden, was kept away from her son's body because it was evidence. She was denied the rights of a mother, a sad fact reminiscent of pre–Civil War times, when as a slave she would have had no legal claim to her offspring. McSpadden learned of her new identity as a mother of a dead son from bystanders: "There were some girls down there had recorded the whole thing," she told reporters. One girl, she said, "showed me a picture on her phone. She said, 'Isn't that your son?' I just bawled even harder. Just to see that, my son lying there lifeless, for no apparent reason." Circling the perimeter around her son's body, McSpadden tried to disperse the crowd: "All I want them to do is pick up my baby."

McSpadden, unlike Mamie Till Mobley, seemed to have little desire to expose her son's corpse to the media. Her son was not an orphan body for everyone to look upon. She wanted him covered and removed from sight. He belonged to her, her baby. After Brown's corpse was finally taken away, two weeks passed before his family was able to see open coffin and allowed photographs to be taken and published of her dead son's disfigured body.

Mobley's refusal to keep private grief private allowed a body that meant nothing to the criminal-justice system to stand as evidence. By placing both herself and her son's corpse in positions of refusal relative to the etiquette of grief, she "disidentified" with the tradition of the lynched figure left out in public view as a warning to the black community, thereby using the lynching tradition against itself. The spectacle of the black body, in her hands, publicized the injustice mapped onto her son's corpse. "Let the people see what I see," she said, adding, "I believe that the whole United States is mourning with me."

It's very unlikely that her belief in a national mourning was fully realized, but her desire to make mourning enter our day-to-day world was a new kind of logic. In refusing to look away from the flesh of our domestic murders, by insisting we look with her upon the dead, she reframed mourning as a method of acknowledgment that helped energize the civil rights movement in the 1950s and '60s.

The decision not to release photos of the crime scene in Charleston, perhaps out of deference to the families of the dead, doesn't forestall our mourning. But in doing so, the bodies that demonstrate all too tragically that "black skin is not a weapon" (as one protest poster read last year) are turned into an abstraction. It's one thing to imagine nine black bodies bleeding out on a church floor, and another thing to see it. The lack of visual evidence remains in contrast to what we saw in Ferguson, where the police, in their himself from nothing. He has grown up with the rhetoric and orientation of racism. He has seen white men like Benjamin F. Haskell, Thomas Gleason, and Michael Jacques plead guilty to, or be convicted of, burning Macedonia Church of God in Christ in Springfield, Massachusetts, just hours after President Obama was elected. Every racist statement he has made he could have heard all his life. He, along with the rest of us, has been living with slain black bodies.

We live in a country where Americans assimilate corpses in their daily comings and goings. Dead blacks are a part of normal life here. Dying in ship hulls, tossed into the Atlantic, hanging from trees, beaten, shot in churches, gunned down by the police, or warehoused in prisons: Historically, there is no quotidian without the enslaved, chained, or dead black body to gaze upon or to hear about or to position a self against. When blacks become overwhelmed by our culture's disorder and protest (ultimately to our own detriment, because protest gives the police justification to militarize, as they did in Ferguson), the wrongheaded question that is asked is, What kind of savages are we? Rather than, What kind of country do we live in?

In 1955, when Emmett Till's mutilated and bloated body was recovered from the Tallahatchie River and placed for burial in a nailed-shut pine box, his mother, Mamie Till Mobley, demanded his body be transported from Mississippi, where Till had been visiting relatives, to his home in Chicago. Once the Chicago funeral home received the body, she made a decision that would create a new pathway for how to think about a lynched body. She requested an to feel temporarily bad about black suffering, there really is no mode of empathy that can replicate the daily strain of knowing that as a black person you can be killed for simply being black: no hands in your pockets, no playing music, no sudden movements, no driving your car, no walking at night, no walking in the day, no turning onto this street, no entering this building, no standing your ground, no standing here, no standing there, no talking back, no playing with toy guns, no living while black.

Eleven days after I was born, on September 15, 1963, four black girls were killed in the bombing of the 16th Street Baptist Church in Birmingham, Alabama. Now, fifty-two years later, six black women and three black men have been shot to death while at a Bible-study meeting at the historic Emanuel African Methodist Episcopal Church in Charleston, South Carolina. They were killed by a homegrown terrorist, self-identified as a white supremacist, who might also be a "disturbed young man" (as various news outlets have described him). It has been reported that a black woman and her five-year-old granddaughter survived the shooting by playing dead. They are two of the three survivors of the attack. The white family of the suspect says that for them this is a difficult time. This is indisputable. But for African American families, this living in a state of mourning and fear remains commonplace.

The spectacle of the shooting suggests an event out of time, as if the killing of black people with white-supremacist justification interrupts anything other than regular television programming. But Dylann Storm Roof did not create

The Condition of Black Life
Is One of Mourning

CLAUDIA RANKINE

A friend recently told me that when she gave birth to her son, before naming him, before even nursing him, her first thought was, I have to get him out of this country. We both laughed. Perhaps our black humor had to do with understanding that getting out was neither an option nor the real desire. This is it, our life. Here we work, hold citizenship, pensions, health insurance, family, friends, and on and on. She couldn't, she didn't leave. Years after his birth, whenever her son steps out of their home, her status as the mother of a living human being remains as precarious as ever. Added to the natural fears of every parent facing the randomness of life is this other knowledge of the ways in which institutional racism works in our country. Ours was the laughter of vulnerability, fear, recognition, and an absurd stuckness.

I asked another friend what it's like being the mother of a black son. "The condition of black life is one of mourning," she said bluntly. For her, mourning lived in real time inside her and her son's reality: At any moment she might lose her reason for living. Though the white liberal imagination likes fear—without others' fear—wherever we choose. I've lived in New York City for almost a decade and have not stopped walking its fascinating streets. And I have not stopped longing to find the solace that I found as a kid on the streets of Kingston. Much as coming to know New York City's streets has made it closer to home to me, the city also withholds itself from me via those very streets. I walk them, alternately invisible and too prominent. So I walk caught between memory and forgetting, between memory and forgiveness.

and hoped to join. Instead of meandering aimlessly in the footsteps of Whitman, Melville, Kazin, and Vivian Gornick, more often I felt that I was tiptoeing in Baldwin's—the Baldwin who wrote, way back in 1960, "Rare, indeed, is the Harlem citizen, from the most circumspect church member to the most shiftless adolescent, who does not have a long tale to tell of police incompetence, injustice, or brutality. I myself have witnessed and endured it more than once." Walking as a black man has made me feel simultaneously more removed from the city, in my awareness that I am perceived as suspect, and more closely connected to it, in the full attentiveness demanded by my vigilance. It has made me walk more purposefully in the city, becoming part of its flow, rather than observing, standing apart.

But it also means that I'm still trying to arrive in a city that isn't quite mine. One definition of home is that it's somewhere we can most be ourselves. And when are we more ourselves but when walking, that natural state in which we repeat one of the first actions we learned? Walking—the simple, monotonous act of placing one foot before the other to prevent falling—turns out not to be so simple if you're black. Walking alone has been anything but monotonous for me; monotony is a luxury.

A foot leaves, a foot lands, and our longing gives it momentum from rest to rest. We long to look, to think, to talk, to get away. But more than anything else, we long to be free. We want the freedom and pleasure of walking without gation and socialization—every city has its own. It was the arbitrariness of the circumstances that required them, an arbitrariness that made me feel like a child again, that infantilized me. When we first learn to walk, the world around us threatens to crash into us. Every step is risky. We train ourselves to walk without crashing by being attentive to our movements, and extra-attentive to the world around us. As adults we walk without thinking, really. But as a black adult I am often returned to that moment in childhood when I'm just learning to walk. I am once again on high alert, vigilant.

Some days, when I am fed up with being considered a troublemaker upon sight, I joke that the last time a cop was happy to see a black male walking was when that male was a baby taking his first steps. On many walks, I ask white friends to accompany me, just to avoid being treated like a threat. Walks in New York City, that is; in New Orleans, a white woman in my company sometimes attracted more hostility. (And it is not lost on me that my woman friends are those who best understand my plight; they have developed their own vigilance in an environment where they are constantly treated as targets of sexual attention.) Much of my walking is as my friend Rebecca once described it: A pantomime undertaken to avoid the choreography of criminality.

Walking while black restricts the experience of walking, renders inaccessible the classic Romantic experience of walking alone. It forces me to be in constant relationship with others, unable to join the New York flaneurs I had read about fellow detainee. Deference to the police, then, was sine qua non for a safe encounter.

The cops ignored my explanations and my suggestions and continued to snarl at me. All except one of them, a captain. He put his hand on my back, and said to no one in particular, "If he was running for a long time he would have been sweating." He then instructed that the cuffs be removed. He told me that a black man had stabbed someone earlier two or three blocks away and they were searching for him. I noted that I had no blood on me and had told his fellow officers where I'd been and how to check my alibi—unaware that it was even an alibi, as no one had told me why I was being held, and of course, I hadn't dared ask. From what I'd seen, anything beyond passivity would be interpreted as aggression.

The police captain said I could go. None of the cops who detained me thought an apology was necessary. Like the thug who punched me in the East Village, they seemed to think it was my own fault for running.

Humiliated, I tried not to make eye contact with the onlookers on the sidewalk, and I was reluctant to pass them to be on my way. The captain, maybe noticing my shame, offered to give me a ride to the subway station. When he dropped me off and I thanked him for his help, he said, "It's because you were polite that we let you go. If you were acting up it would have been different."

I realized that what I least liked about walking in New York City wasn't merely having to learn new rules of navime. "Against the car!" In no time, half a dozen cops were upon me, chucking me against the car and tightly handcuffing me. "Why were you running?" "Where are you going?" "Where are you coming from?" "I said, why were you running?!" Since I couldn't answer everyone at once, I decided to respond first to the one who looked most likely to hit me. I was surrounded by a swarm and tried to focus on just one without inadvertently aggravating the others.

It didn't work. As I answered that one, the others got frustrated that I wasn't answering them fast enough and barked at me. One of them, digging through my already-emptied pockets, asked if I had any weapons, the question more an accusation. Another badgered me about where I was coming from, as if on the fifteenth round I'd decide to tell him the truth he imagined. Though I kept saying—calmly, of course, which meant trying to manage a tone that ignored my racing heart and their spittle-filled shouts in my face— that I had just left friends two blocks down the road, who were yes, sir, yes, officer, of course, officer, all still there and could vouch for me, to meet other friends whose text messages on my phone could verify that, it made no difference.

For a black man, to assert your dignity before the police was to risk assault. In fact, the dignity of black people meant less to them, which was why I always felt safer being stopped in front of white witnesses than black witnesses. The cops had less regard for the witness and entreaties of black onlookers, whereas the concern of white witnesses usually registered on them. A black witness asking a question or politely raising an objection could quickly become a me for an old enemy, but found out soon enough that he'd merely assumed I was a criminal because of my race. When he discovered I wasn't what he imagined, he went on to tell me that his assault was my own fault for running up behind him. I blew off this incident as an aberration, but the mutual distrust between me and the police was impossible to ignore. It felt elemental. They'd enter a subway platform; I'd notice them. (And I'd notice all the other black men registering their presence as well, while just about everyone else remained oblivious to them.) They'd glare. I'd get nervous and glance. They'd observe me steadily. I'd get uneasy. I'd observe them back, worrying that I looked suspicious. Their suspicions would increase. We'd continue the silent, uneasy dialogue until the subway arrived and separated us at last.

I returned to the old rules I'd set for myself in New Orleans, with elaboration. No running, especially at night; no sudden movements; no hoodies; no objects—especially shiny ones—in hand; no waiting for friends on street corners, lest I be mistaken for a drug dealer; no standing near a corner on the cell phone (same reason). As comfort set in, inevitably I began to break some of those rules, until a night encounter sent me zealously back to them, having learned that anything less than vigilance was carelessness.

After a sumptuous Italian dinner and drinks with friends, I was jogging to the subway at Columbus Circle—I was running late to meet another set of friends at a concert downtown. I heard someone shouting and I looked up to see a police officer approaching with his gun trained on buildings, stylish residents, and buzzing streets. Onward into Washington Heights, the sidewalks spilled over with an ebullient mix of young and old Jewish and Dominican American residents, past leafy Inwood, with parks whose grades rose to reveal beautiful views of the Hudson River, up to my home in Kingsbridge in the Bronx, with its rows of brick bungalows and apartment buildings nearby Broadway's bustling sidewalks and the peaceful expanse of Van Cortlandt Park. I went to Jackson Heights in Queens to take in people socializing around garden courtyards in Urdu, Korean, Spanish, Russian, and Hindi. And when I wanted a taste of home, I headed to Brooklyn, in Crown Heights, for Jamaican food and music and humor mixed in with the flavor of New York City. The city was my playground.

I explored the city with friends, and then with a woman I'd begun dating. She walked around endlessly with me, taking in New York City's many pleasures. Coffee shops open until predawn; verdant parks with nooks aplenty; food and music from across the globe; quirky neighborhoods with quirkier residents. My impressions of the city took shape during my walks with her.

As with the relationship, those first few months of urban exploration were all romance. The city was beguiling, exhilarating, vibrant. But it wasn't long before reality reminded me I wasn't invulnerable, especially when I walked alone.

One night in the East Village, I was running to dinner when a white man in front of me turned and punched me in the chest with such force that I thought my ribs had braided around my spine. I assumed he was drunk or had mistaken as soon as it opened for reoccupancy, but my adoptive aunt, Maxine, who hated the idea of me returning to a hurricane zone before the end of hurricane season, persuaded me to come to stay in New York City instead. (To strengthen her case she sent me an article about Texans who were buying up guns because they were afraid of the influx of black people from New Orleans.)

This wasn't a hard sell: I wanted to be in a place where I could travel by foot and, more crucially, continue to reap the solace of walking at night. And I was eager to follow in the steps of the essayists, poets, and novelists who'd wandered that great city before me—Walt Whitman, Herman Melville, Alfred Kazin, Elizabeth Hardwick. I had visited the city before, but each trip had felt like a tour in a sports car. I welcomed the chance to stroll. I wanted to walk alongside Whitman's ghost and "descend to the pavements, merge with the crowd, and gaze with them." So I left Kingston, the popular Jamaican farewell echoing in my mind: "Walk good!" *Be safe on your journey,* in other words, *and all the best in your endeavors.*

I arrived in New York City, ready to lose myself in Whitman's "Manhattan crowds, with their turbulent musical chorus." I marveled at what Jane Jacobs praised as "the ballet of the good city sidewalk" in her old neighborhood, the West Village. I walked up past midtown skyscrapers, releasing their energy as lively people onto the streets, and on into the Upper West Side, with its regal Beaux Arts apartment his suspicion. "No one waves to the police," he explained. When I told friends of his response, it was my behavior, not his, that they saw as absurd. "Now why would you do a dumb thing like that?" said one. "You know better than to make nice with police."

A few days after I left on a visit to Kingston, Hurricane Katrina slashed and pummeled New Orleans. I'd gone not because of the storm but because my adoptive grandmother, Pearl, was dying of cancer. I hadn't wandered those streets in eight years, since my last visit, and I returned to them now mostly at night, the time I found best for thinking, praying, crying. I walked to feel less alienated—from myself, struggling with the pain of seeing my grandmother terminally ill; from my home in New Orleans, underwater and seemingly abandoned; from my home country, which now, precisely because of its childhood familiarity, felt foreign to me. I was surprised by how familiar those streets felt. Here was the corner where the fragrance of jerk chicken greeted me, along with the warm tenor and peace-and-love message of Half Pint's "Greetings," broadcast from a small but powerful speaker to at least a half-mile radius. It was as if I had walked into 1986, down to the soundtrack. And there was the wall of the neighborhood shop, adorned with the Rastafarian colors red, gold, and green along with images of local and international heroes Bob Marley, Marcus Garvey, and Haile Selassie. The crew of boys leaning against it and joshing each other were recognizable; different faces, similar stories. I was astonished at how safe the streets felt to me, once again one black body among many, no longer having to anticipate the many ways my presence might instill fear and how to offer some reassuring body language. Passing police cars were once again merely passing police cars. Jamaican police could be pretty brutal, but they didn't notice me the way American police did. I could be invisible in Jamaica in a way I can't be invisible in the United States.

Walking had returned to me a greater set of possibilities. And why walk, if not to create a new set of possibilities? Following serendipity, I added new routes to the mental maps I had made from constant walking in that city from childhood to young adulthood, traced variations on the old pathways. Serendipity, a mentor once told me, is a secular way of speaking of grace; it's unearned favor. Seen theologically, then, walking is an act of faith. Walking is, after all, interrupted falling. We see, we listen, we speak, and we trust that each step we take won't be our last, but will lead us into a richer understanding of the self and the world.

In Jamaica, I felt once again as if the only identity that mattered was my own, not the constricted one that others had constructed for me. I strolled into my better self. I said, along with Kierkegaard, "I have walked myself into my best thoughts."

When I tried to return to New Orleans from Jamaica a month later, there were no flights. I thought about flying to Texas so I could make my way back to my neighborhood sweater. Khaki pants. Chukkas. Sweatshirt or T-shirt with my university insignia. When I walked I regularly had my identity challenged, but I also found ways to assert it. (So I'd dress Ivy League style, but would, later on, add my Jamaican pedigree by wearing Clarks Desert Boots, the footwear of choice of Jamaican street culture.) Yet the all-American sartorial choice of white T-shirt and jeans, which many police officers see as the uniform of black troublemakers, was off-limits to me—at least, if I wanted to have the freedom of movement I desired.

In this city of exuberant streets, walking became a complex and often oppressive negotiation. I would see a white woman walking toward me at night and cross the street to reassure her that she was safe. I would forget something at home but not immediately turn around if someone was behind me, because I discovered that a sudden backtrack could cause alarm. (I had a cardinal rule: Keep a wide perimeter from people who might consider me a danger. If not, danger might visit me.) New Orleans suddenly felt more dangerous than Jamaica. The sidewalk was a minefield, and every hesitation and self-censored compensation reduced my dignity. Despite my best efforts, the streets never felt comfortably safe. Even a simple salutation was suspect.

One night, returning to the house that, eight years after my arrival, I thought I'd earned the right to call my home, I waved to a cop driving by. Moments later, I was against his car in handcuffs. When I later asked him—sheepishly, of course; any other way would have asked for bruises— why he had detained me, he said my greeting had aroused

What no one had told me was that I was the one who would be considered a threat.

Within days I noticed that many people on the street seemed apprehensive of me: Some gave me a circumspect glance as they approached, and then crossed the street; others, ahead, would glance behind, register my presence, and then speed up; older white women clutched their bags; young white men nervously greeted me, as if exchanging a salutation for their safety: "What's up, bro?" On one occasion, less than a month after my arrival, I tried to help a man whose wheelchair was stuck in the middle of a crosswalk; he threatened to shoot me in the face, then asked a white pedestrian for help.

I wasn't prepared for any of this. I had come from a majority-black country in which no one was wary of me because of my skin color. Now I wasn't sure who was afraid of me. I was especially unprepared for the cops. They regularly stopped and bullied me, asking questions that took my guilt for granted. I'd never received what many of my African American friends call "The Talk": No parents had told me how to behave when I was stopped by the police, how to be as polite and cooperative as possible, no matter what they said or did to me. So I had to cobble together my own rules of engagement. Thicken my Jamaican accent. Quickly mention my college. "Accidentally" pull out my college identification card when asked for my driver's license.

My survival tactics began well before I left my dorm. I got out of the shower with the police in my head, assembling a cop-proof wardrobe. Light-colored oxford shirt. V-neck nights found me racing against dawn. My mother would often complain, "Mek yuh love street suh? Yuh born a hospital; yuh neva born a street." ("Why do you love the streets so much? You were born in a hospital, not in the streets.")

I left Jamaica in 1996 to attend college in New Orleans, a city I'd heard called "the northernmost Caribbean city." I wanted to discover—on foot, of course—what was Caribbean and what was American about it. Stately mansions on oak-lined streets with streetcars clanging by, and brightly colored houses that made entire blocks look festive; people in resplendent costumes dancing to funky brass bands in the middle of the street; cuisine—and aromas—that mashed up culinary traditions from Africa, Europe, Asia, and the American South; and a juxtaposition of worlds old and new, odd and familiar: Who wouldn't want to explore this?

On my first day in the city, I went walking for a few hours to get a feel for the place and to buy supplies to transform my dormitory room from a prison bunker into a welcoming space. When some university staff members found out what I'd been up to, they warned me to restrict my walking to the places recommended as safe to tourists and the parents of freshmen. They trotted out statistics about New Orleans's crime rate. But Kingston's crime rate dwarfed those numbers, and I decided to ignore these well-meant cautions. A city was waiting to be discovered, and I wouldn't let inconvenient facts get in the way. These American criminals are nothing on Kingston's, I thought. They're no real threat to me.

The streets had their rules, and I loved the challenge of trying to master them. I learned how to be alert to surrounding dangers and nearby delights, and prided myself on recognizing telling details that my peers missed. Kingston was a map of complex, and often bizarre, cultural and political and social activity, and I appointed myself its nighttime cartographer. I'd know how to navigate away from a predatory pace, and to speed up to chat when the cadence of a gait announced friendliness. It was almost always men I saw. A lone woman walking in the middle of the night was as common a sight as Sasquatch; moonlight pedestrianism was too dangerous for her. Sometimes at night as I made my way down from hills above Kingston, I'd have the impression that the city was set on "pause" or in extreme slow motion, as that as I descended I was cutting across Jamaica's deep social divisions. I'd make my way briskly past the mansions in the hills overlooking the city, now transformed into a carpet of dotted lights under a curtain of stars, saunter by middle-class subdivisions hidden behind high walls crowned with barbed wire, and zigzag through neighborhoods of zinc and wooden shacks crammed together and leaning like a tight-knit group of limbo dancers. With my descent came an increase in the vibrancy of street life—except when it didn't; some poor neighborhoods had both the violent gunfights and the eerily deserted streets of the cinematic Wild West. I knew well enough to avoid those even at high noon.

I'd begun hoofing it after dark when I was ten years old. By thirteen I was rarely home before midnight, and some neighborhood could mean your last day. No wonder, then, that my friends and the rare nocturnal passerby declared me crazy for my long late-night treks that traversed warring political zones. (And sometimes I did pretend to be crazy, shouting non sequiturs when I passed through especially dangerous spots, such as the place where thieves hid on the banks of a storm drain. Predators would ignore or laugh at the kid in his school uniform speaking nonsense.)

I made friends with strangers and went from being a very shy and awkward kid to being an extroverted, awkward one. The beggar, the vendor, the poor laborer—those were experienced wanderers, and they became my night-time instructors; they knew the streets and delivered lessons on how to navigate and enjoy them. I imagined myself as a Jamaican Tom Sawyer, one moment sauntering down the streets to pick low-hanging mangoes that I could reach from the sidewalk, another moment hanging outside a street party with battling sound systems, each armed with speakers piled to create skyscrapers of heavy bass. These streets weren't frightening. They were full of adventure when they weren't serene. There I'd join forces with a band of merry walkers, who'd miss the last bus by mere minutes, our feet still moving as we put out our thumbs to hitchhike to spots nearer home, making jokes as vehicle after vehicle raced past us. Or I'd get lost in Mittyesque moments, my young mind imagining alternate futures. The streets had their own safety: Unlike at home, there I could be myself without fear of bodily harm. Walking became so regular and familiar that the way home became home.

Black and Blue

GARNETTE CADOGAN

"My only sin is my skin.
What did I do, to be so black and blue?"
—Fats Waller, "(What Did I Do
to Be So) Black and Blue?"

"Manhattan's streets I saunter'd, pondering."
—Walt Whitman, "Manhattan's Streets
I Saunter'd, Pondering"

My love for walking started in childhood, out of necessity. No thanks to a stepfather with heavy hands, I found every reason to stay away from home and was usually out—at some friend's house or at a street party where no minor should be—until it was too late to get public transportation. So I walked.

The streets of Kingston, Jamaica, in the 1980s were often terrifying—you could, for instance, get killed if a political henchman thought you came from the wrong neighborhood, or even if you wore the wrong color. Wearing orange showed affiliation with one political party and green with the other, and if you were neutral or traveling far from home you chose your colors well. The wrong color in the wrong

world. Visually, I'm not so fresh. I wear the same thing every day. But I am a Southern black worker, committed to building stank-ass art rooted in honesty, will, and imagination.

This weekend, I'm going to drive down to Grandmama's house in central Mississippi. I'm going to bring my computer. I'm going to ask her to sit next to me while I finish this essay about her artistic rituals of labor vis-à-vis OutKast. I'm going to play *ATLiens* and *Aquemini* on her couch while finishing the piece, and think of every conceivable way to thank her for her stank, and for her freshness. I'm going to tell Grandmama that because of her, I know what it's like to be loved responsibly. I'm going to tell her that her love helped me listen, remember, and imagine when I never wanted to listen, remember, or imagine again. I'm going to read the last paragraph of this piece to her, and when Grandmama hugs my neck, I'm going to tell her that when no one in the world believed I was a beautiful Southern black boy, she believed. I'm going to tell Grandmama that her belief is the only reason I'm still alive, that belief in black Southern love is why we work.

house I'm staying in this year as the writer in residence at the University of Mississippi. I planned on inviting Grandmama, too. Between the four of us, I thought we could get to the bottom of some necessary stank, and maybe play a game of "Who's Fresher?: Georgia vs. Mississippi." But the interviews fell through, and Grandmama refused to come up to Oxford because I'm the only black person she knows here, and she tends to avoid places where she doesn't know many black folks.

I kept imagining the meeting, though, and I thought a lot about what in the world I would say to Big Boi and André. As dope as they are, there's nothing I want to ask them about their art. I experienced it, and I'm thankful they extended the traditions and frequencies from whence we came. Honestly, the only thing I'd want to ask them would be about their grandmamas. I'd want to know if their grandmamas thought they were beautiful. I'd want to know how their grandmamas wanted to be loved. I'd want to know how good they were at loving their grandmamas on days when the world wasn't so kind.

The day that my grandmama came home after work without the stank of chicken guts, powder, perfume, sweat, and Coke-Cola, I knew that her time at the plant was done. On that day—when her body wouldn't let her work anymore—I knew I'd spend the rest of my life trying to honor her and make a way for her to be as fresh and remembered as she wants to be.

Due to diabetes, Grandmama moves mostly in a wheelchair these days, but she's still the freshest person in my

In the middle of Dre's verse, he nudges us to understand that there's something more happening in this song: "Hope I'm not over your head, but if so you will catch on later."

Big Boi alludes to the book of Revelation, mentions some ballers trying to unsuccessfully repent and make it to heaven, and then rhymes about getting his family and heading to the Dungeon, their basement studio in Atlanta—the listener can easily imagine it as a bunker—where he'll record one last song. The world is ending. He grabs the mic: "I got in the booth to run the final portion." Of course, this ending describes the very track we're hearing, thus bringing the fictional apocalypse of the song into our real world.

I was reading Octavia Butler's *Kindred* at the time *Aquemini* came out. Steeped in all that stank, I conceived of a book within a book within a book, written by a young Southern black girl whose parents disappear. "I'm a round runaway character" was the first sentence my narrator wrote. I decided that she would be an emcee, but I didn't know her name. I knew that she would tell the world that she was an ellipsis, a runaway ellipsis willing to do any and all things to stop her black Southern community from being written off the face of the earth. I scribbled these notes on the blank pages of *Kindred* while *Aquemini* kept playing in the background. By the time the song "Liberation" was done, *Long Division*, my first novel, was born.

I thought about interviewing André and Big Boi for this piece. I was going to get them to spend the night at this huge *cation* had me expecting a lot more from my male heroes. A month later, OutKast dropped *Aquemini.*

Deep into the album, the song "West Savannah" ends with a skit. We hear a young black boy trying to impress his friend by calling a young black girl on the phone, three-way. When the girl answers, we hear a mama, an auntie, or a grandmama tell her to "get your ass in here." The girl tells the boy she has to go—and then the boy tells her that his friend wants some sex. The girl emphatically lets the boy know there is no way she's having sex with him, before hanging up in his face. This is where the next song, "Da Art of Storytellin' (Pt. 1)," begins.

In the first verse, Big rhymes about a sexual experience with a girl named Suzy Screw, during which he exchanges a CD and a poster for oral sex. In the second, André raps about Suzy's friend Sasha Thumper. As André's verse proceeds, he and Sasha are lying on their backs "staring at the stars above, talking bout what we gonna be when we grow up." When Dre asks Sasha what she wants to be, Sasha Thumper responds, "Alive." The song ends with the news that Sasha Thumper has overdosed after partnering with a man who treats her wrong. Here was "another black experience," as Dre would say to end another verse on the album.

Hip-hop has always embraced metafiction. In the next track—"Da Art of Storytellin' (Pt. 2)"—Big and Dre deliver a pair of verses about the last recording they'll ever create due to an environmental apocalypse. We've long had emcees rhyming about the potency of their own rhymes. But I have never heard a song attribute the end of the world to a rhyme.

they'd wrassle it out, talk more shit, hug, and come back ready to out-fresh each other, along with every artist who'd come before them in the making of lyrical art.

OutKast created a different kind of stank, too: an urban Southern stank so familiar with and indebted to the gospel, blues, jazz, rock, and funk born in the rural black South. And while they were lyrically competing against each other on track after track, together Big and Dre were united, railing and wailing against New York and standing up to a post-civil-rights South chiding young Southern black boys to pull up our pants and fight white supremacy with swords of respectability and narrow conceptions of excellence. *ATLiens* made me love being black, Southern, celibate, sexy, awkward, free of drugs and alcohol, Grandmama's grandbaby, and cooler than a polar bear's toenails.

Right out of Oberlin, I earned a fellowship in the MFA program at Indiana University, to study fiction. For the first time in my life, I was thinking critically about narrative construction in everything from malt liquor commercials to the Bible. It was around that time that Lauryn Hill gave my generation an elixir to calm, compete with, and call out a culture insistent on coming up with new ways to devalue black women. In *The Miseducation of Lauryn Hill*, I saw myself as the intimate partner doing wrong by Lauryn, and she made me consider how for all the differences between André and Big Boi, they shared in the same kind of misogynoir on their first two albums. (Particularly on the song "Jazzy Belle": ". . . even Bo knew, that you got poked / like acupuncture patients while our nation is a boat.") *Misedu-*

in the presence of older Southern black folk my entire life, but I'd never heard it connecting two rhymed verses. Art couldn't get any fresher than that.

By the mid-nineties, hip-hop was an established art form, foregrounding a wide, historically neglected audience in completely new ways. Never had songs had so many words. Never had songs lacked melodies. Never had songs pushed against the notion of a hook repeated every 45 seconds. Like a lot of Southern black boys, I loved New York hip-hop, although I didn't feel loved or imagined by most of it.

When André said, "The South got something to say and that's all I got to say," at the Source awards in 1995, I heard him saying that we were no longer going to artistically follow New York. Not because the artists of New York were wack, but because disregarding our particular stank in favor of a stink that didn't love or respect us was like taking a broken elevator down into artistic and spiritual death.

With OutKast, Dre and Big each carved out their own individual space, and along with sonic contrast—Big lyrically fought and André lyrically conjured—they gave us philosophical contrast. When Dre raps, "No drugs or alcohol so I can get the signal clear as day," I remember folks suggesting there was a smidgen of shade being thrown on Big Boi, who on the same album rhymed, "I got an ounce of dank and a couple of dranks, so let's crank up this session." If there was ever shade between them back then, I got the sense, they'd handle it like we Southern black boys did:

page to probe and to remember through essays and sometimes through satire. I was imitating, and maybe interrogating, but I'm not sure that I had any idea of how to use words to imagine and really innovate. All my English teachers talked about the importance of finding "your voice." It always confused me because I knew we all had so many voices, so many audiences, and my teachers seemed only to really want the kind of voice that sat with its legs crossed, reading *The New York Times.* I didn't have to work to find that cross-legged voice—it was the one education necessitated I lead with.

What my English teachers didn't say was that voices aren't discovered fully formed, they are built and shaped—and not just by words, punctuation, and sentences, but by the author's intended audience, by the composition's form, and by subject. It was only after listening to *ATLiens* that I realized in order to get where I needed to go as a human being and an artist, in order to release my own spacey stank blues, I had to write fiction. Dre and Big showed me it was possible to create fake worlds wholly concerned with "what if" and "maybe" and "what really was."

I remember sitting in my tiny dorm room under my huge Black Lightning poster, next to my tiny picture of Grandmama. I was supposed to be doing a paper on "The Cask of Amontillado," but I was thinking about OutKast's "Wailin'." The song made me know that there was something to be gained, felt, and used in imitating sounds from whence we came, particularly in the minimal hook: the repeated moan of one about to wail. I'd heard that moan

Da Art of Storytellin' (a Prequel)

KIESE LAYMON

From six in the morning until five in the afternoon, five days a week, for thirty years, my grandmama Catherine's fingers, palms, and wrists wandered deep in the bellies of dead chickens. Grandmama was a buttonhole slicer at a chicken plant in central Mississippi—her job was to slice the belly and pull out the guts of thousands of chickens a day. Grandmama got up every morning around 4:30 a.m. She took her bath, then prepared grits, smoked sausage, and pear preserves for us. After breakfast, Grandmama made me take a teaspoon of cod liver oil "for my vitamins," then she coated the area between her breasts in powder before putting on the clothes she had ironed the night before. I was ten, staying with Grandmama for the summer, and I remember marveling at her preparations and wondering why she got so fresh, so clean, just to leave the house and get dirty.

"There's layers to this," Grandmama often said, when describing her job to folks. She went into that plant every day, knowing it was a laboratory for racial and gendered terror. Still, she wanted to be the best at what she did— and not just the best buttonhole slicer in the plant, but the best, most stylized, most efficient worker in Mississippi.

She understood that the audience for her work was not just her coworkers or her white male shift managers, but all the Southern black women workers who preceded her and, most important, all the Southern black women workers coming next.

By the end of the day, when the two-tone blue Impala crept back into the driveway on the side of our shotgun house, I'd run out to welcome Grandmama home. "Hey, baby," she'd say. "Let me wash this stank off my hands before I hug your neck."

This stank wasn't *that stink.* This stank was root and residue of black Southern poverty, and devalued black Southern labor, black Southern excellence, black Southern imagination, and black Southern woman magic. This was the stank from whence black Southern life, love, and labor came. Even at ten years old, I understood that the presence and necessity of this stank dictated how Grandmama moved on Sundays. As the head of the usher board at Concord Baptist, she sometimes wore the all-white polyester uniform that all the other church ushers wore. On those Sundays, Grandmama was committed to out-freshing the other ushers by draping colorful pearls and fake gold around her neck, or stunting with some shiny shoes she'd gotten from my aunt Linda in Vegas. And Grandmama's outfits, when she wasn't wearing the stale usher board uniform, always had to be fresher this week than the week before.

She was committed to out-freshing herself, which meant that she was up late on Saturday nights, working like a wizard, taking pieces of this blouse from 1984 and sewing them into these dresses from 1969. Grandmama's primary audience on Sundays, her church sisters, looked with awe and envy at her outfits, inferring she had a fashion industry hookup from Atlanta, or a few secret revenue streams. Not so. This was just how Grandmama brought the stank of her work life into her spiritual communal life, in a way that I loved and laughed at as a kid.

I didn't fully understand or feel inspired by Grandmama's stank or freshness until years later, when I heard the albums *ATLiens* and *Aquemini* from those Georgia-based artists called OutKast.

One day near the beginning of my junior year in college, 1996, I walked out of my dorm room in Oberlin, Ohio, heading to the gym, when I heard a new sound and a familiar voice blasting from the room of my friend John Norris, a Southern black boy from Clarksville, Tennessee.

My soliloquy may be hard for some to
    swallow
But so is cod liver oil.

I went into John's room, wondering who was rapping about cod liver oil over reverbed bass, and asked him, "What the fuck is that?" It was "Wheelz of Steel," from *ATLiens.* John handed me the CD. The illustrated cover looked like a comic book, its heroes standing back-to-back in front of a mysterious four-armed force: Big Boi in a letterman jacket with a Braves hat cocked to the right, and André in a green turban like something I'd only seen my Grandmama and Mama Lara rock. Big Boi's fingers were clinched, ready to fight. André's were spread, ready to conjure.

John and I listened to the record twice before I borrowed my friend's green Geo, drove to Elyria, and bought *ATLiens* for myself. Like *Soul Food* by Atlanta's Goodie Mob, another album I was wearing out at the time—their song "Thought Process," which featured André, had nudged me through the sadness of missing Mississippi a year earlier— *ATLiens* was unafraid of the revelatory dimensions of black Southern life. Like *Soul Food*, *ATLliens* explored the inevitability of death and the possibility of new life, new movement, and new mojo.

But something was different.

I already knew OutKast; I loved their first album, *Southernplayalisticadillacmuzik*, in part because of the clever way they interpolated funk and soul into rap. *ATLiens*, however, sounded unlike anything I'd ever heard or imagined. The vocal tones were familiar, but the rhyme patterns, the composition, the production were equal parts red clay, thick buttery grits, and Mars. Nothing sounded like *ATLiens*. The album instantly changed not just my expectations of music, but my expectations of myself as a young black Southern artist.

By then, I already knew I was going to be a writer. I had no idea if I would eat off of what I wrote, but I knew I had to write to be a decent human being. I used ink and the

• • •

When President Obama broke into "Amazing Grace" at the funeral for those killed at Mother Emanuel, it was mere hours after the Supreme Court declared gay marriage legal, and barring it as unconstitutional. There it was strange yet strangely fitting to hear him sing that song written by the reformed slaver while at sea. I like to think the slaves who took the song over and made it a Negro spiritual were not the same kinds of *wretch* as its author.

Of course you can see why anyone would want to be black: being black is fun. Don't tell nobody.

This morning I woke from a "deep Negro sleep," as Senghor put it. I then took a black shower and shaved a black shave; I walked a black walk and sat a black sit; I wrote some black lines; I coughed black and sneezed black and ate black too. This last at least is literal: grapes, blackberries, the ripest plums.

Summer 2015

stage: as either a joke or a set of jailed youths and stooped old people.

Even the president, who started up a Twitter feed weeks before the Dolezal incident, was inundated by racists posting pictures of nooses and equating him to a monkey or worse. It is only when one feels such stereotypes as real that one might find being in blackface freeing—not because you believe the stereotypes, but because you want to establish other, corny ones.

Sinking feeling: blackfaced person always occupies a bigger public stage than a black one.

Standing back, maybe it's true: not that being black is only comic or tragic, but that too often white thinking or acting out about it, as demonstrated in Dolezal's hoax and the Charleston murders, remains only polarized: comic or tragic. Both are nullifying.

Amid the bewilderment and grief, for just a moment I wondered how onetime NAACP chapter leader Dolezal would've responded, as surely she would have sought to, had she not been unmasked. Where's our fearless leader now? I thought. Then I didn't think of her again.

I came out as black as a teenager. Before then, I was simply a boy. After, I was sometimes, still.

stant shifting set of stories to explain her identity (it's complicated), an array of attempts to be not just someone else as anyone might, but to be exotic, even in her birth (which she said was in a teepee or tipi). When asked directly on the teevee if she was born in a teepee, she answered, "I wasn't born *in* a teepee," emphasis allowing that maybe, just maybe, she could later say she was born near or under one. The hoaxer is always leaving the pretend teepee door ajar.

Dolezal also says she was abused, and claimed to have lived in South Africa. It is true that her actual parents did live there, but not with her, only her siblings—many of whom were actually adopted and black. She apparently earlier equated their alleged beatings (that several of them have denied) with slavery. Given her disproven lies, abuse does not so much provide an explanation for her behavior as much as a distraction: true or not, like her making slavery a mere metaphor it would seem part of a scenario of victimhood, which to her is also, inherently, black.

Borrowed blackness and nativeness provide her the ultimate virtual victimhood.

Finally the chief problem with racial impostors or blackface: it can be only, as James Weldon Johnson said of stereotypical black dialect, comic or tragic. Ultimately, it conforms to white views of "the blacks" themselves, off-

• • •

Whenever I tell a white person about the injustices at the airport, or on the street, the daily snubs, or that my white neighbor's farewell to me as I was moving out of my apartment last year was *Goodbye, nigger* and that no one in the condos or its board, both painted white, did a thing about it, they too grow silent.

Part of grief, I've found, is silence. Protest too, at times. What the no-longer-neighbor wanted from me most, I knew instantly, was a reaction. *Bye*, I said. Good riddance, I meant.

I've heard even Dolezal's paintings of black faces while in school as a white graduate student at Howard were actually plagiarized. Our Dolezal didn't just want to disappear into blackness, but disappear. For her, blackness was not a private thing, which ultimately may be where blackness best tells us what it knows. It is this private, shifting, personal blackness that cannot be borrowed. What can be: wigs, tanning booth, rhetoric.

Dolezal's righteous rage looks more like self-righteousness — or is it other-righteousness?

What no one seems to say is just how Dolezal's actions, over many years, conform to the typical hoaxer's: a conness don't mean hiding. Sunday meant rest, and a respite, wearing a different kind of white, black hair crowned by lace.

Blackness too often veers between two poles in the public eye: opaqueness and invisibility. For [racist killer], blackness wasn't just opaque but conspicuous. It named an enemy and provided a uniform that allowed mass judgment—and murder.

Rachel Dolezal could be conspicuously outraged all the time, filing lawsuits, marching, because she didn't have to save any energy for just being herself.

Dolezal's drama didn't just start recently. The persecution complex, the past lawsuits (when she was white) against a historically black institution like Howard University no less, seem like the whitest thing ever. It's like when you are with a white friend and they experience racism, likely for the first time, alongside you: they usually go wild, protesting no one and everyone; you shrug as much as shout. Some things are just part of the daily dose of being black. The cab will drive away with a white friend in it rather than drive you too. It's dealing with blackness that black people have perfected—or at least gotten practiced at.

Racism's daily injustices are almost an inoculation against it. Almost.

In a place like the South that loves its tall tales, why do people take their Confederate stories hyperseriously? As gospel? *Everyone's a colonel,* someone joked with me about the South when I was at the University of Georgia, where I taught for five years.

It was my first job, and I was regularly thought by strangers at the university to be passing for a student (and not a grad student). *You look too young to be a professor,* surprised interrogators would say, usually after asking what year in school I was. (It's true I was only twenty-five, but had a book already and a degree or two.) After a while, I began to translate the comment about looking young to be a more polite way of saying what they couldn't: *You look too black to be a professor.*

Maybe blackness is only a look, one we're told cannot ever look back?

Far more interesting and provocative than a white mother in blackface would be a white mother with black children. Wouldn't that provide a much more complex identity than any blackface? You get the feeling that, for Dolezal, blackness equals hiding.

For the deaconess at the church who had to make her way by cleaning white people's houses during the week, black-

111

and answered the question of whether she was black or not with *I don't understand the question*, came the murders in cold blood at Mother Emanuel Church in Charleston. Both cases didn't seem just coincidental, but near-simultaneous misapprehensions not just of blackness but of whiteness too.

After the killings in Charleston, several things happened: Dolezal's story went back to merely being ridiculous. Talk shows moved on to something else and those who somehow willed Dolezal sublime retreated. Flags flew at half staff—except the Confederate flag on South Carolina statehouse grounds. It took a black woman to climb up and take that down.

They gave the assignment to a black man to raise the "rebel flag," the stars and bars, back up. Like Sally Hemings, he might not have minded, but he certainly couldn't have refused.

Soon the Confederate battle flag would be voted down by the state assembly, but flag sales would soar. Customers began to hoard them like guns once most major outlets suspended sales. Yet given the killer's postings of himself with Confederate flags and separatist slogans, easy slogans like "heritage not hate" stood naked. The proof here only increased as a pro-flag rally brought out the American Nazi flag, side by side and even mashed up with the Confederate one.

Strom Thurmond had him a black daughter out of wedlock; the only people surprised by this were the white voters he courted by vehement racist rhetoric. Of course, this behavior, demeaning blacks while desiring at least one, descends from slavery and is how we got most light-skinned folks who "look white" in the first place.

Why doesn't Rachel Dolezal seem to know that a white person can have a black child (see one-drop rule above)? (See Obama.) (See Hemings.) (See Jefferson.) See . . .

Being black is not a feeling. *I don't always feel colored.* Nor is it simply a state of mind.

Blackness: a way of being.

It would be one thing, I think, if in her house, to her pillow or family, Dolezal said she felt black. I imagine many white households across the country don blackface and grab banjos and have themselves a good ol' time when no one else is around. It's when that somehow translates to what she does, when she teaches black studies as if she's a black person—not a teacher, but a mind reader—that it becomes a problem. She wears the mask not to hide but to gain authority over the very thing she claims to want to be. How very white of her!

After Rachel Dolezal had mumbled her way through various news shows looking like Gilly from *Saturday Night Live*

• • •

So when the killer [name withheld] walked into Mother Emanuel Church in Charleston one week after the Dolezal story broke, I am not surprised that the black worshippers there welcomed him. Welcome is an integral part of the African American Christian tradition; it is especially so in the African Methodist Episcopal one, begun over two hundred years ago when the Methodist church prevented blacks, mostly freedmen and women, to pray beside its whites, even pulling them off their knees.

How long did [name redacted] sit there waiting, deciding to deny the evidence of humanity before him? Nothing, it appears, could have convinced him not to kill blacks, whom he believed—and spewed hate about—preyed on white people, especially women. One suspects he may not've known any women besides his family.

Thomas Jefferson hated black people but slept with one who bore his children, six of them. (*Misery is often the parent of the most affecting touches in poetry.*—*Among the blacks is misery enough, God knows, but no poetry*, he wrote in *Notes on Virginia*.) That Sally Hemings was also his wife's half-sister neither stopped him nor did it make him reevaluate his stance toward black thought, which he saw as an impossible paradox.

Jefferson had black heirs who he, and for centuries his (sorta) white heirs and white defenders, denied. In our time,

While black folks often hear the beat, and set it, doesn't mean when anyone else hears it, that she gets to be black.

Every church I know of had a white lady who arrived one day. Ours in Topeka did. After she hung around awhile, and proved herself she wasn't a tourist, "Mrs. Pete" was accepted and seen as part of the AME congregation, even singing in the choir (which was a high bar, as it were). But we never thought she was, or somehow became, black. *She's good people*, folks would say.

She did get herself a perm: I mean a white, curly one, instead of a straightened, black one; a clarification that's one more sign we're awfully mixed up. There's the joke: *You didn't get yourself a perm, but a temporary.*

There is the other, far rarer passing, which we may call reverse-passing, of whites living as black. The most prominent I know of may be Johnny Otis—who was successful enough that many race women and men I know aren't aware he was actually born white. Or the Baseball Hall of Fame inductee, owner of a Negro League team who likely wasn't black herself. What's interesting is to wonder what the black people around them thought, usually accepting them—not necessarily as what they said they were, but how they acted. It isn't that they weren't judged, just that when they were, they weren't found wanting.

• • •

Like Rachel Dolezal, I too became black around the age of five. I first became a nigger at nine, so I had me a good run.

The problem isn't just that Rachel Dolezal can wash off whatever she's sprayed on herself (it just don't look right), or that blackness is a choice, but that what she's wearing isn't just bronzer, but *blacker*: a notion that blackness is itself hyperbolic, excessive, skin tone only. Well, and wigs.

This last, some black observers have praised.

Did Dolezal really fool those black folks around her? I have a strange feeling she didn't, that many simply humored her. You have to do this with white people, from time to time.

Black people are constantly identifying and recognizing those who look like secret black folks—many light-skinned people I know get identified as white by white people, but we know they're black. (This isn't passing, btw.) Most look like one of my aunties. Knowing they are black, it is hard to see them another way.

It's one of the advantages of my folks being from Louisiana—there's lots of folks who don't "look black" but are (which of course should make us stop and reevaluate what "looking black" is). Because of the one-drop rule, though begun as a controlling race law, black people themselves adapted and even invented and accepted a broader blackness. In general this has made black people—I am speaking for every single black person without exception here, of course—wary yet accepting.

Those surprised by a white lady darkening her skin and curling her hair haven't been out of the house or online in a while.

There was the rather white-looking bank manager in Athens, Georgia, who chatted me up one day and mentioned a couple key black striver things—a black sorority here, the Links there—that let me know she was black too. It was brilliant, and in no way calculated; hers was smart survival.

It was also a test to see if I was woke, or a striver, too.

Teaching a class about blackness doesn't mean you are black. Blackness isn't a bunch of facts to memorize, or a set of stock behaviors; nor darker skin color neither. It's like the jazz heads I've seen, often white, who can tell you every sideman on every session, but seem in the daylight unable to find the beat. The beat is there always; doesn't mean you can always hear it.

• • •

One of the best things about being black is that, barring some key exceptions, it's not a volunteer position. You can't just wish on a dark star and become black. It's not paid either. It's more like a long internship with a chance of advancement.

I've never seen the TV show *Blackish* all the way through. (I hear it's quite good now.) From what I've seen, *Fresh Off the Boat*, another of ABC's offerings, seems to me a more accurate portrayal of the complexity of racial identity, even black identity. (This is despite the worries of its creator, chef and author Eddie Huang.) The young Asian immigrant who's the main character identifies with hip-hop in order to be both American and remain and help explain being *nonwhite*. It's funny, and frequently brilliant: How *do* you become American?

Is this the same as becoming black?

Traditionally, pretend blackness was the fastest route to becoming white. This is true for Irish and Jewish immigrants, who adopted blackface in large numbers in the late nineteenth and early twentieth, and soon assimilated; and for Northerners, for whom blackface helped them imagine themselves a nation since blackface's advent in the 1830s.

Cue that f'in caricature of Jim Crow dancing.

of Life" (from Victor LaValle); "Blackish Like Me" (mine too). Now things done got serious.

When you are black, you don't have to look like it, but you do have to look at it. Or look around. Blackness is the face in the mirror, a not-bad-looking one, that for no reason at all some people uglify or hate on or wish ill for, to, about. Sometimes any lusting after it gets to be a drag too.

Every black person has something "not black" about them. I don't mean something white, because despite our easy dichotomies, the opposite of black is not white. This one likes European classical music; that one likes a little bit of country (hopefully the old stuff); this one is the first African American principal ballerina; this one can't dance. Black people know this—any solidarity with each other is about something shared, a secret joy, a song, not about some stereotypical qualities that may be reproducible, imitable, even marketable. This doesn't mean there aren't similarities across black people or communities or better yet memory—just that these aren't exactly about bodies and not really about skin at all, but culture.

There is a long tradition of passing—of racial crossing the line, usually going from black to white. You could say it was started, like this country, by Thomas Jefferson.

and say, "another black poem."
Maybe I'm scared people won't think
of the poem as a poem, but as a cry for help.

Maybe the poem is a cry for help.

Maybe I come from a place where people
are always afraid of dying.
Maybe that's just what I tell myself
so I don't feel so alone in this body.
Maybe there's a place where everyone is both
in love with and running from their own skin.
Maybe that place is here.

Maybe that's why I'm always running from
the things that love me. Maybe I'm trying
to save them the time of burying darkness
when all they have to do is close their eyes.

Queries of Unrest

CLINT SMITH

After Hanif Willis-Abdurraqib

Maybe I come from the gap
between my father's teeth.
Maybe I was meant to see a little
bit of darkness every time he smiled.

Maybe I was meant to understand that
darkness magnifies the sight of joy.
Maybe I come from where the sidewalk
ends, or maybe I just read that in a book once.
It can be hard to tell the difference sometimes.

Maybe that's because when I was a kid
a white boy told me I was marginalized
and all I could think of was the edge
of a sheet of paper, how empty it is—
the abyss I was told never to write into.

Maybe I'm scared of writing another poem
that makes people roll their eyes

PART II

RECKONING

This doesn't mean that I don't honor and claim the myriad other aspects of my heritage. I do, in ways serious and silly. I read Philip Larkin and Seamus Heaney and love all things Harry Potter and *Doctor Who*. I study French and Spanish and attempt to translate the simplest poems by Pablo Neruda and Federico García Lorca into English (and fail awfully). I watch obscure French movies with subtitles. I attend powwows and eat fry bread and walk along the outside of the dancing circles with a kind of wistful longing because I want to understand the singing so badly, because I want to stomp the earth in exultation and to belong in that circle, too. But I imagine that my ancestors from Sierra Leone and Britain, from France and the Choctaw settlements on the Mississippi bayou, from Spain and Ghana—all those people whose genetic strands intertwined to produce mine—felt that same longing, even as they found themselves making a new community here at the mouth of the Mississippi. Together, they would make new music, like blues and jazz and zydeco, and new dances, second lining through the streets. They would make a world that reflected back to them the richness of their heritage, and in doing so discover a new type of belonging.

percent European—a mixture of British, Irish, French, German, Scandinavian, Iberian, Italian, and Ashkenazi—32 percent sub-Saharan African, a quarter Native American, and less than 1 percent North African. For a few days after I received my results, I looked into the mirror and didn't know how to understand myself. I tried to understand my heritage through my features, to assign each one a place, but I couldn't. All I could see was my hair: hair that grows up and out instead of falling flat, like my father's; hair that refuses to be as smooth and tidy as my mother's but instead bushes and tangles and curls in all directions at once. Mine is a mane that bears the strongest imprint of my African ancestors, hair that my stylist combed out into a voluminous afro during one of my visits to New York City, so that I walked the streets with a ten-inch halo that repelled the rain and spoke of Africa to everyone who saw it.

That's how I remembered myself. I remembered that people of color from my region of the United States can choose to embrace all aspects of their ancestry, in the food they eat, in the music they listen to, in the stories they tell, while also choosing to war in one armor, that of black Americans, when they fight for racial equality. I remembered that in choosing to identify as black, to write about black characters in my fiction and to assert the humanity of black people in my nonfiction, I've remained true to my personal history, to my family history, to my political and moral choices, and to my essential self: a self that understands the world through the prism of being a black American, and stands in solidarity with the people of the African diaspora.

ture of British, Irish, French, German, Scandinavian, and Iberian—41 percent sub-Saharan African, and 3.4 percent Native American.

My parents' results gave them the concrete proof of their ancestry that they'd always been denied. My father, a former member of the Black Panther party, proudly claimed his Native American heritage by registering with the Choctaw tribe of Slidell, Louisiana. My mother could at last make educated guesses about the parentage of her great-grandparents. It was as if 23andMe had taught them to read the language of their family histories, enabling them to finally understand the incomprehensible book of their ancestral pasts: to read what had been gibberish.

Yet I found my own results both surprising and troubling. I was raised in Mississippi, in a family and a community that identified as black, and I have the stories and the experiences to go with it. One of my great-great-grandfathers was killed by a gang of white Prohibition patrollers. My mother helped to integrate the local elementary school in the 1960s. My father was run out of segregated Pass Christian's beaches and the local park. I was the only black girl at my private high school in Pass Christian, the target of my classmates' backward ideas about race. Despite my parents' sense of their mixed roots, I had thought that my genetic makeup would confirm the identity that I'd grown up with—one that located Africa as my ancestors' primary point of origin, and that allowed me to claim a legacy of black resistance and strength.

So it was discomfiting to find that my ancestry was 40

it wasn't. You order a kit online, the professor explained, and get it in the mail a week or so later, then register it on the company's website, spit into a test tube, seal it, and send it back in the provided box. Around six weeks later, you receive your results. The professor said that his girlfriend had spent hours poring over hers, fascinated by her genetically based health analysis. (Due to an FDA crackdown, 23andMe no longer provides that particular service.) But I was interested in genetic testing for a different reason.

I ordered tests for my father, my mother, and myself. We submitted our samples, then waited for the company's scientists to decode the ancestral information in our DNA.

My mother and I were sitting at her kitchen table when her test came back. My father was at my sister's house, surrounded by his children, when he received his. Their results confirmed some of the notions we'd had about our ancestry, as passed down through family lore, and subverted others. My father, who'd always believed himself to have Native American heritage, and who had a strong affinity for Native American history and culture, found that he is 51 percent Native American, as well as nearly equal parts sub-Saharan African and European (British, Irish, Spanish, and Ashkenazi)—23.5 percent and 22.5 percent, respectively— and just over 1 percent North African. My mother, who has told me story after story about her white great-grandparents taking their mixed-race children to visit their families in Kiln, Mississippi, only to hide the kids in the trunk of the car at the end of every visit when the sun set and it was no longer safe, found that she is 55 percent European—a mixsions on the coast. On the local TV station, she watched commentators discuss what it meant to be a proper Creole, women who were darker than her asserting that true Creoles have only Spanish and French ancestry. Theirs was part of an ongoing attempt to write anyone with African or Native American heritage out of the region's history; to erase us from the story of the plantations, the swamps, the bayou; to deny that plaçage, those unofficial unions, during the time of antimiscegenation laws, between European men and women of African heritage had ever taken place.

It's impossible for most black Americans to construct full family trees. Official census records, used by so many genealogy enthusiasts to piece together their families' pasts, don't include our non-European ancestors. Both my mother's and my father's family name is Dedeaux (I bear my paternal grandmother's last name), and several relatives on my mother's side have traced their lineage through European Dedeauxs back to France, but building a family tree of people of color is far harder. I always understood my ancestry, like that of so many others on the Gulf Coast, to be a tangle of African slaves, free men of color, French and Spanish immigrants, British colonists, Native Americans— but in what proportion, and what might that proportion tell me about who I thought I was?

I was at a dinner with some professors from Spring Hill College in Mobile, Alabama, when one of them told me about the genetic-testing company 23andMe. It cost ninety-nine dollars—that was my first surprise. I imagined that the price of such a service would be exorbitant, but evidently or so down the road, houses graced with front-facing balconies so that the wealthy white families who lived in them could gaze out at the flat pan of the water and the searing, pale sand, where mangrove trees had grown before they'd bulldozed the land.

Put simply, my father grew up as a black boy in a black family in the deep South, where being black, in the sixties, was complicated. The same was true in the eighties, when I was growing up in DeLisle, a town a few miles north of Pass Christian. Once, when I was a teen, we stood together in a drugstore checkout line behind an older, blondish white woman. My father, an inveterate joker, kept shoving me between my shoulder blades, trying to make me stumble into her. "Daddy, stop," I mouthed, as I tried to avoid a collision. I was horrified: Daddy's going to make me knock this white woman over. Then she turned around, and I realized that it was my grandaunt Eunice, my grandmother's sister—that she was blood. "I thought you were white," I said, and she and my father laughed.

Coastal Mississippi is a place where Eunice—a woman pale as milk, with blond hair and African heritage—is considered, and considers herself, black. The one-drop rule is real here. Eunice wasn't allowed on the beaches of the Gulf Coast or Lake Pontchartrain until the early seventies. The state so fiercely neglected her education that her grandfather established a community school for black children. Once Eunice graduated, after the eighth grade, her schooling was done. She worked in her father's fields, and then as a cleaning woman for the white families in their man-

Cracking the Code

JESMYN WARD

When my father moved to Oakland, California, after Hurricane Camille wrecked the Mississippi Gulf Coast, in 1969, strangers he encountered from El Salvador and Mexico and Puerto Rico would spit rapid-fire Spanish at him, expecting a reply in kind. "Are you Samoan?" a Samoan asked him once. But my father, with his black, silky hair that curled into Coke-bottle waves at the ends, skin the color of milky tea, and cheekbones like dorsal fins breaking the water of his face, was none of these things. He attended an all-black high school in Oakland; in his class pictures, his is one of the few light faces. His hair is parted in the middle and falls away in a blowsy afro, coarsened to the right texture by multiple applications of relaxer.

My father was born in 1956 in Pass Christian, a small Mississippi town on the coast of the Gulf of Mexico, fifty miles from New Orleans. He grew up in a dilapidated single-story house: four rooms, with a kitchen tacked onto the back. It was built along the railroad tracks and shook when trains sped by; the wood of the sloped floor rotted at the corners. The house was nothing like the great columned mansions strung along the man-made beach just half a mile

March 1956, 101 members of Congress issued the Southern Manifesto, declaring war on the *Brown* decision. Governors in Virginia, Arkansas, Alabama, Georgia, and elsewhere then launched "massive resistance." They created a legal doctrine, interposition, that supposedly nullified any federal law or court decision with which a state disagreed. They passed legislation to withhold public funding from any school that abided by *Brown*. They shut down public school systems and used tax dollars to ensure that whites could continue their education at racially exclusive private academies. Black children were left to rot with no viable option.

A little more than half a century after *Brown*, the election of Obama gave hope to the country and the world that a new racial climate had emerged in America, or that it would. But such audacious hopes would be short-lived. A rash of voter-suppression legislation, a series of unfathomable Supreme Court decisions, the rise of stand-your-ground laws, and continuing police brutality make clear that Obama's election and reelection have unleashed yet another wave of fear and anger.

It's more subtle—less overtly racist—than in 1865 or even 1954. It's a remake of the Southern Strategy, crafted in the wake of the civil rights movement to exploit white resentment against African Americans, and deployed with precision by Presidents Richard Nixon and Ronald Reagan. As Reagan's key political strategist, Lee Atwater, explained in a 1981 interview: "You start out in 1954 by saying, 'N——, n——, n——.' By 1968 you can't say 'n——'—that hurts you. Backfires. So you say stuff like 'forced busing,' 'states' rights,' and all that stuff. You're getting so abstract now you're talking about cutting taxes, and all these things you're talking about are totally economic things, and a byproduct of them is blacks get hurt worse than whites. And subconsciously maybe that is part of it. I'm not saying that." (The interview was originally published anonymously, and only years later did it emerge that Atwater was the subject.)

Now, under the guise of protecting the sanctity of the ballot box, conservatives have devised measures—such as photo ID requirements—to block African Americans' access to the polls. A joint report by the NAACP Legal Defense and Educational Fund and the NAACP emphasized that the ID requirements would adversely affect more than 6 million African American voters. (Twenty-five percent of black Americans lack a government-issued photo ID, the report noted, compared with only 8 percent of white Americans.) The Supreme Court sanctioned this discrimination in *Shelby County v. Holder*, which gutted the Voting Rights Act and opened the door to twenty-first-century versions of nineteenth-century literacy tests and poll taxes.

The economic devastation of the Great Recession also shows African Americans under siege. The foreclosure crisis hit black Americans harder than any other group in the United States. A 2013 report by researchers at Brandeis University calculated that "half the collective wealth of African-American families was stripped away during the Great Recession," in large part because of the impact on home equity. In the process, the wealth gap between blacks and whites grew: Right before the recession, white Americans had four times more wealth than black Americans, on average; by 2010, the gap had increased to six times. This was a targeted hit. Communities of color were far more likely to have riskier, higher-interest-rate loans than white communities, with good credit scores often making no difference.

Add to this the tea party movement's assault on so-called Big Government, which despite the sanitized language of fiscal responsibility constitutes an attack on African American jobs. Public-sector employment, where there is less discrimination in hiring and pay, has traditionally been an important venue for creating a black middle class.

So when you think of Ferguson, don't just think of black resentment at a criminal justice system that allows a white police officer to put six bullets into an unarmed black teen. Consider the economic dislocation of black America. Remember a Florida judge instructing a jury to focus only on the moment when George Zimmerman and Trayvon Martin interacted, thus transforming a seventeen-year-old, unarmed kid into a big, scary black guy, while the grown man who stalked him through the neighborhood with a loaded gun becomes a victim. Remember the assault on the Voting Rights Act. Look at *Connick v. Thompson*, a partisan 5–4 Supreme Court decision in 2011 that ruled it was legal for a city prosecutor's staff to hide evidence that exonerated a black man who was rotting on death row for fourteen years. And think of a recent study by Stanford University psychology researchers concluding that when white people were told that black Americans are incarcerated in numbers far beyond their proportion of the population "they reported being more afraid of crime and more likely to support the kinds of punitive policies that exacerbate the racial disparities," such as three-strikes or stop-and-frisk laws.

Only then does Ferguson make sense. It's about white rage.

pretend is a face. Those who wear blackface reduce black-ness to skin in order not to be white. The implication of course is that black people are just miscolored or extra-dark white people. Many a joke told for my benefit in my Kansas grade school reinforced the same. *Know why black people's palms are white?*

But if you are white but truly "feel black" then why do you have to look like it?

My next nonfiction book, *Unoriginal Sin*, is about hoax-ers and impostors, plagiarists and phonies. I finished it last week and sent it in to my publisher, elated and relieved. Now I have to take time to write about Rachel Dolezal too?

I can't decide if Dolezal, the woman revealed to have been merely pretending to be black, lecturing as such and even leading her local Oregon NAACP, is the natural extension of what I've been saying in my next book, or a distraction from this larger point: that quite regularly, faced with the paradox of race, the hoax rears its head. It turns out, I now know, it rears its rear too.

When Rachel Dolezal first broke, and was simply a joke on Black Twitter, I identified some of my favorite Twitter titles for the inevitable, anticipated memoir: "Their Eyes Were Watching Oprah" (that one's mine); "Imitation of Imitation

Blacker Than Thou

KEVIN YOUNG

It was never easy for me. I was born a poor black child . . .

The beginning of Steve Martin's *The Jerk* still makes me laugh with its twist on Once Upon a Time. The dissonance between what we know of the white comedian Martin, his relative success, and his obviously false declaration sends up not only the tragic showbiz biography but the corny black one: in both, the worser, the better. It also suggests his character's transformation, his overcoming—after all, he's clearly white now!—not to mention his current lot in which he's as smudged, bummy, apparently destitute. His isn't blackface, but his face half-greased is certainly part of the effect—it's a familiar one, in other words, to black people used to watching white people only claim blackness as a "poor me" stance.

Now, why does this jerk remind me of Rachel Dolezal?

There's a long-standing American tradition of whites donning blackface, or redface, or any other colored mask they on its latest incarnation with Barack Obama's ascent to the White House. For every action of African American advancement, there's a reaction, a backlash.

The North's victory in the Civil War did not bring peace. Instead, emancipation brought white resentment that the good ol' days of black subjugation were over. Legislatures throughout the South scrambled to reinscribe white supremacy and restore the aura of legitimacy that the antislavery campaign had tarnished. Lawmakers in several states created the Black Codes, which effectively criminalized blackness, sanctioned forced labor, and undermined every tenet of democracy. Even the federal authorities' promise of 40 acres—land seized from traitors who had tried to destroy the United States of America—crumbled like dust.

Influential white legislators such as Rep. Thaddeus Stevens (R-Pa.) and Sen. Charles Sumner (R-Mass.) tried to make this nation live its creed, but they were no match for the swelling resentment that neutralized the Thirteenth, Fourteenth, and Fifteenth amendments, and welcomed the Supreme Court's 1876 *United States v. Cruikshank* decision, which undercut a law aimed at stopping the terror of the Ku Klux Klan.

Nearly eighty years later, *Brown v. Board of Education* seemed like another moment of triumph—with the ruling on the unconstitutionality of separate public schools for black and white students affirming African Americans' rights as citizens. But black children, hungry for quality education, ran headlong into more white rage. Bricks and mobs at school doors were only the most obvious signs. In

White Rage

CAROL ANDERSON

When we look back on what happened in Ferguson, Missouri, during the summer of 2014, it will be easy to think of it as yet one more episode of black rage ignited by yet another police killing of an unarmed African American male. But that has it precisely backward. What we've actually seen is the latest outbreak of white rage. Sure, it is cloaked in the niceties of law and order, but it is rage nonetheless.

Protests and looting naturally capture attention. But the real rage smolders in meetings where officials redraw precincts to dilute African American voting strength or seek to slash the government payrolls that have long served as sources of black employment. It goes virtually unnoticed, however, because white rage doesn't have to take to the streets and face rubber bullets to be heard. Instead, white rage carries an aura of respectability and has access to the courts, police, legislatures, and governors, who cast its efforts as noble, though they are actually driven by the most ignoble motivations.

White rage recurs in American history. It exploded after the Civil War, erupted again to undermine the Supreme Court's *Brown v. Board of Education* decision, and took

I imagine Phillis and John, what their moments together might have been.

Maybe Peters thought Wheatley was beautiful. He was drawn to her delicate face, to her very dark skin, her full lips, her tight, kinky hair, to the ring in her nose that might have been an ornament she carried from across the water. (Look very closely at that engraving in her book. Use a magnifying glass and you will see that nose ring.)

And maybe Wheatley thought Peters handsome. He might have looked like her relatives, back in the Gambia that she wrote about. She and Peters might have shared a hankering for a place that lived only in their memories. He might have been born in America—we probably will never know—but in any case, he would have been of African heritage. Maybe at night, when they settled down together in their rickety bed, they talked in whispers, telling each other stories of that faraway place across the water. Folktales or proverbs that had been passed down.

He possessed ambitions, the same as she, and instead of stories, maybe they talked about the future, their hopes for his fledgling businesses and her new book of poetry, the glories that would be accomplished by their children. Anything was possible in that time, when messages of liberty abounded.

Maybe he was a tender lover and they laughed and cried and clutched. The words they spoke after their passion were to be believed, even though they came from the mouths of black folk.

a free lineage that did not include the Wheatleys. If nothing else, a treatment of precolonial West African history, along with the eighteenth-century culture of that region, would be an appropriate and respectful introduction to Wheatley's life in America.

In addition, I'm waiting for someone to include a compassionate, well-fleshed depiction of John Peters, which considers how he fit into African American intellectual, commercial, and activist life of the Revolutionary era. Perhaps I seem naïve or silly, but I'd like scholars to view him as a natural occurrence in Wheatley's trajectory, instead of a low-down disruption that led to her demise. Oddly, no account that I've read of Peters gives the most obvious, commonsense reason for why Wheatley might have married him.

Maybe he didn't trick her. She wasn't desperate or temporarily out of her mind. They married because they were deeply, passionately in love.

Is that explanation so ridiculous? Why wouldn't they love each other? American people of African descent did fall in love back then, and, if allowed by local power structures, they legally married. They did this in the midst of war, slavery, economic chaos, and/or posttraumatic stress over being torn from their homelands and sent over the horrific Middle Passage. I think it's logical to assume that many, many black folk fell in love with many, many other black folk. This assumption is a rational consequence of acknowledging black humanity.

At times, when I'm impatiently waiting for scholars to reexamine the complicated realities of these two people, would be left to rely upon? Precious little. Yes, a chronicle that may not be fully accurate is more than exists for most eighteenth-century, formerly enslaved black folks, but really, these traces provide a pitiful tribute to the woman who is the mother of African American literature.

Never mind that controversial, beginning line of her poem "'Twas mercy brought me from my *Pagan* land . . ." Wheatley is much more than that. She proved something to white people about us: that we could read and think and write—and damn it, we could *feel*, no matter what the racists believed. We already knew those things about ourselves. I'm pretty positive about that, but during her time, philosophers were arranging the "nations" with Africans at the bottom, while other Europeans measured black people's skulls alongside those of orangutans to determine if the two species were kissing cousins. In the midst of these soul assaults, Wheatley's poems carried the weight for African people on this side of the Atlantic. As a result, Wheatley—along with black soldiers and sailors who fought on the winning side of the American Revolution, black intellectuals and writers, and various individuals of African descent asserting their God-given rights of liberty—helped to sway many white Americans and Europeans that slavery was wrong.

Yet I'm waiting for someone to write a more emotionally charged book about Wheatley, one that would take into account her pre-American existence. Although she was a little girl when she arrived in Boston, and although the Wheatleys were "kind" to her, she did have African birth parents. Her life did not begin in America or with slavery. She had cussing the unproven connection between Odell and the Wheatley family:

> [It] is distressing that, in 176 years, scholars have not questioned Odell's right to speak for Phillis Wheatley. This blind trust continues the disturbing historical trend of African Americans, and black women in particular, needing white benefactors to justify their lives and history.

The thing is, I have fallen in love with Wheatley and I want to do right by her legacy. I want to get everything correct, but if I'm not the one to uncover new information, if someone else finds it, that isn't a problem for me. I just want it to be found. I have hoped that by pointing to the absence of documentation on Odell, researchers will take notice and renew the search for her genealogy. If no family records can be identified, then the responsible, professional cause of action would be to cease using Odell as a primary source for Wheatley's life. The other option would be to categorize *Memoir* as historical fiction, but whatever the categorization, someone must directly challenge Odell's authority to provide the most enduring depiction of Wheatley, and of her husband as a sycophant and a hustler.

I've tried to be pragmatic when it comes to the work of Wheatley biographers and scholars. Research is hard. It's time-consuming and frustrating; I know that from personal experience. Furthermore, there often isn't much information to go on. For example, if Odell's *Memoir* were to be eliminated as a primary source for Wheatley's life, what else of a never-published letter (dated June 2, 1791) between the printers Ebenezer T. Andrews and Isaiah Thomas. In this letter, Andrews refers to a "proposal" for "Wheatley's Poems," and that he had promised Peters that they would "print them" and split the "neat profits with him." But bewilderingly, that second book never appeared.

Carretta notes that Peters died in 1801; he was fifty-five at the time of his death. He never was able to pay off his debts, but he left some nice belongings behind. A horse, a desk, some leather-bottomed chairs. Books, which meant he not only was literate, but may also have enjoyed reading.

When you look at Peters's life, okay, the brother "did a couple bids," but at least he didn't leave behind any *people* that had to be sold to erase his debts, as Jefferson did. Families were broken up, auctioned off, and sifted like chaff. That would be the fate of the slaves of Monticello after Jefferson died. I can't help but wonder what Odell would have thought of his actions.

I have continued my research on Wheatley. I regularly search for new information; I read new articles about her, and always, I check the notes and the bibliography. Periodically, I look for primary materials to see if any new information on her has emerged. When finances permit, I travel and do my primary research in person.

In the meantime, I publish poems based upon Wheatley research. In 2010, I published an essay on her as well, mentioning my sighting of Peters on that 1790 census, dishigh during this period. It was not uncommon for parents to lose several offspring in infancy or childhood, even those parents who fed, clothed, and loved their children. There would have been nothing for Peters to forestall a child's death from a disease such as measles. As for Wheatley's passing and whether Peters had a direct or indirect hand in it, there is no proof that he pushed her into an early grave, either. In the eighteenth century, life spans were short for whites, and even shorter for African Americans. Wheatley died around the age of thirty-three, which, unfortunately, is in keeping with life expectancies for black women in America at that time.

Carretta supplies evidence that, at the time of Wheatley's death, Peters was living in Massachusetts indeed, but he was in prison because he couldn't pay his bills. (In twenty-first-century terms, he had bad credit.) This is not a crime by our contemporary standards, but it was during Peters's time. There was an economic depression in New England, in the aftermath of the American Revolution; many people in Massachusetts, black and white, couldn't pay their bills or even afford food. Starvation was not unheard of.

Peters was released from jail, and, according to Carretta, for the next sixteen years, he continued to aspire to the role of gentleman. And now we have definitive proof that Peters also kept trying to publish the second book of poetry that his late wife had written. In October 2015, I corresponded (by e-mail) with the assistant curator of manuscripts at the American Antiquarian Society. Knowing my interest in the Wheatley-Peters marriage, she shared with me an excerpt

As a white woman of the nineteenth century Odell fits in perfectly with her era, too. It doesn't take much speculation to deduce that she believed Peters to be an uppity Negro. He was a black man who had the nerve to possess high self-esteem, who cajoled Wheatley away from her white friends. Even though Odell dedicates her book to "friends of the Africans," her tone ridicules his ambitions: "[Peters] is said to have been both too proud and too indolent to apply himself to any occupation below his fancied dignity." In other words, how dare a black man want to be anything other than a day laborer with calluses on his hands? Who did he think he was, to desire property and not *be* property, to style himself as a business owner, to marry a high-status, accomplished woman of his own race?

There are other second- or third-hand, derisive accounts of Wheatley's husband, all by whites. Carretta quotes from Josiah Quincy, who claims to have met John Peters in court, and who didn't think much of the encounter. While doing my own research, I found a footnote in the November 1863 *Proceedings of the Massachusetts Historical Society*, which claims that an acquaintance of Obour Tanner told someone else that Tanner had told her—keep up, now; this is getting complicated—that Tanner did not like Peters, that Wheatley had "let herself down" by marrying him. But this same footnote giving this ostensible inside information also gets Wheatley's death date wrong, by ten years.

Even if Wheatley did, as Odell claims, give birth to children who died in infancy—and at present, there is no documentation for that—infant mortality rates were disturbingly herself as "Phillis Peters"; thereafter, whenever she refers to herself in print, she always uses her married name.

In the years leading up to the Revolution and directly afterward, Massachusetts was the site of black political agitation. Just as I had heard the name of Phillis Wheatley in elementary school, so had I learned about Crispus Attucks, a biracial African American and the first to fall during what became known as the Boston Massacre. Over the years, I would learn the names of others, like Lemuel Haynes, a minister who had fought in the Revolution, and Prince Hall, who founded the African Masons. There was Belinda, who petitioned the Massachusetts Assembly for a pension in her old age. And I would read the words of Felix, an unidentified black man—and presumably a slave—who petitioned the same body, demanding his freedom and that of other African American men:

> We have no Property. We have no Wives. No Children. We have no City. No Country. But we have a Father in Heaven, and we are determined, as far as his Grace shall enable us, and as far as our degraded contemptuous Life will admit, to keep all his Commandments. . . .

When I view Peters through the lens of the eighteenth century, he fits in quite easily with his brethren. Carretta depicts him as a smart, hard worker, trying his hand in different business enterprises: law, commerce, real estate, even medicine. (The latter was not the profession that we know today, and required no specific schooling.)

up Odell in the New England Historic Genealogical Society. I did, and I found Margaretta Matilda Odell of "Jamaica Plain, Massachusetts"—and that's all I found. Nothing else.

I returned to the texts on Wheatley. In each, I double-checked the notes and indexes several times, sure that I had overlooked something. Every night, back in my fellow's room, I took hours to draft possible genealogies of the blood relatives and in-laws of Susannah and John Wheatley, and those of their twins, Mary Wheatley Lathrop and Nathaniel Wheatley. I uncovered no documentation connecting Odell to the white Wheatleys. There was no establishment of family bona fides. Rather, it appeared that the only proof that Odell had been related to Susannah Wheatley, the former mistress of Phillis Wheatley, was that *she had said so.*

Vincent Carretta, the author of *Phillis Wheatley: Biography of a Genius in Bondage* (2011)—to date, the most comprehensive biography of the poet—has unearthed a treasure trove of previously unpublished material on Phillis Wheatley and her husband: legal documents, newspaper notices, records in Boston's *Taking Book*, along with other important minutiae. Still, even Carretta doesn't know how or when Wheatley met Peters. There is a reference to a "young man" in a letter she wrote her friend Obour, on October 30, 1773, but we don't know his identity. We do know that in 1778, Phillis Wheatley and John Peters, "free Negroes," married during the tumultuous period of the American Revolution. In a letter to Obour (dated May 10, 1779), the poet signs completely two more times and took pictures of the relevant pages.

I sat there, confused. Rather than verifying facts about America's first black poet, which had been my intention, I realized literary history had entrusted the story of Wheatley and Peters to a white woman who may have made assumptions about Wheatley's husband that might not just be wrong, but also the product of racial stereotypes.

Why *would* Peters have moved farther south after the Revolution? This piece of it didn't make sense to me. Why would a free, black man in his natural, right mind move south, taking his body to slaveholding territory, where white men would be waiting to place him in chains?

Wheatley had died in 1784, but the census had been taken in 1790. It's possible, then, that Peters had been in Boston through that decade, which meant that Peters may have been in Boston when Wheatley died. What could this mean? Had the young couple been separated? Had he left her for another woman? Had she left him? Maybe they had remained together. Maybe he hadn't abandoned her. Maybe Odell misrepresented their relationship. And if Odell had misrepresented the relationship of Wheatley and Peters, maybe she had done the same about her relationship to the white Wheatleys.

I drove back to the AAS and huddled with my mentor and the research librarian. I asked them what Odell meant in her book when she claimed to be a "collateral descendant" of the white Wheatleys? A cousin? A niece? An in-law married to a direct descendant? Both of them advised me to look nearly twenty years, I wasn't formally trained as a historian, but as the research librarians remarked, I was quick and a self-starter. In only a matter of days, I found references to Odell's *Memoir and Poems of Phillis Wheatley, A Native African and a Slave.* Looking through the bibliographies in texts on Wheatley, I noticed that they either cited *Memoir* directly or they summarized Odell and listed a relative of the Wheatley family as a reference. There was no overt tracing of Odell's lineage, no proof of how she was related to the Wheatleys, no way to establish Odell's authority.

In July, around the middle of my fellowship term, I drove from Worcester to the Northeast National Archives in Waltham, Massachusetts. It was at the urging of my mentor at the society that I made the drive, even after she told me that records would be on microfiche; the very mention of microfiche made me sick to my stomach. I spent a couple hours looking through the census records, and as I feared, it was not the exhilarating process I'd hoped for. My eyeballs ached and the lobster roll from the day before threatened to repeat on me.

I was ready to return to Worcester, when I saw John Peters on the 1790 census of Suffolk County, Massachusetts—the city of Boston. He was listed as a free man of color.

No, it wasn't a mistake. There was Peters's name.

Swallowing my nausea, I rechecked the entire census, just to be sure. There was no other black John Peters, the narcissistic man who had abandoned his wife off and on, and then—as Odell had written—supposedly had moved farther south after his wife's death. I looked the census over

Journey.
Let's call it that.

Let's lie to each other.

Not early descent into madness.
Naked travail among filth and rats.

What got Phillis over the sea?
What kept a stolen daughter?

Perhaps it was *mercy*,
Dear Reader.

Mercy,
Dear Brethren.

However, until I traveled to Worcester, Massachusetts, to the American Antiquarian Society, I had no idea that the devastating picture of the naked, gap-toothed child wrapped in a carpet may have been Odell's imaginary reflection. It was 2009, and I was the recipient of the society's artist fellowship. Its archives house one of the largest collections of printed material from early colonial days through 1876, about the United States, the West Indies, and Canada. I was on a mission to write a series of poems based upon Wheatley's life, and I was in search of primary resources.

At the beginning of my fellowship, I was ready to get to work. Though I'd been conducting archival research for tion, which persisted into the 1960s and continues into contemporary times.

My encounter with Gates's article started me on a Wheatley reading jag. For the next six years, I read everything I could find on her. I checked books out from the library, I downloaded scholarly articles, and I began to think deeply about her most (in)famous poem, "On Being Brought from Africa to America." This eight-line poem begins with discordancy, with seeming racial self-hatred combined with religious fervor. The tone of these verses earned Wheatley sharp, ugly criticism from other black poets, most notably the Black Arts Movement poet Amiri Baraka (né LeRoi Jones):

'Twas mercy brought me from my *Pagan* land,
Taught my benighted soul to understand
That there's a God, that there's a *Saviour* too:
Once I redemption neither sought nor knew.

As a woman in my (then) thirties, I had a different take from Baraka. I thought about a little girl's pain at being torn from her parents in Africa, her trauma on board a slave ship. I thought of her mother's grief, her wondering what had become of her child. I thought about my own and other black folks' beliefs in a benevolent God, in spite of our history in this country, the brutality enacted against us. And in a burst of empathy, I wrote these lines:

Mercy: what Phillis claimed
after that sea journey.

Odell) three pregnancies. From there, Odell opines, Wheatley's destruction was a foregone conclusion: There was terrible poverty. Each of the three children born to Wheatley fell sick in infancy and died. And at the age of thirty-three or -four, Wheatley herself died from an illness exacerbated by her "extreme misery" in living in "a filthy apartment" with a "negligent" husband.

This is the story branded into literary history.

In 2003, while working on my third book of poetry, I read an essay on Wheatley written by Henry Louis Gates, Jr., in *The New Yorker*. It was an excerpt from his soon-to-be-published book, a treatment of Wheatley juxtaposed against the racism of Enlightenment scholars such as Immanuel Kant, and more specifically, Thomas Jefferson. As someone who explored American history in my poetry, I found Gates's thesis fascinating: He believed Wheatley was important in dispelling derisive eighteenth-century notions about black humanity; her poetry had rebutted Kant's ordering of the nations with Africans down at the very bottom. Because of Wheatley's important symbolism for black humanity, Thomas Jefferson's negative response to Wheatley's poetry—"[t]he compositions published under her name are below the dignity of criticism"—was a symbol as well. It meant that the struggle for black equality on all fronts was not yet won. And thus, Gates argues, an intellectual movement was born, one that triggered a wave of eighteenth-century black literary and scholarly produc-

and they did not raise their voices publicly or act overtly against the institution of slavery. Odell seems to think that Phillis was living the kidnapped African's dream, however, and that, after the death of Susannah, that dream collapsed:

> At this period of destitution, Phillis received an offer of marriage from a respectable colored man of Boston. The name of this individual was Peters. He kept a grocery in Court-Street, and was a man of very handsome person and manners; wore a wig, carried a cane, and quite acted out "the gentleman." In an evil hour he was accepted; and he proved utterly unworthy of the distinguished woman who honored him by her alliance. He was unsuccessful in business, and failed soon after their marriage; and he is said to have been both too proud and too indolent to apply himself to any occupation below his fancied dignity. Hence his unfortunate wife suffered much from this ill-omened union.

Having written in great, flattering detail about the poet's years with the white Wheatleys, Odell uses her talents to draw a contemptuous likeness of John Peters. She informs us that Phillis never used the last name of her husband— and, it's implied, we should assume that this decision had something to do with Peters's qualities as a mate. Odell accuses him of possible abuse, writing in delicate terms that while Phillis was in very bad health, she wouldn't have been "unmindful . . . of her conjugal or matronly duties." In other words, Peters pressed his frail wife into sexual service when he shouldn't have, which resulted in (according to ences Africa in several of her poems, too. "To the Right Honorable William, Earl of Dartmouth" contains lines about her involuntary—and possibly violent—migration from her native land:

Should you, my lord, while you peruse my song,
Wonder from whence my love of Freedom sprung,
Whence flow these wishes for the common good,
By feeling hearts alone best understood,
I, young in life, by seeming cruel fate
Was snatch'd from Afric's fancy'd happy seat:
What pangs excruciating must molest,
What sorrows labour in my parent's breast?

Odell paints the Wheatleys as kind masters, and draws an especially sympathetic portrait of Susannah, who acted as an eighteenth-century stage mother to push forward Phillis's career. Susannah wrote to Selina, Countess of Huntingdon, a philanthropist and a leader in the Methodist movement, in an attempt to secure her patronage for the young poet. (The countess replied to this letter on May 13, 1773.) Phillis herself speaks lovingly of Susannah, and she continued to live with the Wheatleys after receiving her freedom. In a letter to Obour (dated March 21, 1774), Phillis writes of the death of her former mistress, and how a white woman treated Phillis as less a "servant" and more a "child." But as we look back on this era, kindness must be viewed through a complex prism, for slavery was a scatological, morally bankrupt enterprise. Besides Phillis, the Wheatleys owned at least one other slave of cloth tied around her like a skirt. Once the child was taken home,

> A daughter of Mrs. Wheatley, not long after the child's first introduction to the family, undertook to learn her to read and write; and, while she astonished her instructress by her rapid progress, she won the good will of her kind mistress, by her amiable disposition and the propriety of her behavior.

And with the help of Susannah, the smart and well-behaved Phillis began writing poetry. Odell doesn't give specific dates about Phillis's journey to freedom, but later biographers of the poet do. On May 8, 1773, she sailed to London (accompanied by the Wheatleys' grown son, Nathaniel) to promote her work, staying there six weeks. According to Wheatley scholar Vincent Carretta, on September 9, 1773, advertisements appeared for Phillis's only book of poetry, *Poems on Various Subjects, Religious and Moral.* We know that upon her return from London, her owners freed her, because Phillis mentions this fact in a letter dated October 18, 1773.

We can't know if Phillis hoped to return to her African homeland after receiving her freedom, but we do know that she retained a connection to the continent and its people. She developed a years-long friendship with Obour Tanner, a fellow kidnapped African who lived in Newport, Rhode Island. For several years, these two women exchanged fervent, spiritual thoughts in their letters. Phillis dedicated a poem to "S.M., A Young African Painter," and she refer-voice. My mother had fought her way up from backwoods poverty in rural Georgia and she cautioned me: One wrong step with a man could land me in perdition; living in a shack or a one-room apartment surrounded by my screaming, misbehaved progeny. As a formerly poor person, my mother looked down her nose at poor, black folk who had not escaped to tell the advisory tale, as she had.

I thought of Wheatley, the "Ethiop" genius, taken in by Peters's charms, falling from her magnificent perch. I pictured her, beguiled by a man who whispered in her ear, told her lies to get into her starched, Good Negro bloomers.

Much of the information on Wheatley's personal life comes from *Memoir and Poems of Phillis Wheatley, A Native African and a Slave*, a book published in 1834, fifty years after the poet's death. The author, Margaretta Matilda Odell, identifies herself as a "collateral descendant" of Phillis's former mistress. In her biography of Wheatley, she pushes a well-meaning abolitionist message: Black folks do not deserve to be slaves, and someone like Wheatley is the example of what her brethren could be, if they only had a chance.

According to Odell, the child-who-would-be-renamed-Phillis was "supposed to have been about seven years old, at this time, from the circumstance of shedding her front teeth" when she arrived in Boston. Susannah Wheatley, the wife of a merchant, was looking for a "faithful domestic in her old age." Instead, she found "the poor, naked child" with a piece

African woman on this side of the Atlantic to publish a book of poetry. Neither of my parents liked her poetry much, but that wasn't the point. The point was loyalty to the race, to African American men and women. This probably wasn't my first lesson about the responsibilities of being a black person, but it's the first one I remember and the most lasting.

I don't recall my elementary school teachers or my parents ever mentioning Wheatley's husband. I believed she never had married before dying at the young age of thirty-four, and I found it heartbreaking that she did not have someone to love from her native land, someone who looked like her and shared the same cultural memories. All she had was the white people who used to own her. When I first encountered information about Wheatley's husband, John Peters, in my junior year of college, I was confronted with the dominant negative stereotypes of black men. Those thirty-five words describe him as an arrogant good-for-nothing who deserted his family.

Talladega College, where I was studying at the time, was founded by former slaves. The campus is situated in a rural Alabama town, but smack in the middle of the 'hood. As I read the words portraying Peters, how he had abandoned Wheatley and their children, leaving them to poverty and then eventual death in the midst of squalor, images of black men came to me: the shiftless brothers who hung at the edge of campus, townies waiting for college girls. They sometimes shouted to us and promised pleasures of all kinds. These were the young men my doggedly middle-class mother had warned me about, in her alto, cigarette-tuned

"The Dear Pledges of Our Love":
A Defense of Phillis Wheatley's Husband*

HONORÉE FANONNE JEFFERS

As a little girl in the seventies, I memorized the names of prominent African Americans for Black History Month. These were the images that my teachers would trace from construction paper, then tack to the bulletin boards in my school. How I loved those dark silhouettes.

My school was 99 percent segregated; the laws had changed in the South but custom had not. My teachers celebrated black "firsts" to shore up our self-esteem, to fortify us against our smaller and shabbier schools and a pervasive white unfriendliness from those outside our enclave.

To my teachers, the eighteenth-century poet Phillis Wheatley was the *first* of the firsts, a beacon for black children. My parents were teachers, too, and at home they filled in the details. Wheatley was a child stolen from across the Atlantic and enslaved. A young genius whose playthings were the poems of Homer and Terence, she was the first

---

*The title of this essay uses a line from Phillis Wheatley's "To a Clergyman on the Death of His Lady," published in *Poems on Various Subjects, Religious and Moral* (1773).

North Carolina while seeking help after a car accident. It is as if we have reentered the past and are living in a second Nadir: It seems the rate of police killings now surpasses the rate of lynchings during the worst decades of the Jim Crow era. There was a lynching every four days in the early decades of the twentieth century. It's been estimated that an African American is now killed by police every two to three days.

The outcomes in Staten Island and Ferguson and elsewhere signal, as in the time of Jim Crow, that the loss of black life at the hands of authorities does not so much as merit further inquiry and that the caste system has only mutated with the times. From this, we have learned that the journey is far from over and that we must know our history to gain strength for the days ahead. We must love ourselves even if—and perhaps especially if—others do not. We must keep our faith even as we work to make our country live up to its creed. And we must know deep in our bones and in our hearts that if the ancestors could survive the Middle Passage, we can survive anything.

African Americans made after enslavement, during the cracked window of opportunity known as Reconstruction. The newly freed people built schools and businesses and ascended to high office.

But a conservative counterreaction led to a gutting of the civil rights laws of that time and to the start of a Jim Crow caste system in the South that restricted every step an African American could make. Any breach of the system could mean one's life. African Americans were lynched over accusations of mundane infractions, such as stealing a hog or 75 cents, during a period that lasted into the 1940s.

Six million African Americans fled that caste system, seeking asylum in the rest of the country during what would become the Great Migration. Denied the ballot, they voted with their bodies.

Their defection put pressure on the country, North and South, and freed them to pursue their dreams of self-determination. But in the North, they were met with hostility from the onset—redlining, overpolicing, hyper-segregation, the seeds of the disparities we see today. The past few months have forced us to confront our place in a country where we were enslaved for far longer than we have been free. Forced us to face the dispiriting erosion that we have witnessed in recent years—from the birther assaults on a sitting black president to the gutting of the Voting Rights Act that we had believed was carved in granite.

And now police assaults on black people for the most ordinary human behaviors—a father tasered in Minnesota while waiting for his children; a motorist shot to death in

Where Do We Go from Here?

ISABEL WILKERSON

Before the summer of 2014, before we had seen Eric Garner dying on a Staten Island street and Michael Brown lifeless in the Missouri sun for hours, before the grand jury decisions and the die-ins that shut down interstates, we may have lulled ourselves into believing that the struggle was over, that it had all been taken care of back in 1964, that the marching and bloodshed had established, once and for all, the basic rights of people who had been at the bottom for centuries. We may have believed that, if nothing else, the civil rights movement had defined a bar beneath which we could not fall.

But history tells us otherwise. We seem to be in a continuing feedback loop of repeating a past that our country has yet to address. Our history is one of spectacular achievement (as in black senators of the Reconstruction era or the advances that culminated in the election of Barack Obama) followed by a violent backlash that threatens to erase the gains and then a long, slow climb to the next mountain, where the cycle begins again.

The last reversal of black advancement was so crushing that historians called it the Nadir. It followed the leaps acid-free archival storage boxes in a municipally provided laboratory space, await reinterment.

Because I worried that I would lose track of the archaeologists' report among the bills, magazines, and student papers that littered my desk, for many months I kept it beside my bed, on the floor beneath my nightstand. Each morning the radio woke me with news of the war, a pop star's addiction, dismal predictions for the American economy. Later, I put the report in my backpack, its pages flat against my spine. At some point, I am not sure when, I grew accustomed to its weight and stopped noticing I was carrying it around.

damaged by heavy rain and a redirected sewer line that flooded the grave shaft during excavation. Decades of a sewer pipe lying across the child's midsection also contributed to this poor state, despite the fact that the coffin was found to be in relatively good condition. Directly beneath that body were the remains of a male person between twenty-one and forty years of age in Burial 12 whose bones were very soft also due to the high water table of the soil. At present, it is impossible to tell if these two people were buried at the same time or possibly even generations apart. The coffinless remains of persons in Burials 2B, 3B, 4B, 5B, and 7B were discovered beneath the sidewalk. Dental fragments and hand bones from a person not presently attributed to Burial 2 but found nearby are all that exists of the person in Burial 2B. Twelve teeth represent the person in Burial 3B. One tooth each indicates persons in Burials 4B and 5B, and a femur shaft fragment resting atop the child's coffin in Burial 7 is all that was found of the person in Burial 7B.

The boundaries of Portsmouth's African Burying Ground are still a mystery, as they have been for more than one hundred years, but plans to build a formal memorial are under way. Public discussions led by the state's archaeologists have asked city residents to consider whether a part of either street should be closed to vehicular traffic. Some Portsmouth residents have submitted samples of their DNA to see if they are in any way related to those people whose remains, now stored in Ethafoam, 0.002 mil polybags, and

Archaeologists recovered only extremely fragile fragments of the cranium and major long bones. The part of the mandible that was still intact suggests participation in a West African puberty ritual as there is a long-healed-over gap where lower and lateral incisors would have been. Stains in the soil represented most of the coffin wood. Only thirty teeth, small fragments of bone, some twenty wood and coffin nails accounted for the person of twenty-one to forty years of age in Burial 4. Those remains were extremely damaged by erosion and the unintentional intrusion of the excavator.

Pipe laid around 1900 across the bottom of the coffin of the male person aged twenty-one to forty in Burial 5 eventually disintegrated his lower extremities. Shovel marks on the coffin base indicate where a crew member either hit his coffin accidentally or attempted to cut through it.

The head of the female person in Burial 6 was located under the sidewalk, which had to be caved in to allow for her removal. Only the upper portion of her coffin was found intact. Her lower legs, cut off where they intersected with a utility trench and a ceramic sewage pipe installed around 1900, revealed evidence of a bone infection and severe inflammation of the shins. Her left arm appeared to be laid across her torso, and her cranium, now missing the face, pointed to the right side of the coffin. Her upper central incisors were shaved, possibly according to a West African cultural tradition, and represent the earliest documented case of such dental modification in North America.

The person in Burial 7 was a child between the ages of seven and twelve, of unknown sex, whose remains were ing out from the bottom of his coffin, which was made of white pine and was hexagonal in shape. All of his mandibular and some of his maxillary teeth were present, but like most of those recovered at the site, his teeth exhibited traces of enamel hypoplasia, a sign of previous infection or nutritional stress. His bones revealed a calcified blood vessel in his right lower leg and prolonged shin splints. A pumpkin seed of unexplained significance was found in his coffin as well as a metal object, probably a shroud pin, suggesting he was naked at burial.

In Burial 2, the remains of another male person between twenty-one and twenty-six years of age were found in good condition despite the fact that part of his skull had been unintentionally crushed by the excavator, leaving only his mandible and several teeth. A gas line running through the foot portion of his coffin meant that many bones in his right foot also were missing. His body was slumped to the left side, probably due to his coffin being tipped during burial, and his hipbone was broken in several places. His right hand lay over his thigh. Further analysis of his bones showed signs of repetitive forearm rotation and possible inflammation of the right leg, presumably from heavy shoveling, lifting, or other strenuous work. Salt, either used as a preservative before burial or for some other ritual, and a single tooth of unknown origin found between his knees, further distinguished his remains.

Burial 3 contained the remains of a person of indeterminate sex, thought to be approximately thirty to fifty years of age with the head facing east, perhaps toward Mecca.

Archaeologists removed the remains of thirteen people from beneath the intersection of Chestnut and State streets with the help of some machinery, but they did most of the digging by hand. Once in the laboratory, they used potters' tools and paintbrushes to remove excess soil from the bones and teeth. The exact dates associated with each burial remain unknown, but it is assumed that all were interred during the eighteenth century. Four males and one female could be identified by sex, but they found it impossible to determine the sex of the other eight, though most were believed to be in early adulthood, between the ages of twenty-one and forty years. Heads of the deceased generally faced west, suggesting a burial in the Christian tradition. In no cases were all the bones of an individual represented, perhaps due to the commingling of remains during previous installations of gas and sewer lines, the stacking of coffins, or a high water table in the soil. Thus no cause of death could be determined for any of those recovered. Archaeologists noted, however, that the lack of visible traumatic defects, cut marks, fresh or healed fractures does not rule out the presence of trauma. The teeth of each person, which in several cases constituted the entirety of the remains, appeared to be better preserved than their bones, which were found wet, free of flesh, colored gray or black, and, in the case of long bones, often missing the ends.

Pieces of the skull, portions of the upper and lower limbs, shoulder girdle, ribs, spine, and pelvis of a male person between the ages of twenty-one and thirty years represent Burial 1. An excavator operator noticed his leg bones stick-me from behind the circulation desk with a smile and thin wave. Seduced by all of it, I thought, *I love my new library.*

When I asked the reference librarian about the report, he told me it was now shelved in the local history section in the regular stacks. I thought, *Now it's all out in the open. Now there's nothing to hide.* I grabbed it off the wall, took a seat at one of the new blond reading tables, and thumbed through it lightly as if it were a mere tabloid magazine. I took notes from the acknowledgments, introduction, and background chapters, but when I got to the section describing the removal of the coffins—those same pages I had copied nearly a year before—a shrill noise came up from the back of my throat at the pitch of a full teakettle in a rolling-boil whistle. I cleared my throat and went back to reading, but my din started again. It was sharp enough for anyone to hear, so I decided I had better leave—but not before making a fresh copy of the report to take with me.

When a story is unpleasant, it is hard to focus on details that allow you to put yourself in the place of the subject, because the pain of distortion starts to feel familiar. Paying attention often requires some sort of empathy for the subject, or at the very least, for the speaker. But empathy, these days, is hard to come by. Maybe this is because everyone is having such a hard time being understood themselves. Or because empathy requires us to dig way down into the murk, deeper than our own feelings go, to a place where the boundaries between our experience and everyone else's no longer exist.

When I asked a reference librarian if I could see it, she hesitated and wanted to know if I planned on making copies. I told her I was not sure if I wanted to make copies because I hadn't yet seen the report. She then consulted with the head reference librarian, who told me that the burial site is a very sensitive issue for the city and that he needed to consult with the city attorney's office before releasing it. He took down my information—name, city of residence, and school affiliation—then asked me to wait while he placed the call.

The librarian was worried about how I might represent Portsmouth in a piece on the subject, because he cared about the town. I liked the town, too. It is pretty, easy to navigate, and surprisingly friendly for New England. I felt guilty and ashamed about my affinity for the town because at the time I could not muster more than a diffuse intellectual identification with the people who were buried just a few streets over.

Before copying the report, I remembered how easy it was for me to ignore what was already obvious, so I wrote down some details to remind myself of what I shouldn't forget: people were carried like chattel on ships to America; they were sold to other people; they were stripped of their names, spiritual practices, and culture; they worked their entire lives without just compensation; they were beaten into submission and terrorized or killed if they chose not to submit; when they died they were buried in the ground at the far edge of town; and as the town grew, roads and houses were built on top of them as if they had never existed.

I spent the long summer with my friends at the beach,

drinking Bloody Marys and eating lobster rolls on the open-air deck of a clam shack in Galilee, Rhode Island, while the Block Island Ferry, serried with tourists, made its lethargic heave past the docked commercial fishing boats. Once school started, I turned my attention back to the spiritless tedium of lesson planning and grading papers. In all that time I did not once touch the archaeologists' report.

I could make something up about why I let the report sit in a manila folder on my desk for nine months without ever once attempting to read it—something about wanting to let the dead rest or about how loneliness swells and recedes—but I won't. The reason is not clear to me even now. What I do know is that holding the copy I had made of the report near the Xerox machine by the dimly lit front door of the Portsmouth Public Library that previous spring made me feel more than I had felt during any of my grave-site visits, like a balloon in my chest was expanding and taking up all the space I normally used to breathe.

Intense discomfort, I had thought. *Maybe that's enough.*

But by January I was driving back up to Portsmouth, irritated with myself for not reading the copy of the report I had already made but even more irritated with myself for not being able to let it go unread. The once tattered and gloomy public library had moved to a brilliant new building a few streets over, and as I walked around the landscapers installing the brick steps, I caught the sign on the door that said, "Welcome to Your New Library." In the breezeway, three junior high school girls gathered around a computer terminal and giggled. A woman in a purple cardigan greeted

Portsmouth such as the *New Hampshire Gazette* printing office where Primus, a skilled slave, operated a press for fifty years; the Town Pump and Stocks, where black leaders were elected in a ritual following loosely from the Ashanti festival tradition of Odwira; and St. John's Church, where the records indicate that Venus, most likely a poor but free black woman, received a gift of one dollar from the church in 1807 on Christmas Day.

I sat on a bench overlooking the Memorial Bridge, which crosses the Piscataqua River from Kittery, Maine, to where captive Africans would have first encountered Portsmouth, the wharf at what is now Prescott Park. The first known African captive arrived in Portsmouth around 1645 from Guinea, and slave ships started landing regularly as early as 1680 carrying small loads of mostly male children and adolescents. I tried to imagine what it felt like to come into this swiftly moving river harbor after a long journey across the Atlantic in the cargo hold of a ship—after having been starved, beaten, shackled, and covered in the feculence of the living and dead. Did seeing the flat, tidy fronts of buildings outlining this colonial settlement for the first time make them feel hopeful? So many rectangles. How far away the rest of the world must have seemed.

I ended my walk at the Portsmouth Public Library, which held no significance on the trail, but, according to the first news story I heard about the burial ground, had in its collection a copy of the archaeologists' report on the burial site.

cemeteries and an eight-foot wrought-iron fence facing Farewell Street, God's Little Acre is comparatively pastoral, and most of the grave markers are missing as a result of vandalism or landscaping contractors running tractor mowers through it for many years. The inscriptions on those few slate stones still standing are fading due to the way weather and pollution wear on them. Many are now just barely legible.

A white woman with a backpack was taking pictures of the scant stones. She told me she teaches courses on American graveyards at a school in Connecticut. Pointing to one of the graves, she said, *He must have been loved by his "family" because stones were very expensive back then.* I wanted to say, *So were people.* And then I remembered reading an inventory from the estate of Joseph Sherburne, whose house has been preserved at the Strawbery Banke Museum. The linens were listed as worth forty dollars while the African woman who washed and pressed them had a line-item value of fifty dollars.

My trip to Newport made me realize that I knew almost nothing about the lives of blacks in Portsmouth during slavery and I wondered if *that* was the reason I was so unmoved by my visit. So I drove back up to New Hampshire to walk the Black Heritage Trail, put together by a retired schoolteacher and local historian, Valerie Cunningham, in order to learn about the experiences of Africans and African Americans in Portsmouth. Some of the sites on the Black Heritage Trail highlight historic accomplishments of blacks in she had looked for information on African graves on the Web before she left her home in Seattle. The woman told me she was originally from Connecticut, but when she decided to marry an African American man in the 1970s, her family disowned her. She had four children with him, none of whom ever met her parents. She had brought her youngest daughter back east to visit historical sites for a vacation and confessed that she was glad she no longer lived in New England. *I couldn't take all of this "in your face" history. Like Thames Street, the blue stones*, she said, referring to the pavers on a road that edges Newport's harbor. *Each one of those stones represents an African. Every stone was from the ballast of a slave ship and was carried by a slave as he or she debarked.* When I called the Newport Historical Society to confirm this, the reference librarian and genealogist Bert Lippincott III, C.G., insisted that stones like that were used as ballast on all ships coming into Newport, not just slave ships. He added, *Many Newporters bankrolled ships in the trade, but Newport was not a major destination for slave ships.* When I mentioned the article in the *Providence Journal* that claimed most Africans in colonial Newport were slaves, he said, *Many were third-generation Americans. Most were skilled, literate, and worked as house servants.*

At God's Little Acre on the edge of Newport, three stones stand erect, three others appear jackknifed into the ground at a forty-five-degree angle. One lies level to the ground. Only these seven tombstones remain in the graveyard that commemorates the contributions of Africans to the city's early history. While surrounded on three sides by larger, crowded a euphemism for "slave" in New England and how there is a presumption that Africans here were somehow "smarter" and treated better than those in the South. *This mispercep-tion*, he pushed, *is because people don't want to remember the dehumanization.* Without hesitating, he went on to say, *Slavery is violent, grotesque, vulgar, and we are all impli-cated in how it denigrates humanity.*

According to a series of articles by Paul Davis running that same week in the *Providence Journal*, Newport was a hugely significant port in the North Atlantic slave trade, and from 1725 to 1807 more than a thousand trips were made to Africa in which more than a hundred thousand men, women, and children were forced into slavery in the West Indies and throughout the American colonies. Ms. Guzmán Stokes explained how African people built many of the prominent colonial houses throughout New England, including those in Newport, and while many of those buildings remain restored in one form or another, just a handful of graves of Africans who made this contribution to the town's development can be found.

On my way to God's Little Acre, I came upon the tiny Newport Historical Cemetery #9, which Theresa Guzmán Stokes had also mentioned during her talk, but I could not figure out which graves belonged to Africans and which belonged to whites. A white woman was taking pictures of stones, so I asked her if she knew. She pointed to two graves in the corner. *These over here*, she said and then explained

Ground had been housed at the museum before they were transported to the temporary laboratory. I assumed that my own lack of feeling was due, in part, to the randomness with which I had selected Portsmouth as the place to try to make sense of the remains of slavery in America. I had no personal connection to New Hampshire, no familial bond to any of the people buried there, and I became certain that was the reason I couldn't feel anything while standing on those Africans. I thought maybe I needed to visit a slave grave site more closely related to my life if I was going to experience some true cathexis.

So once back in Rhode Island, I went to a talk given by Theresa Guzmán Stokes at Newport's Redwood Library about that city's largest African burial ground, called God's Little Acre, a cemetery founded in 1747. For more than twenty years, without city support, she had been maintaining its grounds out of personal respect for those buried there, clearing away litter and weeds and eventually establishing a fund to protect it. She runs a website about the cemetery, and she and her husband, Keith Stokes, former executive director of the Newport County Chamber of Commerce, are writing a book on the subject.

While introducing his wife, Stokes assured the small audience, *We're not interested in slavery. It's emotional and it separates people.* But the absurdity of slavery means it is practically impossible for anyone to contain all the contradictions that arise when speaking of it. So despite his promise seconds earlier to refrain from talk of slavery, Stokes started by explaining how often the term "servant" is used as *this city block for a 'Negro Burial Ground.' It was close to town but pushed to what was then its outer edge. By 1813, houses were built over the site.* I got back in my car to write notes about what I found. This is when I realized my car was probably sitting on top of people. I knew I should feel something about that, but all I felt was a familiar loneliness creeping in on me.

The trip to Portsmouth had not elicited much outrage in me, even after I discovered that one of the oldest known grave sites of blacks in New England was neither green nor sacred space. I accepted the reality that the historic colonial houses—now the business residences of attorneys, hairstylists, insurance agents, and doctors—were considered by most people to be more valuable than the bodies down below them. But while I had thought that my lack of feelings while standing on people would allow me to forget that I had been standing on people, it didn't. I had no intuition about how these dead Africans might have felt about being paved over, no feelings of ancestral connection to those buried below, and I heard no discernible voices calling to me from the depths of that darkness. I wondered if the woman at the museum had been right. Maybe the corner *was* just an intersection.

The ambivalence the folks at the Strawbery Banke Museum expressed for those buried beneath Portsmouth's downtown was all the more surprising when I later learned that the first bodies exhumed from the African Burying

When the young couple asked about the role of the Native population in the development of Portsmouth, Charles explained that they were not a factor: *Most died out before the town became sizable, after catching diseases from their contact with the Europeans*, he said.

At the end of the tour, I returned to Stoodley's Tavern to ask for directions to the slave graves mentioned in the radio report. Charles told me, *You can't see anything. There's nothing there.* I thought he meant that the site had not been commemorated or officially rededicated, but his reaction made me wonder if there was even a historical marker indicating the graveyard's boundaries. The woman who had sold me a ticket said, *They've been reinterred.* I told them I still planned to go and asked if Chestnut Street was close, since Portsmouth's downtown area is quite small. *Or should I drive?* I said. She responded tersely, *It doesn't matter. It's just an intersection.*

It was sharply cold and the wind was picking up when I arrived at Chestnut Street near the corner of Court. Several restored colonials now serving as lawyers' and doctors' offices lined its east side. On the west side there was a beauty salon and a sign indicating a "Drug Free School Zone." Other than these buildings, it seemed that there *was* nothing to see. As I rounded the corner at Chestnut and State, I noticed a brass plaque affixed to the clapboards of a house: *In colonial Portsmouth, segregation applied in death as in life. City officials approved a plan in 1705 that set aside* originally on board had survived. The rest had been picked off by sharks or drowned.

After looking through a few of the houses in Puddle Dock, the Old Mainer, his wife, and I fell behind the guide and the young couple, who kept bragging about the beehive stove in an eighteenth-century farmhouse they were thinking of buying and restoring. They asked questions about the interior design of every home we toured. I took copious notes on Portsmouth's history and in this, felt my dour mood lightening. Details were comforting. Charles told us that Portsmouth was an Anglican, not Puritan, settlement and that among its original inhabitants were seventy-two Africans and eight Danes. Many of the wealthiest families in town made their fortunes in "the trade" first by shipping food, lumber, livestock, and other goods to British colonies in the West Indies and then by carrying captured Africans to the Caribbean, Virginia, and Portsmouth from the late seventeenth century through much of the eighteenth. Throughout the tour Charles occasionally used the word "servant" but never the word "slave."

In an alcove at the top of a staircase in a house built in 1790, the Old Mainer said to me, *I'd never live in one of these old houses. They're too cold.* There were two pictures on the mantel over the fireplace in the dining room. One called *An Emblem of Africa* featured a black woman walking with a feathered headdress next to a tiger in the background. The other picture, *An Emblem of Europe*, featured a white woman with a globe at her feet holding a book and a horn of plenty filled with fruit and flowers at the crook of her arm.

The museum turned out to be a neighborhood of restored colonial houses at the edge of the Piscataqua River. The main entrance was closed, so I followed an elderly white couple into Stoodley's Tavern, which served as the museum ticket office on weekends. An older white woman with silver-bobbed hair sat at a table covered with pamphlets advertising local tourist attractions. *Are you here for the tour?* she asked. I nodded yes. *Ten dollars.* Charles, our docent, chatted about the weather with the five of us who waited for the tour to begin: me, the senior couple from Kittery, Maine, and a very young, blond couple just recently moved to Vermont from Tahoe, Nevada.

We walked across the street into the original settlement founded in 1630, known as Puddle Dock. The Old Mainer wanted to know: *Where were the borders of the marsh before the houses were built? Where had the water been pushed back to?* He was wearing a cap that said *USS Indianapolis.* Charles asked him if he was on the ship during WWII and he said yes. Charles said, *Were you on it when it went down?* The Old Mainer told us that he had gone ashore at Pearl Harbor just before the ship had set sail for Guam. Charles enthusiastically told us the story of how the ship went down, as if its history illuminated an unseen aspect of the tour. On July 30, 1945, the ship, en route from Guam to the Gulf of Leyte, was torpedoed by the Japanese. More than nine hundred sailors were hurled into cold, choppy water. Although they radioed U.S. forces for help as they went down, no one came for four days. By August 8, at the end of the rescue effort, only 317 men of the 1,196 deal with those exhumed, as well as the fact that as many as two hundred people might still be buried at the site.

Perhaps if I had not already spent more than a couple of weeks being so down in the dumps, if talk about the expected duration of the wars in Iraq and Afghanistan suggested a time frame other than the interminable, if images from my trip to New Orleans were not so powerfully present to me, then maybe the NPR report would have floated past me that morning. But something about hearing that Africans are buried beneath a public street in a small, coastal New England town gave me a new context to reconsider what is obvious and how one might learn to live with it. I knew I had to go there to see the people, even if they were still tucked in tight, if I was ever going to start letting go of the expectation that I could someday feel less lonely in America.

The first time I drove the two hours north from Providence to Portsmouth I had no idea what I was going to do when I got there. It was a Sunday in late February, the day after a large snowfall had dumped about six inches of snow along New England's southern coast. By morning, the roads were no longer wet and the snowdrifts at the side of the road glowed while ghostly wisps of fine powder swirled in the winnows of eighteen-wheelers trying to close the distance on Monday. From the interstate, I saw a sign for the Strawbery Banke Museum, which had been mentioned in the radio report, and I followed its direction.

too much that was obvious about the way class and race work in America. More than I wanted to see. More than I was capable of seeing.

This is when I realized my loneliness had deeper roots than I had initially suspected, and that, in addition to personal disappointments, it came from having a profound sense of disconnection from what I thought America was, and who, in that context, I knew myself to be. My post–New Orleans loneliness seemed to emanate from a place that preceded my own memory and stretched across time into a future that extended far beyond my vision. It was as if I had been thrown overboard into the sea and was paralyzed by the shock of it. I could neither breathe nor drown. I could not sink or return to the surface.

Then early one morning in January as I was listening to Boston's public radio station, I heard a story about the 2003 discovery of a grave site in Portsmouth, New Hampshire. As city workers attempted to dig a manhole near the corner of Court and Chestnut streets in the seaside town, a pine coffin was discovered with leg bones sticking out. An independent archaeological firm had been brought in immediately to lead an exhumation. Eight coffins and the remains of thirteen people were removed. The report noted that a combination of forensic evidence and DNA testing had confirmed that at least four of the remains in question were of African ancestry, most likely slaves buried there during the 1700s. The archaeologists' report had just been released to the city of Portsmouth, which was engaged in public discussion about the most appropriate and respectful way to planning to return. On this visit, Holt felt strangely serene; unlike the rest of the city, it appeared not to have changed in any significant way. In fact, I might have wandered among the unknown dead for hours had I not heard my mother frantically shouting from the car. *Wendy, come on! We've got to get to Constantinople before dark!*

We picked up Aunt Lou from Chester's and drove over to Constantinople, a street in the Magazine district, to meet up with her childhood friend who had survived the flood trapped with her son in the attic of his house for a week before being rescued. Because none of the traffic lights were working, my mother was nervous and complained all the way there about how I had lingered too long in the cemetery. She chided me that one should let the dead rest. *That's right,* Aunt Lou said. I interrupted: *I just wanted to make sure that our people hadn't floated away.* They went quiet.

But I took a walk around, and it looked like everybody was still tucked in tight.

I returned from New Orleans more miserable than when I left. As much as I had wanted to come back from that trip with a sense of conviction, inspired to action that would distract me from my loneliness, I could not find a singular source of outrage on which to fixate—not poverty, racism, the failure of the federal government, a history of community self-destructiveness, a river, a lake, or a hurricane. Not a house without a roof, a felled tree across a path, a tumbled-down tombstone, or a wayward corpse. I was faced with appeared stained and tumbled over by water. In the early 1900s a portion of Holt was used as a "pauper's field" for the poor and indigent, and during segregation it was one place where blacks could be buried. Our family crypt had been there longer than anyone could remember, but its precise location was unknown; its marker had been stolen in 1969, just weeks after my great-grandmother was laid to rest. Up close I could see new grass, slender and gold-green, appearing in short tufts at the foot of the headstones, most of which were pitched in one direction or another toward the ground. Handmade markers in wood or cement were adorned with bottle glass, sea shells, or not at all, with the names and dates of the deceased written in by hand. Some had been decorated with Mardi Gras beads and silk flowers. I walked down the dirt path to the part of the cemetery where most of the stones were missing and called out to my ancestors. *I have no idea where you are. Tell me where you are.* But I heard nothing.

Ten years ago, when I last visited Holt, the grounds had not been well tended, and even then many of the grave markers were missing, in disrepair, or toppled down. Back then I had only a piece of scrap paper with a row and plot number written on it to guide me to the crypt's location. The ground, deeply sunken where bodies were buried, looked as if waves were passing through it in slow motion. On that visit I worried that I could not read the names of the people I was walking over to apologize directly for the disrespect of having done so. Hastily I laid some flowers and a note where I thought the crypt should be and left without ever lay across the front lawn. When we opened the front door, dirt, mud, debris, and seaweed covered the hardwood floors and the sofa, which had floated over to the opposite wall from where it had been set. The house looked like someone had picked it up and shook it hard before setting it back down onto its cinder-block frame. We put on face masks and gloves, and booties over our shoes. A chifforobe sitting in water for weeks had gently exploded and still-wet clothes poked out of holes in the sides. Black and brown mud blotted the wall next to an antique brass bed. In the back room, the ceiling had caved in and wires and other debris hung low from what was left of the roof, like snakes in trees.

Aunt Lou said, *My house is tore up.*

Radio and television news reports about New Orleans mentioned that several of the city's cemeteries had been badly damaged by the flooding, and Chester's wife said coffins had been turning up all over the city. So I convinced my mother to drive over to Holt Cemetery, where our family crypt is situated, but she wouldn't get out of the car to check on it with me. Instead she shouted from its window, *Watch out for water moccasins!* as I walked through a rusty and twisted wrought-iron fence bolstered by rotten tree stumps into a field of tall, dead grasses and sun-bleached tombstones. Cypress trees sheltered the perimeter, branches reaching like veins across a heart.

Despite the fact that most of the graves at Holt are below-ground, unlike many cemeteries in New Orleans, it looked to me that Holt had kept hold of its dead better than the grave sites near the end of Canal Street, where mausoleums leave my bungalow by entering the world with a sense of purpose, or at least a sense of direction.

It was with this ambition that I had gone to New Orleans to help my great-aunt Louise come to recognize that her home there had been destroyed, even though my gumption was clearly tainted with dread. Sitting in a cold house listening to the radio was painful enough, but the thought of actually walking through so much loss made me worry that I would have to face more of the obvious than I could be distracted from noticing. As our plane flew over the Gulf Coast it was hard to tell how bad things actually were on the ground. Muddy patches of brown and tan signaled the normally slow growth of a Southern winter. I saw the edge of Lake Pontchartrain, into which, during the early 1920s, my great-grandmother Susie had thrown her wedding ring when she needed to affirm a point that her husband would not accept. On our descent I began to see blue tarps stretched over large holes in people's roofs.

When we arrived at Aunt Lou's tiny red-brick, railroad-style house, her nephew met us. Chester was a former longshoreman. He had returned to the city a few weeks after the water had been pumped out and had been living in a FEMA trailer while he gutted his own house. Even though he had warned my mother and Aunt Lou on the phone that the house was in very bad condition, he wanted to make sure we understood this before we entered it, because from the outside, there appeared to be little structural damage. About four feet from the ground, a black, bathtub-ring-like watermark circled the exterior. Garbage and a broken ladder to cure myself of optimism as a strategy to ward off future misery. The value of this approach was confirmed by a self-help book I kept on my nightstand. When I dared to open it, I could read only a single chapter at a sitting because each reiterated a simple point that I just could not seem to accept—that to become free from disappointment one must acknowledge the obvious, then learn to live with it.

By mid-January, the United States' war with Iraq was coming to the end of its fourth year, the war in Afghanistan was intensifying again, and the shortcomings of the federal government that had been noted after Hurricane Katrina were fading from media attention, which was now absorbed with a surge of reports that, come summer, another movie star couple would be expecting their first biological child. I found myself momentarily enthralled in speculation: How long would this new relationship last? What did his ex-wife think of the sudden pregnancy of his new girlfriend? Who would take time off from their career to care for the family? These questions, though deeply irrelevant to my own life, served to distract me from the obvious fact that an unpopular war, entered into on misinformation, was showing no signs of ending. I studied the news reports on the radio every morning, which covered many subjects: planned highway construction projects, politics, movie stars, pop music stars, television stars, impending diseases, lying politicians, local sports, bank robberies, soldiers killed in Iraq. I suppose I was hoping the radio would serve as a kind of personal oracle, that stories of real human struggle might release me from solipsistic self-pity and show me how to

my neighborhood, or near any of the places where I con-
duct my life. My cultural memory of slavery, which I don't
think is so unlike that of many other Americans, suggests
that it was primarily a Southern phenomenon, one confined
to the borders of plantations, which, if they haven't been
transformed into shopping complexes or subdivisions, exist
now only as nostalgic, sentimentalized tourist attractions.
The landscapes associated with slavery, however, extend far
beyond the South.

My home is in New England and in the winter my house
feels slight against the wind as its windows tremble with
every blustery gust, which makes me want to stay in bed,
though I am not at all the type of person who likes to linger there once awake, unless circumstances are such that
I am not alone, and then, even in that rare case, I can be
restless and ready to set forth at sunrise. In the winter of
2006, I was not working at my regular job, which might
have been a good thing had I not been prone to a melan-
choly obsession over recent personal disappointments. I
began to notice pains in my body I had never felt before: a
tendon pulling across the length of my leg when I sat down,
a sharp twinge in my side when I stood up, and sometimes
when I'd shower my skin was so sore I could barely stand
to feel the water on it. I knew these pains were likely psy-
chosomatic, evidence of how deeply I was suffering from
loneliness. Because I suspected that the hope of escaping my
loneliness was adding to my discomfort, I had been trying

Lonely in America

WENDY S. WALTERS

I have never been particularly interested in slavery, perhaps because it is such an obvious fact of my family's history. We know where we were enslaved in America, but we don't know much else about our specific conditions. The fact that I am descended from slaves is hard to acknowledge on a day-to-day basis, because slavery does not fit with my self-image. Perhaps this is because I am pretty certain I would not have survived it. I am naturally sharp-tongued, suffer from immobility when I am cold, and am susceptible to terrible sinus infections and allergies. My eyesight is poor. Most of the time I don't think about how soft the good fortune of freedom has made me, but if I were to quantify my weakness of body and character I would guess that at least half the fortitude my enslaved ancestors must have possessed has been lost with each generation in the family line, leaving me with little more than an obtuse and metaphorical relationship to that sort of suffering.

I resist thinking about slavery because I want to avoid the overwhelming feeling that comes from trying to conceive of the terror, violence, and indignity of it. I do not like to think of it happening in my hometown, where I work, in to have prepared himself well for his black death, his mortality, and even better, his immortality. Indeed, he bested all of them, because he wrote it all down. And this is how his memory is carried. On the scent of wild lavender like the kind in his yard, in the mouths of a new generation that once again feels compelled to march in the streets of Harlem, Ferguson, and Baltimore. What Baldwin knew is that he left no heirs, he left spares, and that is why we carry him with us. So now when people ask me about James Baldwin, I tell them another truth: He is my brother, he ain't heavy.

ramparts of his home in another country? I wanted someone else to understand the private, black language found in one of Baldwin's last conversations with his brother David. Frail, sick, being carried to his deathbed in his brother's arms, what the world thought of him might as well have been an ocean away. In that moment, Baldwin didn't refer to French poets, or to the cathedrals of his genius, he instead returned to a popular Hollies song. He loved music, and he told his brother: So it is true what they say—he is my brother and he's not heavy.

Baldwin once wrote, "Life is tragic simply because the earth turns and the sun inexorably rises and sets, and one day, for each of us, the sun will go down for the last, last time. Perhaps the whole root of our trouble, the human trouble, is that we will sacrifice all the beauty of our lives, will imprison ourselves in totems, taboos, crosses, blood sacrifices, steeples, mosques, races, armies, flags, nations, in order to deny the fact of death, the only fact we have. It seems to me that one ought to rejoice in the fact of death— ought to decide, indeed, to earn one's death by confronting with passion the conundrum of life. One is responsible for life: It is the small beacon in that terrifying darkness from which we come and to which we shall return."

Because I am telling you this now, writing it all down, I am finding time to regard memory and death differently. I'm holding them up in the light and searching them, inspecting them, as they are not as I want them to be. On that hill, in Saint Paul de Vence, I wanted to alter fate, and preserve things. But why? They did not need me—Baldwin seemed raphy shaped the authors and our collective vocabulary. By next year, Baldwin's house will just be another private memory for those who knew it.

I do not know if I will ever see his house again. If I will be able to pull sour oranges from his trees and wonder if they were so bitter when he lived there. I do know that Baldwin died a black death.

For a while when I came back to the States, I started to send desperate e-mails to people who knew him that read:

> For the last two days, I've basically found myself frantically, maniacally looking for everything that I could find about Baldwin's life there. To be honest, I'm not at all sure what I am looking for, but when I walked up that steep little hill, past the orange and cypress trees out onto the main road, and looked back at his house, I just felt a compulsion to start asking people who knew him about his life in that house. The compound is almost gone, as they are in the process of demolishing it, and yet something about it and him seemed to still be very much there.

I sent those notes—feeling as hopeless as I sounded—because I wanted to save that building. Because I was scared that no one else would ever be able to see that Baldwin had a rainbow kitchen—an orange sink and purple shelves—in his guesthouse. I wanted someone else to wonder what he ate from this kitchen, who he loved, who stayed in this annex of his estate; did his love feel free in this kitchen, in this house where two men could embrace in private behind the them at all. He preserved himself so he could stay alone. In France, I saw Baldwin didn't live the life of a wealthy man but he did live the life of a man who wanted to travel, to erect an estate that held a mood of his own design, where he could write as an outsider from the noise, alone in silence, with fearlessness.

Decades after his death in 1987, what I found left behind in Baldwin's house was something similar to what we experienced when I waded through my grandfather's effects after his house had burned down. Two months later, my grandfather would die from shock and stress caused by the fire. Baldwin's death, too, came at him hard and fast. In both houses, I found mail strewn on dirt piles in rooms that no longer had doors or windowpanes, entryways nailed over to prevent trespassers like us. In each case, clearly someone had forced entry in order to drink beer. The scattered, empty beer cans were recent additions, as were the construction postings from the company that was tasked with tearing the house down. So that nothing remained. No remembrance of the past. Not even the sense that a great man had once lived there.

James Baldwin lived in this house for more than twenty-five years, and all that was left were half a dozen pink tea-cups and turquoise saucers buried by the house's rear wall, orange trees that were heavy with fruit, but the fruit was bitter and sharp to the taste. We see Baldwin's name in connection to the present condition more often than we see Faulkner's, Whitman's, or Thoureau's. We can visit houses and places where they lived and imagine how their geogto have the demand for dignity be at absolute odds with the national anthem.

From the outside, Baldwin's house looks ethereal. The saltwater air from the Mediterranean acts like a delicate scrim over the heat and the horizon, and the dry, craggy yard is wide and long and tall with cypress trees. I had prepared for the day by watching clips of him in his gardens. I read about the medieval frescos that had once lined the dining room. I imagined the dinners he had hosted for Josephine Baker and Beauford Delaney under a trellis of creeping vines and grape arbors. I imagined a house full of books and life.

I fell in love with Baldwin, because Baldwin didn't go to France because it was France. He was not full of naïve, empty admiration for Europe; as he once said in an interview: "If I were twenty-four now, I don't know if and where I would go. I don't know if I would go to France, I might go to Africa. You must remember when I was twenty-four there was really no Africa to go to, except Liberia. Now, though, a kid now . . . well, you see, something has happened which no one has really noticed, but it's very important: Europe is no longer a frame of reference, a standard-bearer, the classic model for literature and for civilization. It's not the measuring stick. There are other standards in the world."

Baldwin left the States for the primary reason that all emigrants do—because anywhere seems better than home. This freedom-seeking gay man, who deeply loved his sisters and brothers—biological and metaphorical—never left

Baldwin joined the pantheon of black people who were from that instructional generation of civil rights fighters.

On that train to Baldwin's house I thought more about this generation and about the seemingly vast divide between Baldwin and my grandfather. They had very little in common, except they were of the same generation, the same race, and were both fearless men, which in black America says a lot. Whereas Baldwin spent his life writing against a canon, writing himself into the canon, he was a black man who was recording the Homeric legend of his life himself; my grandfather simply wanted to live with dignity.

My grandfather liked to look on the bright side. Even when I visited him in Los Angeles for one of the last times, he insisted things weren't so bad. He was eking out a living on the money we sent and social security. My mother asked him to come east to stay with us, but he refused. He had lived in this building for almost fifty years, but now the upstairs neighbors were what he called "young bloods," guys who threatened to shoot him when he complained about their noise. The landlord wanted him out to raise the rent; he needed more money for the place. All my grandfather had were a few worn tracksuits and his rusted golf clubs. No one needed an eighty-year-old carpenter, no matter how clever he was: he'd worked hard but had made next to nothing. California had once been fertile ground for him, but in the end it, too, was bound to the country that had long seen him and us as subservient human beings. But my grandfather preferred not to focus on that sort of thing. What Baldwin understood is that to be black in America is of the magazine, the security guards, the delivery guys, the office manager, and the folks at the front desk; among them the United Nations was almost represented. With them, I did not have to worry that one word pronounced wrong or one reference not known would reflect not just poorly on me but also on any black person who might apply after me.

I also didn't have to worry about that in that storeroom. There I could think. I realized three things spending a week in the back of that dismal storeroom. That yes, I was the only intern asked to do manual labor, but also that I was surrounded by two hundred years of the greatest American essays ever written, and I discovered that besides the physical archives and magazines stored there, the storeroom was also home to the old index card invoices that its writers used to file. In between my filing duties, I spent time searching those cards, and the one that was most precious to me was Baldwin's. In 1965, he was paid $350 for an essay that is now legend. The check went to his agent's office. There is nothing particularly spectacular about the faintly yellowed card except that its routineness suggested a kind of normalcy. It was human and it looped a great man back to the earth for me. And in that moment, Baldwin's eminence was a gift. Because he had made it out of the storeroom. He had taken a steamer away from being driven mad from maltreatment. His excellence had moved him beyond the realm of physical labor. He had disentangled himself from being treated like someone who was worthless or questioning his worth. And better yet, Baldwin was so good they wanted to preserve his memory. I would look at that card every day of that week.

years ago, but he was not certain if she really "counted" as black. I was also alerted later to there being one editor who was half Filipina, half white. But when I asked how this dismal situation could be possible I was told that the lack of diversity was due to the lack of applications from people of color. As awkward as these comments were, they were made in the spirit of oblivious commonwealth. It was office chatter meant to make me feel like one of the gang, but instead of comforting my concerns they made me feel like an oddity.

On good days, being the first black intern meant having my work done quickly and sounding extra witty around the water cooler; it meant I was chipping away at the glass ceiling that seemed to top most of the literary world. But on bad days I gagged on my resentment and furiously wondered why I was selected. I became paranoid that I was merely a product of affirmative action, even though I knew I wasn't. I had completed the application not once but twice and never did I mention my race. Still, I never felt like I was actually good enough. And with my family and friends so proud of me, I felt like I could not burst their bubble with my insecurity and trepidation.

So when I was the only intern asked by the deputy editor to do physical labor and reorganize all of the old copies of the magazine in the freezing, dusty storeroom, I fretted in private. Was I asked because of my race or because that was merely one of my duties as the intern-at-large? There was no way to tell. I found myself most at ease with the other interns and the staff that did not work on the editorial side during a publishing internship. Basically, during a lonely week I had spent in the storeroom of a magazine's editorial office organizing the archives from 1870 to 2005, I had once found time to pray intensely at the altar of Baldwin. I had asked him to grant me endurance and enough fight so that I could exit that storeroom with my confidence intact. I told him what all writers chant to keep on, that I had a story to tell. But later, away from all of that, I quietly felt repelled by him—as if he were a home I had to leave to become my own. Instead, I had spent years immersing myself in the books of Sergei Dovlatov, Vivian Gornick, Henry Dumas, Sei Shōnagon, John McPhee, and bell hooks. Baldwin didn't need my prayers, he had the praise of the entire world.

I still liked Baldwin but in a divested way, the way that anyone who writes and aspires to write well does. When people asked me my opinion on him I told them the truth: that Baldwin had set the stage for every American essayist who came after him. One didn't need to worship him, or desire to emulate him, to know this and respect him for it. And yet, for me, there had always been something slightly off-putting about him—the strangely accented, ponderous way he spoke in the interviews I watched; the lofty, precious way in which he appeared in an essay by Joan Didion as the bored, above-it-all figure that white people revered because he could stay collected while the streets boiled. What I resented about Baldwin wasn't even his fault. I didn't like how many men who only cared about Ali, Coltrane, and Obama praised him as the black authorial exception. I didn't like how every essay about race cited him. I didn't like that he and my grandfather were four years apart in age, but that Baldwin, as he was taught to me, had escaped to France and avoided his birth-righted fate whereas millions of black men his age had not. It seemed easy enough to fly in from France to protest, whereas it seemed straight hellish to live in it with no ticket out. It seemed to me that Baldwin had written himself into the world—and I wasn't sure what that meant in terms of his allegiances to our interiors as an everyday, unglamorous slog.

So even now I have no idea why I went. Why I took that high-speed train past the sheep farms, and the French countryside, past the brick villages and stone aqueducts until the green hills faded and grew into Marseille's tall, dusky pink apartments and the bucolic steppes gave way to blue water where yachts and topless women with leather for skin were parked.

It was on that train that I had time to consider the first time I started to revere Baldwin, something that had occurred ten years earlier, when I was accepted as an intern at one of the oldest magazines in the country. I had found out about the magazine only a few months before. A friend who let me borrow an issue made my introduction, but only after he spent almost twenty minutes questioning the quality of my high school education. How could I have never heard of such an influential magazine? I got rid of the friend and kept his copy. But still I had no idea of what to expect.

During my train ride into the city on my first day, I kept telling myself that I really had no reason to be nervous; after all, I had proven my capability not just once but twice.

Because the internship was unpaid I had to decline my initial acceptance to instead take a summer job and then reapply. When I arrived at the magazine's offices, the first thing I noticed was the stark futuristic whiteness. The entire place was a brilliant white except for the tight, gray carpeting.

The senior and associate editors' offices had sliding glass doors and the rest of the floor was divided into white-walled cubicles for the interns and the assistant editors. The windows in the office looked out over the city, and through the filmy morning haze I could see the cobalt blue of the Manhattan Bridge and the water tanks that spotted some of the city's roofs. The setting, the height, and the spectacular view were not lost on me. I had never before had any real business in a Manhattan skyscraper.

Each intern group consisted of four people; mine was made up of a recent Vassar grad, a hippie-ish food writer from California, and a dapper Princeton grad of Southeast Asian and Jewish descent. We spent the first part of the day learning our duties, which included finding statistics, assisting the editors with the magazine's features, fact-checking, and reading submissions. Throughout the day various editors stopped by and made introductions. Sometime after lunch the office manager came into our cubicle and told us she was cleaning out the communal fridge and we were welcome to grab whatever was in it. Eager to scavenge a free midday snack, we decided to take her up on the offer. As we walked down the hall the Princeton grad joked that because he and I were the only brown folks around we should be careful about taking any food because they might say we were looting. I had forgotten about the tragedy of that week, Hurricane Katrina, during the day's bustle, and somehow I had also allowed the fact that I am black to fade to the back of my thoughts, behind my stress and excitement. It was then that I was smacked with the realization that the walls weren't the only unusually white entities in the office—the editorial staff seemed to be strangely all white as well.

Because we were interns, neophytes, we spent the first week getting acquainted with each other and the inner workings of the magazine. Sometime toward the end of my first week, a chatty senior editor approached me in the corridor. During the course of our conversation I was informed that I was (almost certainly) the first black person to ever intern at the magazine and there had never been any black editors. I laughed it off awkwardly, only because I had no idea of what to say. I was too shocked. At the time of my internship the magazine was more than one hundred and fifty years old. It was a real *Guess Who's Coming to Dinner* moment. Except that I, being a child of the eighties, had never watched the film in its entirety, I just knew it starred Sidney Poitier, as a young, educated black man who goes to meet his white fiancée's parents. The film was set in the 1960s; I had been born in 1981.

When my conversation with the talkative editor ended I walked back to my desk and decided to just forget about it. Besides, I reasoned, it was very possible that the editor was just absentminded. I tried to forget it but I could not, and finally I casually asked another editor if it was true. He told me he thought there had been an Algerian-Italian girl many

I lay awake turning over in my mind the inevitable, that soon Sallie Mae or some faceless, cruel moneylender with a blues-song-type name would take my mother's home—she had cosigned for me—and thus render my family homeless. In my mind, three generations of progress would be undone by my vain commitment to tell stories about black people in a country where the black narrative was a quixotic notion at best. If I knew anything about being black in America it was that nothing was guaranteed, you couldn't count on a thing, and all that was certain for most of us was a black death. In my mind, a black death was a slow death, the accumulation of insults, injuries, neglect, second-rate health care, high blood pressure and stress, no time for self-care, no time to sigh, and in the end, the inevitable, the erasing of memory. I wanted to write against this, and so I was writing a history of the people who I did not want to forget. For many years, I taught during the day and wrote at night—long pieces, six thousand words for which I was paid two hundred bucks. I loved it; nothing else mattered because I was remembering, I was staving off death.

So I was in London when a check with one comma hit my account. It wasn't much but to me it seemed enormous. I decided if I was going to spend any money, something I was reluctant, if not petrified, to do, at the very least I would feel best about spending it on James Baldwin. After all, my connection to him was an unspoken hoodoo-ish belief that he had been the high priest in charge of my prayer of being a black person who wanted to exist on books and words alone. It was a deification that was fostered years before

The Weight

RACHEL KAADZI GHANSAH

It was an acquaintance's idea to go there, to Baldwin's house. He knew from living in Paris that Baldwin's old place, the house where Baldwin died, was near an elegant and renowned hotel in the Côte d'Azur region of France. He said that both places were situated in a medieval-era walled town that was scenic enough to warrant the visit. He said we could go to Jimmy's house and then walk up the road for drinks at the hotel bar where Baldwin used to drink in the evening. He said we would make a day of it, that I wouldn't regret it.

For the first time in my life I was earning a bit of money from my writing, and since I was in London anyway for family obligations I decided to take the train over to Nice to meet him. But I remained apprehensive. Having even a tiny bit of disposable cash was very new and bizarre to me. It had been years since I had I bought myself truly new clothes, years since going to a cash machine to check my balance hadn't warranted a sense of impending doom, and years since I hadn't on occasion regretted even going to college because it was increasingly evident that I would never be able to pay back my loans. There were many nights where

We think we can still outrun 'em.

Who threw that rock at the gator?

Don't know   *Where Toya?*

Y'all there?

We here.

Gator comin, boy, run

Don't see no gator, cuh   *Well, gator see us, nigga*

Runnnnnnnnnnnnnnnnnnnnnnnnnnnnnnnnnnnnnnnnnnnnnnnnnnnnnnnn
nnnnnnnnnnnnnnnnnnn

so we run

fast

cuz gator made for water   but children born for land.

stop eating pork and why he got separate meat and when all the women become Nefertiti bangles and headwraps and all us named like Muslims. Our cousins who couldn't make it because he died on the wrong Friday, wadn't payday, and our cousins who did and their many children tearing up the front yard. Our decision to sneak into the woods with red cups, black and milds, Jim Beam, a blue lighter plucked from the card table, and Toya's gold cap kept in her change purse. The pot of greens we brought out with us and the mosquitoes keeping company like we wasn't down in the swamps to bury our dead.

Our cousins know the dark and the heat, but we haven't been home in so long. Our back sweating and this old bra sticky so more and more from the red cup. Our cousin say, *Lemme top it off for youse*, so we oblige and when he said pull, we pulled and when he said blow, we blew smoke over our shoulder and then into his open mouth, giggling. Our cousin say, *You know they found him in the bed, right?* And we nod cuz sleep don't come easy no how. He say, *Just like that.* And our cousin clap when he say *that* and we think of Grandaddy setting his glasses down on the nightstand one last time. Our cousin say, *You missed me?* And we smile cuz his hand is on our hip and it's hot out and he smell good and it's the darkest Charleston has ever been. The dead of night is forgiving when you're kin. Grandaddy gone and we sitting up in the woods with brown liquor, necking, our cousin hard on our thigh. Toya say, *Keep watch for them copperheads*, but copperheads ain't never kill nobody—we got our eyes trained for gators.

Homegoing, AD

KIMA JONES

Here's the down south story we didn't tell you: sixteen hours in and Jack can't feel her feet but we never stop. Our uncle asleep at the wheel and we that closer to death with each mile. Turned around again and again, before GPS, we learned North Carolina is a long state: tobacco taller than us, the fields and fields of it, no washing it out of our clothes, the air so wet and thick of it, choking us.

Jack won't fly. Full grown with a dead granddaddy and still she won't fly, she tells us I-95 has always been the way back home so we gun it. Straight through, no stopping, sixteen hours and Jack doesn't care how bad we need to pee, she says, *Hold it.* Sixteen hours till we saw the palmetto trees and smelled the paper mill and knew Savage Road was in sight.

Georgie 'n' em got Grandaddy laid out in the front room like a piece of furniture and ushers fanning the top of Grandmama's head. We couldn't find our place in the business of departing: hams out the oven, lemon cake iced, organ tuned, tea made, napkins folded, the children's black patent leather shoes set out for the dirt road come morning.

Here's the down south story we didn't tell you: Leroy barking at us from the grill because when did everybody

PART I

LEGACY

beautiful . . . people who cannot suffer can never grow up, can never discover who they are. . . . Everything now, we must assume, is in our hands; we have no right to assume otherwise. If we—and now I mean the relatively conscious whites and the relatively conscious blacks, who must, like lovers, insist on, or create, the consciousness of others—do not falter in our duty now, we may be able, handful that we are, to end the racial nightmare, and achieve our country, and change the history of the world. If we do not dare everything, the fulfillment of that prophecy, re-created from the Bible in song by the slave, is upon us: *God gave Noah the rainbow sign, No more water, the fire next time!*

I hope this book makes each one of you, dear readers, feel as if we are sitting together, you and me and Baldwin and Trethewey and Wilkerson and Jeffers and Walters and Anderson and Smith and all the serious, clear-sighted writers here—and that we are composing our story together. That we are writing an epic wherein black lives carry worth, wherein black boys can walk to the store and buy candy without thinking they will die, wherein black girls can have a bad day and be mouthy without being physically assaulted by a police officer, wherein cops see twelve-year-old black boys playing with fake guns as silly kids and not homicidal maniacs, wherein black women can stop to ask for directions without being shot in the face by paranoid white homeowners.

I burn, and I hope.

to this because I feel it: all these essays give me hope. I believe there is power in words, power in asserting our existence, our experience, our lives, through words. That sharing our stories confirms our humanity. That it creates community, both within our own community and beyond it. Maybe someone who didn't perceive us as human will think differently after reading Garnette Cadogan's essay on the black body in space, or after reading Emily Raboteau's work on urban murals. Perhaps after reading Kiese Laymon's essay on black artists and black love and OutKast, or after reading Mitchell S. Jackson's piece on composite fathers, a reader might see those like me anew. Maybe after reading Rachel Kaadzi Ghansah's essay on Baldwin or Kevin Young's hilarious essay about Rachel Dolezal and what it means to be black, a reader might cry in sympathy and then rise to laughter, and in doing so, feel kinship.

At the end of *The Fire Next Time*, Baldwin writes:

This past, the Negro's past, of rope, fire, torture, castration, infanticide, rape; death and humiliation; fear by day and night, fear as deep as the marrow of the bone; doubt that he was worthy of life, since everyone around him denied it; sorrow for his women, for his kinfolk, his children, who needed his protection, and whom he could not protect; rage, hatred, and murder, hatred for white men so deep that it often turned against him and his own, and made all love, all trust, all joy impossible—this past, this endless struggle to achieve and reveal and confirm a human identity, human authority, yet contains, for all its horror, something very not be as tidy as I thought. But race in the United States is not a tidy matter. Only three of the submitted pieces explicitly referenced the future. Most of them were concerned with the past and the present. And that told me two things. First, it confirmed how inextricably interwoven the past is in the present, how heavily that past bears on the future; we cannot talk about black lives mattering or police brutality without reckoning with the very foundation of this country. We must acknowledge the plantation, must unfold white sheets, must recall the black diaspora to understand what is happening now. Second, it reveals a certain exhaustion, I think. We're tired. We're tired of having to figure out how to talk to our kids and teach them that America sees them as less, and that she just might kill them. This is the conversation we want to avoid. We're tired of feeling futile in the face of this ever-present danger, this omnipotent history, predicated as this country is, founded as this country was, on our subjugation. But the pieces in this work that do invoke the future—Daniel José Older's letter to his wife and future child, Natasha Trethewey's poem about the many planes on which time exists, and Edwidge Danticat's essay exploring the idea that people of the black diaspora are refugees—help me to believe that I might be able to have that conversation with my child in the future. These pieces give me words that I might use to push past the fear and exhaustion and speak to my daughter, my nieces and nephews. This work helps me to believe that this is worthwhile work, and that our troubling the water is worthy.

If I were smarter, perhaps I wouldn't say this, but I attest help me puzzle this out. I knew that a black boy who lives in the hilly deserts of California, who likes to get high with his friends on the weekend and who freezes in a prickly sweat whenever he sees blue lights in his rearview, would need a book like this. A book that would reckon with the fire of rage and despair and fierce, protective love currently sweeping through the streets and campuses of America. A book that would gather new voices in one place, in a lasting, physical form, and provide a forum for those writers to dissent, to call to account, to witness, to reckon. A book that a girl in rural Missouri could pick up at her local library and, while reading, encounter a voice that hushed her fears. In the pages she would find a wise aunt, a more present mother, who saw her terror and despair threading their fingers through her hair, and would comfort her. We want to tell her this: *You matter. I love you. Please don't forget it.*

The Fire Next Time is roughly divided into two parts: a letter to Baldwin's nephew, which looks forward to the future, and an essay about religion and the Nation of Islam, which concerns itself with Baldwin's past and present. I initially thought that *The Fire This Time* would be divided into three parts, roughly inspired by Baldwin's chronological division: essays or poems about the past, deemed legacy, essays or poems about the present, labeled reckoning, and essays or poems about the future, or jubilee, and all of them would wrestle with the specters of race and history in America, and how those specters are haunting us now. But as the pieces of work my editor and I solicited came in, I realized that the structure I envisioned for the work would the quality journalism of the time, with so much of it published online, meant that I couldn't go to one place for it all. I couldn't fully satisfy my need for kinship in this struggle, commiserate with others trying to find a way out of that dark closet. In desperation, I sought James Baldwin.

I read Baldwin's essay "Notes of a Native Son" while I was in my mid-twenties, and it was a revelation. I'd never read creative nonfiction like Baldwin's, never encountered this kind of work, work that seemed to see me, to know I needed it. I read it voraciously, desperate for the words on the page. I needed to know that someone else saw the myriad injustices of living while black in this country, that someone so sharp and gifted and human could acknowledge it all, and speak on it again and again. Baldwin was so brutally honest. His prose was frank and elegant in turn, and I returned to him annually after that first impression-forming read. Around a year after Trayvon Martin's death, a year in which black person after black person died and no one was held accountable, I picked up *The Fire Next Time*, and I read: "You can only be destroyed by believing that you really are what the white world calls a *nigger*. I tell you this because I love you, and please don't you ever forget it." It was as if I sat on my porch steps with a wise father, a kind, present uncle, who said this to me. Told me I was worthy of love. Told me I was worth something in the world. Told me I was a human being. I saw Trayvon's face, and all the words blurred on the page.

It was then that I knew I wanted to call on some of the great thinkers and extraordinary voices of my generation to

My schoolmates were white. I was not. Trent Lott took a whip as long as a car off his office table, where it lay coiled and shiny brown, and said to my one male schoolmate who grinned at Lott enthusiastically: *Let's show 'em how us good old boys do it*. And then he swung that whip through the air and cracked it above our heads, again and again. I remember the experience in my bones.

I know little. But I know what a good portion of Americans think of my worth. Their disdain takes form. In my head, it is my dark twin. Sometimes I wonder which of us will be remembered if I die soon, if I suffocate in that closet. Will I be a vicious menace, like Trayvon Martin? An unhinged menace, like Tamir Rice? A monstrous menace, like Mike Brown? An unreasonable menace, like Sandra Bland? A sly menace, like Emmett Till? I imagine I will be as black and fetid as the horde at Scarlett's heels, crowding her wagon, thundering to rip it apart, wheel by rivet.

Replace ropes with bullets. Hound dogs with German shepherds. A gray uniform with a bulletproof vest. Nothing is new.

I needed words. The ephemera of Twitter, the way the voices of the outraged public rose and sank so quickly, flitting from topic to topic, disappointed me. I wanted to hold these words to my chest, take comfort in the fact that others were angry, others were agitating for justice, others could not get Trayvon's baby face out of their heads. But I could not. The nature of the application, even the nature of before Zimmerman shot him. I, too, grew up in a place that could sometimes feel as limiting and final as being locked in an airtight closet, the air humid and rank with one's own breath and panic. A place where for all the brilliant, sun-drenched summer days, there is sometimes only the absence of light: America, and the American South. A place where the old myths still hold a special place in many white hearts: the rebel flag, Confederate monuments, lovingly restored plantations, *Gone with the Wind*. A place where black people were bred and understood to be animals, a place where some feel that the Fourteenth Amendment and *Brown v. Board of Education* are only the more recent in a series of unfortunate events. A place where black life has been systematically devalued for hundreds of years.

In December 2002, my then senator, Trent Lott, attended a function honoring the outgoing Senator Strom Thurmond, who is famous for opposing the Civil Rights Act of 1957 so strenuously he conducted the longest lone filibuster ever, one that lasted twenty-four hours and eighteen minutes. At this event, Lott, who is from a small town on the Mississippi Gulf Coast around twenty-five miles from mine, said: "We're proud of it [voting for Thurmond in the 1948 presidential election]. And if the rest of the country had followed our lead, we wouldn't have had all these problems over all these years, either." It was dismaying to hear this, to see what those in power thought of people like me, but it wasn't a surprise. After all, when I participated in Presidential Classroom in Washington, D.C., I, along with around five of my high school classmates, met Senator Trent Lott.

big in the way that children's eyes are—I saw a child. And it seemed that no one outside of Black Twitter was saying this: I read article after article that others shared on Twitter, and no major news outlet was stating the obvious. Trayvon Martin was a seventeen-year-old child, legally and biologically; George Zimmerman was an adult. An adult shot and killed a child while the child was walking home from a convenience store where he'd purchased Skittles and a cold drink. Everything, from Zimmerman stalking and shooting Trayvon to the way Trayvon was tried in the court of public opinion after his death, seemed insane. How could anyone look at Trayvon's baby face and not see a child? And not feel an innate desire to protect, to cherish? How?

And then I realized most Americans did not see Trayvon Martin as I did. Trayvon's sable skin and his wide nose and his tightly coiled hair signaled something quite different for others. Zimmerman and the jury and the media outlets who questioned his character with declarations like *He abused marijuana* and *He was disciplined at school for graffiti and possessing drug paraphernalia* saw Trayvon as nothing more than a wayward thug. They didn't see him as an adult human being, either, but as some kind of ravenous hoodlum, perpetually at the mercy of his animalistic instincts. Although this was never stated explicitly, his marijuana use and adolescent mischief earned this hoodlum in a hoodie his death.

I knew that myth. It was as familiar to me as my own eyes, my own nose, my own hair, my own fragile chest. It was as familiar to me as the air I grew up in, air as dense and heavy and close and hot as the air Trayvon breathed

Introduction

JESMYN WARD

After George Zimmerman shot and killed Trayvon Martin on February 26, 2012, I took to Twitter. I didn't have anywhere else to go. I wanted to hear what others, black writers and activists, were thinking about what happened in Sanford, Florida. Twitter seemed like a great social forum, a virtual curia, a place designed to give us endless voice in declarations of 140 characters or fewer.

I found the community I sought there. I found so many people giving voice to my frustration, my anger, and my fear. We shared news and updates and photos, anything we could find about Trayvon. During that time, I was pregnant, and I was revising a memoir about five young black men I'd grown up with, who all died young, violent deaths. Every time I logged in or read another article about Trayvon, my unborn child and my dead brother and my friends sat with me. I imagined them all around me, our faces long with dread. Before Zimmerman was acquitted of second-degree murder and manslaughter in July 2013, I suspected Trayvon's death would be excused. During this period, I returned often to the photo of Trayvon wearing a pale hoodie. As I gazed on his face—his jaw a thin blade, his eyes dark and serious, too

The Tradition

JERICHO BROWN

Aster. Nasturtium. Delphinium. We thought
Fingers in dirt meant it was our dirt, learning
Names in heat, in elements classical
Philosophers said could change us. *Star Gazer.*
Foxglove. Summer seemed to bloom against the will
Of the sun, which news reports claimed flamed hotter
On this planet than when our dead fathers
Wiped sweat from their necks. *Cosmos. Baby's Breath.*
Men like me and my brothers filmed what we
Planted for proof we existed before
Too late, sped the video to see blossoms
Brought in seconds, colors you expect in poems
Where the world ends, everything cut down.
John Crawford. Eric Garner. Mike Brown.

THE FIRE THIS TIME

CONTENTS

Contents

To Trayvon Martin
and the many other black men, women, and children
who have died and been denied justice
for these last four hundred years

SCRIBNER
An Imprint of Simon & Schuster, Inc.
1230 Avenue of the Americas
New York, NY 10020

First Scribner hardcover edition August 2016

SCRIBNER and design are registered trademarks of The Gale Group, Inc.,
used under license by Simon & Schuster, Inc., the publisher of this work.

For information about special discounts for bulk purchases,
please contact Simon & Schuster Special Sales at 1-866-506-1949
or business@simonandschuster.com.

The Simon & Schuster Speakers Bureau can bring authors to your live event.
For more information or to book an event contact the Simon & Schuster Speakers
Bureau at 1-866-248-3049 or visit our website at www.simonspeakers.com.

Interior design by Erich Hobbing

Manufactured in the United States of America

1   3   5   7   9   10   8   6   4   2

ISBN 978-1-5011-2634-5
ISBN 978-1-5011-2636-9 (ebook)

Copyright notices continued on page 225.

THE FIRE
THIS TIME

A New Generation
Speaks about Race

EDITED BY
Jesmyn Ward

SCRIBNER

New York London Toronto Sydney New Delhi

Also by Jesmyn Ward

Men We Reaped: A Memoir
Salvage the Bones: A Novel
Where the Line Bleeds: A Novel